Children of the Incubi

V: Dead Party

A Novel Series by

Lana M. Wiggins

Black Dragons Press
New Orleans

Children of the Incubi: Dead Party

Black Dragons Press
New Orleans, LA
www.blackdragonspress.com
www.lanawiggins.com

Children of the Incubi Series:
Book I: Marriage of Heaven and Hell
Book II: Blood Mark
Book III: Banquet of the Lesser Gods
Book IV: Gods in the Onyx
Book V: Dead Party
Book VI: Revelations

ISBN-13:9781729259368

Acknowledgements:
Special thanks to Black Dragons Press. **Cover art** from Pixabay. A million thanks to Cheryl Estrada, Bobbi Elisi, Meredith Beck-Wiggins, Karen Hollier, Theresa Wiggins, my soldier, Tommy Wiggins, my prodigious and silent hero, and Nate Wiggins, my inspiration for everything I do. Special thanks to Tom Wiggins, Marie Hollier, Gary Hollier, Rhonda Robison-Berkeley, Cynthia Martin, Sufyan Jarushi, David Zheng, Declan Flannagan, Brian Innes, and Susan Laird for shelter, support, guidance, and Gaelic words. To the Dragons, Josh, Rick, Kyle, Michelle, and Kerry F., thank you all for saving my life in more ways that I can count. Jessie, Mark, Keith, and Sam, I will see you at the Gates. Frank Adams, thank you for the beautiful dance moves and ethereal art that inspired the sparring scenes. Rest in Peace, my friend. I'll see you in Gael, on an alabaster stage, fanning a blue kilt.

For Tommy, Theresa, and Nate

Scribe's Note

Sylvia Plath once wrote, "The floor seemed wonderfully solid. It was comforting to know I had fallen and could fall no farther."

That line rolled over and over in my head as I lay sprawled out on the floor, face down, comfortable in the knowledge that although the floor was a hard stop, it was a stop nonetheless. I stopped writing. I stopped working. I tried to stop breathing, but my lungs refused to cooperate. The body always wants one last pull of air. I didn't die, but I stopped living. I couldn't face the world. I couldn't face Louise. I couldn't face the guests. I couldn't face Samael and Drake either. I couldn't face the fact that Marduk was dead. I knew that his death meant the end of the world. Amon and Marduk were inextricably linked, and if Marduk was dead, Amon was sure to follow. I didn't want to live in a world where there was neither a God nor a Devil. More specifically, I didn't want to live in a world without Marduk. There was no one to take his place. No one could possibly replace Marduk in the Colonies, in the book, in my heart.

"She's not going to recover on her own this time."

"I hate to say it, Drake, but…I think you're right. She's not getting better. She needs professional help."

"Don't bother. It's the end of the world. Just let me lie here until the world implodes. It'll happen any minute now," I said softly.

"The world hasn't ended, Lily," Samael said in a droll tone. "It's still spinning. No implosions."

Samael's harsh words made me cry like a small child as I dug my fingers into the rug beneath me. "There's nothing left without Marduk. Amon will die too. It's over. The world is over. The book is over. We failed. No point in writing another word."

Samael groaned loudly in an eerie moan that reverberated throughout the cabin. "It isn't that tragic, Lily. People die every day."

"He's not… people! He's Marduk! Who's gonna rid the world of evil? Who's gonna avenge Aramanth? Poor little Samoset. He just got his Papa back. Cain too. Marduk didn't even get to say goodbye to Lilith," I sobbed loudly, then in soundless heaves as I pressed my face deeper into the floor. "My life is over."

I heard Drake's footsteps as he made his way toward me. His hand was comforting on my back. "I didn't know you loved him this much, Lily," he said in a soft, sad whisper.

"I never expected to love him, Drake. I thought he was gonna be the bad guy in this story. But he wasn't. He wasn't wicked. He took on the role of the Devil to save Amon…to make sure Amon never had to face the darkness of the world. He took it all on his own shoulders. He took care of everyone, but nobody took care of him. He never knew love."

I let out a blood curdling scream that frightened even me, but not enough to make me move from the spot on the floor where I'd been lying since Marduk died.

"I thought losing Issa was hard, but…Marduk. I have no words. I can't… I just can't go on without him."

"That's not how life works. The sun still comes up with or without Marduk. The world is still spinning, Lily." Drake replied softly.

I lifted my head a half inch and read Drake's thoughts. "He's still alive in our memories," I said in a childlike voice. "Thank you for letting me chronicle Marduk's life to keep his memory alive." I rolled over onto my back and stared blankly at the ceiling. "I think I'll just die now. Take me home, Samael. There's nothing left for me here."

Samael leaned forward and took my hand in his. "There's more to the story. I know it's painful, but the story isn't finished."

"Nope. Can't write another word. It's finished."

"But what about Declan and Caraye? Mia? Cain? Don't they deserve your love too?"

"They'll be fine without me. I'm just gonna lie here until I die."

"You'll be there a long time, Lily. You're not getting out of the contract. Whether you finish the story or not."

"Not."

"Lily, you can't leave the story hanging like this. With no end. What will people think?"

"People will think I died."

"But you're not dead. They'll think you copped out. Do you wanna be remembered as a quitter? And what about Marduk? What kind of legacy will you leave him if you don't finish his story?"

"That's not fair," I almost shouted, but it came out like a thick-throated croak.

"Fair? What the fuck is that? There's no such thing in this world. It's all arbitrary. Haven't you learned that by now? If you love him so much, don't leave Marduk's legacy hanging on a limb. Finish the book."

"Samael's right, Lily. You'll be doing a grave injustice to Marduk if you leave the story unfinished."

I groaned loudly, huffed half a dozen times, then slowly pulled myself into a sitting position. "Get me some fucking Scotch. If I have to live without Marduk, I'm gonna need a lotta Scotch. And before I write another word, we're having a funeral."

"A funeral?" Drake asked in a comical tone.

"Don't laugh at me, Drake! Yes. A funeral for Marduk. Lots of Scotch. We'll blow up a bunch of helium balloons and… No! Sex dolls! We'll put blonde wigs on them, blow them up all legs and curves, just the way Marduk liked his women, then we'll release the dolls into the air! Like balloons, but blondes," I yelled as I sniffed loudly with a budding grin.

"It's not a bad idea," Samael said while nodding his head. "What about dragons?"

"Kites! Yes! We can fly dragon kites and blonde blow-up dolls in his honor! Steal everything we need, Drake. I need a shower."

"I thought you'd never say that. Lily. Your feet. And your breath, my love. Both kicking. Humans are so nasty," Samael replied with a shudder.

"We're nasty by design. You sky people fucked up," I quipped. Samael smirked.

"That's a lot to steal, Lily. Can't we buy the stuff this time?" Drake huffed loudly.

"Why pay for it when we can steal it? You never get caught, Drake. C'mon. For Marduk." I pouted and let out a soft sob.

Drake growled loudly. "Alright. But this is the last time I steal," he said adamantly.

"Get a black dragon kite. And don't forget the helium," I added.

"Make the blondes thick, Drake. You know how much Marduk loved round hips on his lasses," Samael said in a slightly wicked tone. He lit a cigarette and leaned back with a dreamy, boyish grin.

"This is the most ridiculous thing I've ever done," Drake said angrily as he drifted away, cursing beneath his breath.

I took a deep, ragged breath, then turned toward Samael with a fierce scowl. "Fair warning, Samael. If I lose another character, I'm done with this book."

His eyes were mischievous as he slowly scanned my legs, my breasts, then finally lifted his gaze to my eyes. He squinted and took a long drag from the cigarette, then grinned crookedly when he handed it to me. "The story isn't finished, Lily. You may not have lost any characters." He grinned mysteriously as he ran his hands through his hair in a charming move, then scowled and shifted uncomfortably when he caught me in a dazed stare, as though he were suddenly bored with my adoration. I didn't think I could feel any worse until he spoke again.

"You stink, girl. Run some water over yourself. Soap. Shampoo. I'm taking you to a Dead Party, but you're not the guest of honor," he said with a pronounced sneer.

"We call them funerals here, Samael." I took a long drag from the cigarette as the sting of his rejection settled deep in the core of my being.

"Not the same thing."

"Is it like a Jazz funeral? Dancing and music?"

"Not exactly. Dead Parties are nothing like any funeral you've ever been to."

"What's it like?" I asked in child-like awe and wonder.

Samael furrowed his brow, crossed his legs at the ankles, then began rubbing his toes together. "A Dead Party is…" he scrunched up his face and pursed his lips. "More like a masked Ball, but with better secrets. Revelations and hidden alliances. Sex, Lily. Lots of sex." He smiled when he saw that I was intrigued enough to lift myself from the floor. "There's my girl. Get yourself all dolled up, baby. You are cordially invited to Dorcha. To the Onyx Lair where Lilith is hosting a Dead Party in Marduk's honor."

"I'm really going to the Dead Party?"

Samael stood in one graceful move, then took two steps closer to me. He wrinkled his nose and pulled away from me an inch or two. Maybe a foot.

"Not in this condition. I'll take you to the best fuckin party you'll ever go to in all your many lives, Lily. If you take a fuckin shower." He lifted the cigarette from my fingers and flashed a seductive grin.

"What's the dress code?" I called out excitedly as I ran to my closet and began to rifle through it like a teenaged girl with a last minute second chance at a first date.

"Black, of course…and sexy," Samael said as he suddenly appeared behind me and began to rifle through the closet with me. He pulled out an outfit that made his black hole eyes widen with curiosity.

My cheeks blushed at the memory of the one time I wore this skin-tight black leather dominatrix outfit to a party in Manhattan.

"Is there a story behind this outfit?" Samael asked with a seductive grin. "There's definitely a story behind it…spill it, Lily," he teased.

"I have to shower." I smirked and walked away from him with a sway of my hips in a catwalk prance as I stripped naked and stepped into the shower.

"Look at you, all sassy and sexy," he said in a hoarse whisper, then slowly slithered toward me with his intentions evident. "I like this confident Lily."

Samael stripped off his shirt, then slowly lowered his jeans to proudly stand naked before me. Samael was the most beautiful creature I could possibly imagine, like nothing I'd ever seen before. His tightly corded, chiseled perfection was beyond my wildest definition of magnificence. My knees nearly gave way, but I managed to stand and take a step back.

"The contract, Sam," I said breathlessly.

"Contract says no sex. No copulation." He bit his lip and scanned every inch of me appreciatively as he stepped into the shower with a charming smile, then began to gently lather my hair, my neck, my shoulders. "Touching is allowed."

"I like touching," I said like a simpleton, but the hoarseness of my voice lent an air of sensuality Samael responded to immediately as he pulled me toward him.

He grinned devilishly, then lowered his lips over mine tenderly as warm water sprayed over both of us. He gently bit my bottom lip, then whispered softly against the corner of my mouth, "Tell me the story behind that outfit."

The Red Dragon

"He's dead. Nobody can lose this much blood and live. Not even the fucking Devil." The Red Dragon smiled wickedly as she walked around the abandoned warehouse where Marduk was shot. She touched the blood stains on the wall, licked her bloody fingers, then walked to the center of the room and dipped one booted foot in the thick pool of congealed blood on the floor. She bent to scoop up two test tubes full of Marduk's blood, snapped rubber caps over the tubes, then grinned victoriously when she held them up to the light. She turned again to cast a dark, narrow glare toward the other redhead pacing in circles across the room.

"You were sloppy, and you don't have what I asked for." The tall, elegant redhead walked around the room slowly, as she surveyed the damage with tight lips. "You'll get half the reward…when you find his body and bring me that fucking amulet. The cost of the window repair is coming out of your pay."

"Where am I supposed to look for the Devil's body?" The second redhead asked with a withered brow as she continued to pace back and forth in a narrow path.

"Why don't you ask your idiot son? He should be able to track his own father." She sat back and crossed her legs elegantly, then lit a black cigarette. "And what the fuck is this, Shannon?" The elegant redhead tossed a newspaper with the front-page picture of Amon and Aaden in the restaurant. "Why the hell didn't I know he was here? What do we pay you for?" She stood abruptly and charged toward Shannon, slapping her with enough ferocity to bring Shannon to her knees. "I want them all! This was our only chance to get the White One, you idiot! You're losing your focus!" She paced in a slow circle around Shannon, then kicked her viciously. "You better find that body. And keep looking for the sons. I want all of them," she said through a clenched jaw, then headed toward the door in heavy steps. "Clean up this fucking mess."

Shannon turned to her son with an angry scowl. "You see what you did? I told you to shoot him, Braedon! Now she's pissed and it's all your fault!" Shannon pulled herself up from the floor and wiped her hands on her skirt.

"I did shoot him, Mama! Look at all this blood! I shot him. I shot the Devil, just like you told me to, Mama."

"Then how did he get away?" Shannon shouted while waving her hands in the air.

"Cuz he's the Devil. He can't get dead, Mama. She's wrong. The Devil ain't dead," Braedon said softly while eyeing the bloody mess on the floor.

Shannon scoffed and groaned loudly. "You're the stupidest person alive, Braedon. How the hell did I end up giving birth to the stupidest person alive?"

"Cuz you fucked the Devil, Mama. That's how you ended up with me." Braedon held his hands up to his face when his mother charged at him and slapped him across the cheek. "Stop it, Mama. I'm just answering your question."

"I didn't ask a fucking question, Braedon."

"You asked how you got me, Mama. She says you fucked the Devil, and that's why I ain't as bright as the other kids in the program."

"Clean up this mess, Braedon. And don't try to think," she spat out.

"I ain't touching devil blood, Mama!" Braedon said loudly, then shirked away from the blood stains on the chair Marduk had been chained to when Shannon stabbed him.

"Don't be stupid, Braedon. Blood is blood. Besides, you're already touched by devil blood. It's in your veins, boy." She smiled wickedly at the shocked look on Braedon's face.

"Stop saying that, Mama. I ain't the Devil's son. I'm your son. I do what you tell me to do. I ain't never listened to the Devil, Mama," Braedon said as he pulled a mop and bucket to the center of the room where Marduk's blood covered half the floor. He sniffed and cried softly as he mopped up the blood that ran into a massive slick mess covering nearly the entire floor.

"Blessed are the meek, for they shall inherit the Earth," Braedon repeated over and over while mopping up the bloody mess he and his mother made in their clumsy attempt to appease the Red Dragon.

"Keep saying them scriptures, Braedon. God's watching you, Son," Shannon said in a dark tone meant to frighten Braedon. "He knows every bad and stupid thing you ever did." She laughed wickedly when Braedon began to weep softly.

"I'm sorry I made a mess, God. I'll do better next time." Braedon's shoulders slumped as he continued to mop up Marduk's blood. "Don't send me to hell, God, please don't let me burn in hell," Braedon prayed while mopping up his mess.

Shannon sat back lazily while watching him with squinted eyes and pursed lips. "You keep missing the same spot over and over, Braedon. To the right."

Braedon turned to his mother with a pinched face. "I ain't even finished yet, Mama! Gimme a minute. This is hard!" Braedon sniffed hard twice, then turned back to his task and scrubbed a little harder.

"Not there, you idiot! To the right! Jesus fuckin Christ, Braedon! How the hell can you not see it? Right! My right, Braedon!"

Braedon stopped crying and slumped against the wall. "Why didn't you say that in the first place. Your right…" He looked left to right with a strained grimace, then slapped his hands over his head. "How does it go again, Mama?"

Shannon groaned loudly and stormed toward Braedon with an angry scowl. "Braedon, how have you not learned this by now? You have to see things from my point of view! Not your own! My right is your left, idiot! The hand you write with, Braedon…that's your left, and my right!"

"Mama, if you just say…your left, Braedon, it would be a whole lot easier for me to get it," he whispered softly, then sobbed loudly as he looked back and forth from his left hand to his right in confusion.

"For fuck's sake, Braedon, just mop it all again!"

The Red Dragon walked out of the warehouse with her fire-red hair blowing wildly in the river breeze. She pulled her coat around her shoulders, then briefly glanced over her shoulder. She spotted Titus in an alley across the street from the warehouse, watching her with a confused look on his face. She slowed her pace, hoping he would follow her.

Titus did follow her, but he was more confused than ever. The device wasn't tracking her. The tracker was still in the warehouse she'd just left.

Titus scratched his bald head and wrinkled his brow. "I'm certain she's the one, but…" He'd been following her all night, but something was different about her today. She was more poised. He looked up at the warehouse, then back at the redhead walking away from the tracking device. "She must've found the tracker and ditched it. Fuck," Titus growled.

The Red Dragon smiled victoriously at Titus's confused hesitation as she ducked into a corner bar. She ordered a drink, then sent a text message to Shannon.

Titus pulled his coat around his body and followed her to the bar. He stopped just before stepping inside when the tracking device began to vibrate again.

"What the fuck?"

Titus finally put it all together when he looked over his shoulder and saw the second redhead a block away, scurrying out of the warehouse with her son.

"For fuck's sake…two of 'em?"

Titus backed out of the bar and sprinted across the street, then quickly doubled back around the block to the alley where he had a perfect view of both the warehouse and the bar. He watched Shannon and Braedon climb into the dark van, looking over their shoulders anxiously, then turned his attention back to the elegant redhead. He was mesmerized by her poise as she slowly sipped her Martini in the bar while half a dozen men closed in around her.

Titus looked back and forth between the two women and did a quick assessment. He wavered in his decision several times, but finally made a definite decision to follow the elegant redhead instead of the tracking device.

“I’ll be fuckin damned. I finally got ye,” he said under his breath as he pulled his hood over his head and settled into the alley for a long night of dramatic intrigue.

Chapter One

Marduk cringed and cowered defensively against the blackness of the void and jumped with a start when the first set of hands touched him. He pulled away quickly and ran right into a thick, dark mountain of flesh with a hundred and one hands dragging him farther and farther into a cavernous void. He screamed, growled, and howled, but no sound came from his mouth. The void was completely silent. He felt himself panting, gasping for air, but there was none. The last of the air from his lungs came out in a wisp of ice blue smoke that twisted and twirled into a tightly woven coil.

The blue light of his breath illuminated the cavern, and Marduk's voice finally broke through in a growling howl when he saw thousands of dead souls closing in on him with wicked grins and fiery eyes. He swung his fists as hard as he could, taking out a few dozen with the first punch, but he was immediately fatigued and doubled over from the searing pain in his chest.

He looked up just in time to see the coil of air turn blood red, then morph into a snake that slithered toward him with a wide mouth that grew enormously as it approached him. Marduk was mesmerized by its ice-blue eyes. He couldn't move, not even when the snake swallowed him whole.

Marduk gasped for air when he suddenly realized he could breathe inside the snake. He curled up in the fetal position, as though he were in a warm womb, then began to pant like a dog. He took in several deep breaths, then expelled a series of ice-blue coils. The coils turned into a dozen red and black snakes wriggling toward him. Marduk swung his fists and kicked wildly when the snakes began to strike against his ankles, then his thighs. He tried to grab them, but the snakes scattered, then came together again to form a huge coil that morphed into a raging bull charging at him. Marduk smiled when he punched the bull right in the nose, and it fell backward with a loud wail. He stopped fighting when he heard Omega's voice.

"Life or Death, Marduk?"

"Get me out of here, Father! Please…get me out of this snake. I have to find Bella!" Marduk screamed her name over and over, but there was no answer. "Where is she, Papa? Where is Bella?"

"Life or Death, Marduk?" Omega repeated.

"Bella!" Marduk screamed, then dug his fingers into the flesh of the snake, ripping his way through the belly. He gagged when the snake's blood dripped into his eyes, his nose, his mouth, and the stench of it filled his nostrils, but he fought through it, clawing and tearing the snake's flesh until he tore a hole large enough to crawl through.

Invisible hands grabbed him immediately and pulled him back into the cavern, scratching, clawing, tearing his flesh, and this time, the cavern was filled with the thunderous roar of thousands of desperate voices calling his name over and over and over, until the sound became a pulsing, primal rhythm pounding in his head as he was carried farther and farther into the void.

The void became silent again when he was suddenly struck in the chest by an unseen force, and he once again released the last breath of air in his lungs. He watched in awe as the coil morphed into a red dragon this time. He cowered at the red beast snorting smoke at him, but his fear subsided when he finally saw Bella in the distance beyond the dragon. Bella's smile was radiant as she held out her graceful hand to him.

Marduk burst into tears when he saw the full-bodied specter of Princess Arabel in all her glorious beauty. Her dark hair flowed in perfect waves around her shoulders. Her cheeks were flushed and plump in a pinkish hue that matched her lips. Lilith's lips. He suddenly found the strength to shirk off the dark souls grabbing and clawing him, then fiercely marched toward Bella in determined steps.

Come play with me, Papa, Bella said softly, but the roaring cry of the dead rose to a crescendo, becoming louder and louder with each step he took.

"Are you certain you want to go forward, Marduk?" Omega asked in a thunderous voice.

"I have to save her, Papa. I cannot leave Bella in this hell alone," Marduk screamed as he struggled to get to Bella, but the weight of his own body was too much for him to carry. He fell to the ground and crawled past the dragon, ducking its fire and clawing the ground to get closer to Bella. Her tinkling, child-like laughter floated in the air as she led him deeper into the void.

When Marduk finally made it to Bella, he was met by a pack of wild dogs foaming at the mouth, and Bella disappeared into the darkness.

"You must make 3 negative confessions," the dogs said in unison.

"I have never killed anyone that did not deserve it," he said quickly. The dogs growled fiercely and moved closer. Marduk began to sweat when he realized that although he did not personally kill Sekhmet's victims, he was responsible for their deaths. He wiped his brow and dropped to his knees.

"I have never killed anyone with anger or malice in my spirit. I have never taken anything that did not belong to me. I have never lifted angry hands to my wife," he choked out, and the dogs suddenly disappeared. Marduk's breathing was heavy as he gingerly stepped through the gate that creaked open slowly. He began to cry again when he saw Bella standing at the end of the pathway.

Come, Papa. It is almost over…then you can play with me.

Marduk finally reached Bella again, only to be met by the fire-breathing dragon blocking her from his view. Marduk stood perfectly still, except for the shivers running up his spine as the dragon spewed fire all around him, but he was untouched by the flames.

"Three negative confessions."

"I did not cheat on my wife and lovers…until they cheated on me. I never left the innocent defenseless in times of desperate need. I never fucked a woman who did not want me to fuck her."

The dragon disappeared in a ball of fire, and another gate slowly creaked open. Marduk followed Bella's voice until he hit a brick wall, and a Gryphon with bloody talons perched on his back. The creature leaned forward to stare into his eyes.

"Three negative confessions."

Marduk began to sweat when he realized he had no more negative confessions to make. "I had to do these things! It was my duty! To refuse would have disrespected my father, Amon, and the Elders! I did not disrespect my father! Nor did I disrespect Amon. The Elders did not receive my full respect, but neither did they receive the full brunt of my wrath."

Marduk was surprised when the creature flew away with a loud screech and the brick wall, the third gate, slowly opened.

Omega appeared in front of the wall and held his hands against Marduk's chest. "Once you go through this gate, Marduk, there is no turning back."

"I have to find Bella! I cannot leave her, Father…let me through. I made my confessions!"

Omega nodded slowly, sadly, then gingerly stepped aside. "Welcome to your death, Marduk."

Chapter Two

13 Weeks Later

Mia slowly made her way through the hallways of the Crystal Palace in heavy steps. She was feeling lonely today and badly missing New Orleans, or so she thought. Mia didn't really know who or what it was she was missing, but she was never more aware of how far from home she was. She was also aware that she had no one to lean on. Declan and Caraye's romantic bliss was evident to everyone, so was Jade and Killian's. Both were constant reminders that the romantic attachments she hoped to develop had all recently detached from her. Including Cain.

Mia stopped near the central rose garden and let out a deep, sad sigh as she watched the silver fairies fluttering around the roses. She thought it was the most romantic thing she'd ever seen, but all her romantic interests were gone. Cain was in Dorcha with Lilith. She suspected Raven was there too. Mia hadn't seen either of them in weeks. Her friendships and family connections were tenuous as well. Caraye was always with Declan, who hovered over her like one of the fairies hovering over Nahemah's roses, with wings flapping softly against the petals. Jade and Killian were training for the Revolution, and falling deeper in love with each other. They had been working day and night, and she hadn't had any alone time with her son for weeks. The

Army ship still hadn't returned from the rescue mission after four months, and they were long overdue.

Mia breathed in the ambrosial scent of the roses and closed her eyes as her shoulders dropped. "The romance in Gael ain't all it's cracked up to be."

Mia started back toward her suite with a heavy spirit, walking through the short hallway, gingerly running her fingertips along the crystal walls, and wishing she could read the history of those walls. She wanted to know so much more about Gael. She knew she could find her answers in Declan's library, but the books seemed fruitless without Cain or Declan to answer her barrage of questions.

Mia turned the corner into the long hallway, and stopped short when she spotted two tall figures at the other end. She stopped breathing for 10 seconds, then shivered slightly when she recognized Lugh with a young man who looked exactly like him.

Aaden stepped up to Lugh and playfully held up his fists, then let out a rebel yell as he and Lugh circled each other with wide smiles. Lugh grabbed Aaden's neck, and held him in a wrestle hold, then gathered him into his arms as he kissed the top of his head.

"Welcome to Gael, Aaden. This was my home…before I met your mother and we began our family. I love Earth, don't get me wrong, but Gael is full of magic you're not going to believe. It's good to be home. Even better with you here."

"I could use a little magic in my life. I hope the lasses in Gael are as beautiful as Amon said they were." Aaden chuckled and snuggled closer to Lugh.

"I think ye'll be happy with our Gaelic Princesses," Lugh replied with a hearty laugh.

Mia instinctively knew the young man was Lugh's son, and she was afraid Lugh's wife had come to Gael as well. Her heart began to pound in her chest, but her cheeks flushed when she realized that it was just Lugh and his son walking the hallways together. She took two steps forward, but her legs went weak at the sight of Lugh's golden hair pulled back in a messy bun as he approached in a Navy-blue Army uniform and knee-length boots. She took in a deep breath and let it all out in a breathy sigh. Golden Lugh was back in Gael, and the air suddenly filled with romance again.

Mia leaned against the wall and grinned as she watched Lugh in the distance with light and bouncy steps as he held his arm around the young man's shoulders. She looked over Lugh's shoulder for Marduk. Her heart sped up at the thought of seeing him again, marching down the hallway with his kilt swinging around his long, lean legs. Mia fanned herself as her cheeks flushed again, and she stretched her neck further to look for him. Her eyes lit up when Amon rounded the corner several feet behind Lugh with a full procession of Soldiers. She drew in her breath, then sighed dreamily over the regal elegance of Amon walking slowly and somberly while the Soldiers gathered around him in a tight formation, holding their swords over his head. She tried to look over Amon's shoulder to see if Marduk was in that procession, but she couldn't see past the Soldiers. She groaned softly when she saw a young woman with pale blonde hair walking arm-in-arm with Amon, and several young women and men trailing behind them. She hoped they weren't Lugh's wife and children. There was a family resemblance between the young men and women, but they had a wide variety of coloring. There were three giggly girls with bright red hair mingling with an overprotective young lad with slick, dark hair. He stood out from the crowd because of his sullen frown and stiff shoulders.

Mia lifted her hand to her chest when she saw the resemblance between Amon and the girl on his arm. She knew it was Aramanth. She suddenly got a little teary-eyed at that thought of what she'd just been through. Mia's soft heart instinctively wanted to mother her. She wanted desperately to be useful in any possible way.

"The procession of the Gods. That's something you don't see every day. Look at Amon with his swagger on. I'll be damned. God got game," Mia chuckled and crossed her arms over her chest, then stretched her neck to search for Marduk again. She was once again disappointed by his absence.

Lugh was ecstatically happy to have Aaden with him in Gael, and was more than pleased that Aaden accepted the truth of his existence without question. Aaden couldn't deny it, and didn't want to. Aaden was immediately in love with Gael, and more enchanted than ever with his father. It all made sense now. Aaden was relieved to finally know what he'd suspected all his life about his father. He wasn't a mere mortal.

"Dad, this place fuckin rocks. I wanna learn everything." Aaden looked around the Crystal Palace with wide, shiny eyes, noting every detail in the intricately carved crystal walls and ceilings. He wanted to remember everything, so he could tell Maggie when he returned to Bethel Woods. He couldn't believe he was actually here, in Gael. In the magical mystery place his father talked about all his life. It was better than he imagined from Lugh's detailed descriptions.

"Aye. Ye will, Aaden. I'll teach ye myself. Me and you, Son…we're gonna rock this place harder." Lugh pulled

Aaden to him and tousled his hair. “Declan is here, ye know.”

Aaden’s eyes widened. “Uncle Declan is alive?”

“Aye. He’s alive. He’s been in Gael all this time. Declan is Amon’s Heir. He’s been tucked away for years, learning and preparing to rule.”

“I’ll be damned. Ye knew this? And didn’t tell us? Cheap shot, Dad.” Aaden grinned and aimed his right fist at Lugh’s face, but punched Lugh in the gut with his left instead. Lugh doubled over in pain, with a wide grin on his face.

“Ye’ve perfected that move, kiddo. Ye finally got me.”

Aaden grinned. “Ye’re getting old, dad. Finally.”

Lugh squinted playfully and pulled Aaden into a fierce choke hold.

“Respect your elders, lad,” Lugh chuckled, but shivered when he thought about introducing Aaden to his Elders.

Aaden broke free from Lugh’s hold and proudly bounced alongside his father. “Why is Declan the Heir, Dad? Why not you?”

“Declan’s the First Son. I’m the Second Son.”

“Hmmph… if it goes by birth rank, then I’m screwed. I’m way down on that list.” Aaden grinned.

“Being the second son, or the seventh, has its advantages. I was able to live my life on Earth for a season. To marry your mother and raise my brood alongside her.” Lugh hugged Aaden again. “Declan was confined all this time.”

Lugh wasn’t ready to explain the details of Declan’s disappearance, nor his confinement with the Elders. He wanted to ease Aaden into the story, but he was anxious for

Aaden to get to know Declan. Lugh clearly saw the commonalities between the two of them, and knew they would find themselves in each other.

"I can't wait for ye meet your Uncle Declan, Aaden. My big lug of a brother is the best thing about Gael."

Lugh was anxious to see Declan again, but was a bit worried about how to broach the subject of Caraye with Aaden. He decided to cross that bridge when he came to it. For now, he was happy to be home, with Aaden at his side.

Lugh missed a step when he spotted Mia leaning against the wall. His cheeks turned bright red, and his heart began to pound so loudly he was afraid Aaden would hear it. He was inclined to scoop Mia up into his arms, but he wanted to ease Aaden into Gael first, and ease him into the idea of his father with another woman as well.

"Welcome home, Lugh," Mia called out with a brilliant smile.

Lugh nodded politely and pulled Aaden close to him. "I got my son with me." He grinned, and bounced his steps toward her. "This is Aaden. My youngest. Aaden, this is Mia. She's Declan's guest." Lugh scanned her body quickly while he drew in a sharp breath. He gently kissed her hand, then squeezed it lightly, but didn't hold it long.

Aaden looked Mia over from head to toe very slowly with undisguised appreciation. "Pleasure to meet ye, Mia. You're right about the Gaelic Princesses, Dad." Aaden kissed her hand, then ran his thumb along the back of it while his sea-green eyes glowed with obvious interest.

Mia gave him a playful smirk and raised an eyebrow. Aaden looked just like Lugh, but his mannerisms were more like Declan's. "Very nice to meet you, Aaden. I look forward to getting to know you," Mia said in her most regal manner and flashed her infamous smile. Both Aaden and Lugh drew in their breath quickly, then let it out in an airy whistle. Mia grinned at their synchronicity, then raised her skirt an inch to do a little curtsy, showing off her firm thighs. The display didn't escape notice from neither father nor son.

Lugh bowed gracefully to Mia with a shy smile, and gave her another quick but thorough once over, then stepped away from her without another word. He pulled Aaden along with him, but Aaden glanced back over his shoulder and winked at her.

Even though Lugh was preoccupied and barely acknowledged her, Mia's body and spirit were suddenly on fire. The stale air in Gael was blowing again. She knew this transition with Aaden wasn't going to be easy, so she sadly resigned herself to a shadow existence in Lugh's vision for the time being.

Mia turned back to watch Amon and Aramanth approaching, but couldn't help looking past them for any sign of Marduk. He was still nowhere in sight, but she smiled broadly when she caught Aramanth's eye and saw a sparkle in them.

"You must be Declan's wife. I'm Aramanth. I've waited so long to meet the woman who would steal my brother's heart." Aramanth scanned Mia's face for a sign of Issa, but she didn't see it.

Amon stepped forward to kiss Mia's cheek gently, then wrapped his long arms around her gently as he held her against his chest for a moment. "Mia, you are a rare and beautiful sight for my weary eyes."

"Welcome home, Amon," she whispered, then breathed in his musky scent. Everything was normal again with Amon back in the Crystal Palace.

"Aramanth, this is Mia LeBlanc. Declan's wife is Caraye. You will meet her soon. Mia and Caraye are best friends…sisters…and more." Amon touched Mia's cheeks softly and smiled shyly. "We will have a feast tonight to celebrate our return. Everyone is invited, and you will sit near me at the banquet table, Mia. We have much news to share with Gael," Amon said in a soft voice. Despite the turmoil and tragedy of his journey, Amon was relieved to be home, back in his Crystal Palace where he knew the protocols, and knew every single face. He couldn't wait to see Makawee. He sent Angelus to retrieve her from the Citadel the moment they landed on the shores of Gael.

Aramanth smiled shyly at Mia as a spark of recognition dawned on her. "I'm very happy to meet my new sister's sister. Welcome to Gael, Mia. Sit next to me tonight, okay?"

Mia felt an instant kinship with Aramanth. She'd just been through a horrific ordeal, but she was on her feet and seemed none the worst for her ordeal.

"You got it, sister," Mia said with a firm nod. Mia admired Aramanth's fortitude as well as the scrappiness in her demeanor. Aramanth was exactly what she hoped she would be. "Who are these young folks?" Mia added as she looked over the group of young people shadowing Amon.

"These are my nieces and nephews from Críoch. They will join us for dinner tonight. Tomorrow they will be returned to their mothers in the Citadel."

The dark-haired lad with a bored scowl bowed reverently and took Mia's hand. "Prince Scotch, Son of Seth." He gave Mia a thorough scan, then waved his hand at the others while rolling his eyes. "These are my sisters and cousins. Boring bunch of twits of no importance," he continued in a droll tone and a sneering smirk. "Our fathers are in prison…thanks to you."

Mia pulled her hand away from Scotch immediately and opened her mouth to give Scotch a much needed scolding, but Amon's deep, sad sigh stopped her.

"Forgive my nephew, Mia. He is misinformed and in dire need of discipline that I and the Elders will give him straight away." Amon shot Scotch a fierce look, then bowed his head reverently to Mia and led Aramanth down the hallway with a shy blush creeping up his cheeks. The young Princesses gawked at her with open curiosity, maybe a hint of admiration while Scotch sneered angrily at Amon's back.

Mia watched them all with a wide smile until they disappeared around the arc of the hallway. When she turned around again, she drew in a sharp breath at the tall, dark-skinned man standing directly in front of her with a wide grin and curious eyes.

"I am Draco, Son of Li Jing." He leaned in closer and scanned her face with an awestruck grin.

Mia's heart pounded wildly. Draco was the most handsome man she'd ever seen. He wasn't beautiful like Lugh and Cain, nor was he fiercely savage like Marduk. He was handsomely chiseled, with high cheekbones, smooth mahogany skin, and dark, almond-shaped eyes that glowed with wisdom. Mia couldn't breathe with Draco standing so close to her. She had a strong urge to touch him, to read his entire life. Mia was unbearably intrigued by Draco, and wanted to know his history in the Colonies. He was an African man with a Chinese name, living among the Gaelic Gods. Draco, Son of Li Jing was a layered mystery Mia wanted to peel in small bits.

"Mia LeBlanc," she said in a hoarse whisper.

"Mia the White." Draco held one hand to her face and gently ran his fingertips across her cheek bone. "But you are amber." He scanned her wild hair standing on end around her face. "And gold," Draco added softly, then bowed gracefully to her before he followed Amon down the hallway. Draco couldn't resist looking back at her once with a wide grin and sparkling eyes.

Mia's knees went weak and she nearly fell over. She had to lean against the wall to hold herself up. Her King of Spades, the dark warrior, had arrived. She couldn't wait to tell Caraye.

Mia turned around to look for Marduk again, but he still hadn't made an appearance in the hallway. A cold shiver ran through her body. Something was wrong with this triumphant return to Gael. Mia took slow steps forward in hopes of finding Marduk, but the halls were still empty of his commanding presence. Mia walked a little faster as her heart pounded wildly in her chest. Dark thoughts filled her mind, but she willed them away.

Mia braced herself as she finally reached the end of the hallway. She closed her eyes, held her breath, and stepped around the corner. Nothing. Marduk wasn't on either end of the long, winding hallway. Her shoulders slumped as she raised her hand to her lips.

"No," she said softly, then turned to make her way back down the hallway with a confused and withered face. She took five steps forward, then stopped when she felt a wave of energy behind her.

Mia gasped loudly when she turned and finally saw Marduk leaning lightly on a cane in his right hand; his left arm was in a sling, He was pale and thinner, but still took up the entire hallway.

Marduk sauntered toward her in heavy steps. His kilt swayed lighter than usual around his legs as he approached her with a slight limp and a stoic face. His eyes slowly ran the full length of her body and back up again before he closed the gap between them to stand in front of her with his shoulders squared.

"Welcome home, Marduk," Mia said barely above a whisper. The air in the inches between them crackled and made her shiver as the hair on the back of her neck stood on end. Her unruly curls plumped up and spread wide from the massive amounts of energy Marduk exuded.

Marduk's eyelids were heavy as he looked past her at the visage of Maddie on Mia's shoulder. He leaned in closer to Mia and growled in a low tone. His lips lingered near hers, but he didn't kiss her.

Mia stared up at him wide-eyed, barely breathing in short, staccato breaths. She leaned in closer to him, but didn't move in for the kiss she wanted so badly from Marduk's thick, wine-stained lips.

Marduk scanned her face, then growled once more before he blinked and looked away. He tucked his cane under his arm and walked away from her without saying a word. She watched him walk away with only a hint of a limp as his kilt swayed and fanned out majestically around his legs. Marduk never looked back.

"Watch this, Mom," Jade called out as she dove into the wheel and gracefully made seven rotations without slamming her face into the floor. She pressed one foot on the pad behind her and reversed her spin as she grabbed the bars of the wheel, flipped her legs outside the wheel, and held a graceful pose as the wheel rolled slowly. She slipped back inside in perfect time to catch the roll of it as though she were an extension of the wheel. She managed to hold on in an upside-down rotation, then stopped the wheel with her left foot, just before it rolled into a red line. She stepped out with a sassy grin and bowed gracefully.

"Bravo, Jade!" Killian called out as he clapped slowly and let out a New Orleans rebel yell. "You mastered the wheel!" Killian's maple eyes shined with a romantic fire as he scanned Jade's long, lean body that had become sleek, toned, and more limber than ever. Killian wanted to run into the circle to kiss her and run his hands along her body, just as they did every night when they dove off the ledge together, sharing ardent kisses in the weightless anti-gravity shaft, but Killian didn't want to ruin her shining moment.

"Ye did it, Jade! Seven rotations!" Declan yelled out with a wide smile. He leaned in and kissed Caraye's grinning cheek. "Our daughter is so graceful, *mo shíorghrá*." Declan's cheeks blushed at the soft look of love in Caraye's eyes as she watched Jade's triumphant moment. He knew for certain she'd be an attentive mother to his son as well. Rory would be well-loved.

"Jade, that was amazing! You're so graceful, kitten!" Caraye made a start toward her, but Declan stopped her with a worried look on his face.

"There are trigger wires, my love. Stay behind the lines. We don't want Rory to go through that." Declan winced as he pointed above him at the maze in the rafters.

Caraye looked up at the monstrous contraption above her and shivered slightly. She instinctively held her hand to her belly. "I wanna try that wheel myself. After Rory is born." She smiled up at Declan as she held onto his arm.

"I'll teach ye, my love. I taught Jade." Declan puffed up with pride and blushed at Caraye's gentle hand on his face.

"Jade is blossoming under your training, Declan. She's more graceful than I've ever seen her. And fierce! Thank you for taking care of my baby girl," Caraye said softly.

"She's my baby girl, too," Declan said proudly as he watched Jade go through her routine one more time with fierce determination. "I want her well-trained for this battle." He wrapped his arms around Caraye when he felt her tense up at the mention of Jade in a battle. He rested his forehead against hers before kissing her tenderly. "Ye're the most beautiful pregnant woman I've ever seen, Caraye. Jade will figure it out soon if we don't tell her." Declan bit his lip and sighed a deep, contented sigh. He'd never been happier in his entire life and wanted this euphoric feeling to last, but there was a nagging pull on his spirit that he couldn't push away.

"I was kinda hoping to do it tonight. I wanted to make sure that I made it past the first trimester," Caraye said softly. "But all is well with our little boy. It's time to make our announcement, Declan."

"I can hardly wait to see her face when she hears the news. Aye, *mo shíorghrá*, tonight we'll announce Rory."

Declan looked back at the circle with a furrowed brow when he heard a sharp yelp from Jade. His eyes widened when he saw the iron claw pick her up by the waist and lift her into the air toward the maze above. Caraye yelled out and made a move toward Jade, but Declan held her back.

"No! The traps, Caraye! I'll rescue Jade. Stay right here." Declan took two steps toward Jade, but stopped when he heard a loud shriek behind him. He turned to see a young man with golden hair run past him right into one of the trigger lines.

"I got this," the golden boy yelled out loudly as another claw took him up to the rafters right behind Jade, who was being tousled by the padded mechanical arms punching her in the gut. Jade fell to the floor and screamed loudly as the stranger made his way through the tunnel, gliding around the mechanical arms with grace and ease, flipping and ducking over and beneath them seconds before they hit him. His laughter rang out loudly through the gym.

"For fuck's sake, this is awesome!"

Declan squinted as he watched this display with interest while wondering who this young man was. The answer dawned on him when he saw his golden hair flying wildly as he dove over a series of traps.

The golden stranger reached Jade in seven quick moves, then dove to the floor beside her and threw his body over hers. He bit his lip when he looked down at Jade with a wide, flirtatious grin on his face.

"I'm Aaden. At your service, Princess." Aaden drew in his breath, then ducked just before a mechanical fist popped out, narrowly missing his head.

Jade stared into his sea-green eyes and felt like she'd just been hit in the gut. She couldn't take her eyes from his angelic face, inches away from hers as he scanned her with open admiration.

"Jade," she answered breathlessly.

"Your eyes match your name, lass," Aaden said softly, then leaned down a little closer. "It seems ye're in need of rescuing. For the low, low price of a single kiss, I'll be your champion, lass." Aaden lifted one eyebrow with a cocky grin and didn't wait for Jade's answer before lowering his mouth over hers while running his hands through her hair.

Jade's lips burned from Aaden's warm mouth against hers. She couldn't stop herself from touching his cheek. The warmth of his blush burned her palm.

Killian also felt like he'd been hit in the gut as he watched this golden stranger kissing Jade as though it were his right. Killian stepped toward the red line, but Declan held him back.

"She'll be down before ye make it up there."

Declan draped his arm around Killian's shoulders and winced at the pain in Killian's eyes as he watched Aaden lift Jade in his arms to carry her through the maze as he dodged each blow in graceful steps, laughing and yelling wildly.

Jade couldn't take her eyes from Aaden's blushing cheeks as she giggled and squealed while holding her arms around his neck. She was amazed by his grace, as well as the wild shine of determination in his eyes.

Aaden kept his eyes on the mechanical arms swinging toward his head, and the sharp pendulums ahead of him, but he was very aware of Jade's eyes on him. He cast a sexy grin at her when he finally made it to the end of the maze, but took a hard blow to his left side with ease before diving down the winding silver slide with Jade in his arms. He struck a cocky pose at the end of it, then set Jade on her feet, but he held her around the waist firmly. He winked as he leaned in again for a second kiss, but Killian stepped forward and pulled Jade from his arms.

"You okay, baby? Are you hurt?" Killian cupped his hands around Jade's face and kissed her fiercely. He wanted to wipe away the kiss of this bold stranger who was gawking at them with an open mouth and squinted eyes.

Aaden was more than curious about the young lovers. He wondered how closely bonded they were, and whether he could get a fingernail's wedge between them. His heart pounded and sank simultaneously when he noticed that there was no light between them at the moment.

Jade giggled as she wrapped her arms around Killian. "A little bruised, a little embarrassed, but I survived. Thank you, Aaden." She turned to Aaden and smiled sweetly, but rested her head against Killian's chest.

Killian smiled at Aaden with tight lips, but there was no real malice in his demeanor. "Thanks for rescuing my girl. I would've done it myself, but you beat me to the red line. I'm Killian." He held out one hand, but kept the other around Jade.

"Aaden. Pleasure was all mine." Aaden stepped forward and took Killian's hand while winking at Jade. "That was fuckin awesome! Right, Jade? Let's do it again sometime. Ye should try the maze yourself, Killian. If ye're brave enough." Aaden spinned gracefully and kicked the air above Killian's head, barely touching the tips of his curls that fluttered from the force of Aaden's kick.

"I'm brave enough," Killian said while holding his position at Jade's side. He neither blinked nor flinched at Aaden's reckless display.

"Ye don't have the look of a warrior, Killian," Aaden said with a raised eyebrow as he crossed his arms over his wide chest.

"Looks are often deceiving, Aaden. Like that cocky stance of yours. Most people would think you're confident in your abilities, but it tells me a different story. You're not as badass as you want to be."

Aaden laughed loudly, then squared his shoulders. "Care to make a wager on my badassery, Killy-boy?"

"I'm not a fucking boy!" Killian spat out as he stood eye to eye against Aaden's grinning face.

Jade stepped in between them, holding her hands against their chests to push them apart. Aaden touched Jade's hand and rubbed his thumb along the back of it, but never took his eyes away from Killian.

"Okay, guys. You're both fierce. You're both badass. Put the testosterone to the test on the obstacle course. We're not fighting each other." Jade rolled her eyes and shook her head, then walked toward the edge of the ring to watch the scene she knew was about to unfold.

Declan turned slowly and drew in his breath when he saw Lugh standing in the back of the gym with a wide grin on his ruddy cheeks as he jogged toward Declan with his arms held out.

"Brother! I'm home! With my son. That's my Aaden," Lugh said proudly. Lugh wrapped his arms around Declan and lifted him off his feet slightly.

Despite all the turmoil in Declan's spirit, tears welled up in his eyes, and he hugged Lugh fiercely. His heart broke, and so did his anger. He couldn't deny the fact that Lugh's presence lit up the room significantly. It lit up Caraye's face too. She wedged in between the two of them and basked in the glow of love while her husband and father kissed her flushed, rosy-pink cheeks simultaneously.

"Welcome home, Lugh," she said breathlessly.

"It's good to be home, lass. I've missed my big lug of a brother!" Lugh said in a spirited growl. "Aramanth is safe, Declan. Our little sister is home safe, and she's dying to meet ye, Caraye."

Declan's chest expanded against his will when he saw the undisguised affection in Lugh's eyes as he looked at Caraye. He saw what he needed to see in Lugh's eyes in that moment. He breathed his first sigh of relief, but there were still unanswered questions and a long discussion to come.

Lugh noticed the glow in Caraye's cheeks, and grinned wider. He held her gently and didn't swing her around the room as he wanted to.

"Declan…I see a glow on my daughter's face that I am very familiar with. Congratulations, brother. Ye're going to be a father." Lugh gingerly touched Caraye's belly, and let out a happy chuckle as tears formed in the corners of his eyes.

"Aye. We're having a baby. Be careful with my wife, brother. I couldn't part with her for the world. Anyone who attempts to harm my wife will die by my hands. Even you, little Lugh," Declan said firmly.

Lugh looked deep into Declan's eyes and easily read the pain and betrayal in them. He knew Declan well enough to read his thoughts further. Lugh's face fell as he blushed softly.

"Brother…" Lugh broke into sad tears as he pulled Declan away from Caraye. Declan went reluctantly at first, but Lugh pulled harder and whispered into Declan's ear. "I didn't mean to hurt ye, Declan. And I wouldn't hurt your wife, my daughter, for anything…or anyone. Not even for you." Lugh pulled away, and stared into Declan's eyes tenderly, then pressed his forehead against Declan's.

"I learned of it from Samuel. Tough blow, Lugh. Ye should have told me yourself," Declan said through tight lips.

"Aye, I had my own turmoil, Declan, but I should have told ye," Lugh said quietly. "Can we get past this, brother?"

"In time, Lugh. Give me some time," Declan whispered back.

"I'm home now and have nothing but time." Lugh clapped Declan on the back. "Ask anything ye want to know. I'm an open book, and my page is turned to your story. Anything ye need to know, brother, just ask."

"Aramanth is safe, ye say?" Declan asked softly.

"Aye. She rescued herself, Declan. Ye should have seen her! Our little sister beat the snot out of Malachi." Lugh's wide shoulders shook as he wiped away his tears and grinned like a young boy. "We taught her well." Lugh wanted to bring back a happy smile to Declan's face, but Declan merely offered a slight nod.

"Aye, Aramanth is strong," Declan replied with a withered face. Declan knew he'd have to face Aramanth and Amon now too. The idea of it stung his heart.

"We're home, but the journey was far from easy. We lost Marduk, Declan."

"How the fuck can ye lose Marduk?" Declan asked with a chuckle, but the sadness in Lugh's eyes told him this was a serious matter.

"He was attacked in New York. Shot and stabbed. Marduk died, Declan."

"Marduk is dead?" Declan whispered.

Lugh saw the shock on Declan's face as the blood drained from his face, so he continued quickly. "He was dead, for several minutes… but Amon brought him back. It took three whacks in the chest with those big ham-fists to bring Marduk back from the dead. He's alive, Declan, though hardly well." Lugh hung his head and sighed heavily when he thought about the day Marduk died. It was the heaviest and darkest moment Lugh had ever faced in his life. "Everyone is home safe."

Declan released a heavy rush of air. "Is Marduk alright? Lugh…is Marduk whole?" Declan's chest was so tight he could barely breathe. His knees went weak as he waited for Lugh's answer.

"He's whole. Scarred and badly battered, but he'll be fine, in time. Scariest thing I ever witnessed, Declan. Not his death…his fuckin return to life. He was pissed at us for taking him from his peace. He fought like the fuckin devil's devil. Clawing at the air, crying out for Bella with a monstrous grimace. He screeched and screamed like a fuckin demon. It was the most wicked sound I've ever heard. Then he hit Amon square in the nose and wrestled me and Draco until he finally passed out again. He hasn't been the same since. His body is fine, but his spirit, Declan…" Lugh shivered when he recalled the violent way Marduk returned to his body. Marduk was recovering from his physical wounds, but his psyche was still fragile from his ordeal.

"I have to see him," Declan said absently and swallowed back tears. He was familiar with the weight of death on his shoulders, and he knew he might be the only one to pull Marduk fully back into life. "I'm glad ye're home, little Lugh. I'm glad everyone is home safe."

Declan's heart was heavy at the news of Marduk, and he felt the fragility of life acutely. He didn't have the energy to hold his anger against his betrayers, his family. He wanted answers and would get them in time. Until then, his own family was his priority.

Declan nodded politely, coolly, then made his way back to Caraye. He draped his arms around her from behind, lacing his fingers gently over her belly. He was determined to protect his unborn son at any cost.

Lugh's heart broke at Declan's aloof attitude. He wanted a hero's welcome from his brother, but he knew he would have to earn Declan's trust again. He wiped the tears from his eyes, and turned to watch Aaden in the ring, circling Killian with a cocky grin.

"I'm taking my wife to safety, brother. There are trigger wires in the gymnasium. Do not cross the line, Lugh," Declan said in a hushed tone, then led Caraye out the gym. He never looked back.

Lugh's face withered into a heavy grimace. He'd lost so much over his decision to reincarnate Issa. He couldn't bear the thought of losing Declan too. Lugh sat heavily on the bench and focused his attention on Aaden. Right now, Aaden was all he had for certain, and he hoped that wouldn't change after Aaden learned all the secrets hovering in the air above him.

Aaden let out a loud yell and flipped mid-air, then ran to the sparring course to begin a series of powerful moves. He ran the entire course, kicking, sweeping, and bouncing off each of the sparring boards with graceful ease. He did a double flip in the air and grinned when he noticed Jade staring at him with wide eyes full of admiration. He added another extra flip at the end of the course, then landed solidly on his feet. He bowed with his arms held out wide and his eyes fixed on Jade.

The exchange wasn't lost on Killian, who moved into his own series of moves, matching Aaden's steps exactly, flip for flip, kick for kick. Killian also landed gracefully on his feet next to Aaden, then held his hand out to him with a confidant smile on his face. Jade's eyes were on Killian again, which made his chest puff up a little.

Aaden raised both eyebrows as he took Killian's hand. "Impressive," he said in a friendly tone. "Let's do it again. Triple kicks…if ye can." Aaden winked at Jade before going through the course again with more power this time. He held a fierce face as he watched Killian's long, lean body follow his moves with precision. He'd never felt more alive in his entire life. He reversed the course, and moved toward Killian with fierce determination. When the two of them met in the center of the circle, Aaden took up a warrior's stance with a gleam in his eyes.

"Let's see how ye measure up against a real man, Killian."

"When you become a real man, Aaden…let me know," Killian said as he marched off the floor toward Jade.

Jade barely noticed Killian coming towards her. She was staring wide-eyed at Aaden pulling his golden hair into a tight bun as he grinned crookedly at her. Jade's heart was in her throat; she couldn't breathe.

Chapter Three

Marduk took slow strides through the Onyx Lair with an easy swagger that covered his limp as he made his way down the dark hallways. His entire body ached, but he ditched his cane in the shuttle, along with his arm sling. He wasn't going to let anyone in Dorcha see him limping in pain. Especially Lilith.

He squared his shoulders and cleared his mind of the doubts, self-deprecation, and fear burning in his mind, as well as the searing pain burning in his body. He focused instead on the burning passion under his kilt and turned toward Lilith's suite.

The entire time Marduk was in the Onyx, Lilith was the focus of his mind's eye. Her failures, for the most part, and all the ways in which he couldn't forgive her. But when he hovered between life and death, he couldn't remember a single one of her failures. Instead, he remembered her bold, feisty spirit, her playful seductions, her curvy body, her sculpted cheekbones, her wild mane of hair, and most of all, her wicked craftiness that never failed to excite him. He finally realized that he could no longer live without her. No one else awakened his entire being like Lilith, and he wanted a fresh start with her. He wasn't sure how he was going to manage, it, but he was determined to give his marriage another chance. Not just for himself and Lilith, but he was certain Bella would return if he and Lilith were together again.

Mia's face flashed in his head for a second, but he willed it away. In his mind, he failed Mia in losing the Red Dragon again. He didn't avenge her mother's murder, and he was still stinging a little from her rejection. He clearly saw today that she wanted him, and part of him wanted her too. But Cain's declaration of love and intent to win her back was a line Marduk wasn't willing to cross. He wanted a second chance with Cain as well, despite his deception with Lucian. He wanted to give Cain a chance to turn it all around, or confess, at the very least. Marduk wanted his family back, but more than anything, he wanted Lilith, his familiar lover, his Queen that he'd held at arm's length far too long.

Marduk adjusted his kilt as his erection began to stir beneath it, and limped a little faster toward Lilith, who he knew for certain wanted his love. Lilith had never refused his love in the 3000 years since he found her dancing near the rose garden and was stung by her thorn. That thorn was Marduk's constant reminder of Lilith. Today, he didn't need a thorn to remind him how much he loved her.

Lilith rolled onto her side, pulling Raven closer to her as she arched her back and purred softly against Raven's cheek. "You are so tender. I love that about you."

Raven smirked and rolled her eyes. "I'm not tender. And don't even mention the "L" word around me. I don't do the love thing."

Lilith chuckled softly and kissed Raven passionately. "I did not mean it like that, Raven. I love

Marduk. Only Marduk. But I love your body…your spirit, and your tongue." Lilith grinned and bent her head to Raven's tiny breast. She drew the hardened nipple into her mouth, while wrapping her long, lean legs around Raven's hips. "The love we make is tender, but you, my little bird…you are as hard as nails. Like a lad. I like it," Lilith said seductively.

Raven leaned forward and kissed Lilith deeply. "You are all woman, Lilith. I had no idea what to expect at first, but this is good."

"Am I your first female lover?" Lilith asked softly as she ran her fingers through Raven's hair.

"Yep. I always kinda liked girls, the look of them, anyway. But I never acted on it, ya know. My dad was convinced it was a deadly sin, and my stepmom would've locked me up in a nuthouse if I had brought a girl home. Or killed me."

"There is nothing sinful about love, Raven. In any form," Lilith sighed deeply, and tenderly ran her fingers across Raven's cheek. "You are my first lass as well, but only because I never had the opportunity to be with a female before. I rather like it," Lilith grinned.

"Seems like your husband gives you free rein in the bedroom. Why haven't you ever been with a woman before?"

Lilith shrugged, then rested her head against Raven's shoulder. "Aye, Marduk is lenient with my sexual activities, for the most part. I suppose the only reason I've never been with a lass before is because the line of lovers at my bedroom door ran long and deep, and they were all lads." Lilith laughed in a sultry tone that set Raven's heart on fire.

"Long and deep, huh?" Raven teased as she slide her hand between Lilith's thighs. "I'm guessing your husband didn't like that very much. What's he gonna say about us?"

Lilith sighed sadly as an image of Marduk crossed her mind. "Marduk…" she began, then winced when she realized just how much she missed him. "…has abandoned me. He no longer loves me, and no longer cares who I share my bed with," Lilith whispered softly as tears welled up in her eyes.

"Aww…don't cry, Lilith. If your husband is dumb enough to let you go, then you're better off without him. You got me…and your long line of deep lovers," Raven replied as she placed soft kisses along Lilith's cheek, neck, and shoulder.

"Marduk is anything but dumb, Raven. He is fierce, and he may have your head if he finds out about us."

Raven grinned as she grabbed a handful of Lilith's hair and pulled her closer for a passionate kiss. "Lucky for us…Marduk is far, far away," Raven whispered as she dove under the sheets, kissing Lilith's firm, flat belly all the way down to her legs, spread wide open. Raven slipped two fingers inside before she closed her warm mouth over Lilith's wet curves.

Marduk grinned wickedly as he approached Lilith's suite. He stopped to take a deep breath and smooth his hair and beard before he sauntered into Lilith's private quarters without knocking. She no longer had the privilege of privacy she had as a Queen, and he wanted to take her by surprise while he conjured up a hundred ways to love her. He marched quickly toward her bedroom and swung the door open wide, but stopped dead in his tracks when he clearly saw movement beneath the sheets and heard Lilith's familiar love moans, soft giggles, and breathless whispers from beneath those sheets.

Marduk growled as he took long, heavy steps to Lilith's bed and pulled the sheets away. His face went from fierce anger to shocked surprise when he saw Lilith's lover.

"What the fuck?" Marduk said with a withered face as he stared at Lilith's lazy grin and delicate hands running freely over her lover's body.

Raven yelled and tried to hide, but Marduk held the sheets in his massive hand, and there was nowhere to hide from those piercing eyes. Raven shivered in fear at Marduk's fierce scowl as she tried to cover her body with her hands.

"Loophole, Marduk. I found a loophole in your rules," Lilith said with a sly grin as she pulled Raven close to her, then kissed her neck tenderly. Raven's eyes were wide with fear as she pulled away from Lilith.

Marduk paced at the foot of the bed with squinted eyes and a hard-set jaw.

Raven began to cry softly, but she relaxed when she saw the budding grin on Marduk's face.

"I cannot believe ye would be so bold, Lilith!" Marduk said as his laughter filled the room. "A lass. Ye found a lass to love ye."

Marduk continued to laugh loudly while he paced and scanned the messy bedsheets and the two naked women huddled together in them. His eyes shined with passion and mischief as he slipped out of his boots, then slowly unbuttoned his shirt.

Lilith grinned like a cat as she watched her dark, brooding husband strip naked, except for his kilt, then dip one knee on the bed. Lilith was taken back by the wide bandage over his left shoulder, but she wasn't curious enough to ask about it yet. All she needed and wanted right now was Marduk. He was home, in her bed, nearly naked, and fully erect.

Marduk moved toward Raven first and took her slight body into his arms, then kissed her with an open mouth. He growled with pleasure when he tasted Lilith on her tongue.

"Carry on, lass," Marduk said while he bit his thick bottom lip and stared intensely into Raven's wide, blue eyes.

"Hell no! I am not into this! You two work this shit out between you. Without me in the middle." Raven slinked out of Lilith's bed and gathered her clothes from the floor, then ran out the room naked.

Marduk laughed loudly in a deep menacing tone, and pulled Lilith into his arms. "It seems I've scared away yer loophole, Lilith. It's just the two of us… again." He kissed her tenderly, then pulled her roughly to his chest. "Would it kill ye to be loyal to me for two fuckin months?" he asked through gritted teeth, but there was a gleam in his eye Lilith hadn't seen in hundreds of years.

Lilith stretched and pressed herself against Marduk's warm, naked body that was vibrating with energy. "It has been a bit longer than two months, Marduk. But you are in my bed now, and I am not letting you get away," She whispered as she straddled him, then leaned in to kiss him passionately.

Marduk wasn't surprised to taste Raven on her tongue. "Mmm…yer skinny lass tastes like honey. Carry on, Lilith." Marduk grinned as Lilith dove under the kilt with a steamy look in her eyes. His mouth opened wide, and he growled with pleasure as he watched her head bobbing under his kilt. He finally let out a breathy yell and lifted his buttocks off the bed.

"That is new," he said in a stifled whisper. He pulled Lilith up to his face and stared into her eyes with a fierce glare. "Where did ye learn that?" He drew her in for a deep kiss as he brushed the hair from her face, then turned her over to lay beneath him. He entered her with one quick thrust and rode the waves of pleasure fueled by the passion in Lilith's eyes.

"Raven. She has a tongue of gold," Lilith replied in a sultry voice as she met Marduk's thrusts easily and fiercely. Lilith stared into his heavy-lidded eyes as a wave of comforting love washed over her.

"Does she now?" Marduk growled softly, then thrust slowly, deeply against Lilith until she screamed out in pleasure and clawed his back. "Can her tongue do that, Lilith?" He pounded into her fiercely, then grinned when she became submissive to him and gave herself over to his savage love.

Marduk thrust hard into Lilith, releasing all the frustration and anger between them in his attempt to forgive her. He finally did when she responded by meeting each of those thrusts until they collapsed against each other breathlessly.

Lilith draped herself across Marduk's chest and purred softly as she ran her hands over his familiar body that never failed to satisfy her. She reached up to lightly touch the bandage on his left shoulder, but when Marduk flinched at her touch, she backed away and gently kissed his full, wine-stained lips instead.

"Welcome home, Marduk," she whispered as he pulled her into his arms.

"I actually missed ye. My little whore." He grinned crookedly at her and flipped her over. "Let me show ye what I learned." He growled against her ear as he entered her slowly and tenderly, lifting her buttocks with each swirling motion. He pulled her legs together, then straddled her as though riding the waves of the sea, swirling his hips slowly in the reverse motion he usually used on her.

"Oooo…that is new, too. Where did you learn that?" Lilith asked breathlessly.

Marduk laughed softly and thrust deeper. "I always knew it. But I forgot this move…until a pretty blonde reminded me," Marduk said in a sultry growl as he thrust just hard enough to make her cry out in pleasure.

"You are a whore too, Marduk." She laughed seductively and moaned under this intense pleasure as she bucked against him wildly.

"Aye. We are well matched, Lilith," he growled as he gently pulled her hair and rode her hard.

Lilith screamed out as a fierce orgasm washed over her. Marduk's face broke into a wide grin as he felt her clamp down on his enormous erection. He spilled all the pent-up love he'd been holding back for months, holding himself up with his right hand as his body crumpled against hers. He kissed her shoulders, neck, and back, then buried his face in her hair.

"Damn ye, Lilith…ye're the most delicious thing I have ever known." Marduk turned her over and grinned crookedly at her while shaking his head slowly. He sucked in his breath, then let it out in an airy whistle before he kissed her tenderly. "Ye may keep yer lass." He grabbed a handful of her hair and pulled her up to his lips. "But if I ever find another lad in yer bed…I will torture ye both until ye beg for my mercy. And ye know I have little mercy in my composition." Marduk's eyes turned ice-cold as he scanned her face.

Lilith was unaffected by Marduk's vicious stare. She'd seen it thousands of times before. She grinned and bit her lip. "I have no need for another lad in my bed as long as you are here, Marduk. No lad, nor lass, has ever measured up to you, my love." Her eyes were heavy with passion. Her body was on fire from the kilt burns and Marduk's arms around her so tightly.

Marduk sucked his teeth arrogantly and lifted one eyebrow. "More?"

Lilith purred against his ear and bit his neck gently. "More."

"Let's ye and I go another round then, Lilith," he said as he lifted her off the bed, holding her tightly around the waist. Marduk wrapped her legs around his waist and kissed her thoroughly, savagely, but with tender passion that slowly drove up the heat between them. Marduk wanted this rediscovered passion to linger before dousing the flame entirely. Lilith, back in his arms, was everything he needed to erase the events of the past four months. He'd never felt so alive, so in love. With Lilith. With life. With this dream-like womb of surreality where everything in his life was suddenly set right.

"I thought we lost each other this time, Lilith," Marduk said tenderly. His eyes filled with hot tears as he scanned her face. When he died, he was certain he'd never see her face again. Now he was afraid he'd never see Bella again. He was given a choice between life and death, Bella and Lilith. He chose to live. He chose Lilith.

"I thought so too, Marduk. I do not want to lose you," Lilith answered back softly with a girlish pout while running her hands through his hair. "I cannot live without you, my love."

"I've been away four months, Lilith. Yet ye're still alive, and Patrick's fuckin jacket is draped over yer chair. Again." His eyes narrowed slightly, but his hands on her body were tender as he held her against him. He gently stroked her face, then lowered his mouth over hers tenderly.

Lilith laughed seductively and wrapped her arms around his neck. "I am a whore. Your father made me this way."

"Aye, but ye're my whore. Don't forget that fact, Lilith," Marduk said in a hushed whisper against her lips.

"You have to remind me of that fact now and again, Marduk. If you expect me to remember it."

He grinned crookedly and laughed softly. "Aye, I believe I just reminded ye, Lilith," Marduk whispered hoarsely while adjusting her legs away from the raw skin on his back. Marduk playfully smacked her bottom, then lay back on the pillows with his fingers laced behind his head.

"Show me what else ye learned while I was away."

Lilith grinned playfully as she pulled Marduk's hair around his shoulders. Marduk's coffee, amber, and gold hair drove Lilith to madness when she wrapped her hands in it and pulled gently. She kissed him seductively, then playfully bit his thick bottom lip.

"Patrick learned new tricks too," she answered in a sultry voice.

Marduk growled and squinted. "I'm going to fuck that little Incubus next time I see him." He grabbed her hair to pull her closer. He didn't kiss her. He hovered over her mouth, then spread his lips in a wide grin when she answered.

"Patrick is indeed a little Incubus, Marduk. No need to hurt the wee lad," Lilith said seductively, and Marduk's heart swelled with love for her. He knew he was caught in Lilith's trap again, but he didn't mind it this time. Despite the love spree he knew she'd been on while he was away, she still wanted him. Despite her new lover, and her old ones, she was happy to be back in his arms. He thought he'd lost her, and now he was determined never to let her get away, even if it meant giving up his war against her.

After Samael and I released the black dragon kite, I filled up the first sex doll with helium and giggled, dancing around like a little girl at her first birthday party.

"He's alive! Marduk is alive!" I howled while the doll inflated quickly with her arms and legs popping out as though she were celebrating Marduk's return to life with us.

"I told you it wasn't that tragic. Nor the end of your life," Samael said as he ran his hands through the blonde wigs with a devilish grin. "These are expensive and luxurious wigs, Draco. Where did you get them?"

"In the Garden District. From an older lady's bedroom. They were just sitting in her closet collecting dust. She went red a few years ago, so I thought I'd bring these back to life. She's a wealthy woman, Samael. You might be able to get some favors from her."

"How wealthy? How old?" Samael asked with budding interest on his face.

"Hold up, guys. This is Marduk's funeral. We're not talking business tonight."

"He's not dead, Lily," they said simultaneously.

"Birthday party, then. The rebirthing of the new and improved Marduk, Son of Omega!"

"I think you've had too much Scotch. Set the blonde free. First one's for Amon. For bringing Marduk back to life." Samael held up the bottle of Scotch to the heavens, then drank heavily from it. He slapped my hands away when I reached for it.

"Gimme the fucking Scotch! I can't celebrate Marduk without Scotch!"

"You have to write tonight. No more Scotch. Let's set all the blondes free at once!" Samael's face lit up, and the infinite black holes where his eyes were supposed to be, sparkled. "It's what Marduk would want. All 13 lasses at the same time."

"Thirteen plastic virgins with virtual vaginas." I grinned. "Totally Marduk's style."

"Blondes, yes. Vaginas, yes. Virtual virgins? Not so much. And there are 14 virtual virgins," Drake said as he carried the rest of the dolls to the helium tank. He put a doll on the pump, then pulled the Scotch from Samael's hand and gave it to me. "Let Lily have her Scotch. She's been through a traumatic experience. You made her believe Marduk was dead. Cruel joke, Samael."

Samael held up his hands and scoffed. "Devil. Hello?" He shook his head slowly, and I imagined he rolled his eyes that were hidden behind the black holes.

"Why 14 dolls, Drake? You know 13 is Marduk's number," I said, then drank heavily from the bottle of Scotch.

"Fourteen wigs, Lily, and there were exactly 14 dolls in the first shop I went to. I took it as a sign and grabbed them all."

"In true Marduk style," I giggled, then put the wigs on the dolls as Drake blew them up one at a time. I was so excited about the wigs and dolls, I missed Samael sneaking up on me to snatch the bottle from my hand. He stepped back quickly with a wide grin.

"Not quick enough for the Devil, Lily." He took a big swig and smack his lips. "Cheap Scotch. Marduk would have my fuckin head for this. We need money, Drake. Tell me about this redhead in the Garden District."

I turned to him with a scowl and my hands on my hips, like a teacher about to scold the entire classroom. But before I could get a single word out, the last doll on the helium tank blew up, literally, into a million shards of plastic that erupted into the air like a synthetic volcano. The helium tank went haywire and blew a burst of air pressure that sent 13 dolls simultaneously floating into the air with their wigs falling haphazardly over their faces. Their legs were spread wide open, their mouths framed in a perpetual O, as though the sudden lift-off surprised them.

"Marduk's alive," I said with a romantic gleam in my eye. I bent to pick up the 14th silky, silver blonde wig from the ground and slipped it over my black hair.

Samael's face lit up like daybreak as he moved closer. I blushed at the remembrance of our shower together earlier and struck a sexy pose. "You like?" I asked in what I hoped was a seductive tone.

"Not really," he said adamantly while shaking his head. "But a grand idea just crossed my mind."

"Oh shit…what now, Samael?" I asked as I pulled the wig off quickly.

"Leave it on, Lily. It's perfect for the Dead Party," he said softly as he pulled me closer and arranged the wig on my head and draped the soft hair around my shoulders and over my breasts.

"Drake, find me a black kilt," he commanded before he lifted me off the ground and kissed me savagely.

Chapter Four

Amon paced the floor of his suite while waiting for Makawee to return to the Palace. He couldn't wait to see her, and share his adventures with her. He wanted to see Declan and Caraye too, but his heart was burning for a glimpse of Makawee first. His heart jumped, his cheeks flushed bright red when the door opened and Makawee ran inside in her slightly clumsy gait that Amon loved about her.

"Amon! You are home," Makawee said softly and ran into his open arms. He gently scooped her up and lifted her for a tender kiss while pressing his forehead against hers.

"Aye, my Queen. I am home. I never want to leave Gael again…not without you." Amon's shoulders finally relaxed after being away from Gael and his beloved Makawee for so long.

"Is Aramanth safe?" Little Lugh?" Her voice was tender, as though she were afraid to hear the answer to her question.

"All safe, Makawee. Even Marduk." Amon let out a deep breath as tears filled his eyes. He'd come so close to losing Marduk. It was the most painful ordeal Amon had ever gone through. Even more painful than losing Issa. Marduk had been in Amon's life ever since the day they were born five days apart, 12,000 years ago. Marduk's death would have taken down Amon as well. It would have been the final straw he could carry on his back. Amon shivered now thinking about how close it all came to falling apart. The balance of the entire Multiverse would have been shaken to its foundation with the loss of either King. No one, not even Declan, was prepared to take either Crown.

Amon set Makawee on her feet and shook off the heaviness of this journey. Everyone was safe, everyone was home. He smiled tenderly at her while brushing his fingertips across her face.

“I have so much to tell you, my love. We went to Earth! To New York. I ate in a grand dining hall with humans who came out of their homes just to meet me. Angelus arranged it all. They did not like me very much…but I did not like them either. They ate flesh, Makawee. Like beasts! And drank vile potions that gave me a wicked ache in my belly. A young lass asked me to sign my name on paper. Why did she want my name on paper, Makawee? Oh, and look at this!” Amon pulled the dollar bill from his pocket and handed it to Makawee. He was bursting with excitement, and wanted to tell her every detail of his journey through the Onyx River and his walk among humans in the Living Colony.

“What is it, Amon?” Makawee asked with bright eyes. She hadn’t seen him this alive and energetic in years. She wanted to know everything he’d seen and done since he left. Her own life had been on hold, it seemed, but she was back home now, back in the arms of Amon, and he had strange objects from his journey that he wanted to share with her. It was these simple things between them that made Makawee happy. Not that she was a simple woman. Makawee was uncomplicated, unspoiled, and happily so. Her life was a dream, a gift she cherished every day. It was that trait that kept Amon under her spell. She was his rock, his leaning post, an uncomplicated salvation in Amon's very complicated world.

He smiled as he moved a little closer to her. "I do not know, Makawee. I hoped you would tell me what it is. Earth was your home." He glanced at her with a twinkle in his eye that spark a mirror twinkle in hers.

"I have never seen this, Amon. It is very pretty. Such a lovely shade of green. But I do not know what it is." Makawee said as she turned the dollar over and over in her hands and held it up to the light.

Amon's tiger-gold eyes shined like amber in sunlight as he leaned his temple against hers. "Do you think it is a message? Look at this…there are geometrical shapes. Someone on Earth knows of my Mathematics, Makawee. There might be a message hidden here," Amon said excitedly, and Makawee's eyes lit up as he held the dollar to the light and saw the shapes he saw.

"I know these things, Amon. The objects in the drawings are familiar to me."

Amon smiled and pulled her closer. "Perhaps you and I can figure it out together, Makawee. A secret project between us."

Makawee stood on her tiptoes and tried to kiss him, but he was too tall, even standing on the tip of her toes. Amon bent to kiss her gently with graceful sexiness Makawee hadn't seen in him before. She drew in her breath and marveled at his newfound confidence as she leaned against him seductively.

"Amon, my love…you have changed."

"Aye. I found courage, Makawee. I also found Queen Nahemah. She forgave me everything I did to her…which is such a weight off my shoulders. Makawee, we faced beasts, the undead, militant armies, and human beings who meant to kill us. I learned how strong and brave I really am, Makawee. Even in the face of death, I was brave." Amon puffed up a little, and smiled shyly.

"I would like to have seen that, Amon. You facing danger, challenging death itself, and winning," she whispered as she pressed her body close to his.

Amon flashed a sexy grin and pulled her closer. "Makawee…I saw your face in my dreams every night. I felt your kisses in my sleep. My body burned from my dreams of you. But when I woke, you were not there, my love. I do not ever want to leave you again. The time seemed to crawl by. I wanted to see your face so badly," Amon whispered.

"Amon…time is nothing to us. If you had not gone away, we would not have this tender reunion between us. And this lovely green paper that will be our secret project." Makawee held his dimpled cheeks in her hands and chuckled softly. Her kind, gentle giant was home again, safe.

"Tell me everything," she said as they strolled arm-in-arm toward Amon's desk where they sat together most nights while Amon poured his heart out to his gentle Queen.

"Marduk was gravely injured, Makawee. We lost him." Amon's handsome face broke into a tortured grimace.

Makawee's jaw hung open, and her eyes filled with tears. "Marduk is dead?" she asked in a horrified whisper.

Amon smiled through his tears and wiped his cheeks roughly. "He was. We managed to bring him back to life, but it was so close." Amon hugged her gently and let out a deep sigh of relief.

"Oh Amon…I cannot imagine life without Marduk. Thankfully, he is alive. Were you injured? I did not know this journey would be so dangerous." Makawee shivered and held Amon tighter.

"I am not injured, my love. Marduk was alone when he was attacked by humans." Amon kissed the top of her head and leaned against her heavily when he thought about his own walk among the violent humans who might have taken his life as well, if not for Aaden. "Little Lugh's son is in Gael, Makawee. Aaden. I met Maggie and all Lugh's children. Maggie is the fiercest lass I have ever seen! She hit Lugh over the head with a cooking pan! And he liked it!" Amon shook his head. "Human traditions are so strange."

Makawee giggled and lay her head against his massive chest. "I hit Ahanu once with a thick stick. He did not like it, though."

Amon chuckled softly and his handsome face lit up like the sunrise. "I would not like that either, Makawee. Please do not hit me with a stick." Amon's face shined as he bent again to kiss her tenderly on the corner of her mouth, and congratulated himself on the smooth move.

Makawee blushed as she held his face against hers. "Amon, I cannot even reach your head to kiss you, I do not think I can reach it to hit you. Even with a stick." She laughed softly and kissed the opposite corner of his mouth.

Amon lay his forehead against hers and closed his eyes to soak up her energy. He missed her positive and happy energy so much these last few weeks. Amon had to hold himself together without her support all this time, and now that he was home, all he wanted to do was lean on her and soak up her presence.

"Tell me about little Lugh's family. What is Aaden like? Will I meet him, Amon?"

"Of course, my love. Tonight, we will have a feast to celebrate our victory, and to introduce Aaden to Gael."

"A feast! Yes, Amon. The Palace needs a family gathering. I will cook!" She smiled happily as her eyes lit up at the prospect of creating her own brand of magic for her returning heroes. Then her face fell when a dark thought crossed her mind. "Amon…is Aramanth well enough for a feast?" Makawee's face was tender with worry, and Amon's heart swelled with love again.

"Aramanth is fine, my dear. I will let her tell her own story tonight, but she handled herself like the Soldier we always knew her to be." Amon cupped her cheeks softly and smiled proudly. Amon had never been prouder of Aramanth, and couldn't wait to let her share her news tonight at the victory feast.

Makawee blushed at the tender look in Amon's eyes. She grinned like a little girl, then spilled her own news. "Amon, I also have news. I think you will want to hear this in private. It is only a rumor, but…" She held her elegant hands to her face to hold back her emotions, but she couldn't. Her tears spilled over onto her cheeks. "Declan and Caraye are having a child. Your sister, Hecaté, who has become my friend, told me she saw it in her magic fires."

Amon's face went from glowingly happy to ecstatically flustered, to the greatest sense of relief he'd ever felt in his life, and finally to unabashed tears of joy that he couldn't hold back. He was glad he was alone with Makawee while he broke down in tears. The overwhelming range of emotions hit him so hard, he lost all decorum and control. He didn't want anyone else to see him like this. These moments of Amon's life were private. He only shared them with Makawee, his foundling human wife who was his mirror. She was a quiet observer of life, like Amon, and took nothing at face value but her heart, her discerning intuition, and Amon's rare moments of emotional release.

Makawee knew the legend of the great unwavering Amon was a façade that he wore well in public, but in his own space with Makawee, Amon let down all pretenses.

Right then, in the safety of his Palace and his wife's arms, the great unwavering Amon lost all his logic, reason, and restraint, and cried like a small child finding innocence again after a painful ordeal. Not only was Marduk alive and well, but Declan, Amon's pride, his heart, his First Son and Heir, was having a child of his own. Declan would finally secure his own place in the Dynasty of the Incubi. Declan was the person Amon knew he'd disappointed the most in his life, but this made up for it all. Declan regained everything he lost and more.

"Makawee…thank you for telling me this in private. I cannot hold myself together…and I would not want the world to see me like this," he said softly. "Declan will finally have his own child." Amon lay his head upon Makawee's shoulders and let out all the pain he'd been holding since he found out Caraye was Issa. He wanted to tell Makawee, but he couldn't spoil this reunion, or this beautiful moment of her revelation about Declan's Heir.

Makawee also wanted to tell him that Issa was home, but she didn't want to spoil this moment either.

"Amon, you are so dear to me. I do not have the words to tell you how much you mean to me. I love you… hardly seems enough. I adore you. That does not capture my feelings either. I do not have the words." Makawee blushed and smiled at Amon shyly. "If you will come to bed with me, my love…" she stood and held out her hand to him. "I will show you how much I love and adore you."

Amon breathed a deep sigh, wiped the tears from his eyes as he stood slowly, then leaned in to kiss Makawee fiercely. He scooped her up in his arms and carried her to the bedroom with passion burning in his golden eyes.

"I had a selfie with three beautiful lasses at the dining hall," Amon said softly while carrying Makawee toward the bed they shared against Amon's own protocol. He loved sleeping next to Makawee, and loved waking up to her even more.

Makawee wrinkled her brow and held back a wave of panic. "What is that, Amon? A selfie." She was afraid to imagine Amon in a sexual situation with other women. She wrapped her arms around his neck and lay her head on his shoulder.

"It was a photograph, I believe. They were beautiful lasses, Makawee. They kissed my cheeks." Amon blushed profusely and lowered his eyes shyly.

Makawee giggled softly. "Did you enjoy that kiss, my love? With your three beautiful lasses?" she asked while Amon softly placed her on the bed, then leaned in close to her face.

"I will admit it, I did enjoy that moment." Amon laughed and kissed her tenderly, lingering close to her face with a soft look in his eyes. "But it was always you in my thoughts, Makawee."

Amon took her in his arms and held her tightly as they stripped each other naked while kissing fiercely. Makawee could hardly breath while she clung to him, wrapping her legs around his broad back.

"Amon…I missed this more than I knew," she said breathlessly while Amon grinned and adjusted her legs to enter her slowly. He thrust into her tenderly and flipped over so she was on top of him. He ran his hands over her breasts, and lower to her hips as she swayed and swirled against him while they worked up a feverish passion between them.

Amon grinned devilishly as he flipped her over again and gave Marduk a run for his title as the King of the Incubi, the King of Love, for the first time in his life.

Chapter Five

The Crystal Palace Dining Hall was alive with laughter and chatter as Caraye, Declan, and Jade approached the open doors. Jade started to run inside when she spotted Killian sitting with Mia and Amon, but Caraye pulled her back.

"Jade, I have something to tell you." Her eyes were shiny with mischief as she pulled Jade toward her. "I want to tell you privately before we make the announcement."

Jade's curiosity was piqued. "What is it, Mom? Is it about Salem?" Jade asked with her jaw set firmly in an angry scowl.

Caraye was a bit taken back by Jade's anger. Jade was developing an air of confidence and ferocity Caraye had never seen in her before. She was becoming a warrior, and she was just beginning her training. Something about this strange Colony they'd landed in was redefining Jade, and shaping her into a force to be reckoned with. Although Caraye missed Jade's playful sarcasm and kittenish claws, she breathed a sigh of relief as her fears about Jade's safety began to subside.

"Salem has nothing to do with this…it's a family secret. We're having a baby," she whispered then held one finger up to her grinning lips.

Jade's eyes widened as she mouthed her reply, "A baby?" She clapped her hands together and squealed softly.

Caraye smiled when she saw a brief glimpse of the old Jade. "It's a boy," Caraye whispered breathlessly while Declan stood behind them with a wide grin on his face. He was waiting to catch Jade's eye to assess her reaction for himself.

Jade glanced in his direction and grinned like a little girl. "A little brother. Awww, Declan, your first son. I'm so happy for you," she whispered before she threw her arms around Declan's waist and lay her head against his chest. She heard his heart thumping wildly and relaxed against the sound as though it were her lifeline. In the back of her mind, however, Jade was calculating how badly her little brother would complicate things if she decided not to fight in the Revolution.

"Thank ye, Jade. Ye'll play a big role in raising our little Rory. He's going to need all the love and family he can get. Rory must be protected at all costs. Ye understand, right?" Declan asked softly.

Jade nodded and let out a whoosh of air. "Wow. My little brother is your Heir. Declan, he'll be a good King. Like you, and Amon." Jade smiled, but the smile didn't quite reach her eyes. She was a bundle of confusion, and she desperately wanted Killian's advice.

"Better than both of us, I hope," Declan answered softly. He was dreading this meeting with Amon. He didn't want to face it yet, and certainly not in public. But the moment was here, and although Declan wasn't sure he could pull it off, he knew he had to keep his emotions under control tonight.

"Come on, ladies. The big guy is home. Let's eat." Declan tried to smile, but his heart was racing. He took a deep breath, squared his broad shoulders, then led his family into the Dining Hall stiffly.

Amon's face lit up when he saw Declan and Caraye. He jumped up from the table abruptly and took long steps toward them with wide open arms. His sapphire robe billowed beautifully around him as he glided across the room. Amon hoped Declan would make his announcement tonight so they could openly celebrate the impending arrival of the next Heir to the Dynasty.

"Declan! Caraye, Jade. I have missed you all so much." Amon wanted to embrace them all, but Declan stepped in front of Caraye and Jade, then held his hand out to Amon with a stoic face.

Declan didn't expect the rush of bitter emotions to hit him so hard. He was a bundle of confusion about his family's intentions to Caraye. He wanted to protect her, not only because of the child, but because he'd come to love Caraye more than he'd ever loved anyone before. She was his great loves in one, and that one was carrying his child.

"Welcome home, Amon." Declan smiled stiffly and bowed to Amon, then led his girls to the far end of the table.

Amon's face withered at Declan's cool reception. His heart was heavy as he watched Declan turn his back on him to seat Jade and Caraye as far away from him as possible.

"Declan, your place is at the head of my table, not the rear," Amon said in a reasonable tone, but the command was clear.

Declan turned to him with stiff shoulders. The betrayal and disappointment was written all over Declan's face, anger blazing from his eyes.

Amon's heart fell to his stomach when he realized why Declan was so cold. He knew about Caraye.

"We will sit where ever ye command us to sit, Amon," Declan said solemnly. He led Caraye and Jade back to the head of the table, positioning himself between Amon and Caraye. He didn't even look at Amon when they passed by.

"Declan, what's the matter with you?" Caraye asked as she looked at him quizzically, then turned to Amon with a wide grin.

"Amon! Welcome home! I'm so happy to see your face again." She threw her arms around his neck, and kissed his cheek. Amon blushed softly as Caraye and Jade showered him with affection. He kissed them tenderly, then walked with them past Declan to the head of his table. Amon pulled out Caraye's chair, two seats from his, then placed Jade next to Killian at the first table intersecting the head table. He took in a deep breath, then turned to Declan with a stern glare.

"Son, a private word with you," Amon said loud enough for everyone to hear. He didn't want to give Declan any room to maneuver around this conversation. Amon didn't want to do it, but he knew he had to. He couldn't let this night be ruined with hidden secrets, and anger barely disguised as respect. All Amon's guest hadn't arrived yet, so Declan's cold reception to Amon was only noticed by a few, but the energy in the room was thick and heavy. Amon knew he had to stop this before it went any further.

Declan nodded solemnly, then followed Amon out of the Dining Hall while everyone in the room stared at them open-mouthed and wide-eyed, whispering amongst themselves about this unusual display of animosity between Declan and Amon.

Amon closed the doors of his private suite softly after Declan stepped into the room with his head hanging low. Declan still couldn't look at Amon. He wasn't ready for this conversation, but he had no choice.

"Son, I know you do not understand my reasoning…"

"Reasoning? What fuckin reason could ye have for betraying me again, Amon?" Declan spat out, then winced visibly at Amon's crestfallen face.

Amon pulled himself up to his full height and raised his chin. "You were not betrayed, Declan. Not alone anyway. I had my own share of pain in this revelation, but I buried my pain…for you. I could not bear to hurt you to ease my pain. I could not do it, Declan," Amon said adamantly, but his face softened when he saw the disappointment in Declan's eyes.

"I learned of it from Samuel. If ye'd told me, Amon, I could have accepted it. But once again, ye let me believe I would have Issa. And Samuel took her from me again," he replied bitterly.

Amon crossed the room in two steps and threw his long arms around Declan. Declan tried to pull away, but Amon held him firmly.

"I am sorry you learned of this in such a harsh manner, Declan. My own knowledge of it came rather harshly as well. Lucian. My worst enemy." Amon paused, took a deep breath, then cupped his hands around Declan's cheeks. "The Elders assured me that they would tell you. I could not, Declan. I love you too much, Son. I could not be the one to break you again." Amon's tears fell into his beard, but he held a stoic face. "We both lost Issa…but we both have her again…and more, Declan. We have Issa and Caraye. Jade as well. That darling girl… we would not have her if Lugh and Aramanth had not done what they did. They acted out of love for you, Declan. Lugh lost his family over this." Amon's shoulders relaxed when he noticed Declan's face soften.

"Aye. I know what Lugh suffered. Still… he played with my life. Caraye means the world to me, Amon. Don't take her from me, please." Declan finally broke down and cried softly with his head against Amon's shoulder. "Please, Amon…don't destroy Caraye to bring back Issa. I couldn't bear it."

Amon's face crumbled as he took in a sharp breath. "Is that what you think this is, Declan? How you could think that of me? Son, no one will hurt Caraye. I swear it." Amon understood Declan's position better than Declan knew. Every day, he feared he would lose Makawee by command of a higher authority.

"I don't know what to think any more, Amon. I've been betrayed by everyone I love. Lugh and Aramanth's plan was to bring her here...as a disposable…they created Caraye only to bring Issa back." Declan's eyes were heavy with betrayal and pain. "Did ye know this?"

Amon shook his head vehemently. "No, Declan. I cannot believe that. Surely you are mistaken. Lugh and Aramanth would never do such a thing." Amon paced the floor with his head in his hands and slumped shoulders.

Declan watched him closely and breathed a sigh of relief at Amon's innocent stance. Amon had no nefarious plans against Caraye. Declan was sure of it. Amon was incapable of lying or hiding his emotions. He trusted Amon's reaction, but was still stinging from Lugh and Aramanth's original plan for Caraye.

"I hope I am mistaken, Amon. Because I wouldn't want to fight against my brother, and I don't want to be afraid of my family's intentions toward my wife. But how can I not be afraid? I lost Issa because of my family's secret machinations. I lost Issa twice because of you! But I will not lose Caraye. I will fight to the death for her life, Amon.

Even against you," Declan said painfully. He and Amon stared into each other's eyes, and read each other thoroughly. The anguish each saw in the other's eyes was more than either could bear in their tender spirits.

"It will not come to that, Declan. You have my word. Caraye and Jade are safe. No one will harm a hair on their heads. Nor yours. I will die before I let you or Caraye die. Issa is already lost to us. She has been lost to us for 30 years. Caraye is here. She is your Queen, the mother of your child. I will die before they do," Amon said adamantly.

Declan lifted his chin as tears flowed down his stoic cheeks. He wanted one more test, but it broke him a little not to acknowledge Amon's pledge to die for Caraye.

"I made the Elders write in it blood that she is mine." Declan had to look away from Amon to cover the raw wound so evident in his eyes.

Amon stepped forward and touched Declan's shoulder tenderly. He lifted Declan's chin with one finger and looked deep into his eyes. "Do you require my blood, Declan? I will give it to you. Every drop of it."

Declan's shoulders slumped in relief. He was satisfied now. "No. I don't require your blood, Amon. I only ask that ye keep your fuckin word this time." Declan smiled sadly. But his entire demeanor lifted when Amon spoke his quiet reply with a sly grin.

"You have my word…that I will keep my word." He reached out and ruffled Declan's hair playfully. Declan blushed shyly, then turned back to Amon with a curious grin on his face.

"Ye know about the baby?"

Amon grinned and nodded. "Aye. Makawee told me. She learned of it from Hecaté. Congratulations, Declan. You will finally have a child of your own." Amon's smile was genuine, and so were his tears as he held out his arms, pleading with Declan to come to him. Amon and Declan had been apart far too long, and Amon could no longer accept the distance between them. Neither could Declan. He grinned as he rushed into Amon's arms.

"A son, Amon. Caraye is carrying our Heir," Declan replied enthusiastically, then wiped the tears from his eyes as he relaxed into Amon's arms. He couldn't hold his anger against Amon, and didn't want to. Declan was certain that Amon wouldn't hurt Caraye. Amon gave his word, and Amon's word was law.

"Your First Son, Declan." Amon cried and laughed simultaneously as he hugged Declan tenderly.

Declan and Amon walked back into the Dining Hall arm-in-arm, with wide smiles on their faces and all traces of malice clearly behind them. Amon's step was light as he led Declan to his reserved seat near his right hand, then smiled shyly at Caraye sitting next to Declan.

"My apologies for our behavior, Caraye," Amon whispered softly. "All is well in our Colony now that you are here."

Declan smiled sheepishly as he leaned toward Caraye. "I think the pregnancy hormones are affecting me more than you, my love." Declan laughed genuinely, but the nagging thoughts of Hecaté snooping into his private life sat heavily on Declan's shoulders. He thought about how ill Caraye became on the ship after her magic spell summoning Hecaté. Declan closed his eyes and worked hard to put away those thoughts. Tonight, he would welcome his family back to Gael. Tomorrow, he would go to the Citadel for answers.

Chapter Six

Lugh and Aaden walked across the skyline together in long, bouncy steps while Aaden took in every square foot of the Crystal Palace with wide-eyed awe. He was beyond enchanted with Gael and never wanted to leave. Aaden was enchanted with the women in Gael as well. Jade was the most beautiful girl he'd ever seen in his life; her pale green eyes haunted him more than he cared to admit.

"What's the story with Jade and Killian? Are they engaged or something?" Aaden did a quick kick in the air, then turned to face Lugh with his fists up and a gleam in his eye. "I can take him, ye know?" Aaden's playful nature was evident in his shiny eyes and wide grin.

"Jade and Killian have been through a very difficult ordeal, and they survived it together, Aaden. Let them be." Lugh grinned as he ruffled Aaden's hair.

"Like what? What happened, Dad?" Aaden's sea-green eyes glistened with curiosity and sympathy. He dropped his fists and shoved them into his pockets.

"This is going to sound strange, Aaden…" Lugh began.

"For fuck's sake, Dad. I'm in a Crystal Palace in a Colony of the Gods … on the other side of the fuckin sky. Am I freakin out? No. Tell me everything. Ye said ye would." Aaden slowed his steps. He wanted to hear the whole story before they reached the Dining Hall.

"Jade and Killian were abducted from their homes in New Orleans. They were forcefully taken to another Colony we were at war with. They were held hostage by Amon and Marduk's younger brothers, as leverage for their Crowns. Declan and Cain, Killian's father, rescued them and brought them to Gael. It was Jade's father, Samuel, who took them. Jade was kidnapped by her own father and taken to the most evil entity in the entire world. Killian was Jade's protector. He kinda saved her life." Lugh smiled, and tossed his arms around Aaden's shoulder. Aaden turned inward with a shocked look on his face. Lugh was afraid this was all too much for him. "Are ye alright, lad?"

Aaden's cheeks turned white, then flushed bright red when he realized that he'd misjudged Killian. But his heart ached over Jade's situation. To be betrayed by her own father like that had to be brutal, and he wished he'd been the one to protect her, but it was Killian who kept her safe. He was a warrior after all.

"That's a pretty sad story, Dad. Wow. Abducted by her own father. Did he hurt her?" Aaden looked up at Lugh with teary eyes full of guilt about making such a big deal over Lugh's small betrayal by comparison.

"Aye," Lugh said softly and hung his head. "No one walks away from Lucian's machinations unscathed."

"Poor Jade. She must be devastated." Aaden's heart ached, and his eyes stung with unshed tears. He imagined the worst-case scenarios and hoped none of those scenes occurred. He suddenly wanted to fight. He wanted to slam his fists into Jade's father, but he also wanted to run his hands through Jade's hair again.

"Thankfully Killian was there for her." Aaden hung his head and winced at the thought of the romantic adventure the two of them shared. He knew he could never top that one and resigned himself to stay out of Killian's way with Jade. But he was already attached to Jade. That kiss in the maze was still burning on his lips. He absently reached up and touched them, then sighed heavily.

Lugh laughed softly at Aaden's move, as well as his slumped shoulders. He was reminded of young Declan, when he fell in love with every lass who crossed his path. Aaden had Declan's romantic streak, but he was also a little Lugh with his scrappy nature. Lugh smiled when he had the same thought he'd had for the last 21 years about Aaden. He was either fighting or falling in love. Right now, Lugh was afraid Aaden was falling in love with Jade. He didn't want to see that happen. It would unravel so many secrets Lugh was hoping to hide.

Lugh and Aaden rounded the corner of the Dining Hall and squared their shoulders when they stepped into the room with wide grins as everyone burst into happy cheers at their arrival.

Amon stood up from his chair gracefully, and sauntered toward Lugh with open arms. Aaden was impressed with the changes in Amon now that he was in his own territory. He was no longer clumsy, and he appeared to be in full command of the Colony of Gael.

Declan hesitated a bit, then relaxed his shoulders and slowly approached Lugh with a wide smile. Lugh's heavy heart lifted immediately at the sight of Declan's genuine smile. This was the welcome he hoped for. Lugh bear-hugged Declan, lifting him an inch off the floor. Declan chuckled as he rested his forehead against Lugh's. He wanted to forgive everything, but he had to be certain Caraye wasn't in danger. However, Declan knew this wasn't the moment to have that discussion, and he didn't want to risk pushing Lugh too far away. He needed as many allies as he could muster.

“My big lug of a brother. I love ye, Declan,” Lugh said loudly with shiny eyes and blushing cheeks.

“Love ye more, little Lugh.” Declan cupped Lugh’s chin and smashed his cheeks together like they used to do as young Princes, then kissed him square on the lips. “Who is this young fella? He’s a little, little Lugh!” Declan said with a chuckle as he playfully punched Aaden in the shoulder.

Aaden’s face lit up like daybreak when Declan turned his attention to him. He’d heard stories about Declan all his life, and couldn’t believe he was finally meeting him. Declan was the hero of his house, the enigmatic shadow of Aaden’s family history, and the role model Aaden tried to live up to in every adventure he had in his life.

Declan’s mysterious disappearance had been his family’s project Aaden’s entire life. Maggie made it her personal mission to find Declan, and Aaden himself spent years helping her with phone calls, letters, flyers, and a wide-spread social media campaign that had Declan’s face plastered all over cyberspace. Declan’s disappearance took a hard toll on Maggie, who cried on Aaden’s shoulder more often than Lugh’s over her inability to find a trace of Declan. In this moment, Aaden felt the distance from Maggie acutely and wished he could tell her that Declan was alive.

“I’m Aaden. I knew ye, Uncle Declan, the moment I walked in the door. I’ve heard stories of ye all my life. My mother loves ye very much. My dad, too.” Aaden’s eyes glistened proudly as he took in the full specter of Lugh’s infamous brother who was the subject of nearly every conversation his family had, usually in full fits of laughter while recalling Declan’s colorful antics. Aaden had always been fascinated by Declan, and this magnificent man standing before him with the softest eyes Aaden had ever seen wasn't a disappointment.

"Aye. I love your mother too, Aaden." Declan winked, then clapped Aaden on the shoulder. "One day very soon, ye and I will sit and converse… like the Gods, as we're fond of saying in Gael." Declan chuckled while his eyes threw amber sparks.

Aaden was enchanted by Declan's wide grin and convivial nature. Aaden recognized himself and knew why Lugh and Maggie called him "wee Declan" all his life. "I'll tell ye everything about my 30-year absence, but not tonight. Tonight, we celebrate. Lugh's son is in Gael. Aramanth is safe. Marduk is alive, and we have more than enough revelations to share tonight."

Amon stepped up to his sons and wrapped his long arms around both their shoulders with a wide grin on his handsome face. "Welcome to Gael, Aaden. This is as much your home as your farm house on Earth. We are all family here tonight." Amon pulled Aaden into a gentle wrestle hold and led him toward the table. "Come, your seats are to my left. I am so happy to have my sons at my side again!" Amon said in a loud voice. He was ecstatically happy tonight with all his children under this wing, and more besides. Amon was filled with love and wanted to share it all with his small flock. He hoped they would return this love to others somewhere down the line of life.

Lugh took his seat at Amon's head table, on his left-hand side, while Aaden opted to sit at the intersecting table across from Killian and Jade. He grinned widely at them, and leaned across the table to offer his hand to Killian. Killian didn't hesitate to take his hand.

"Aaden. Good to see you again." Killian's held his shoulders a little stiff, but Killian didn't want to show his insecurities to anyone, especially Jade.

Jade smiled at the exchange and glanced up at Aaden, who smiled shyly at first, then grinned wider when he held her gaze. Jade couldn't hide her attraction to Aaden, and that kiss they shared this morning was still tingling on her lips. Killian noticed the soft glow on her face and groaned slightly.

The group of young Royals from Críoch entered the Dining Hall noisily, with little decorum as they scattered across the room. Three of them made their way toward Jade and Killian. Killian was immediately drawn to the dark-haired young Prince with a long, leonine body, slick hair, and a panther-like gait as he swaggered toward them and held out his hand.

"I am Prince Scotch of Marbh, Son of Seth. These are my sisters, Sherry and Madeira," he said in a bored tone.

Jade held out her hand and made an attempt at Gaelic formality. "Jade, Daughter of Declan. This is Killian, Son of Cain, and Aaden, Son of Lugh." Jade broke into a soft giggle. "You're all named after alcohol."

Scotch lifted one eyebrow and a corner of his mouth as he lifted Jade's hand to his mouth. "Aye. My father and mother are a wee bit too fond of their bottles. I suspect we're all named after the drink they consumed at our respective births." He winked and took the seat next to Jade.

"Or your conceptions," Aaden added, and Jade broke into full-blown laughter.

"Your observation is likely to be more true than mine." Scotch chuckled and drained a glass of wine, then turned to Killian with a sparkle in his eye. "Where's the fun in this pristine prison?" Scotch asked nonchalantly.

"Depends on how brave you are, Scottie." Killian grinned and winked at Jade. She caught on to Killian's game and played along.

"How brave are you? Brave enough to die?" Jade asked with a mysteriously grin meant for Aaden.

"Fuck yeah," Aaden said with bright eyes and no hesitation.

Jade grinned like a little girl. "I knew you were brave, Aaden. You're going to love this." She winked, and Aaden's heart began to pound in his ears. Jade couldn't tear her eyes away from his, until Killian leaned forward to kiss her softly. She blushed at the attention of these two very different but equally attractive young men vying for her affection, but she was more than annoyed at the obvious attempts by Scotch to pull her into an intimate conversation.

"What about me? Am I invited to this mysterious gathering? Surely, you won't leave the newcomers out in the cold?" Scotch asked in a droll tone as he leaned closer to Jade.

"Maybe," Jade replied playfully. "Depends on how well you young folks behave tonight."

Scotch's green eyes lit up significantly as he gave Jade a thorough once over. "The young folks are sitting at the back of the table. I am my father's Heir, and of age to inherit my kingdom, Princess Jade." His thick, dark hair fell seductively across his forehead, but he brushed it all back with one hand and cast her a sultry glance.

"Congratulations." Jade smiled stiffly. "You're getting your inheritance because your father is in jail. For kidnapping me." Jade raised one eyebrow and gave Scotch a harsh glare before turning back to Aaden.

"You're Salem's daughter? Lucian's prized possession?" Scotch asked incredulously.

Jade shot Scotch a fierce glare and had to work hard to hold back her anger. "It's not a joke. My life was ruined by Lucian…and your father," Jade spat out.

"My father had nothing to do with Lucian's machinations. The trial will prove that," Scotch said as he ran his fingers along her arm.

"Tell it to the Elders," Jade replied coldly, then turned her back on Scotch.

Scotch wasn't deterred by Jade's cold shoulder. He leaned in closer and brushed her hair from her shoulder. "I intend to tell the Elders just that, Princess Jade," he replied sarcastically.

"Don't touch me," Jade said harshly.

Scotch sipped his wine and lifted one eyebrow. "My life's mission from this moment forward is to make you to reverse those words."

"You'll be working on that mission a long time, Scottie," Killian replied playfully. "Hands off my girl."

Scotch grinned crookedly as he lifted his hands in the air slowly. "My apologies. I had no idea she was yours." Scotch immediately liked Killian's subtle nature, and knew his way into this group was through Killian.

Jade pulled away from both Killian and Scotch and glared at them both. "I'm no one's property!" She cast a quick glance at Aaden, and was disheartened by his attention to Sherry and Madeira. She turned back to Scotch with a tight jaw. "Your sisters need to learn manners. Aaden isn't a boy toy," she spat out angrily.

Scotch rolled his eyes and groaned loudly. "Sherry, Madeira keep your hands off the humans. They are a bit squeamish, and Jade is jealous."

"No I'm not!" Jade spat out. "Aaden is free to do what he wants."

Scotch lifted one eyebrow sarcastically, and grinned crookedly at Jade. "Apparently, he wants to do my sisters."

Aaden's eyes lit up at the notion of Jade being jealous. "They're my cousins. I don't do blood relations." Aaden grinned and winked. Jade's cheeks flushed instantly at Aaden's attention, but her heart sank when she remembered she was also blood-related to Aaden.

"Fuck," Killian whispered under his breath at Jade's dreamy-eyed stare. He squared his shoulders and mentally prepared himself to fight to keep Jade's attention. "Why don't we all have some wicked fun after dinner? It's a long climb, but totally worth the effort," Killian offered.

"I'm in!" Aaden said as he slipped his arms around the redheads, then winked slyly at Jade.

"I'm in as well," Scotch answered coolly.

"We want to come with you, Scotch! We are going where ever Aaden goes!" The twins quipped playfully, then began to giggle uncontrollably.

Scotch groaned loudly and rolled his eyes. "Not this time, lasses. You have a early curfew, and neither of you are brave enough for the ledge."

Killian turned to him with wide-eyes, trying his best to ignore Sherry and Madeira's whiny pouts. "You know about the ledge?"

"Aye. Everyone in the Colonies knows about the ledge." Scotch extended his hand to Killian and smiled warmly when Killian shook his hand. Then Scotch turned to Jade with a sarcastic smirk. "Don't worry, Princess. Your secret crush is safe in my hands. I'll keep the twins away from your Aaden."

Jade opened her mouth to protest, but was distracted when Aramanth sauntered into the room with Angelus following behind her. He stood in the doorway in his usual position while Aramanth glided into the room to cheers, claps, whistles, and yells.

Declan walked around the table toward Aramanth in long steps. He assessed her thoroughly before he held his hand out to her. Aramanth was exquisite in a pale blue gown with a fitted bodice, and an Empire waistline draped beautifully into a flowing skirt that rustled with each step she took.

"Declan! Ye're all grown-up," Aramanth said sadly as she rushed into his arms. "Ye look happy, brother. Your wife made ye happy again."

Declan wrapped his arms around her, and rocked her back and forth like he'd done her entire life. "Aye. She's made me the happiest Incubus alive." He tried to hold his emotions in check, but Aramanth's sadness was palpable, and he couldn't stop the tears from welling up in his eyes. "Ye're safe, little sister. Malachi will never hurt ye again," Declan whispered in her ear. He knew her fierceness tonight was mostly false bravado. He easily read all the suffering she'd experienced at the hands of Malachi. Declan didn't have the heart to bring up her part in Caraye's situation yet. She seemed to be more fragile than he'd ever seen her. He wiped the tears from Aramanth's cheeks with his thumbs, then kissed her tenderly. "Welcome home, little sister."

"We're all home again, Declan," she said with a soft sob. "But our lives will never be the same."

"Nothing stays the same, Aramanth. Especially for our kind." He gently kissed her forehead, then glided Aramanth toward Amon's table. "Aramanth, this is my wife, Caraye, and our daughter, Jade. My loves, it's my great honor to introduce ye to Gael's new Hero, Princess Aramanth. She only needed the Army to give her a ride home from Marbh. She took down her captor herself. Aramanth is a Soldier. A Warrior Princess."

"I heard of you! My dad told me about you. He said you were a legend in Gael. Princess Aramanth, it's an honor to meet you." Jade curtsied gracefully.

Aramanth was stunned when she looked at Jade. It was as though she were looking at Issa. She glanced at Declan curiously to see if he noticed, but his eyes were locked on Caraye.

Caraye smiled brilliantly and pulled Aramanth in for a hug. "Aramanth, I've heard so much about you from Declan. You're already a legend in my heart." Caraye leaned in and kissed her cheek softly. "I am so happy to finally meet you."

Aramanth melted at the sight of Caraye's warm smile and sweet demeanor, and her heart broke when she recognized Issa's spirit. She wondered how Declan could miss it, as well as Jade's uncanny resemblance to Issa.

"Caraye, you're everything I hoped you would be. You brought my brother back to life, and I love you for it," Aramanth said as tears of joy flowed down her cheeks.

Everyone in the room who knew the story behind Caraye's existence was in tears at Aramanth's words. Especially Declan. He saw it then. A way to believe they didn't create Caraye as a disposable, but as an answer to his prayer instead. Declan pulled all the girls in his arms, and let out another sigh of relief.

"I'm a lucky fucker," Declan said loudly, then broke into a wide grin when he looked up at the doorway. "Speaking of lucky fuckers." He pointed toward Marduk and Lilith standing regally at the entrance of the doorway.

The room fell completely silent at the handsome couple standing together, arm-in-arm, with an undeniable bond between them that surprised everyone, but shook Mia to her core.

"Marduk! Lilith! Welcome to the Crystal Palace!" Amon stood again, but this time he was a little clumsier. Lilith never failed to shake Amon's confidence. He blushed like a schoolboy when he took in her blood-red gown that hugged her curves like second skin, fanning out in a trumpet silhouette around her ankles. The dress glittered like the night sky as Lilith glided into the room gracefully. She kissed Amon's cheek, but she didn't flirt. She didn't give him her usual seductive glances beneath her lashes, either. Lilith only had eyes for Marduk tonight.

Declan sauntered slowly toward Marduk with sad awe and genuine love in his eyes. Marduk was pale and thinner than before, with a barely noticeable limp as he made his way toward Declan, holding his left arm close to his chest. Declan let out the deep breath he'd been holding until he knew for certain Marduk was whole. He gingerly wrapped his arms around Marduk's shoulders, but Marduk scoffed and hugged Declan tightly. He remembered the sad thought he had about never seeing Declan again when he died. He was determined to right all the wrongs against Declan now that he'd been given a second chance. Marduk wanted to come clean with Declan tonight. It was time for Declan to learn the last of the secrets.

"I heard we almost lost ye. But ye're alive. I've never been happier to see yer ugly mug. Are ye alright, Uncle?" Declan's eyes were full of respect and love, but also sad sympathy bordering on pity that Marduk didn't want to see in Declan's eyes.

Marduk smirked, and waved his hand in dismissal. “Aye. I’m fine. Don’t fuss over me, Declan. I expect more from ye. Marriage has made ye soft.” Marduk grinned wickedly, then leaned in and whispered in Declan’s ear. “I need a private word with ye before the night is over.”

Declan nodded solemnly, but felt slightly sick to his stomach. He had no idea what Marduk might ask of him, but he would do whatever he asked. It was his duty. “Of course, Marduk.” Tears welled up in his eyes when he saw something in Marduk’s eyes he’d never seen before. Fear. Uncertainty. Lack of confidence.

Marduk was lighter yet heavier without Bella on his back, and maybe slightly edgier from his brush with death. But there was more than just confidence missing from him. The Red Dragon took a piece of Marduk’s spirit, and it was evident in his eyes.

Declan leaned in and kissed Marduk softly on the lips. “Ye cheated death, Marduk. Ye’re my Hero. Welcome back.”

Marduk’s eyes turned soft and a little misty. He looked at Mia briefly, and felt the weight of the dark spirit on her shoulders.

“I’m no hero, Declan. My attacker was a woman, and if ye tell anyone this, ye’ll not be so lucky to cheat death.” Marduk grinned playfully.

Declan’s eyes widened slightly, but the boyish glint in Marduk’s eyes was hard to resist. “This woman laid ye out like a deck of cards, eh? Never thought I’d see the day.” Declan winked, then kissed Marduk again. “No one will learn it from me. I wouldn’t want to face the wrath of the Black Dragon.” Declan’s eyes were bright with mischief as he leaned in closer. “Was she a blonde?”

Marduk rolled his eyes and shook his head. "A fuckin redhead. They're all mad. Sleep with one eye open, Nephew."

Declan chuckled as he walked with Marduk toward the dining table. They leaned against each other, and Declan's casual arm around Marduk's shoulder seemed normal to everyone. No one noticed Marduk's slight limp. Declan held out his other arm to Lilith, and kissed her cheek respectfully as she smiled sweetly and a little shyly. There were no hidden agendas in Lilith tonight. Lilith was tame and docile, and loyal to Marduk. She couldn't take her eyes off him as he pulled out her seat and grinned devilishly at her. When he pulled her chair to the table and lightly touched her shoulder, Lilith melted under his touch with a sharp intake of breath.

Everyone was surprised to see Lilith so attentive to Marduk, but Mia was heartbroken that Marduk was so attentive to Lilith. She was certain she'd lost her chance with him. She glanced at Lugh, but Lugh only had eyes for Aaden tonight. Mia groaned loudly, and poured herself another glass of wine.

Marduk sat across from Mia and Aramanth, and nodded politely at both, but his eyes lingered on Mia, who was stunning in a black cocktail dress that fit her body snuggly. Her full round breasts were overflowing at the bodice, and Marduk couldn't pull his eyes away from the creamy smoothness of them. He lifted one corner of his mouth as his eyes grew heavy with undisguised passion.

Mia squirmed and blushed under Marduk's intense stare, then drew in a sharp breath when she saw Cain sauntering toward the dining hall with Draco at his side. Cain looked beautifully wicked in a black kilt, black silk shirt, blood-red tie, and heavy boots with his silver and black hair pulled back into a neat half pony-tail, similar to Declan's. Draco was in his Guard uniform that accentuated his wide shoulders and slim hips, but it was his thick, muscular thighs that had Mia flustered.

Aramanth drew in her breath sharply when she saw Cain. She recognized him right away, even though his hair was different. She looked at Declan to assess his reaction, and was shocked when Declan grinned and stood to greet him warmly. Aramanth's confused mind raced with a hundred and one thoughts at once. What was Cain doing in the Colonies, and why was he here in Gael, at their dinner table, with Declan greeting him as though he were his best friend? She glanced at Marduk, who also greeted Cain with affection. Even Amon smiled genuinely as he waved him inside. She stared at Amon with wide-eyes and a hundred questions in her eyes.

Amon's smile faded when he noticed Aramanth's reaction and realized he'd forgotten to tell her about Cain's return. "Cain is welcome here, Aramanth. I will explain it all later, my love. Until then, let us show all our guest the same hospitality."

Amon saw that she didn't understand, and he didn't expect her to. Arabel had been her best friend. Aramanth was deeply affected by Arabel's death, especially after learning that Arabel was murdered 15 minutes after she left Dorcha from a weeklong stay in the Onyx Lair. She'd never felt so helpless, so hopeless in all her life, and threw herself into her training with the Army to cover her loss. Cain was also the reason why Issa was lost. She glanced at his smiling, relaxed persona with all her family gathered around him as though he were the guest of honor, and felt her stomach churn with disgust. She wondered how anyone could ever trust him again.

Cain kissed Mia's cheek before taking the seat next to her with simpering grace and a flirtatious grin when he leaned closer to Mia to whisper in her ear. Aramanth shirked away from Mia as her charms disintegrated significantly in Aramanth's eyes. But when she looked around the room, noting that everyone, except Mia, was enchanted by Cain, she saw an ally.

Draco stood in the doorway with Angelus, grinning playfully at Mia. She held her breath and smiled shyly at Draco leaning casually against the door, staring at her intensely. Mia nearly crumbled under the weight of his stare, but she held her composure as long as she could. She looked everywhere but at the door frame filled with Draco's huge presence, and those liquid onyx eyes lasered on her.

Caraye noticed Draco smiling familiarly at Mia and nudged Declan. "Who's that guy in the doorway? I've never seen him before. He's magnificent."

"That's Draco, Son of Li Jing and Oshun. He's Marduk's General, Angelus's brother, and my friend. Someone I trust with my life. Yours, too. Draco will always be an ally, Caraye. Remember that." He kissed her softly and smoothed her hair. "Are ye feeling well, my love? Happy?" Declan asked sweetly as he scanned her face that was a little pale.

"Happy and well. Rory is famished, though. Where's the food?" Caraye giggled.

Declan pulled a piece of chocolate from his pocket, unwrapped it, and held it up to her lips. She held it half-way between her teeth and crooked her finger at him. Declan grinned widely as he leaned in close to her face.

"I'll take the kiss, lass. But I'll give my share of the chocolate to Rory tonight."

"You're my hero." Caraye giggled softly as she sucked in the chocolate, then kissed Declan tenderly on the tip of his nose, then his lips. She blushed shyly when she noticed Amon watching them with glowing eyes and a full smile. He held his hand over Makawee's and leaned in to kiss her too.

Scotch leaned toward Jade's right cheek while Killian leaned toward her left. She held up both hands to her suitors when they kissed her tenderly, but Jade's eyes were locked on Aaden. He seemed unaware of Sherry and Madeira closing in on him, and absently leaned in to kiss each of their cheeks without ever taking his eyes from Jade.

Marduk leaned in toward Lilith, and touched her hair softly, then ran his fingertips along her neck. She leaned forward to kiss Marduk's full lips in a soft kiss. Marduk looked down at her with adoration he couldn't hide in his heavy-lidded eyes. He laced his fingers in her hair and kissed her savagely, as though they were alone in the room.

Cain was surprised enough by his father's reaction to lean toward Mia for a kiss. Mia held up one hand, and pressed two fingers to Cain's mouth. She raised one eyebrow and gave him her fiercest look. Cain backed away slowly.

"You're missing out, Mia." He reached for her hand under the table and was surprised that she let him hold it.

"I believe ya got dat backwards," she said quietly with a sassy lilt.

Cain squeezed her hand and sipped his wine while he blushed profusely at her rejection. Cain loved his feisty Creole girl who never gave him a minute's quarter. He lightly ran his thumb along the back of her hand. Mia didn't pull away, but neither did she respond. She was angry that Cain had been in Dorcha with Raven. She thought he was back to his old games of keeping his many girls in as many locations. Cain was a master at that game, and no one was more aware of it than Mia.

Lugh watched Mia's move with interest, and smirked at Cain playfully. Cain hung his head and chuckled. He wanted to crawl under the table; the old Cain probably would have, but the new Cain took it like an adult. He respected Mia's wishes, and allowed himself to be the ass of the table. Mia was still holding his hand under the table, and he didn't feel the need to let everyone know it.

Draco let out a deep chuckle at Mia's move; Marduk winced and hung his head. He knew then that Mia didn't reject him personally. Mia wasn't interested in an affair, she wanted love. Marduk wanted to give it to her, because he felt more for Mia than he wanted to admit to himself. But Marduk had been so scarred by love in his past, he couldn't take another chance on it. He always ran back to his familiar Lilith whenever his heart was moved by one of his love interests. Marduk knew exactly what to expect from Lilith. She never failed to disappoint him in her disappointing behavior. He also didn't want to hurt Cain. For the first time in his life, Marduk was growing a heart for his First Son. He saw the changes in him and desperately wanted to believe them, despite the evidence he found in Marbh against him. Everyone wanted to believe in Cain's transformation. Everyone except Aramanth. She didn't believe Cain had changed for a single minute. Aramanth was certain Cain was playing games again and vowed to flush out his secrets.

Aaden couldn't take his eyes off Jade and Killian, deep in an intimate conversation. He felt out of place in that moment. Everyone was in conversation, but he was sitting with strangers. It didn't matter that he was sandwiched between two very pretty girls who apparently adored him.

He felt awkward and was completely disinterested in both of them. It was more than unusual for Aaden, who'd always enjoyed playing the Romeo role with any girl he ever met. But the only girl's attention he wanted was in the arms on his only friend in this place.

Aaden looked up at Declan and Caraye, then grinned when he noticed the halo of love floating around them. He figured this beautiful, golden-haired woman was the reason Declan hadn't left Gael in 30 years. Aaden thought if she were his, he wouldn't leave her either. He stared at Caraye for a long time, and was slightly disturbed by her familiarity. She looked like Caitlyn. Like Lugh. Aaden was puzzled by this revelation, and glanced back and forth between Lugh and Caraye. His mouth hung open when he recognized Lugh in feminine form. He put the thought out of his mind for a minute because he couldn't reconcile the idea that Declan might be married to his own sister. It was too much for his human mind to calculate. Declan shrank a little in Aaden's esteem. They all did for a second or two. Everyone except Lilith. From the moment she walked in the door, Aaden was enchanted by Lilith. He couldn't stop himself from glancing at her every so often, and when he did, he couldn't tear his eyes away. She was the most beautiful woman he'd ever seen in his life. Her perfection was something he'd never seen in any living creature.

Aaden stared blankly at Lilith's perfect profile, with no guise of the adoration in his eyes. Marduk lean forward, and squinted sharply at Aaden. Aaden caught Marduk's cold eye while his twinkled slightly. He grinned widely, shrugged, then draped his arms around each of the redheads.

"Your wife is fuckin beautiful, Marduk." Aaden gave Marduk a reverent nod.

Marduk's face softened a little as he lifted one corner of his mouth. He held his glass toward Aaden, and nodded once. Marduk recognized the same Incubian Romantic streak in Aaden that he recognized in Declan all those years ago, and wondered if he'd just found his next protégée. With Declan out of the Cambion Project, Marduk saw the possibility of his next great Alphan Warrior. He saw hope for the future of humanity, but he also saw a potential rival. Lilith's next lover.

Mia glanced back at Draco, who was still staring at her with a wide smile in his casual stance in the doorway. She wrinkled her brow at him, but he grinned wider. Draco was smitten. Mia was too. She was shaken to the core, and Draco saw right through her. He knew he unnerved her, and enjoyed the furtive glances and blushing smiles they exchanged when their eyes met.

Caraye noticed the flirtatious exchanges between them again and wanted to know the story behind it. "Declan, your friend, Draco, hasn't taken his eyes off Mia since he got here. Is he single?" Caraye's eyes were wide with mischief.

"Ye're going to get yourself in trouble, lass. If Draco is interested in Mia, he'll find a way to her. Let it be."

"Let's make a deal." She grinned and leaned closer to him.

"Oh-oh…she wants to deal. I'm the one in trouble, now. I cannot say no to ye, my love."

Declan's eyes lit up when the food was brought in by the Servants. He immediately filled a plate for Caraye, then held up her favorite food to her lips. She bit into it with gusto, then smacked her lips against his softly.

"Here's the deal. I'll leave Draco and Lugh out of my game play with Mia, if you don't play on Cain's side. Or Marduk's."

Declan's eyes lit up like a naughty little boy. "Marduk? Caraye, is Marduk sniffing around Mia? She's in trouble if that's the case. Marduk is the King of the Incubi, lass. The Chieftain of the Tuatha Dé Danann who taught my generation all we know about love." Declan grinned devilishly and brushed his fingers across Caraye's blushing cheeks. He held up another bite of food to her, and Caraye giggled as she bit into it.

Marduk noticed the romantic affection between them and relaxed his shoulders. Although he was initially skeptical about the family's intentions with Caraye, he was satisfied in the display of love for both Caraye and Jade from everyone in the room. Marduk knew they were safe in Declan's hands. He saw all he needed to see. Declan was in love with Caraye, and no one would dare take her from him.

Marduk thought it was time for him to take a trip to the Elders to get their assurance that she was safe. He also wanted to plead Samuel's case before them in private, before the trial. Marduk was prepared to use every tactic he knew to save Samuel. He made a mental note to visit him tonight to let him know that Caraye was safe, and that he'd gathered enough evidence to clear him while he was in Marbh. Marduk also wanted to personally deliver the news that Malachi, Samuel's jailor, was officially a prisoner of Dorcha. As a citizen of Marbh, Malachi was under Marduk's laws and jurisdiction. It was time to visit Lucian as well. Marduk couldn't wait to tell Lucian his only son was locked in the Dungeon of the Onyx Lair.

Chapter Seven

Amon glanced around the room at all the people he loved gathered in his Dining Hall that was a now a disastrous mess after everyone ate and drank their fill. The noise of happy conversations rang out against the walls and melded into a sweet, pleasurable din. He leaned over to Makawee, and touched her hand tenderly.

"Our flock is home, Makawee." Amon believed he understood the statement better than she did. Makawee thought the same thing.

"I am so happy to have Iris and Ronan here tonight, Amon. Our daughter is happy. Thank you for allowing her to come home with her husband, and for allowing the children of your enemies to come to the feast tonight."

"They are good lads and lasses, Makawee. Despite their fathers…and some of their mothers," Amon said sadly as he looked over the way array of young people in his Palace. He was surprised by their differences, but more so by their similarities. "Makawee…I never thought I would see the children of Gael, Dorcha, Mair, Marbh, and Earth sitting together peacefully at my table. It is a miracle," Amon said wondrously as his eyes filled with tears. He cleared his throat and sat up straight, then continued in a more authoritative voice. "I want them to feel comfortable in this strange situation. A new State, new Colony. Their fathers are in prison and their mothers are locked away in the Citadel…it must be terrifying for them all. I am a bit worried about Delphi's son. I am not certain she is fit to care for him at the moment. The lasses will be a comfort to her, but Scotch is his father's son. He is Omegan, and will need a firmer hand than Delphi's," he sighed heavily. "Perhaps Inuus's daughter would like to remain here in the Palace. She is a lovely young Princess, and more subtle than those two. Aaden may appreciate that." He chuckled and lifted his chin toward Sherry and Madeira fawning all over a reluctant Aaden.

"Riley is another good lad. Ronan's brother." Makawee added. "Iris seems to like him well enough."

Amon nodded in agreement. "Their father, Herne, was a good lad in his youth. Marduk's baby brother. A romantic poet. He fell under Lucian's spell just like all our brothers, but he is harmless. Nonetheless Ronan has made Iris happy. I will assign a suitable position in government for Ronan, and a home in Mair for them as well. Mair is Ronan's home Colony, and Iris seems happy there. I believe Riley should stay with his brother. Now that the Rebellion is over, our families can mend again," Amon said quietly.

"Mended families are often stitched up stronger than before, Amon. I agree with you about Scotch. I think Marduk may be better suited to care for the lad, my love. I would like to keep all the young Princesses here, for Jade's sake. And away from Marduk, for their sakes."

Amon chuckled and patted her hand. "Marduk would never take advantage of the young lasses. Despite his odd wickedness, Marduk is honorable."

"And in love. I have never seen Marduk so smitten," she chuckled softly.

"Aye. Marduk has been smitten with the lasses his entire life." Amon grinned when he remembered Marduk's attachment to Makawee the day she arrived in Gael. He was also reminded of the fight he and Marduk had over Lilith. It nearly broke them apart, like their fathers. He smiled sadly at the thought of Marduk's plight since that day he claimed Lilith as his own. "Many lasses, Makawee. Including you, my dear. But this one… she is eternally embedded under Marduk's skin."

Amon glanced up at Marduk with sad eyes and shivered again when he thought about how close he came to an empty seat at his table tonight with a very different revelation to share with all his loved ones. Amon's eyes filled with tears when he finally saw something he hadn't seen between Lilith and Marduk in thousands of years. They had their own halo of love around them tonight.

Amon caught Marduk's eye and smiled genuinely while nodding his approval of Marduk taming Lilith. Or maybe Lilith tamed Marduk. Either way, they were in love again. But no one knew how long it would last this time.

Marduk grinned like a naughty young Prince, and wrapped his arms around Lilith's shoulders. Lilith leaned in toward Marduk and ran her fingers through his beard. Her cheeks glowed when she touched him. Marduk held Amon's glance and raised one eyebrow, but couldn't wipe the grin from his face. He blew Amon an air kiss, then sent him a tender thought of love and admiration. Marduk knew he owed this moment and every moment he would have from now on to Amon's fierce love and determination to bring him back from the dead. Amon refused to let him stay in the realm of the dead before his time.

Marduk had more tenacity and determination to right the wrongs of this entire fiasco than ever. Tonight, Marduk, Son of Omega was going to take back his power, no matter what he had to do. The Red Dragon took more from him than he was willing to give, and he was going to get it all back. His pride would allow him to do nothing less.

Amon cleared his throat softly and stood to address the table. Everyone stopped talking at once; Amon blushed at the sudden silence. He was happy for the reverence, but he lost his nerve. He glanced at Marduk, who bolstered him with a solid nod.

"Marduk, my brother… my dearest friend who has stood beside me my entire life. I nearly lost you on this journey, which was something I simply could not accept. Thankfully, you responded to my third bang on your chest. You are here. You are alive. You have Marbh again, your strength, your sons, and you have Lilith...again." Amon laughed, and the entire room laughed with him, except Mia. But she did her best to smile anyway. "I have never been happier to see your face at my table than I am now. I love you, Marduk. I do not say that often enough." Amon's eyes glowed with unshed tears that touched Marduk deeply. "I could not bear the thought of losing you. Welcome back to life." Amon raised his glass, and everyone at the table stood to raise their glasses to Marduk. Even those who didn't know the entire story behind Amon's speech, including Lilith.

"Marduk, what is Amon talking about?" Lilith whispered. For a moment, she thought he'd considered permanently leaving Dorcha, the Lair, and her. Her heart clenched with fear at the mere thought of it.

Marduk knew he needed to tell her the truth, but he didn't want her to fall under his spell out of pity or fear of losing him. "I was injured on the journey, Lilith. Just a wee scratch. Nothing to worry about, *mo ghrá gheal*. I'm here now."

Lilith remembered Marduk's new scar, and held her breath for several seconds when it dawned on her that he'd been gravely injured. That scar was much more than a scratch, and from the way Amon and everyone else in the room was looking at him, Lilith knew Marduk had a close brush with death. She had no idea how far on the other side of death he traveled. But he was here now, and she was more determined than ever to keep him. Lilith decided it was time to give up her war against Marduk. She could easily admit defeat after living without him for so long. The silent and bitter years between them were over, and neither wanted to go back to the misery of them. Lilith knew she'd been beaten at her own game and was prepared to take a knee to her master.

Lilith leaned toward Marduk and cupped his face with her delicate hands, then pressed her body against his. "It was more than a scratch, Marduk. Tell me the truth," she whispered against his cheek then closed her lips over his with heated passion that sent an erotic wave around the room as they lost themselves in the kiss. They forgot they'd ever been at war, and that they were in public. The room was completely silent as everyone watched this tender and genuine display of love between Marduk and Lilith.

The Scribe in the corner of the room recorded the third blush of Marduk, Son of Omega as his kilt billowed, and the room went from dead silent reverence to a bawdy din of laughter. The King of the Incubi was alive and well. The Scribe also recorded that Cain, Son of Marduk shed his first happy tear over the fact that his father was alive and well.

Marduk waved his hand in dismissal, then held his glass up to Amon. "Thank ye, brother, for my presence here tonight. If ye hadn't beat me in the chest with your ham-fist a third time, I wouldn't be at this table tonight." Marduk chuckled and nodded to Amon. "I love ye too, Amon. More than ye'll ever know. Though my bones may never recover from your beating, ye fuckin beast, I am happy to be alive." Marduk grinned devilishly and drank his entire glass of wine in one gulp, then turned the floor back to Amon amidst claps and whistles that Marduk dismissed again with a wave of his hand, but the genuine appreciation was evident in his eyes.

"I look around this room and see all the faces of everyone I love. Makawee, my wife. My sons, Declan and Lugh." Amon held his hand to his heart while looking right toward Declan, then left toward Lugh with a glow in his eyes. "My daughters, Rhoda, Gayle, Millicent, Cherish, Aramanth, Iris, and Gael's newest Duchess, Caraye, and my Princesses, Jade…and Mia." Amon smiled and waved his hand toward Mia who blushed slightly under his attention. "My grandsons, Aaden…and Killian." Amon paused when Killian, Cain, and Marduk both sat forward with quizzical looks on their faces at Amon's announcement of Killian as his grandson.

"Tonight is a Night of Revelations. We are all family here. Our lives have been changed forever by knowing each other, by the ethereal connections between us that have brought us here together tonight, in this very room. We are all family. Let us share our revelations, our love, our support, and our congratulations as we share family news, and reveal our secrets. I will begin, if all of you would permit."

Amon held his head high as everyone nodded with interest at Amon's pending announcement. The Incubi in the room were aware of the dinner game, a Night of Revelations, where secrets were revealed by each person in the room. It was an Incubian tradition that had been played for centuries. The secrets would be recorded in the Chronicles of the Gods by the Scribe sitting in the corner of Amon's Dining Hall recording ever word, every action of everyone in the room.

Declan sat on the edge of his seat and hoped Amon wouldn't announce Caraye's secret. Lugh hoped Amon wasn't going to reveal his.

"I have waited a long time to make this announcement, until my whole flock was home safe." Amon turned his glowing eyes to Mia and smiled brilliantly. "Mia LeBlanc…although you have lived a simple life as a human woman, you are Gaelic Royalty, my dear. An Incubian Princess and a Cambion of the highest pedigree. You are my granddaughter, Mia. The daughter of Declan, Son of Amon." Amon waved his hand toward Declan.

Mia's mouth hung open as her eyes widened, and she dropped her wine glass on the floor when she stood abruptly.

Draco stepped into the room to clear the debris, scanning Mia's shapely legs in her pink heels. He reached out his hand to steady her when her knees begun to buckle. He held her up gently and couldn't hide his grin while he looked up at her from the floor. He saw it clearly this morning when he met her in the hallway. She had Declan's eyes, and his wild, gold-streaked hair.

Declan broke into a wide grin as he slowly rose from his chair, then smiled at Caraye as he kissed her cheek gently. "Excuse me for a moment, Caraye, while I love fall in love with your best friend, your sister…my daughter." Declan let out a belly laugh as he held out his arms toward Mia. "Come here, lass."

Mia marched toward Declan, swinging her hips gracefully with each firm step. She was wearing her highest heels tonight and wanted to show off her own brand of femininity. It wasn't lost on anyone in the room. Not even Lilith, who noticed Marduk's sharp intake of breath and his heavy-lidded green eyes glued to Mia's shapely legs in those high heels.

Draco stood with his mouth hanging open as he watched her swinging hips in the black cocktail dress. Cain grinned at the same view as Draco. Lugh was enchanted by her glowing cheeks, and saw the same sparkle in her eyes that he always loved about his brother.

Mia ran into Declan's arms and lay her head against his chest. Mia already loved Declan, but now she had another reason to let her affection for him grow exponentially. She was amazed at the loud thumping of Declan's heart. The rhythm sped up significantly when Declan wrapped his arms around her, then smoothed her hair and kissed her cheek.

"Are ye brave, Mia?" Declan whispered softly.

Mia looked at him with a smirk and rolled her eyes. Declan grinned because he saw himself in her for the first time and wondered how he'd missed it before.

"Who ya talkin' to? I helped ya kicked ass on dat boat, didn't I?" Mia chuckled, then melted into Declan's arms when he lifted them both a foot off the ground. He hovered for a minute with a wide grin, then glided in mid-air and spinned with her twice.

Mia giggled softly while holding her arms around Declan's neck as he glided her back to the floor. Declan smiled softly and blushed shyly for a second, then lifted his eyes to hers in an adoring look.

"Ye're everything I ever wished for in a daughter. Ye're smart. Ye're fierce. And so beautiful." Declan landed softly and gently touched her face. "I just danced the daughter's dance with ye, Mia. To officially claim ye as my own in front of the Scribe in the corner." Declan pointed to a small woman with mousy brown hair furiously writing in a thick book. "Ye have royal status now. Ye're officially my Princess." Declan bowed formally.

Mia couldn't stop her nervous giggle nor the sassy Creole girl from the New Orleans French Quarter who popped out suddenly. Mia gave him a fierce a look, even with a wide grin.

"You owe me a whole lotta child support, Daddy. I want some bling. A Palace. Some goddamn shoes…and some of dem sparkly gowns these Gaelic heifers wear," Mia said in a sassy tone with her hands on her hips and her lips pursed.

Declan burst into laughter and hugged Mia as his massive shoulders shook. Her sense of humor was so much like his. She had his dramatic flair.

"Aye, Princess Mia… ye'll have everything your heart desires. Killian too." Declan looked down at Killian in the chair right in front of him, staring at him with glowing admiration in his maple eyes, then held out his hand to Killian.

"I'm not dancing with you, Declan," Killian chuckled, but stood and hugged Declan fiercely. "I knew there was something between us…but this…it's beyond my wildest dreams."

The entire room burst into laughter and applause. Except Aaden. He looked around the room with a withered brow. Declan's wife was smiling at the announcement as though it were an everyday occurrence to discover that your best friend was your husband's daughter. Declan and Mia seemed to be the same age, and Aaden still wasn't convinced that Declan's wasn't married to his own sister. A sudden panic come over him as his cheeks flushed bright red. He looked at Lugh, who was smiling at Mia with open adoration, and more, on his face.

Aaden turned away from Lugh with a disgusted grimace and discovered Jade looking at him with a sad smile. Jade understood that the protocol of the Incubi, might be difficult for him to process. Aaden had been thrown into it without any warning or knowledge of the otherworlds, just like she'd been. Aaden smiled genuinely without any sign of his usual cockiness. It was clear that he was confused. He found comfort and camaraderie in Jade's eyes, and finally breathed again.

"The strangeness of this place grows on you after a while, Aaden." Jade leaned forward, and stretched out her arm. Aaden fist-bumped her and appreciated the reminder of home.

"Right now, it's gnawing me on, Jade. For fuck's sake, this place is weird." Aaden held Jade's gaze until Killian pulled her into the crowd gathered around Mia and Declan.

Aaden sighed heavily, and turned toward Lilith again. He saw Marduk looking at him with interest, and a slight scowl. Aaden grinned at him, then walked toward Marduk and Lilith in bouncing steps. He thought he'd get a closer look at Lilith, but more than that, Aaden was impressed with Marduk's commanding presence here tonight after his long convalescence on the strange ship that brought him here. Aaden caught glimpses of Marduk limping through the hallways of the Mercuria with a mean scowl as he barked at everyone in his path in a bellowing voice. Aaden steered clear of him on the ship, but this person here tonight was nothing like the angry invalid Aaden met on the journey to Gael. Aaden was amazed at his recovery, and he admired and respected Marduk enough to keep his eyes focused on him and not Lilith. He'd wait until he was formally introduced to her.

"Uncle Marduk, it's good to see ye on your feet again. Strange family we have, eh?" Aaden quipped as he nudged Marduk with his elbow.

Marduk turned his icy stare to Aaden and shielded Lilith from his view. "This is only the beginning of it, Aaden. Hold onto your balls, lad. The night has just begun." Marduk grinned when he noticed Aaden's respect in not ogling Lilith, and Lilith's respect in not ogling Aaden. He squared his shoulders and scratched his back out of habit. "Aaden…this is Lilith. My wife." Marduk said sternly with an emphasis on the word "my." Aaden understood that Lilith was off limits.

When Lilith turned to greet Aaden, Marduk ran his fingers along her neck softly. Lilith didn't flirt with Aaden. She smiled, nodded politely, and graciously welcomed him to Gael.

Aaden was in awe of her perfectly chiseled face that seemed to have been by perfected by design, with precise measurements that gave Lilith both a seductive and innocent look that took Aaden's breath away. He couldn't look away from her. Aaden was calculating the exact space between her eyes, the arc of her pouty lips, and the planes of her cheekbones, while admiring the flawlessness of her skin, and the ice-blue eyes staring lovingly at Marduk.

"Pleasure to meet ye, Lilith. Whoa…ye're a lucky fucker, Marduk." Aaden clapped Marduk on the shoulder, grinning boyishly with a mischievous gleam in his eyes.

"Your wife is the most beautiful woman in this whole fuckin place. Mad respect to ye, Uncle."

Marduk wrinkled his brow and looked at Aaden with a budding scowl, then he broke into laughter he couldn't pull out of easily. Everyone in the room stopped talking and turned to listen to Marduk laughing genuinely for the first time in hundreds of years.

"Ye're a rare breed, Aaden. I look forward to your time in Gael. I have many things to teach ye, lad." Marduk continued to chuckle as he shook Aaden's hand. "Come to Dorcha soon. I have a project ye might be interested in." Marduk winked as he began making plans for Aaden. He believed he'd just found exactly what he needed for his flagging Cambion Project.

Lugh's heart contracted at the sight of Aaden falling under Marduk's spell. Lugh respected Marduk's wisdom and authority, but he wanted to keep Aaden innocent of the ways of the Incubi for as long as possible. The last thing he wanted for his young son was to be pulled into one of Marduk's weeks of debauchery.

Mia joined Declan and Caraye at Amon's table with a wide smile on her face after Amon called the room to order again by holding his hand up. She and Caraye held hands, and rested their heads against each other.

"You're my step-mama, sister. This shit is weird."

"Gets weirder every day, Mia. But at least we're safe here," Caraye said with conviction, but felt a cold chill run down her spine. She glanced around the room to try to find the source of her sudden chill, but it wasn't here tonight. Caraye had a flash of Issa, and the hair on her neck bristled slightly.

"There are more revelations tonight, my loves…more announcements to be made. I pass the floor to my First Son. Declan…do you have anything you want to share with us tonight?" Amon smiled sweetly, and nodded with a quick wink.

Declan lifted Caraye to her feet and leaned in to kiss the tip of her nose gently, then each corner of her mouth. A wave of breathless sighs floated around the table at the love in Declan's eyes when he looked at Caraye.

"Aye, we have an announcement. In five months or so…Prince Rory, Son of Declan will grace us with his presence, and secure the Dynasty for thousands of years to come," Declan announced proudly and raised his and Caraye's hands in the air. The entire room burst into applause, whistles, claps, and cheers. Declan wrapped his arms around Caraye, and kissed her tenderly and slowly.

"We're having a baby, Caraye," he whispered against her cheek.

"A little Declan." Caraye threw her arms around Declan's neck and ran her hands through his hair.

"May the Gods have mercy on us." Declan pulled a face and chuckled as he pulled her closer to his chest. He shot Aramanth a fierce look and wrapped his arms tightly around Caraye.

Aramanth breathed in sharply when she saw that look in Declan's eye. He didn't have to speak a word. The revelation was clear in his eyes. Declan knew everything about Caraye's birth. Aramanth's cheeks turned red as she held his gaze until she could no longer bear the betrayal in his eyes. Aramanth felt the entire weight of her guilt in that moment. Even her part in inviting the Elders to Issa's wedding. She looked back at Declan and was relieved to see a softer look in his eyes, but the disappointment was still evident.

Declan held up his hand and the room turned quiet again. “There are more revelations to come. Aramanth, I pass the floor to ye. Share your revelations, little sister.” Declan waved his hands, then sat next to Caraye with a stoic face.

Aramanth stood with her head held high. She glanced at Angelus standing at the doorway and got the boost she needed by his boyish grin.

“I also have news to share. In about three months or so, Princess Isabel, Daughter of Aramanth will join our world…and I am to be married….to Angelus, Son of Li Jing.”

Once again, the room burst into cheers. Angelus walked forward with a wide grin to stand beside Aramanth. Lugh, Aaden, and Amon came around the table to offer congratulations. Declan slowly made his way to them with a puzzled brow. He knew the child couldn’t be Angelus’s. Angelus was with him in the Onyx until the night Aramanth was abducted. Declan felt a cold chill run down his spine at the notion that Malachi raped Aramanth.

“Who is the father of this child, Aramanth?” Declan whispered as he pulled her into his arms.

“No one ye know, brother,” she whispered back. When Declan started to pull away, Aramanth held him tighter. “Declan…I’m sorry. I never meant to hurt ye.”

Declan sighed and kissed the top of her head. “I know, Aramanth. But ye meant to hurt my wife.” He walked away from her with stiff shoulders, then held out his hand to Angelus. Angelus wanted Declan’s approval almost as much as Amon’s, and felt the weight of uncertainty lift when Declan pulled him in for a bear hug.

“Ye finally won your Princess, Angelus. I thought ye’d never step up. Congratulations, brother. Ye have my blessing…and my sword should ye ever need it. Ye're getting a Soldier bride," Declan laughed.

"Aye. No one will ever stand against the two of us." Angelus grinned, but Declan's heart fell into his stomach when he realized the truth behind that statement. If Aramanth crossed Amon's line, he'd have to fight Angelus, and Angelus was an unstoppable Warrior.

Amon held his hand up and called the room to order again. "Wine for everyone…while Aramanth still has the floor, I hope she will tell the tale of her rescue. This is a good story." Amon chuckled loudly while he made his way back to his chair, next to Makawee, whose eyes shined brightly as Aramanth began to tell the details of her take-down of Malachi.

Marduk leaned toward Lilith, and ran his hands along her neck. "I already know this story, and I have to step away from it. I have business to attend to in the prison tower. Can I trust ye to be loyal, Lilith?" His eyes were heavy with love, but also mistrust. He knew he might be stepping into a fool's paradise with Lilith again, so he only half-expected an honest answer.

Her eyes were soft when she looked at him and touched his face gently. Lilith knew how close she came to losing Marduk, and she never wanted to be in that position again. They finally reached a compromise they could both live with, and Lilith was determined to maintain this new position. She was very aware of Mia's eyes on Marduk, and his eyes on her. Lilith finally gave in to her love war with Marduk. She happily accepted defeat when she nodded her consent and meant it for the first time.

"I will be loyal, Marduk. I swear it."

Marduk smiled lazily and kissed her tenderly, then leaned forward to Cain. “See you mother home safely. I’m going to the Tower,” Marduk said in a droll tone.

Cain’s eyes widened as he clung to Marduk’s arm. He was afraid of Marduk seeing Salem, but more afraid of what Lucian might reveal. Marduk read his thoughts easily.

“Cain…ye’re my son. Nothing will change that.”

“I don’t mean to sound ungrateful, Father…I appreciate the love and forgiveness you’ve shown me, but…is it Lucian or Salem you’re aching to see?”

Marduk sighed softly and winced at the tortured look on Cain’s face. “Both,” he answered honestly.

Cain nodded and attempted to smile, but he couldn’t quite manage it.

“Salem is also my son, Cain, and this reunion with Lucian is long overdue.”

“Father, please…” Cain began, but couldn’t continue. He closed his eyes and hung his head. “I’ll make sure Lilith gets home safely. And alone,” he added with a small chuckle.

Marduk stared intensely into Cain’s teary eyes, then sadly placed a tender kiss on Cain’s lips. He easily read his thoughts, but he wasn’t prepared for Cain’s confessions about his involvement with Lucian yet. He wanted the camaraderie with his son to last a bit longer. But it was time to confront Lucian. He would deal with whatever else he’d learn tonight and take the necessary steps to repair the damage. No matter what happened, Marduk was determined to keep his family. He reluctantly looked away from Cain and motioned for Declan to join him in the hallway.

Declan leaned toward Caraye and kissed her cheek. “I will be right back, my love. Marduk has his own revelations.” Declan winced slightly as he made his way around the Dining Hall toward Marduk. He was afraid to know if he had to count Marduk amongst his betrayers.

Chapter Eight

Marduk held his breath while he and Declan strolled the skyway in slow, light steps. He didn't want to show any weakness, but the wounds on his thighs burned with pain. He ignored it as much as possible as he attempted to figure out how to begin the conversation, but Marduk knew he had to tell Declan the truth regardless. Marduk stepped into a private den, and gently closed the door. He reached for a bottle of whiskey and two glasses, then motioned for Declan to take a seat. He poured two drams, then handed one to Declan.

"I don't even know where to begin this conversation, Declan. So…a toast. To brutal honesty." Marduk held up his glass, then drank his whiskey all at once. Declan eyed him warily and did the same. "Issa is reborn, Declan. Caraye. Your wife is Issa reborn," Marduk said quickly and without emotion, then paused to assess Declan's reaction. He was surprised by the lack of surprise in Declan's eyes. "Ye knew this already?"

Declan poured another dram for each of them. "Aye. I heard it from Samuel a week after my wedding." Declan couldn't look at Marduk. He kept his eye on his glass of whiskey.

Marduk sighed heavily and rubbed his beard fiercely. "It should've been me to tell ye, Declan. If I hadn't left for Marbh so soon after your wedding, I would have told ye." Marduk touched Declan's shoulder lightly.

"Marduk, the fact that ye're telling me now means a lot to me. But ye knew all along…and didn't tell me. That stings a little. I expected more from ye."

"I found out after ye announced your engagement. I tried once to tell ye, lad. The night of your wedding, but ye were so happy. Dreamy, even. I couldn't ruin your wedding night," Marduk said sheepishly, then squared his shoulders and poured another dram. "I also wanted to be certain that Caraye would be safe…from all ye fuckin Alphans, especially Lugh and Aramanth. I'm sorry, Declan, but I had to test ye as well, lad. Ye passed the test." Marduk winked and drained his shot of whisky. "I want ye to know, I was prepared to stand up for her if…" Marduk let his words hang in the air. He didn't want to speak them.

Declan sighed heavily. "I appreciate that. More than ye know. My wife is in no danger from me, Marduk. But I may still need ye to stand up for her. Lugh and Aramanth created her as a disposable. Amon knows who she is, too. I cannot lose my wife, Marduk. If…" Declan also couldn't speak the words either. "I will need ye to stand with me." Declan looked deeply into Marduk's eyes and saw what he needed to see. Loyalty. Marduk did betray him in a sense, but he was honorable enough to tell him now. Declan also knew that Marduk was his best ally if anyone tried to harm Caraye.

"I'll stand with ye to the death, Declan. But it won't come to that." Marduk drank another dram of whiskey. "Aye. Amon knows. But ye have nothing to fear from Amon. He loves ye far too much to take your wife from ye. Amon acted in what he thought was your best interest. Ye cannot blame your father, Declan. He had no part in it, except in not telling ye. Amon lost Issa too. He gave her up, so ye could marry your redheaded lass. Ye have them both now, Declan. No one will take either from ye."

Declan's shoulders slumped as he drank his whiskey. His eyes misted over slightly at the thought of never seeing Issa again, but more so over the betrayal from Lugh and Aramanth. "I've forgiven Amon. Lugh and Aramanth, however…I still don't know what their intentions are."

Marduk clapped him on the shoulder. "Declan, they will not take Caraye from ye. Lugh loves ye…and he loves Caraye. Aramanth loves her too. Don't ye see it in their eyes?" Marduk grinned as his eyes misted over a little. He hated that Declan was being denied Issa again. He also thought about the special commission from the Elders, the Belladonna and Hemlock dream.

"If ye need to worry about anyone, Declan, it would be the Elders. My dream visit on the boat was a commission from the Elders. My task was to keep ye from falling in love with Caraye. But ye know me. Sucker for romance. Ye were already in love with her when I got there. I decided to help ye along instead." Marduk grinned sadly. "I didn't know who she was then, Declan. But the Elders knew. They let ye walk right into this." Marduk downed another dram. "That sits badly in my gut." Marduk sucked his teeth with a hissing sound and squinted.

"Aye, the Elders played a wicked hand with me. But they've ensured her safety as I demanded. It's written in their own blood." Declan grinned devilishly, and Marduk gave him a proud look.

"Ye had the Elders write it in blood? Ye're my fuckin hero, Nephew. One day ye'll have to tell me how ye did that." Marduk chuckled as he poured them each another dram.

"There is someone else I might have to worry about. Hecaté. I'm almost certain she was involved in this. She knew who Caraye was, and moreover, she's been snooping around in my private life lately. She knew Caraye was pregnant before I did. That sits badly in my gut."

Marduk's eyes lit up and a slow grin spread across his face. "Hecaté… I haven't seen her face in thousands of years." He drifted off into a memory while he sipped his whiskey. "I'll handle Hecaté, Declan. Leave her to me. Leave Samuel to me as well. In fact, if ye trust me, Nephew, I will handle the entire investigation into this matter, and have Draco draw up a plan of protection. Let's keep Rory safely inside his mother, and his father out of the line of fire. Congratulations on your beautiful wife and son, Declan." Marduk grinned widely, and pulled Declan close for a tight hug. "Make sure your son stays away from my wife when he grows up." Marduk and Declan laughed together, then poured another dram for a toast.

"Marduk, whatever it is ye're doing with Lilith now, keep it up. I have never seen her so tame."

"She has a lass. I'm allowing it." Marduk shrugged and rolled his eyes.

Declan grinned like a naughty boy. "I heard about Lilith and Raven. Rather surprising news. Even more surprised that ye're okay with it."

"Aye, this new territory has been good for my wife." He smiled tightly and groaned. "She will never be happy with only one lover, even the fuckin King of the Incubi. I have to give her slack in her chain if I want to keep her," Marduk said in a weary voice.

"Maybe ye should do away with the chains altogether, Marduk. She's not one of your dogs."

Marduk tilted his head sarcastically and smirked. "This is Lilith we're talking about. I let her off her chain for half a fuckin hour at the Gathering, with Draco at the fuckin door…and still she found a lover, hidden in the curtains of the Royal suite of the Citadel. I can't let her off her chain, Declan. She runs away every time." Marduk and Declan burst into laughter, and drank a toast to Lilith.

"Speaking of dogs, I hear ye've been sniffing around Mia. Leave my daughter alone, Marduk. If I hear that ye've taken her to Dorcha for a week of debauchery, ye'll answer to me." Declan gave him a playfully fierce look, but he was serious.

"Ahhh…Mia is a lovely woman, Declan. A grown woman." Marduk winked and grinned. "To our growing family," Marduk said genuinely, and clinked glasses with Declan. "Your wife and your daughter are always welcome in my Lair," Marduk said wickedly.

Declan shook his head slowly and gave Marduk the same grin. "Twisted fucker. Leave my wife alone."

"Forty-two days, Declan. One day, I will even that score," Marduk replied.

"Are ye still hung up on the 42-day affair? It was decades ago! Not my wife, Marduk."

"Ye fucked mine. If ye're lucky, I'll grow old before I remember to avenge myself for it." Marduk drained another dram of whiskey and chuckled softly. "I love ye, Declan, but fair is fair."

"Despite your wicked threats…I'm glad ye lived, Uncle." Declan drank his dram then set the glass down softly. "Though I may live to regret those words."

"So ye may, Nephew." Marduk winked.

"How did it happen, Marduk? Why were ye alone and unguarded in the city?" Declan's eyes held more concern than he wanted to show, but the near death of Marduk was heavy on his back. The quiet panic in his body made Declan shiver.

"How much do ye know about the Black Dragon, Declan?" Marduk poured another round of whiskey and turned deadly serious.

"Everything," Declan replied solemnly. "My time with the Elders prepared me for the dual role. Though I'm not prepared to take it on just yet, Marduk."

"Don't fret about it, Declan. The Black Dragon has been around for a long time, and I don't plan on going away any time soon." He clinked glasses with Declan, then drained his Scotch. "When your time does come, ye'll find your own way through it. I'll be there for ye, every step of the way while ye learn." Marduk stood and took off his jacket, and unbuttoned his shirt to reveal the scar on his left shoulder. "This is the first time the fuckin dragons fought back. We are dealing with a rare breed in this Red Dragon. She may have won this small battle against me, but I'll find her again. This is far from over." Marduk wondered if he should tell Declan about Mia's mother, but the sad and worried look on Declan's face was enough to stop him. He knew Declan had enough on his own plate right now.

"A dragon did this to ye? Not a jealous woman?" Declan wrinkled his brow, and drained his Scotch as he noticed how close Marduk's scar was to his heart.

"Aye. A dragoness. My first one." Marduk downed his whiskey and buttoned his shirt again. "I am a wee bit out of element here, Declan." Marduk rubbed his face roughly, then drank straight from the bottle. "Enough about me. Congratulations on the baby, but what else is bothering ye,

Declan. I can feel it gnawing on ye from here," Marduk said solemnly as he slipped back into his jacket gingerly. His shoulder was still a bit tender.

"Aramanth's child. Who is the father?" Declan asked while refilling their glasses.

Marduk took a long deep breath, then let it all out in a heavy huff as he lowered himself gingerly into his chair. He tried hard not to let Declan see the pain burning in his thighs.

"She was returning from a commission when Malachi abducted her. But Malachi is claiming the child. He confessed to seducing Aramanth. She denies that he is the father, but she confessed to giving in to Malachi for the sake of not being forcefully raped. There is no difference in my eyes. He took her against her will." Marduk's face hardened significantly. "Aramanth told me only a little of what she endured, but my bastard brother, Krava, told me the details."

"General Krava? Was he involved in Aramanth's torture?" Declan asked angrily.

Marduk shook his head quickly. "Not at all. In fact, he was her protector, her guardian to the best of his abilities. But Malachi still had his way with her." Marduk's face soured bitterly as he drank another shot of whiskey straight from the bottle.

"Remind me to thank the mysterious General Krava next time I see him," Declan answered. "How the fuck did ye capture him? He's as slippery as an eel. I saw hide nor hair of him when I was in Marbh."

"He surrendered to me before we stepped foot on Marbh. It was Krava who told us where to find Aramanth. I must say, I'm rather impressed with my little brother," Marduk said with a dreamy smile.

"He fought against ye for thousands of years, Marduk. I don't trust him."

"He's in my prison, and will have his day in court. Until then, I will put him to the test. If Krava has nefarious plans for me, I'll know it." He drank again from the bottle, then handed it to Declan. "Malachi is also in my prison. That wicked lad will not escape my wrath. Neither will his father."

"Send Malachi my way when ye're done with him, Marduk. Lucian, however, I'll leave him to ye. I don't want to be tainted by his madness," Declan said in an ominous tone nearly matching Marduk's. "No matter how angry or disappointed I might be in Aramanth, I'll still defend her honor against Malachi."

"If there's anything left of the lad when I'm done with him…he's all yours. In the meantime, I'm off to see my brothers." Marduk slowly made his way out of his chair with a soft groan, then sauntered toward the door in slow steps. "Watch your back, Declan. Call upon me if…"

Chapter Nine

Marduk marched through the long skyway with stiff shoulders in heavy, purposeful steps. His hips swung gracefully with his kilt that hung low on his hip bones, revealing small flashes of his firmly sculpted belly with each step that shook the floor slightly. No one was unaware of Marduk's presence in the Prison Tower. Every Solider stood at attention with their weapons held over Marduk's path, but they held their breath in awe of his dark, regal elegance and the infamous brooding scowl as he approached Patrick, leaning lazily against the first set of doors to the prisoner's cells. Everyone was aware that Marduk was carrying Patrick's jacket in his hand.

Patrick felt the ground beneath him shake, and looked up to see Marduk coming towards him with clenched fists. His cheeks flushed bright red as he stood at attention. His hands were shaking as he tried to unlock the door quickly. Marduk reached him quicker than he thought possible and grabbed a handful of his hair, then shoved his face against the wall. He held up the jacket to Patrick's eye sight.

"Ye left this in my wife's bedroom." Marduk leaned in and pressed his kilt against Patrick's buttocks. Patrick began to whimper when he felt Marduk's stiff erection at his back.

"No… Marduk, please…" he begged softly.

"When ye fuck my wife, ye fuck me. And when ye fuck me…I fuck back."

"Marduk, please, please…" Patrick begged for mercy, but his heart sank when Marduk reached around to rip open the buttons of his uniform pants with one hand.

"Relax. This is gonna hurt, lad, no fuckin way around that. But it'll hurt less if ye relax." Marduk leaned forward to whisper in Patrick's ear, laughing in a low, wicked tone. He pressed harder against Patrick and swirled his hips slowly. "Ye might even enjoy it. I know I will."

"Please, Marduk…do not do this. I am sorry. I will never again cross Lilith's threshold. I swear it," Patrick said in the pleading tone of a terrified child.

"Ye've been in Lilith's bed more times than I can count, Patrick. Now it's my turn to have ye," Marduk said ominously. "But I'm not going to take ye to bed. I'm going to fuck ye right here in front of the entire Army."

Marduk pulled Patrick's pants down with one swift move and bent him over. He rubbed his full erection against Patrick's backside and laughed diabolically. "Take a deep breath and hold it, Patrick."

"I swear it on my life, Marduk! Never again! I will never again make love to Lilith!" Patrick cried loudly.

Marduk pulled Patrick up by the hair and roughly turned him around to face him. Marduk's eyes were bright with anger, and a small hint of mischief.

"If ye ever cross my wife's threshold again, I will fuck ye, Patrick, and ye will not enjoy it." Marduk shoved the jacket into Patrick's chest with one hand and grabbed Patrick's crotch with the other. Marduk's scowl faded, and so did his erection when he began to laugh wickedly. "Lilith was right. Ye are a little Incubus." Marduk released his hold on Patrick, but didn't move an inch away from him. "Open the fuckin door, Soldier."

Patrick shivered as he pulled up his pants quickly, then turned his back on Marduk to unlock the door. He was acutely aware of Marduk towering over him, with the monster inches away while he breathed down Patrick's neck in a deep growl. Patrick held the door open and didn't look at Marduk as he stepped forward in heavy steps. Marduk didn't stop as the next Guard opened the second door quickly and efficiently to allow him through to the cell room without breaking his stride.

Marduk's heavy steps caught the attention of the Lesser Gods as they all stood with wide eyes and open mouths at the sight of Marduk's presence filling up the entire room. His eyes were ice-cold as he sauntered into the room, thoroughly scanning each face coldly. Marduk winced slightly when his eyes met Seth's from across the room.

Seth grinned crookedly and nodded in deference to Marduk. "Well, I'll be fucked. Ye've grown into a fine King, Marduk. How many years since I've seen your face, brother?"

Marduk raised one eyebrow and set his jaw. "Not nearly enough...brother." He sucked his teeth and held his glare, but his stoic face broke when he saw Salem leaning against the bars with a soft smile on his face.

"Papa," Salem said softly as he held his hand through the bars. Marduk crossed over in two steps to take his hand in his.

"Are ye well, Son? I made arrangements for special care. Have ye been treated right?" Marduk asked with a painful grimace. It broke his heart to see Salem behind those bars.

"Aye, Papa. Your instructions have been followed by the Guards. Thank you for the books. They saved my life…and my mind." Salem let out a heavy breath and pulled Marduk closer. "Is Akaia safe? Conall?" Salem's eyes were full of misery and concern. He missed Akaia desperately, and needed assurance that his First Son had been born safely.

"Aye, Samuel. Akaia has given birth to your son. Conall is a fine, healthy lad with silver hair like his mother. They're both safe and well in Dorcha, under my protection. I'll arrange a visit soon."

"I'm a father? Akaia…is she well, Papa? Did she ask about me? Is she angry with me?" Salem went through a range of tortured emotions that Marduk wanted to comfort.

"Aye. Ye're a father, and Akaia is on pins and needles waiting to see ye. Your wife loves ye very much, Samuel. She's a good lass, despite her father." Marduk grinned and tousled Salem's hair when his shoulders slumped. Marduk saw the heavy weight on Salem's shoulders and held him up as best he could through the bars of the prison cell. "There is more news. Caraye is safe. She and Declan are very happy. In love. He will not hurt her. Ye'll not hurt her either, Samuel. Caraye is off limits. Declan as well. Ye shouldn't have told Declan about Caraye. Ye should've left that to me as we agreed. Do not cross Declan's line again, Son," Marduk said adamantly.

Salem nodded and looked up at Marduk with sad eyes. "I was angry, Papa. Declan took Issa from me. She was mine."

"She is no longer yours, Samuel. In truth, she never was." Marduk softly touched Salem's cheeks. "Declan had a claim on her first, and we should never have interfered with their alliance. I blame myself more than anyone. Issa might still be alive if we had honored their betrothal."

"But…then I wouldn't have Jade," Salem said sadly. "And Caraye…she was mine first." Salem's face hardened slightly.

"Samuel…" Marduk began, but Salem cut him off angrily.

"I hate that he has her now…Issa…Caraye. And Jade. They are mine, Papa. It isn't fair!"

"Samuel, ye have Akaia and Conall. They are your family now. Issa is lost, and Caraye is Declan's wife. Legally." Marduk hung his head sadly. "Ye have to relinquish your claim on both Caraye and Jade, Samuel. The Elders have demanded it. They've erased ye from Jade's life history. I'm sorry, Son…but Jade is no longer your legal daughter, and Caraye is not yours. She never was. They both belong to Declan now. Ye must honor this agreement if ye ever want to see the light of day again. If ye want to be part of your son's life, you cannot stake a claim on Caraye, Jade, nor Issa. Do ye understand me, Son?"

"No! She's my daughter! I will not relinquish my claim to her! Especially not to Declan," Salem spat out harshly.

"Ye have no choice, Samuel. Even though ye were Lucian's pawn in this wicked game, ye still played along, and the Elders have erased ye from her life and given her to Declan. That edict cannot be undone. Do not hurt Caraye nor Jade any more than ye already have, Samuel. It's over. Ye've lost them."

Salem's face twisted into a tortuous grimace, but he nodded slowly. "I won't hurt them, Papa. I've lost Jade…and Issa as well. Though it sticks badly in my craw…I will not fight the Elders. My place is with my son, and with Akaia."

"Aye. It is. Ye have a fine wife, Samuel. And ye have a son." Marduk grinned and tousled Salem's hair again. "I'm very proud of ye. Despite all ye've been through, ye have a wife who loves ye. Your son will love ye as well. I'm going to set ye free, Samuel. Ye'll be free to raise your legitimate son with your wife. But ye must keep your hands clean, and your mind straight. Akaia and your mother would like to see ye. Are ye up for that?"

Salem smiled and nodded quickly. "I am, Papa. I want to see my wife…my mother as well. Does she hate me? My mother?"

Marduk's face softened. "Your mother loves ye more than ye can imagine. She always did." Marduk thought about Cain's machinations all those years ago that took Hurit from her son, but managed to swallow the bitter feelings. "I have more news to tell ye, but in private. For now, Samuel…rest easy. Ye'll be free in no time, and our entire family will heal. There will be no more animosity in my Lair. My family will be whole again." He wasn't sure how to tell Salem that he and Cain were reconciled. He was certain Salem wouldn't understand, but Marduk was determined to never lose either son again.

Salem swallowed hard when he read Marduk's thoughts. He didn't want to dwell on the idea of Marduk reconciling with Cain while he rotted in prison, but the bitter bile rose in his throat. He nodded solemnly and vowed to do whatever he had to do to get out of this prison and back into Marduk's good graces. "Cain. He's back in your Lair, and your heart," Salem said sadly and wiped the tears from his cheeks.

"Both my sons are in my heart, Samuel. Aye. Cain and I are reconciling, but that does not take a single ounce of my love away from ye. I love ye as much as I ever have, Son. This old black heart has enough love for ye both." Marduk chuckled and winked, but Salem held his frown.

"I understand, Papa. He's your real son," Salem replied sadly.

Marduk pulled Salem as close to him as possible through the bars of the prison cell. "I have two sons, Samuel. I love ye both, and I will not lose either of my sons again." He kissed Samuel tenderly on the lips and sighed heavily. His tenderness faded immediately when he heard Lucian's wicked laughter from across the room.

"Ye've gone soft, Marduk," Lucian said arrogantly.

Marduk tensed up and leaned closer to Salem to whisper in his ear. "Son, please excuse me while I deal with Lucian. I'm sorry for what ye're about to witness. Don't react to my words…nor my actions." Marduk's face turned ice-cold and hard. "Ye're about to see the devil in me arise, Samuel. Do not be afraid, I mean ye no harm, Son. But my brother will feel my wrath. Avert yer eyes if it offends ye." He gently touched Salem's shoulder and smiled genuinely, then blinked once and his eyes turned ice-cold again.

Marduk turned toward Lucian with a glaring scowl, and sucked his teeth arrogantly. "Soft?" Marduk replied. "Oh brother Lucian, I am harder than steel under this kilt." He strolled slowly toward Lucian's prison cell with fire and blood in his eyes. "I am in the mood to fuck something. Ye're looking awfully good right now, Lucian. That purple kilt suits ye." Marduk unlocked Lucian's cell door, then gave him a thorough once over that shook Lucian to the core.

Lucian made a move to get across the cell to the open doorway, but Marduk's long, leonine frame filled it completely. Marduk grinned wickedly as he sauntered inside the cell, then slammed the door behind him.

"Do not cross the line, Marduk," Lucian said in a harsh tone, then gave Marduk a piercing glare as he approached in panther-like steps. Lucian backed away in slow, easy steps.

Marduk grinned wickedly when Lucian's back hit the wall and the arrogant look on his face dissolved. Marduk grabbed Lucian's collar and turned him around to face the wall. He lifted Lucian's kilt, then pressed his own against Lucian's naked buttocks.

"Yer purple kilt suits me too, Lucian. Easy access to yer skinny arse," Marduk said in a deep growling tone as he rotated his hips against Lucian. "What do ye say, Lucian? A little romance between brothers?"

"Ye're the most twisted fucker I have ever known, Marduk. Yer own son is watching," Lucian spat out.

"He's been warned to avert his eyes." Marduk sucked in his breath, then let it out in an airy whistle. "Yer hair, brother. It smells so lovely. Did ye have a fresh bath, Lucian? Just in time for our brotherly romance."

Marduk grabbed a handful of Lucian's hair and pulled his head back. He towered over Lucian as he leaned forward and bit Lucian's bottom lip, then sucked it into his mouth tenderly. "Ye look like Lucina tonight. I've always wanted to fuck her, to melt her ice-cold shell. After so many years of lusting for my sister, I realized it wasn't Lucina I wanted to fuck. I am above fucking my own sister. I am not, however, above fucking my brother. I finally got ye trapped. Let me love ye, Lucian," Marduk whispered as he leaned in and rubbed his beard against Lucian's smooth cheek, then swirled his hips against Lucian's buttocks again.

Lucian tightened and stiffened his back as he squeezed his buttocks together, then let out one small sob.

Marduk chuckled wickedly, then smacked Lucian's bare buttocks with his massive hand.

"Relax, brother. I'm only rattlin' yer chains." He released his grip on Lucian and strolled away from him arrogantly. "I have no interest in yer tight, skinny arse. Nor Lucina's."

Lucian lowered his kilt, then blushed profusely when he saw Seth's grin from the cell across from him.

Marduk noticed Seth's amusement and gave him back a cold stare when he raised his kilt and one eyebrow. "Are ye aching for some brotherly love too, Seth?" Marduk laughed wickedly when Seth backed away with wide eyes, shaking his head.

"I have nothing but respect for ye, Marduk," Seth replied quickly.

Marduk sent him an air kiss. "Respect from my wayward brother makes me as hard as these brick walls, Seth. Ye're next."

"Lucian is your target, Marduk. Not me. I did nothing to hurt ye," Seth said as he backed away from Marduk's fierce scowl.

"Nothing, Seth?" Marduk spat out and moved closer to the cell bars.

"The price was paid long ago, Marduk."

"By me," Marduk replied with a wicked glare that Seth couldn't hold. He had to look away from Marduk's intense anger.

"I am innocent this time…"

"Ye're just as guilty as me and the Alphans, Seth!" Lucian bellowed in a high-pitched voice.

Marduk turned back to Lucian with a smirk. "So, ye admit yer guilt, eh Lucian? It won't ease yer pain when I'm done with ye, brother, but it's good to hear ye confess."

"That's not what I meant! I meant that Seth is not innocent!"

"None of ye are innocent. But others of ye are guiltier," Marduk spat out as he scanned the faces of each prisoner.

Mahdi and Jacey began to laugh at Lucian finally getting his due from his King, but Inuus was in shock with his hand over his mouth. He stood at the farthest corner of his cell, whimpering and shivering at Marduk's presence in the cell room. Inuus had always been terrified of Marduk, though Marduk hardly noticed Inuus was alive.

Herne sat in the dark corner with sad eyes, but he wore a small grin while he continued writing his love poem to Cadenza. He was never rattled by Marduk's anger; he was charmed by Marduk's romantic nature, even in his fiercest moments. He found his muse in Marduk tonight, and settled in to write the most erotic love poem of his life with a deep sigh of sad contentment.

Marduk locked eyes with Herne for a moment and finally smiled genuinely. "Are ye writing another poem, Herne?" Marduk asked softly. He fought off the urge to open the cell door to hug his younger brothers who he adored in his youth. Especially Seth. Marduk and Seth were best friends in their youth, with Herne always toddling behind them as they tormented Lucian's sullen and sulky nature.

Herne blushed and nodded. "Aye. A love poem to Cadenza. In yer honor." Herne grinned, then suddenly turned serious. "Marduk, surely ye know I never participated in the Rebellion."

Marduk winced. "Aye. I know. Yet here ye are in Amon's prison. Ye'll have yer day in court, Herne."

"I long for the day, brother. I know I will be acquitted and returned to my wife. I belong with her…and to her," Herne said sadly as his shoulders slumped again.

"I have no doubt, little brother." Marduk nodded firmly, then turned back to Lucian with a wicked sneer. "Speaking of belongings, I have something of yers, Lucian. Everything of yers, in fact. Marbh is once again under my command. My Guards are firmly established. My Incubi are free. Yer Fortress… mine as well. I rather like it, brother. Ye have a flair for color. Ye always did." Marduk grinned wickedly with fire shooting from his pale green eyes. He was bolstered by Seth's soft laughter from across the hallway.

"Ye've been to Marbh?" Lucian asked wide-eyed.

"Aye, I have. Marbh is mine again. It always was."

"How did ye get past my Army? Did ye slaughter them?" Lucian asked angrily.

Marduk slowly shook his head while grinning wickedly. "I didn't have to. General Krava easily surrendered to me."

Lucian scoffed and rolled his eyes. "I never trusted that bastard. I knew he would turn on me one day."

"Perhaps if ye'd treated his mother with the respect owed her as Omega's First Concubine, he would still be loyal to ye. I suppose I should thank ye for being the wicked little arse ye've always been."

"Morrigan was well treated under my hand, and Krava was all too willing to serve me…even without his mother's approval." Lucian raised one eyebrow and smirked. "Krava is loyal to himself."

Marduk chuckled. "He appears to be very loyal to me now, Lucian. His respect for his true King is evident to all."

"He appeared to be loyal to me as well, Marduk…with his deep respect evident to all in Marbh."

"The Dukes of Marbh tell a different story, brother. "From what I hear, no one respected ye. Not even yer most loyal supporters. They licked yer balls out of fear, not loyalty, and certainly not respect."

"Who else surrendered to ye, Marduk? I would like to know who I have to kill when I return to Marbh…to my own Fortress."

Marduk's eyes narrowed as he glared fiercely at Lucian. "Still the arrogant fool, eh Lucian? Ye'll never again set foot in my Colony, much less my Fortress. But to answer yer question, all the Dukes of Marbh surrendered to me. Easily. Happily. Some were stripped of their titles. Others were granted new ones. Lachlan, for example. I restored his property, and gave him more. I also had quite a night with yer concubines. Candy. Now there is an interesting…lass." Marduk sucked his teeth arrogantly and chuckled wickedly. "I had no idea yer tastes were so diverse, Lucian."

Lucian stood mute against the wall. He didn't want to remind Marduk of Cain's similar tastes in sexual partners. The last thing Lucian wanted to do was to make Marduk angrier. Despite his arrogant playfulness, Marduk was seething beneath the surface, and Lucian was well aware of it. One wrong word, and Lucian would be back against that wall. He didn't dare play with Marduk in this mood.

"I also have yer daughter and the grandson we share. Akaia is a great beauty. She and Cain have become very good friends…in my Lair." Marduk raised one eyebrow and one corner of his mouth.

Lucian's face withered, and he lost his place in the script he'd planned for his first encounter with Marduk. "Keep your filthy son away from my daughter!" Lucian charged at Marduk, but didn't dare step within Marduk's long reach.

"Filthy sons…something ye're familiar with yerself, Lucian."

"Malachi is not a murderer! And my daughter is innocent! I will take this to the Elders, Marduk!" Lucian turned bright red with anger. The thought of Akaia in Dorcha with Cain and Marduk broke his heart. He couldn't protect her against their legendary depravity. Lucian felt the walls closing in on him; he couldn't breathe. He clearly saw his first mistake in the Rebellion. He married his daughter into Marduk's bloodline. "Let Akaia go to her mother, Marduk. This is beyond protocol!"

"Protocol, ye say? Ye've always worked beyond the lines of protocol, Lucian. Ye set the rules yerself. No rules. I have won this War, brother, but the game is far from over."

Lucian clenched his fists, and took another step toward Marduk. "Ye're better than this, Marduk. As a Ruling King…."

"Oh…ye acknowledge that fact now, do ye? Aye, Lucian. I am yer King, and as such, I have full authority to do with ye as I please. It pleases me to see ye here, in Amon's prison. I wouldn't want ye and yer filthy son together in my prison." Marduk crossed his arms over his chest and gloated as he leaned against the cell bars casually.

His face was stoic, but his eyes glowed with amber sparks when he saw Lucian's horrified face and wide eyes.

"Malachi? Ye have my son?" Lucian charged at Marduk against his better judgement. He regretted it immediately when Marduk slammed him against the bars, then pressed himself against his buttocks again.

"Ye dare to cross the line with me, Lucian? I will fuck ye until ye beg for mercy," Marduk said coldly as he raised Lucian's kilt again, but Lucian elbowed Marduk in his left flank and broke away from him easily. Marduk stiffened, but maintained his stance despite the burning pain on the entire left side of his body.

"Stop it, Marduk. This is beneath ye!" Lucian straightened out his kilt and sat down on the bed, then crossed his legs tightly. Marduk crossed the room in slow, heavy strides, stopping boldly in front of Lucian's face as his kilt billowed slightly.

"Put that damn thing away, Marduk," Lucian said as he waved his hand at Marduk.

Marduk leaned down and squinted into Lucian's eyes. "Are ye scared of my balls, Lucian?" He grinned crookedly as he grabbed a handful of Lucian's hair.

Lucian couldn't help the slight chuckle that rose from his chest. "It is not the balls that scare me, Marduk. It is that monster that lies between them that has me rattled. Sit down, brother. Get that thing out of my face." Lucian pulled away from Marduk with a playful scowl.

Marduk laughed in a low tone. "Yer wife once rode this monster, Lucian. She was rattled too, but Hecaté wasn't afraid." Marduk stepped away and openly gloated again at the flush of Lucian's cheeks.

"I am aware that ye were once entangled with my wife…before ye found Lilith. Need I remind ye that Lilith rode my balls as well? More than once." Lucian gloated momentarily when Marduk's shoulders stiffened.

"Aye, but ye never rattled her." Marduk winked and grinned like a young Prince. "Speaking of balls, Lucian. Yer son's balls have been the subject of much interest lately. Poor Malachi…he may be maimed for life." Marduk made an overexaggerated grimace, but his eyes glowed with amber sparks of mischief under the dim lights in the cell room. His furrowed eyebrows gave him a wicked look that nobody could ignore. Especially Lucian.

Lucian had been the target of Marduk's wrath most of his life. He always made sure his efforts were worth the punishment he knew he'd get from the true Dark God Lucian tried to mimic in his Rebellion. The Dark God Lucian wanted to be in the eyes of humanity, but he never quite measured up. Nobody measured up to Marduk. There was only one Marduk. One Dark God who used his position, his power, and his dark nature to right the wrongs of the world. Avenging Aramanth's abduction and rape was one of Marduk's motives tonight, but Salem's torture was the other thorn in Marduk's back that he was determined to shove into Lucian one way or another.

Lucian's face fell again, and he swallowed back a rush of bile at Marduk's revelation of Malachi's injury. Marduk's torture tactics were legendary, and Lucian shivered at the thought of what Malachi might be suffering at Marduk's hand.

"Ye know the rules of combat, Marduk. No blows below the belt. What did ye do to my son?"

Marduk raised one eyebrow and smirked. "I did not hit yer son below the belt, Lucian. I only leaned a little…below his belt," he answered in a low, sinister tone. "Aramanth broke Malachi's balls. After he abducted her…and forced himself upon her," Marduk continued while fuming through his nostrils. He was determined to make Malachi number three on his hit list tonight, and he was prepared to use his best weapon.

"Aramanth attacked Malachi?" Lucian asked incredulously.

"Attacked? No, Lucian. Aramanth defended herself against Malachi. Yer filthy son is a rapist, and he will face my wrath for it."

"That is not fair, Marduk! My son is not a rapist! He loves Aramanth! He made love to her…he did not rape her! Ye cannot hold my son prisoner for that!"

"Oh, but I can, Lucian…and it is more than fair. And legal. I will hold yer son in my prison…just as ye once held my son in yers." Marduk pushed open the door of the cell and slammed it hard before he locked it again with a loud click.

He slowly crossed the hallway to Seth and Herne's cell and stood arrogantly in front of them with his arms swinging his balled-up fists. But instead of throwing a punch at Seth, he unclenched one hand and firmly grabbed Seth by the collar, then pulled him close to the bars. Marduk ran his hand through Seth's black hair, staring sadly into his bright green eyes, then placed a loud smacking kiss on Seth's grinning lips.

"Welcome home, ye little fucker. I'll face yer arse on the battle ground before this is over, Seth," Marduk chuckled, then released Seth roughly.

Seth chuckled with him and nodded. "Aye, Marduk. I accept yer challenge. Just as we used to do as young lads."

"Are ye so ready to get yer arse kicked again, Seth?"

"Who says ye'll beat me, brother? The last time we fought, I was only a young Prince. I am a full grown Duke now," Seth teased.

Marduk grinned widely and patted Seth on his thickened midriff. "Ye may want to think about shaping up while ye're in here, brother. That wee gut of yers has also grown…along with yer ego."

"Aye, ye may be leaner than me, Marduk, but lean does not always equate with strength. I can still beat ye."

Marduk threw back his head and laughed loudly. "Bold words for an Incubus whose tender arse I kicked every time we scrapped…except that once." Marduk's smile faded and his eyes narrowed.

Seth's smile faded as well. He had to look away from Marduk's harsh glare. "The past…as unfortunate as it was…is past, Marduk. Can we start over from here? New scores to earn?" Seth grinned and held out his hand.

"I will gladly be the Keeper of Scores again." Herne added softly from the dark corner. "Fresh slate?"

"There is no such thing in my world, Herne. Once yer sin is on my slate, it is there until I avenge it." Marduk winked and sucked his teeth arrogantly. "One day soon, Seth, ye and I will be even. Only then will we begin with a fresh slate."

"That means ye're fucked, Seth," Herne chuckled.

Seth groaned and hung his head. "I will drop my kilt this instant and bend over. Let's get this fuckin over with so my brother will love me again."

Marduk shook his head. "Oh no, brother…yer sin isn't washed away that easily."

"Marduk…I'll let ye fuck me, right here, right now, if it will ease yer burden. But let us be friends again."

"I recall Lucian saying those same words time and time again in our youthful days," Herne added with a chuckle.

The three of them laughed loudly at Herne's joke, leaving Lucian to scowl and prance haughtily in his cell. He always hated being the outsider in the triangle of Marduk, Seth, and Herne. Lucian's discomfort went all the way back to his youthful misery when his brothers made his life a living hell with their daily snubs of his begging to play with them. Lucian eventually formed his own trio with Inuus and Lucina. Inuus was the scapegoat the twins bullied and molded to their liking. For the most part, Inuus was their punching bag. Sometimes Hecaté joined them on the pretext of protecting Inuus from the Omegan twins' cruelty, but her own temper and sharp, serrated wit made her the Queen of Lucian's gang of bullies. After her official betrothal to Marduk, however, Hecaté became the 4th in Marduk's gang, and she turned her sharp tongue and eyes on Lucian along with the others.

"Keep writing yer love poems, Herne. Yer wife deserves them. Seth…one day soon…but ye won't be the one getting fucked." Marduk saluted his younger brothers with two fingers, then leaned against Lucian's cell with a casual stance. "Have a nice night, Lucian." Marduk smoothed his kilt, winked, and blew an air kiss to Lucian. "I am away to see yer son, and I am still in the mood to fuck something."

Marduk took long, heavy steps toward the door without turning back to Lucian, but he winked slyly at Salem when he passed by his jail cell on the way out.

Salem held his hand to his chest and smiled at the thought of his fierce, savage Papa fighting so ruthlessly to avenge him. Salem had hope for the first time in 30 years, and although he was behind bars, he felt more free than ever before. His Papa was in control.

Marduk scowled fiercely when he stepped out of the second set of doors to come face-to-face with Patrick's sheepish smile and blushing cheeks. Marduk grabbed him by the back of the neck and stared down into Patrick's terrified face.

"Send my greetings to yer lovely wife, Patrick. Branwen is welcome to return to my Lair any time she wishes. But if I find a fucking hair from yer head in my Lair…" he leaned in closer to Patrick's ear and growled ferociously. "I will have no mercy."

Marduk was feeling more alive than ever today. He was feeling his power. He defeated two enemies in a matter of minutes, in two separate battles that weighed heavily on his back and shoulders for 3000 years. Marduk never actually acted on his threat that was the signature move he used only on the incorrigible dead until now. But the tactic worked like a charm on his wicked brother, as well as Patrick, Lilith's last standing lover. Besides Raven. He chuckled at the entire idea of Lilith's new lover, and was inclined to share Lilith with Raven for the time being. She kept Lilith satisfied, and Marduk didn't feel threatened by this kind of love. It was refreshing to him. He liked that Lilith was exploring new territory, but he would no longer allow her to explore old territory. Marduk believed Lilith found a loophole for both of them, and was satisfied to know that no one else would cross Lilith's threshold but him and Raven. In the meantime, there was another prisoner waiting for him in his Dungeon that made his blood boil for his actions against Aramanth and Salem.

"Three is the charmed number," Marduk said under his breath as he lightened his step and nodded to the Guards as they bowed in reverent awe of Marduk's triumphant walk. He lost his limp completely though his right thigh was still tender, so was his left shoulder where the bullet hit, inches from his heart. The Red Dragon, and humanity itself, dealt Marduk a serious blow, and he was inclined to leave them to their own devices for the time being. He had matters in his own Colony that needed his attention. He would return to the dragoness in time, when he was fully healed, and the mess in his own Colony was cleared up.

Marduk laughed as he relaxed his step and nodded politely to the Guards. He defeated death and no longer feared anything. Every Guard in the Prison Tower knew they were witnessing the night marking Marduk's triumphant return to power and authority in the Colonies. No one was surprised, but everyone was anxious to see what might happen next, now that both Kings were back on their thrones.

Chapter Ten

Jade and Killian ran up the steps alongside Scotch while Aaden took them slowly and stared up at the endless spiral above him, and the countless stairs below him. "For fuck's sake, how far up are we going?"

"Not much farther, Aaden. There's a magic ledge one flight up, with an amazing secret," Jade said in a singsong rhythm that made Aaden's heart thump.

Scotch groaned and rolled his eyes, then leaned toward Killian. "Be careful of that one, Killian. He's got his eye on your girl. Say the word, and I'll do away with him for eternity."

Killian chuckled and clapped Scotch on the back. "I trust Jade. No need to kill anyone, but…let's have a little fun with him." Killian winked. Scotch grinned wickedly and nodded.

"This ledge is the coolest thing you'll ever see, Aaden. Don't be afraid," Killian said in a playful tone.

Aaden scoffed and bounded up the stairs to catch up with them. He walked in sync with Jade's steps, and added a light bounce to his when she glanced up at him admirably, flashing a flirtatious smile.

"I've never been afraid a day in my life." He grinned widely as he ran up the steps backwards with a cocky grin, then sprinted ahead of them. Jade watched his long legs and wide shoulders with a rosy blush creeping up her cheeks.

She couldn't deny her attraction to Aaden. He had a commanding presence and effervescent charm that couldn't be ignored, but she was just as attracted to Killian's quiet, gentle nature. The two young men were polar opposites, and she was being torn in both directions of that pole. It was painful, but the excitement of it was impossible to deny.

When they finally reached the window just a few steps behind Aaden, Jade made a wide, sweeping motion with her hand as she opened the window with a dramatic flair. "Your night of revelations awaits, Aaden."

She smiled brilliantly, and so did Aaden as he stepped through the window. His grin faded immediately when he saw the view of the massive moon hanging in his direct view line.

"That's the most incredible thing I've ever seen in my life. Cool as fuck." Aaden's grin returned as he strolled closer to the edge and peered over. "Whoa…long way down! Can we die here?" He turned to Killian, and was impressed that he knew about this spot, and that he and Jade were brave enough to come up here. Aaden found a new sense of belonging suddenly. He found new friends who were as bold and brave as he was, though not nearly as arrogant about it.

"Yep. We can die here. But the ledge has a secret." Jade stepped to the marked spot and pointed her foot at it. "See this hieroglyph? Your dad and Declan marked it 700 years ago."

"How many…years…ago?" Aaden asked with a withered face and open jaw. He scratched his head and looked at Jade like she'd lost her mind.

"You heard her right. Things are a bit different here, Aaden. Your father is…different. It's easier if you just roll with it. As weird as it is," Scotch smirked at Aaden's shocked face.

"Fuck's sake…this place is poppin, but highkey weird. The 4:00 am subway rides are craic by comparison," Aaden said in a heavy brogue. "I always knew my dad was different, but I had no idea just how different…until I got here. He's 700 years old? Strange fuckin world," Aaden said softly.

Killian stepped up and draped his arm around Aaden's shoulder and grinned. "Your weird shit ain't nothing, Aaden. My dad's 3000 years old, and he was a Vampire until he got the antidote for his virus," Killian said with a chuckle. Scotch snickered and stood closer to Killian.

"Ye're fuckin nuts, Killian." Aaden stepped back with a budding grin. "What kinda drugs ye guys poppin in this place?"

Jade burst into laughter and leaned a bit closer to Aaden. "Seriously, Aaden. His dad was a Vampire. Your dad is an Incubus. Mine too…in a roundabout way," Jade said softly and looked down at her feet.

Aaden's heart contracted at Jade's mention of her father. He wanted to offer words of comfort, but he wasn't certain how fragile her emotional state was over the incident. He didn't think this, 1000 feet in the air on a ledge with no rails, was the place to test that idea. He held out his fist to her, and Jade grinned crookedly as she fist-bumped him.

"We're two of a kind then. This fucker is half Vampire." Aaden chuckled and clapped Killian's shoulder.

"We're three of a kind. My dad is Marduk's son." Killian held up his fist, and the three of them fist-bumped and giggled.

Scotch's jaw dropped open as he stared at Killian incredulously. "You're Marduk's grandson? That makes you my future King," he replied with a facetious bow. "We're four of a kind," he added, then held up his fist to the trio and grinned. "My father is Marduk's brother."

"No kiddin? We're fam, bruh. Hella weird, but fam is fam," Killian answered.

"We're children of the Lesser Gods," Scotch answered in a droll tone. "I say we demand the royal treatment. Starting with lots of lasses."

"I'm down with that," Aaden laughed.

Killian smiled shyly as Jade. "I already got my lass."

Aaden shifted uncomfortably and stepped away from the ledge. "So…show me this secret. I didn't climb up here for a fuckin moon I can peep from the ground floor."

"Okay…here's the deal. You gotta stand right here." Killian walked up to the hieroglyphic symbol. "Don't fight. Stay on the path, and let yourself be light." Killian began in a serious tone.

Jade flinched and took several steps back Scotch ran toward Killian. "For fuck's sake, just jump already!" Before anyone could blink, Scotch pushed Killian off the ledge, then grinned crookedly at Aaden and Jade. "You fuckin half-breeds don't know how to have fun."

Jade set her jaw and balled up her fist, then punched Scotch right in the gut. He fell off the ledge with a loud and wild yell.

Aaden looked at Jade with a withered brow and open jaw. "Ye're fuckin crazy, lass! What the fuck?" Aaden turned white, but relaxed when he heard Killian and Scotch's laughter ringing out. He peered over the edge, but kept his distance and a wary eye on Jade.

"Don't fight the air, stay on the path, and let yourself be light," Jade said as she held out her hand to Aaden. "I thought you were brave," she teased.

Aaden broke into a wide grin as he took her hand. "I am brave, lass. I don't know what's down there, but if Killian and Scotch are laughing about it, it can't be that bad. Let's fuckin do this, eh?"

Jade pulled him forward and held his hand tightly.

"One, two, three!" Jade and Aaden yelled together, then jumped off the ledge hand-in-hand.

Aaden thrashed about for a second, then relaxed when he saw Jade gliding gracefully with her arms out and her eyes closed. She flipped twice, then opened her eyes. Aaden didn't even realize he was floating on air, because his entire world was Jade's eyes in this moment. He stepped forward to touch her, but faltered a little when he felt the air beneath his feet.

"Don't fight the air…" Jade started to repeat the directions.

"Stay on the path, and let yourself be light," Aaden answered, then closed his own eyes as the weightlessness of his fall lifted him suddenly. He did a flip and yelled out loudly, "Fuckin awesome!"

Jade giggled as she descended a little lower. "You good? You got this?"

"Aye, Princess. I got this." Aaden yelled again as he went into a vertical, free form flip that was more graceful than anything Jade had ever seen. Aaden held his body light and flipped again as he watched her descend farther from him, but she held his gaze until she caught up to Killian, then wrapped her arms around his neck.

"Should we tell Aaden our plan?" Killian asked.

"I think he's trustworthy. But let's give him a chance to adjust to life in Gael first."

"I think he'll fight on our side, Jade. His whole family is human. He might even convince Lugh to join us."

Jade smiled as she glanced up at Aaden again. "He's definitely a warrior. But I don't know if he'll fight against his dad."

"I don't think he'll fight against his mom," Killian replied, then flipped gracefully with Jade in his arms.

"Whatever you do, Killian…don't tell Scotch. I don't trust him an inch."

Killian grinned and kissed Jade softly. "He's not a bad guy, Jade. But I won't say anything if that's how you wanna play it."

"That's how I wanna play it," she whispered, then draped her arms around Killian's neck and kissed him passionately.

Aaden watched them with a sting in his heart that made him lose his balance for a second or two, but he recovered quickly, and closed his eyes again as he rode the air with a wide smile.

Scotch landed before anyone else and sat back on the ground with an arrogant grin as the trio landed softly on the ground. "You half-breeds are too slow," he called out.

Aaden took a tumble and rolled into an easy flip, then landed on his feet. He spinned his feet around in a smooth move and laughed loudly with his arms out.

"Most amazing thing I've ever done." His heart jumped to his throat when he looked up at the ledge he'd just jumped from. "For fuck's sake…did we jump from all the way up there? How the fuck did we do that?" Aaden's head was spinning, but he was ready to jump off the ledge again.

"Anti-gravity shaft. Only in that spot, though. Don't try to jump from anywhere else. Gravity applies everywhere but that ledge and the Crystal Field," Scotch said with a smile. He held his hand out to Killian. "No hard feelings, right? I knew you knew the secret," Scotch said with a chuckle.

Killian grinned and slapped a hard handshake onto Scotch's hand. "No problem, Scotch. Just don't ever do it again." Killian genuinely liked Scotch's fearless nature.

Jade, however, was skeptical of Scotch and didn't trust him. When he held his hand out to her, she scoffed, but reluctantly wiggled her fingers against his.

"Are you going to apologize for hitting me?" he asked with a sly grin as he lit a cigarette, then blew the smoke in Jade's face. She coughed and waved the air around her.

"No."

"You punched me in the gut. I could have you whipped for that, lass," he said arrogantly.

"Give it your best shot, whiskey-boy."

Scotch chuckled and shook his head slowly. "Feisty little half-breed." He winked at Jade. "I like it."

"What other secrets can we find in this strange and wonderful world of the Incubi?" Aaden asked with infectious enthusiasm that made Jade blush profusely. Gael enchanted Aaden once again, and Aaden enchanted Jade. She suddenly had the urge to call off her plan to fight against the Incubi. She didn't want to be on the wrong side of Aaden.

"More than we'll probably ever know. But we're determined to find as many as possible," Killian replied mysteriously as he draped his arm around Jade. In the back of his mind, Killian was already on the opposite side of Aaden, but he wasn't quite ready to own up to it.

"Right behind ye, Kill. Maybe ahead of ye in the near future," Aaden said while giving Jade a quick once over. She was glowing from her wild jump off the ledge, or maybe it was because of Killian's arms around her. It didn't really matter to Aaden. Jade was glowing, and his heart was on fire at the sight of it.

"Let's do it again," Aaden said, then started back toward the Palace in long, steady steps. "First one to the ledge gets to hold Jade all the way down." He laughed when Killian and Scotch began a heated race, sprinting far ahead of him. "Dudes fall for that trick every time," he chuckled as he stopped to wait for Jade to catch up, then took her hand and slowly led her away from the Palace with a cocky grin.

"Let's you and me look for something new, eh?"

"Aaden…you know there's a Revolution coming, right?"

Aaden nodded slowly. "Yeah, my dad mention something about it. I don't want any part of it."

"Neither do I."

"But… you're the chosen one. You're gonna lead the Revolution…rumor has it."

Jade shook her head adamantly. "Not if I can help it, Aaden. I refuse to fight against my own people."

"My people, too. But then again…so are the Incubi. Do ye have any options, Jade?"

"Just between you and me? My plan is to learn all their fighting tactics, then turn them back on them."

"Holy fuck! Ye're gonna fight the Incubi?" Aaden asked with wide eyes and a slack jaw.

"If I have to. You in? Or do I have to count you as an enemy?"

Aaden sighed heavily and ran his hands through his thick golden hair. “I don’t wanna fight against ye, Jade. But how the hell am I supposed to fight against my dad?”

“It’s not me you’ll be fighting against, Aaden…It’s either your dad, or your mom. Which one are ye willing to fight against?”

The blood from Aaden’s cheeks drained slowly as he doubled over with a loud groan. “I can’t fight against either of them. Jade…there has to be another way.”

“I think so too, Aaden. Help me and Killian find a way to stop this Revolution. We have to do it before the Elders force this on us. But we have to keep it all lowkey. Your dad can’t find out. Nor Declan. Not even Scotch can know our plan.”

Aaden glanced ahead at Killian and Scotch running and laughing together as though they were already best friends. “Does Killian know that Scotch is the enemy?”

“He’s not an enemy…none of them are our enemies, Aaden. Not yet anyway. But all that might change as soon as the plan is revealed. You in? Or out?” Jade asked solemnly.

“If ye’re in, I’m in.”

Jade breathed a sigh of relief and reached for Aaden’s hand. “We need a plan. And an alternative to this Revolution. I cannot take another life…human or Incubian. I don’t think I can do it.”

Aaden squeezed her hand and led her back toward the Palace in slow, steady steps. “I can take a life if I have to, but I don’t want to. How do we even begin to figure out an alternative, Jade?”

“Declan’s library. It’s…amazing. I’ve never seen so many books in all my life. I’m certain we’ll find our answers in there.”

Aaden grinned and draped his arm around Jade's shoulder. "Count me in, Princess. Show me this amazing library while Killian and Scotch are distracted."

Chapter Eleven

Marduk's light, easy swagger helped to ease the pain in his thighs as he made his way through the Lair, but he stopped dead in his tracks when he saw Raven bolt across the hallway like an apparition. She hit a dead end, turned around quickly, then ran right into Marduk's arms. She gasped as she stared up into his squinted eyes. He held her around the waist, and studied her face intensely. She tried to pull away, but Marduk held onto her.

"Are ye here of yer own will, lass?" he asked in a deep tone with a wrinkled brow.

"I'm not sure what that means anymore," Raven said sadly as she stared at Marduk with wide eyes. She was terrified of many things in this place, but Marduk was her worst nightmare. The stories Cain told her about his father were burned into her brain and rattled her to the core. Marduk's current scowl nearly stopped her heart. Raven shivered and began to cry softly.

Marduk softened his grip as well as his scowl. "Has anyone here…including Lilith, forced ye to do anything ye didn't want to do?"

Raven swallowed hard and shook her head. "Nobody forces me to do anything I don't want to do." She wiped her tears and took a deep breath. "This thing with Lilith…it's new to me, but…she's so beautiful. Nobody can say no to her." Raven threw her hands up and let out a deep huff. "I'm sorry. I won't do it again, I swear." She tried to break free from his grasp, but he easily held her close to him. She stopped fighting when Marduk chuckled softly and hung his head.

"Aye. Even I cannot say no to her. I'm only concerned for your welfare, lass. Ye're in no danger. Ye may carry on with Lilith, if ye so choose. Just do not let anyone force ye into that choice. Do ye understand, lass? If anyone, including Lilith, forces ye to do anything ye're not one hundred percent comfortable with, let me know. I will handle it straight away, if ye cannot."

Raven nodded. "Like I said…nobody forces me to do anything I don't want to."

Marduk lifted one corner of his mouth in an easy smile and finally released her. "Ye have permission to be Lilith's lover, but I will warn ye…and only warn ye once, Raven. Keep her happy in my absence, but in my presence, walk away and do not look back."

Marduk raised one eyebrow, then made a grand sweep of his hand to allow Raven to pass. She blushed but grinned slightly as she passed by him. She got his message loud and clear. She turned back to look at him once and shook her head.

"You two are fucking twisted. You know that, right?" Raven said with a chuckle.

"I am aware. Carry on, lass. Raven…if this ever gets to be too much for ye. Come to me. I'll see ye safely to where ever ye want to go. I swear it. Ye're not a prisoner here, and ye're not to be used against yer will. Ye're allowed to say no. Even to Lilith."

Raven took in a deep breath and nodded. His heavy brogue reminded her of her Irish grandfather who raised her for the first 13 years of her life, before her father dragged her back into his life, and into the Orthodox Fascist cult. Her father was a wicked legend in that cult, and made Raven's life miserable for refusing to fit in. Her life in New Orleans hadn't been easy either. She'd been used and abused by more people than she wanted to count, including Cain.

Here, however, she was free. She was appreciated, and cared for in ways she'd never been cared for before. Although she regretted leaving New Orleans, she wasn't unhappy here in this strange place she landed in through even stranger occurrences she couldn't define. She kept hoping this was a dream she'd wake up from eventually, but in the meantime, she was determined to explore all the pleasures Dorcha had to offer.

Raven's fear of Marduk began to dissolve at his words, as well as the strained tenderness of his tone. Despite his savage ferocity, Marduk was genuinely concerned for her welfare. That surprised Raven more than she thought it would, given all the strange surprises she'd experienced lately.

Raven gave Marduk a full body perusal and blushed at his long, lean legs, and his thick arms crossed over his chest. When she looked up at his face again, she saw a cocky smirk on his lips.

"Only if ye're willing, lass."

"I'm not." Raven pointed toward his kilt. "That's a bit too much for me."

Marduk grinned and nodded. "Only the bravest among ye take this ride, Raven. I can see from here, ye're far from the bravest. Relax, lass. I won't harm ye."

Marduk turned on his boot heel and made his way down the hallway with an arrogant swagger that made his kilt sway majestically. Marduk was feeling more victorious than he'd felt in thousands of years. His journey through the Onyx River invigorated him, his brush with death made him braver than ever, and his victories tonight made him reckless, so he headed down the stairs to his Dungeon with a wide grin on his face, and a budding plot floating in his head.

"Draco!" Marduk yelled out loudly as he approached Draco's office.

Draco rolled his eyes and smirked at Marduk standing in the doorway with a wide, mysterious grin on his face.

"Are ye drunk, my liege?" Draco hadn't seen Marduk this happy or mischievous in hundreds of years, but he was relieved to see Marduk so alive after his violent death and his bittersweet return to life.

"I am not. But that's a good idea, Draco. I'm in the mood for a little romance. Fetch me a bottle of Scotch, scented candles, the pepper salve, and my nephew." He sucked his teeth with a small hissing sound, then grinned wickedly. Marduk's eyes were bright with mischief.

Draco chuckled and shook his head. "The line, Marduk."

"The line was crossed when Malachi forced himself upon Aramanth. She complied in the service of her Army. But the fact remains, he took her against her will. The child she carries…" Marduk let his words hang in the air. He couldn't bear the possibility of Malachi being the father of Aramanth's child. Aramanth insisted that Malachi wasn't the father, but Malachi maintained his claim on the child. Marduk was anxiously awaiting the results of the revelation that might tie Aramanth to Malachi for eternity. The exact moment of conception was difficult to determine in

Aramanth's advanced stage of pregnancy, so they had to wait for the child to be born to determine her parentage.

A hardened flush fell across Draco's cheeks at the very idea of Aramanth giving herself over to Malachi's brutal seduction to save her life. Aramanth was like a sister to him; he was fiercely protective of her, more than ever since she made the announcement of her engagement to his brother. He wanted to make Malachi pay for his actions, but Draco weighed and measured every move he made before making it. He knew well the consequences of acting without forethought. He watched his father die from a bad idea without a solid plan. He watched thousands of humans die from the same lack of introspection.

"Still, he is your nephew, Marduk. Lucian's First Son. The line cannot be crossed," Draco said quietly.

Marduk squinted and smirked with a mischievous grin. "I am in the mood for romance, Draco. Either fetch my wicked nephew or bend over yourself." Marduk crossed his arms over his chest, then crossed one booted foot over the other while glaring at Draco.

Draco raised one eyebrow and set his jaw firmly. Marduk's scowl no longer had an effect on him. "My liege, you could try for a thousand years, but you will never get me to bend over for you. Fetch the lad yourself." Draco crossed his arms over his chest and sat back in his chair.

"Draco…I only mean to frighten the lad. I have never crossed that line, and will not begin with Malachi." Marduk lifted one corner of his mouth slightly, then broke into a wide grin. "I only want to teach him a wee lesson. He tortured my son, as well as your brother…and he raped Aramanth," Marduk said more solemnly. "He needs a little taste of his own tactics. It's my duty, after all."

Draco hung his head, but couldn't hide the smile spreading across his cheeks. "In that case, Marduk. Let us set the stage for a little romance." Draco shook his head as he reached behind him for a bottle of Scotch from the cabinet. He reached for a jar of salve next, but Marduk stopped him.

"That is not the pepper salve, Draco," Marduk said in a serious tone. "The red jar."

"My liege…the fear of *that* in the lad is enough." Draco nodded toward Marduk's kilt.

"The pepper salve, General."

"Ye're a wicked fucker, Marduk," Draco said as he tossed the red jar to Marduk.

"Ye're telling me no news." Marduk caught the jar in mid-air with one hand and squelched his grin as best he could. "Bring him to me naked," Marduk said ominously, then took the bottle of Scotch from Draco's hand and drank from it heavily. "My romantic mood is growing. Don't forget the candles." Marduk turned on his heel and marched toward the private bedroom in the Dungeon.

"Aye, my liege." Draco couldn't stop the chuckle in his chest as he shook his head. "Never a dull day in the Onyx Lair."

Draco set the stage as Marduk directed, then made his way to the prison to collect Malachi for a twisted night of romance with Marduk. He tried not to grin when he unlocked the door to Malachi's cell.

"Come with me, Prince Malachi."

"Where are you taking me?" Malachi asked arrogantly, even as he shivered at the sight of Draco. He was terrified of Draco who stood nearly a foot taller than him and a half foot wider on each side, but he would never let his fear show.

"Tonight is your lucky night, lad. Romance is in the air in Dorcha," Draco said quietly to keep from laughing, as he roughly pulled Malachi from his bed.

"Is Aramanth here? Has she come to see me?" Malachi's eyes were wide with hope.

Draco played into that hope and finally let go of the grin he'd been holding back. "Aye. Princess Aramanth is waiting for you. She requested that you join her… naked."

Draco slowly stripped off Malachi's shirt while he slipped out of his pants. Malachi was a bit shy standing naked before Draco, so he reached for his purple robe on the back of the only chair in his cell.

"Aramanth loves this robe." Malachi grinned as he strolled out the cell door with a light step. Draco had to work hard to keep from laughing at Malachi's simpering arrogance.

"This way, Prince Malachi." Draco opened the door behind him, then led Malachi down the dark hallway toward the private suite in the Dungeon.

Malachi's eyes lit up at the sight of hundreds of glowing candles filling the room with an ambrosial scent that immediately stirred his black little heart, as well as his erection. He saw a shadow moving in the corner of the room and untied his purple robe, slipped it from shoulders, then tossed it to Draco.

"She said she wanted me naked." Malachi waved his hand dismissively as Draco let out a small chuckle.

"Enjoy your evening of romance, Prince Malachi." Draco was proud of himself for keeping a straight face, but he wished he could be a fly on the wall for this scenario.

Malachi closed the door without taking his eyes from the shadow in the corner of the glowing, candlelit room. He lazily sauntered toward the corner with a crooked grin and big dreams of finally winning Aramanth's love.

"I'm so happy you finally came to your senses, my love," Malachi called out as he lazily sauntered toward the bed sprinkled with red rose petals.

Malachi's eyes widened, and he gasped for air when he turned the corner to see Marduk, fully naked and solidly erect, instead of Aramanth.

"Surprise," Marduk whispered hoarsely and reached out one hand to grab Malachi's throat before he could move an inch. He took a long pull of Scotch from the bottle, then held it up to Malachi's lips. "Drink up, Malachi. It'll take the edge off this nightmare ye just stepped into." Marduk grinned wickedly as he moved closer to Malachi.

Malachi shivered as he took a sip of the Scotch. He went for a second sip, but Marduk pulled it back.

"A little at a time, lad. I want ye to remember this night." Marduk pulled Malachi forward, then planted him face down on the rose-covered bed. He closed Malachi's legs and straddled him while rubbing his erection on Malachi's naked bottom. "Hold still, lad. One wrong move, and the monster is inside ye."

Malachi fought against Marduk's hold on him to no avail. He clenched his buttocks together and set his jaw tightly. "Marduk, this is beyond protocol! Even for you! Stop this at once! You will not intimidate me!"

Marduk laughed eerily and leaned down to Malachi's ear. "I don't intend to intimidate ye, Malachi. I intend to fuck ye." Marduk grinned widely, then drank another long sip from the bottle of Scotch. He held the bottle to Malachi's lips as he pushed his hips against Malachi's tight buttocks. "Set the fuckin mood. Drink up."

"Marduk…you are crossing the line…this is beneath you!" Malachi squirmed as Marduk spread his legs, lifted his hips, and pressed his erection to the edge of Malachi's tight, unyielding anus.

"How many times did Aramanth lie beneath ye, Malachi? Against her will?"

Malachi pressed his hips against the bed while attempting to close his legs. "She never lay beneath me against her will, Marduk. I did not rape Aramanth. I seduced her!" Malachi said in a high-pitched whine that grated on Marduk's nerves. He had to work hard to keep from crossing the line. He held his body perfectly still, fuming through his nostrils as he grabbed a handful of Malachi's hair.

"Seduced, ye say? Ye and I will play that game tonight, Malachi. I'm the master of it. I am yer King. The Chieftain of yer Tribe. I'm the fuckin King of the Incubi. Ye'll never again be so royally seduced." Marduk pressed his hips forward in a small movement that made Malachi yell and clench harder.

"Owww…Owww…Owww! Get off me, you fucking animal!"

"Oh, we're not fuckin yet, Malachi. They say the first thrust is magic. A burst of pain that will make yer eyes water and yer head spin while ye fade in and out of consciousness. I'm going to take my time, because I want that magic moment to last for ye, lad." Malachi tried to crawl away from Marduk, but Marduk's grip on him was solid. So was his erection. "Hold still, my beauty…and take a deep breath," Marduk whispered against Malachi's ear in a foreboding tone.

Malachi collapsed against the bed and began to cry loudly when he recognized the same words he spoke to

Aramanth the night he abducted her and held her down while he 'seduced' her into submission.

"Marduk, don't do this. I didn't hurt Aramanth. She didn't fight me. She wanted me. I swear it. I love her, Marduk. I did not hurt her."

Marduk sighed and pulled back slightly as he rolled his eyes. "Don't cry, lad. Ye never know…ye might like it," Marduk said in a sweet, seductive lilt as he leaned over and playfully grinned at Malachi. Marduk could hardly keep a straight face as he tucked Malachi's hair behind his ear and hovered near his cheek. "Some of my lads do…after the tenth time or so. Once they open up to me." Marduk lightly pressed against Malachi again. "Oooo, so tight, lad. I love first-timers," Marduk growled in Malachi's ear. Marduk's mischievous grin grew at the sight of Malachi's heaving shoulders.

"Relax, lad." Marduk held up the jar of salve to Malachi's line of sight. "I have a magic salve that will ease yer pain, and prolong my pleasure." Marduk growled again and nibbled on Malachi's ear gently, then thrust his tongue deep into Malachi's ear.

"This is cruel! I am your nephew! Please, Marduk. Don't do this to me. I never did this to your son!"

"Never?" Marduk asked in a mock quizzical tone. "Are ye sure, Malachi? Yer reputation says otherwise. Or is all yer bravado only a false flag?" Marduk slipped on a glove and opened the jar of pepper salve. "Let's see how brave ye truly are, lad." He dipped his gloved fingers into the pepper salve, then rubbed a large scoop of it around Malachi's anus. He counted to three, then slipped the tip of one finger inside. "Oops…told ye to hold still, lad," Marduk said as he smacked Malachi's buttocks hard.

Malachi cried out in a loud scream, then crawled out from beneath Marduk, who eased himself up to hover over the bed with one eyebrow cocked.

Marduk slipped the glove off his hand and tossed it at Malachi, then laughed in a deep, sinister tone at the sight of Malachi rubbing his bare bottom on the sheets as tears stung his eyes, and the pepper salve stung his swelling anus. Marduk took a long swig of Scotch, then hiked up one leg on the bed frame. He still had a solid erection.

"This is the cruelest thing you have ever done, Marduk!"

"Not by far, Malachi." Marduk shook his head and grimaced playfully before he took another swig of Scotch. He handed the bottle to Malachi with an arrogant smirk. Malachi drank deeply from it, wincing hard as he rubbed his buttocks against the sheets again.

"You're an animal!" Malachi cried out, then drank more of the Scotch until Marduk took it from him again.

Marduk leaned over and pulled Malachi's head down to an inch away from the infamous monster that was his best weapon. "Count yer blessings that the pepper salve is the only thing in yer arse right now, Malachi," he said in a heavy brogue.

Marduk pushed Malachi away from him, then stepped off the bedframe. He picked up his kilt from the floor, then slowly wrapped it around his waist while he squinted fiercely at Malachi, who was whimpering like a wounded animal. Marduk was unaffected by Malachi's tears. He'd seen the same reaction thousands of times with the incorrigible dead.

Marduk sent Malachi a playful air kiss, then walked away from the bed in heavy steps to wash the pepper salve from his hands thoroughly.

"You're not going to rape me?" Malachi asked breathlessly.

Marduk stopped in his tracks and turned to his prisoner with a wide grin. "Ye sound so disappointed, Malachi. Ye almost make me want to, but ye've soiled yerself, lad. The romance is over." Marduk shrugged, then tossed a towel to Malachi and marched toward the door in heavy steps with his chest puffed up with satisfaction.

Marduk opened the door to Draco nervously pacing the hallway where he stood guard. Marduk laughed like a naughty schoolboy as he strolled toward Draco with an easy swagger.

"That lad will never want to face me again. In an hour, allow him an enema of milk, chamomile, and aloe vera, then burn the sheets."

Draco's face fell. "Marduk, what did you do?"

"I avenged Aramanth." Marduk couldn't wipe away his wicked grin as he took a long swig of Scotch, then handed the bottle to Draco.

Draco drank deeply from it, but kept a wary eye on Marduk. "Is the lad intact?"

Marduk pulled a face and scoffed. "Of course he's intact." He grinned again and tossed the jar of pepper salve to Draco. "Mostly."

Marduk laughed the entire way down the hall as he marched in heavy strides toward Lilith's suite. He burst through her door, and was more than surprised to find her alone in bed. She sat up and gave him a seductive smile as her hair tumbled around her bare shoulders. Marduk's heart skipped a beat at the sight of his beautiful Lilith, finally alone in her bed, finally docile, but more important to Marduk, finally loyal.

Marduk slowly unbuckled his kilt and let it fall to the floor. Lilith's eyes widened as he strolled toward her in slow, precise steps. He usually wore his kilt to bed, mostly to punish her with the rough, raw wool that marked her body with itchy red streaks that lasted for days and kept her from her lovers.

Lilith let her eyes wander over his body with no guise of her appreciation of the rare glimpse of Marduk, Son of Omega fully naked. She'd almost forgotten how magnificent Marduk's long, leonine body was, even with the new scars on his shoulder and thighs, and the old scars around his waist from his kilts, the hundreds of cuts and scratches from Bella, as well as the unevenly laced scars along his lower back from his multiple attempts to cut out the thorn from it. Lilith's thorn. Marduk hadn't found it in 3000 years, but he had Lilith back, and he was determined to remind her that she belonged to him.

Marduk dipped one knee on the bed and slowly pulled her to him by the ankles. He was drunk on Scotch and power, but more so on the passionate love in Lilith's eyes. He finally won her back, and he was going to keep her this time, no matter the cost. He leaned forward and kissed her belly, the spot between her breasts, then her neck before he made his way to her lips. He tenderly pulled her bottom lip into his mouth while he ran his hands through her hair.

"Let me romance ye, *mo ghrá gheal.*"

Lilith's eyes lit up at the sound of Marduk's tender whisper. "Romance is something we have not shared in hundreds of years, Marduk."

"Thousands. I will make it up to ye tonight, my love. If ye're willing."

Lilith responded by draping her arms around Marduk's neck and her legs around his back, then she pulled him in for long, sensual kiss. "I am willing," she whispered against his cheek, as though disclosing a secret.

He bit his lip, grinned lazily, and for the first time in thousands of years, Marduk made love to Lilith instead of fucking her.

Chapter Twelve

Declan and Caraye were deep into their own throes of passionate romance, tangled together under the sheets, and joined in a massive orgasm that sent them both into a screaming frenzy.

Angelus heard their screams and was reluctant to knock on the door, but Amon had summoned Declan for another conference. Lugh and Aramanth were there too. Both were on pins and needles, waiting for Amon's verdict to crash down upon their heads.

Declan was floating on a love cloud with Caraye in his arms, and was ready to make love to her again when he heard a loud thumping in his ears.

"Do ye hear that, lass? Ye've got my heart beating so loud, I hear it myself. Come here, woman. Let me love ye again," Declan whispered against her lips.

Caraye moaned and tilted her hips forward, then grabbed a handful of his hair to pull him down for a series of kisses. "Declan…as much…as I want…to believe…it's your heart…it's not." She groaned loudly and tilted her hips forward one more time. "Someone is knocking on our door."

Declan grinned widely, then kissed Caraye slowly, tenderly. "Let them knock. We're not home." He bit his bottom lip and was about to flip her over on top of him when he heard the second round of banging that wouldn't stop. He rolled his eyes and growled loudly before lowering his mouth over her full, round breast. “Hold that thought, my love. I’ll be right back.” He sucked her bottom lip tenderly, then stepped out of bed and was about to walk out the door naked, but Caraye called him back.

“You might want to cover that thing, luv. It might be Jade. Or Mia.” She giggled when his face broke into a blushing grin.

“Aye, I wouldn’t want my daughters to see my naked nethers,” he said sheepishly, then slipped into a pair of jeans with a heavy sigh when the third round of banging began. “How odd that Mia is my daughter, eh? This is going to be fun, Caraye. She’s got my flair for drama…and comedy.” Declan leaned over the bed to kiss Caraye in a lingering, breathy kiss. “Be right back. Don’t go anywhere, lass.”

“I’m tucked in for the night. Hurry back, lover,” she said seductively.

“Aye*, mo shíorghrá*. Five minutes.” He kissed her again, then ran toward the door with a happy grin. Not even the urgent banging could lift the cloud of love around Declan’s head. He opened the door with a smirk, but turned serious when he saw Angelus in an official stance. He held his arm across the threshold and held his breath.

“Angelus…why are ye at my door in the middle of the night?”

“Amon has summoned you, Declan.”

“Can it wait until morning?” Declan asked with a withered scowl on his face. “I’m making love with my wife.”

Angelus tapped Declan on his bare stomach with the back of his hand. “You’re always making love with your wife, Declan. Amon cannot wait for you to finish.” He grinned like a young boy. "He's in his private office. Waiting anxiously," Angelus said in a more serious tone.

Declan looked at the bedroom, then back at Angelus with a budding scowl. He didn't like the thoughts running through his head. He didn't want to leave Caraye alone, but he had no idea who to trust to watch over her. Angelus was armed, only a few feet away from his pregnant wife. That didn't sit well in Declan's gut, despite Amon's declaration that Caraye was safe. He suddenly wished Marduk was still in Gael. Oddly enough, Declan trusted Caraye with Marduk more than anyone in Gael. The revelation wasn't as comforting was Declan wanted it to be.

"I'll be there shortly." Declan nodded, then closed the door despite Angelus's insistence that he come right away. Declan sprinted to the bedroom and took in a sharp breath when he saw Caraye posed beautifully on the bed with a bold look in her eye. She crooked her finger at him and blushed.

"*Mo shíorghrá*, I am breathless…and speechless." Declan climbed in the bed beside her, pulled her to him fiercely, then cupped her face gently. "I've been summoned," he sighed.

"Amon?" Caraye asked softly. "What's going on with you two?"

Declan blushed as he fell back on the bed with a heavy sigh. "It would take a lifetime to explain it."

"Luckily, we have a lifetime or two…explain it to me later. Right now, you have no time. The big guy is calling." She giggled like a girl in an attempt to pull Declan from his dark and distant reverie. Caraye was almost certain this new rift with Amon was about Issa. "You want me to come with you?" she whispered as she wrapped her arms around his waist.

"I would like nothing better," he whispered and pulled her closer. "But Amon isn't thrilled about surprise guests. Would ye like to visit Mia? Or Jade? I'll escort ye there myself, *mo shíorghrá*."

Caraye's eyes lit up at the mention of Mia. She and Mia hadn't had much time together lately and she was curious to know if there was news of her love triangle, or quadrangle now that Draco entered the picture.

"I would love to spend some time with Mia! Jade is with Killian and Aaden. They're a cute little trio, aren't they? I like Aaden. He's a little Lugh. Have you seen the way he looks at Jade? Could be a little trouble brewing there." Caraye pulled a face and sucked in her breath.

Declan had indeed seen Aaden's furtive glances at Jade, and he noticed Jade's undisguised attraction to Aaden as well. Declan felt Killian's pain more acutely than anyone knew. It was all too similar to his triangle with Issa and Salem.

"I've seen it. Aye. There may be trouble brewing." Declan said while pulling himself up from the bed. He held out his hand to Caraye with a wide smile and bowed gracefully. "If ye'd be so kind as to let me escort ye to my daughter, my love."

Caraye took his hand with a flirtatious smile. He pulled her closer to him, then kissed the tip of her nose gently. "Lady Godiva…please put on a dress. I cannot face Amon with this…" He gently pressed her hand to his erection, and growled under his breath when she arched her body against his. "Ye're not helping, lass."

Caraye giggled softly as she reached into the closet for a loose flowing dress, then slipped into a pair of silk slippers. "Better?" She held out her hands and twirled.

"It's going to take another round or two with ye to tame this monster." He grinned as he looked her over slowly and thoroughly. "I'm in so much trouble."

"You're going to be in real trouble if you don't answer Amon's summons. C'mon. Take me to Mia. I gotta know what's going on with Draco!" Caraye's eyes lit up brightly.

"I thought we had a deal?" he teased while they walked together through the suite.

"I said I wouldn't meddle…didn't say I wouldn't gossip."

Declan leaned in to kiss her before he opened the door, then led her to Mia's suite.

"Caraye, what is bling?" Declan asked curiously.

"Have you been sharing sex memories with Cain again?"

Declan laughed, then winced at the memory of his twisted night with Cain. "No, lass…the whiskey was the devil that night. My apologies, my love." He blushed and looked at her from beneath his lashes. "Mia said she wanted bling. I'm inclined to give to her, but I don't know what it is, and I wouldn't want to disappoint her with a guess."

"It's jewelry. Bling is a slang word. Ya know, shiny stuff. Bling," Caraye said with a wide grin and girlish giggle. She was happy to be able to teach Declan something about her world. He was teaching her everything about his.

"Oh…I'll have an entire set of jewels made for her." Declan grinned and blushed. "Do you like jewelry, Caraye? I'll have every jewel in the Colony made for you if ye do."

"Every girl likes bling," Caraye replied in a sassy tone.

"Then Jade will get bling as well."

Mia came to the door with a puzzled brow, messy hair, and puffy eyes, but her face lit up when she saw Caraye. She pulled her inside her suite, then smirked at Declan. "I need your wife. Just da wife. Go drink something. Or fight. Girl talk." Mia grinned widely.

Declan feigned indignation. "Well, that's a fine way to greet your father, lass! Just when I was planning a bling party for ye. With new shoes and all." Declan chuckled and leaned toward Mia to kiss her cheek.

"Diamonds and Rubies. Red looks really good on me. Oh, and pink peep-toes. High, high heels. I got the legs for it. Black pumps. Red ones too. Bye, Daddy…love ya," Mia said playfully and grinned before she slammed the door on Declan's withered face and sparkling eyes.

"Can I at least kiss my wife?" Declan called out from behind the door.

Mia smirked at Caraye who was in a fit of giggles. "What?"

Caraye giggled as she walked back to the door and opened it to Declan leaning against the door frame with a sexy grin.

"I knew ye'd come back." Declan pulled Caraye to him and kissed her with a loud smack. "Stay here with Mia until I come for ye. Don't go anywhere with anyone else." His eyes turned serious for a second, and Caraye felt another cold chill.

"You're scaring me, Declan. What's going on?"

Declan lowered his eyes and smiled shyly. "There's nothing going on, lass. I'm just looking out for your safety, and Rory's." He gently touched her belly. "I won't be long. Have fun with Mia."

"It's impossible not to have fun with Mia. We'll talk later, okay? I wanna know what this mysterious summons is all about."

"Aye, and I wanna know all about Mia's love life. Share our gossip later?" Declan's eyes lit up like a young boy.

Caraye nodded enthusiastically. "It's a night of revelations. Go before you get in trouble." She pushed him away and scowled playfully. She didn't want to see a repeat of that disturbing display of animosity between Declan and Amon.

Declan grinned at her sudden ferocity. "Irish lasses." He held his hand to his heart and stepped away, watching her until she closed the door, then sprinted to Amon's private suite with a hundred questions running through his mind.

Angelus breathed a sigh of relief when he saw Declan approaching. "Finally! Amon was about to take my head off." Angelus quietly ushered Declan inside, and all Declan's questions funneled down to one when he saw Lugh and Aramanth sitting at Amon's conference table. His first instinct was to run back to Caraye, but he had no safe place to take her. His heart began to race as he looked at the chair that Amon was holding out for him. It left his back exposed and was far from the door.

"Have a seat, Son. Family conference," Amon said resolutely. He was determined to put an end to this animosity between his children tonight. He finally had his entire flock home again, and he wasn't going to let secrets ran rampant through his Palace to tear his family apart.

Declan sat in the chair closest to the door as he set his jaw stubbornly. "I'm fine right here, Amon."

Amon rolled his eyes. "Do not be so dramatic, Declan. Sit at my table," he said in his usual commanding tone.

Declan didn't budge. Amon was beyond frustrated with the discord and was inclined to drag him to the table, but Declan had already suffered enough, and Amon wouldn't add to his discomfort.

"Your mother, Declan. We have news of Nahemah," Amon said quietly, and almost laughed when Declan's fierce look melted into child-like curiosity when he got up from the chair to join Lugh and Aramanth without looking at them.

"She is safe in her own Palace that Marduk secured for her in Marbh. The Armies agreed to a peace treaty in keeping the Lower Colonies and the Onyx Caves safe. General Dante's Elite Guards will keep the shores of both Marbh and Mair safe."

Declan wrinkled his brow. "General Dante? I've never heard of this General. Someone new?"

Amon chuckled and exchanged glances with Lugh. "Aye. Someone new. Dante is a newly appointed General under Marduk's command. He is not Incubian. Nor human."

"He's a *lusus nature*. A giant freak of nature. No one knows what he is," Lugh said with small chuckle.

"Why would Marduk appoint a *lusus naturae* to guard the shores of Críoch? Did ye agree to this, Amon?"

Amon nodded firmly. "Aye. I did. Dante's Army has agreed to stay off the shores of Marbh and Mair to allay the fears of the Incubi under the watch of Lachlan and Brian. Marduk worked out an agreement between the two Armies. Dante has his preternatural army under tight command, and Dante is under Nahemah's even tighter command. The Lower Colonies are secure, and Nahemah is married."

"Married? To who? Or dare I ask… what?"

Lugh broke into a chuckle and attempted to pull Declan closer to him, but Declan pulled away. Lugh's face fell again. He thought they'd worked through their issues at the banquet. He stared at Declan with soft eyes, but Declan refused to look at him.

"What. Nahemah is married to General Dante," Amon said more solemnly.

Declan finally looked at Lugh, then Aramanth. "Ye left our mother in the hands of a beast?" Declan spat out angrily.

Lugh laughed again. "Declan…it's Nahemah. The Dragon Queen. She's the beast in her marriage. She rules Dante, though he is larger than Amon."

Declan couldn't help the chuckle that spilled out. "Impossible. No one is bigger than Amon." He nudged Lugh, then remembered that they were at odds and composed himself stoically.

Amon grinned and paced the floor. "Larger by a foot, Declan. I could not believe it myself."

"Is she well? When I saw her last, the virus had overtaken her."

"She agreed to the antidote," Amon said.

Declan ran his hands through his hair and sighed heavily. "I knew Marduk planned to give her the antidote, but was afraid she'd refuse. Still, I don't understand why Marduk left her in the hands of a fuckin beast. Why didn't ye insist that she come home?" Declan looked from Amon to Lugh with a withered brow. "She's our fuckin mother! Ye should have taken her home, Lugh!"

"She's in love, Declan!" Lugh replied fiercely. He was stinging from Declan's harsh tone and cold shoulder.

Amon touched both their shoulders lightly to settle them down. "Queen Nahemah and Dante are two of a kind. She is cured Declan. She is safe and out of the caves. She will remain in Marbh with her new husband…and children."

"Children? With her *lusus naturae*? The poor wee bastards," Declan said as he shook his head and groaned.

Lugh turned to Declan with a sad smile. "She loves those little monster bastards, as well as Dante. Though he's a beast. He's no threat to Nahemah, Declan. Dante is on our side, and may fight with us in the Revolution."

Declan's face withered significantly as the mention of the Revolution, as well as the idea of Nahemah's army of freaks fighting against humanity, landed heavily on his shoulders. The entire idea of the Revolution had soured for him now that he had a human family.

"Lugh…a *lusus naturae* army will devastate humanity. They cannot be controlled."

"Marduk is working on a plan to keep them under control. The Revolution is something you and I will discuss with Marduk on another night of revelations, Declan. Tonight is about Nahemah… and Caraye. Aramanth and I would like to explain everything. I'm begging ye, brother, hear us out."

Declan closed his eyes and sighed, then stood abruptly and squared off against Lugh. "I want one question answered before we go any further with this discussion."

Amon pulled himself to his full height and towered over Declan. "Sit down, Son," he commanded, but Declan didn't back down.

"Not until they answer my fuckin question! Is my wife safe?"

"Aye!" Lugh and Aramanth both answered simultaneously.

Lugh took two steps closer and gripped Declan's shoulder to keep him from running. "I love her, Declan. I didn't know what to expect at first, but now that I know her…not even for you, nor for Amon, would I hurt her. Aye, in the beginning, the plan was to bring Issa back for ye. But things changed when ye fell in love with her. We changed the plan. As soon as ye told me how ye felt about her, we called it off."

Declan shirked off Lugh's grip on his shoulder and stepped back angrily. "What was the plan, Lugh? To lure her to Gael so ye and Aramanth could kill her? How did ye plan to do it? Were ye going to snap her neck? Lock her in Amon's laboratory while ye drained her blood? What was the fuckin plan?!" Declan yelled through a clenched jaw.

"Caraye wasn't supposed to make it to Gael. She was supposed to die along the way. Hecaté worked a spell. But we called it off, Declan. The plan was called off before ye even set sail. We knew ye were already in love with her," Lugh replied.

Declan paced and fumed while glaring at Lugh and Aramanth. Amon stood in the background with his head hung low. He couldn't believe what he was hearing. He felt an overwhelming sense of guilt for mourning Issa so long. He believed his own grief over Issa's loss was the catalyst to this tragedy.

"Hecaté. She keeps popping up all over this situation. Hecaté's spell nearly took Caraye's life! She saved her in the end, but… did she really save her? What the fuck did she do to Caraye in Marbh?" Declan ran his hands over his face and took a deep breath. He led Hecaté right to

Caraye, trusting that she would heal her. Now he was terrified that she might have cursed her further.

"How could ye do this, Lugh? Aramanth? My wife and my child may in danger this very moment! Hecaté's spells are very powerful. Ye know this! Ye took my life into your fuckin hands without consulting me! I am furious with both of ye!" Declan paced and glared at them with painful, angry betrayal in his eyes. No one in the room was unaffected by the raw emotion in Declan's eyes.

Aramanth made a move toward Declan, but he stepped away from her. Her shoulders slumped as she began to cry. She couldn't bear the thought of losing Declan.

"So much of your hardship is my fault, Declan. I did this. Lugh was only along at my insistence. If ye're going to hate anyone, hate me. I created the seed. I contacted Hecaté. She played a large role in creating Caraye, but I am the one to blame."

"Aye, I fuckin blame ye for this, Aramanth!" Declan growled and clenched his fists as he paced back and forth. The sudden silence in the room was deafening. Then Declan remembered what Aramanth had just been through, and his own guilt at not protecting her overrode his anger. His shoulders slumped as he hung his head and paced slowly. "I will never understand why ye did this. Your reasoning behind it all makes no sense to me. Ye overstepped your boundaries, lass!" he screamed through gritted teeth. But as soon as Aramanth burst into tears, his anger began to dissolve. "Aramanth…we've all been through enough. We've all suffered so much since Issa's death. We lost each other, for 30 years. We were all separated…then your abduction…the baby. I hate what ye've done, make no fuckin mistake about that, but…I cannot hold my anger against ye. Ye're my little sister. If ye swear to me that ye mean no further harm to my wife, and if stand with me to protect her from Hecaté and the fuckin Elders, I will eventually forgive ye. I just fuckin need time!"

"I swear it, Declan. I will stand with ye as I always have. I will not harm Caraye nor your son. I made a mistake that I tried to make up for. And I did…Caraye is still here."

"But Issa is not," Declan said sadly.

"The Elders, Declan. The Elders took Issa…and they took control of Hecaté's spell," Lugh answered adamantly. "I will fight beside ye to keep her safe from the Elders. Caraye will not suffer a single day if we all stand side-by-side."

"She has already suffered!" Declan stepped up to Lugh with an angry glare. "Ye already hurt my wife, Lugh!"

"She's not just your wife, Declan! She's my daughter! I will protect her with or without your fuckin permission," Lugh spat out angrily. "I'm not your fuckin enemy! No one in the room is your enemy!"

"When ye hurt my wife, ye hurt me! And ye fuckin hurt her, Lugh! Ye left her alone in the world! No fuckin father and no mother, because ye chose a selfish bitch of a mark to bear Issa! Ye fucked up, Lugh!"

"I didn't choose the fuckin mark, Declan! Hecaté did!" Lugh faced off against Declan until Amon stepped in and pulled them apart.

"Enough! I will not have animosity between my children under any circumstances!" His booming voice was enough to dispel the heavy tension in the room. "Lugh, Aramanth…I am so disappointed in the two of you for this! You had no right to interfere in Declan's life! Neither of you have the authority to create nor take a life for your own purposes! And if either of you dare to harm Caraye, the future Queen of Gael, you will answer to me!" He fumed angrily at the two of them, then turned toward Declan. "I am disappointed in you as well, Declan, so wipe that smug look off your face! Aye! Lugh and Aramanth made a grave mistake, but they are pledging their loyalty to you now to stand with you against anyone who dares to harm your Queen. Even against the Elders! You are a fool if you do not accept this pledge! You cannot stand alone in this fight to save her, Declan! You need Lugh and Aramanth if we are to save our fucking Dynasty and the fucking Alphan Crown! I will not allow this animosity to continue in my fucking Palace!" Amon yelled until he was red in the face.

Declan, Lugh, and Aramanth were shocked to see Amon so angry. The three of them stood mute with wide eyes and slack jaws.

Declan let out the first chuckle, then Lugh joined him. Aramanth held her hands to her mouth to cover her giggles, then the three of them burst into uncontrollable laughter.

Amon cleared his throat and blushed profusely. "Aye. I said 'fuck.' Three times." He cleared his throat again, then burst into laughter with them. "It felt good! I should use the word more often," Amon said resolutely, then lifted his eyes upward and blushed. "Forgive me, Alpha. I know you hate that word, but it was necessary." He hunched up his shoulders as though waiting for a lightning bolt to come down upon his head. Amon's move sent Declan and Lugh into another round of laughter as they hugged each other, then pulled Aramanth into their circle.

"I do need ye both," Declan said softly as his laughter turned to tears. "My wife and my Heir are at risk. I need ye at my side. Ye've both sworn loyalty to my wife, so I have to accept this…and forgive both of ye. Besides… we have to stand together to keep Amon from saying 'fuck' ever again. I never want to hear that word coming from his mouth again. I'll be disturbed for eternity at the memory of it."

Lugh pulled himself together, then pulled Declan into a bear hug. "I swear my loyalty to ye, Declan. To Caraye and your unborn child as well. Your child will be my grandson, brother. Don't forget that. I will die before they do."

Declan's shoulders slumped as the last of his anger disappeared. "I had forgotten that wee fact. I trust ye, Lugh. Aramanth…" Declan's face withered as the tears rolled easily down his cheeks. "I cannot fight with my little sister, and I cannot hate ye. I love ye too much," he said softly. "No more tricks. No more interference in my life." Declan pulled Aramanth close to his chest. "We'll all stand together to protect Caraye against the Elders…and Hecaté. They are far from innocent in this plot, and I want answers." Declan's face hardened again as the thought about Hecaté's spell.

Amon finally let out his breath and wrapped his long arms around all three of his children. He was determined to keep the peace between them, even at the expense of his beloved little sister, Hecaté.

Aramanth and Lugh exchanged furtive glances and made a mental promise to each other not to reveal the final secret in the fiasco just yet. It was Hecaté's secret to reveal in her own time.

Chapter Thirteen

Marduk and Lilith lay in each other's arms, kissing tenderly and glowing under the romantic candles as the sweet scent of their love-making floating in the air all around them.

"Ye looked so beautiful in the new red gown tonight, Lilith," Marduk whispered against her cheek as he pulled her closer. "More beautiful than I have ever seen ye."

"Thank you for replacing my red dress, Marduk. It is more lovely than the original one. I did not know you were going to New York on this journey." Lilith ran her hands through his hair and kissed him in a lingering, tender kiss that left her breathless.

Marduk pulled her closer to him, placing soft kisses along her neckline to her shoulder. Lilith purred and smiled lazily. She was no longer invisible and was determined never to leave Marduk's line of sight again.

"Amon wanted to meet Lugh's family," Marduk said quietly as the events of New York flooded his memory. He shivered visibly, then wrapped his arms and legs around Lilith to calm his anxiety.

Lilith turned to him with tenderness in her eyes he hadn't seen in hundreds of years. "Amon said you nearly died." Lilith moved in closer and draped her arms around him possessively. "What happened on this journey, Marduk? Was there a battle in Marbh?" She kissed him tenderly and cupped her hands around his cheeks. Lilith's eyes were heavy with love, and Marduk finally trusted it enough to tell her the truth.

"I took Marbh by storm, *mo ghrá*. I easily won that battle." He grinned devilishly and pulled her closer. "The battle wasn't in Marbh. I was assaulted in New York. Shot and stabbed. I crossed over, Lilith. I was dead until Amon revived me by banging his fist on my chest. Three times. The third one brought me back to life," he whispered softly. He didn't think it was necessary to tell her about losing Bella. Marduk was certain Bella had returned. Although he couldn't see her, he felt her spirit hovering in the room somewhere, but he didn't want to spook her. He knew this tender time with Lilith would draw her back to him. Bella could never resist the tender moments between him and Lilith.

"Shot? Stabbed? Oh Marduk…who did this to you? You died?" she asked breathlessly. "Are you alright, my love?" Lilith's eyes filled with tears when she thought about how close she came to losing Marduk permanently. The idea of it took her breath away and made her head spin in a moment of panic. She shivered as she wrapped her arms tighter around him.

"Aye. I'm fine, Lilith. It was just some random criminals with guns and knives."

"Why were you in New York alone, Marduk? Why were you so close to random criminals without protection? Where was Draco?" Lilith's genuine concern touched him, but he didn't want her pity. Marduk didn't want her to see him as weak and wounded.

"Draco had his own troubles. It wasn't his fault," Marduk replied quietly with a grin as he recalled Draco's story about his arrest that he told over and over while sitting in the chair beside him during his recovery. Draco never left Marduk's side the entire ten weeks when the Mercuria was docked until Gael's Physician's pronounced Marduk healthy enough to travel.

"I wanted to meet with Michael. He's the designer who makes all yer pretty gowns, Lilith, and speaking of …" He sat up slowly and tried not to wince in pain, but Lilith saw his pained grimace and helped him up without making a fuss about it. Marduk leaned on her despite his pride. "I have more dresses for ye, *mo ghrá gheal*."

Marduk grinned and ran his hands through her hair, but jumped with a start when Bella suddenly leaped onto his back. He heard her sigh in the background of Lilith's sharp intake of breath at the mention of gowns.

Pretty dresses, Papa? Bella whispered in his ear, then made a soft high-pitched purring sound against his cheek. Marduk's eyes teared up, but he held a stoic face for Lilith's sake.

"Lots of pretty dresses," he choked out, then relaxed his shoulders as he felt the familiar weight of Bella on them again.

Lilith's eyes lit up as she threw her arms around his neck excitedly. "May I see them?"

"How can I say no to this face?" Marduk cupped her chin and kissed her tenderly, then groaned happily as he slid out of bed to march toward Lilith's vestibule. He felt normal again with the added weight of Bella on his shoulders, but Bella wasn't as heavy now. She was back, but she was here on her own terms.

No bones ache, Papa. Bella whispered in his ear softly. *You have to see me as I am. Dead. Bella is dead, Papa.*

"Aye, I know," he whispered back. Marduk realized he could no longer keep Arabel a prisoner of his back after experiencing it himself. "No more aching bones," he whispered.

Bella purred softly and clung to his neck without digging her claws into his skin. They finally reached a comfortable compromise both of them could live and die with. The shards of their relationship had finally smoothed enough to allow them to coexist in their natural and unnatural states as they were.

Marduk grinned devilishly as he pulled a thick garment bag from the closet and casually strolled back to the bed where Lilith was sitting up in a seductive pose with her messy hair falling over her shoulders. Marduk couldn't take his eyes off her. The two of them had each other's full attention, until Bella jumped off Marduk's back and sat on the pillow beside Lilith. Marduk got a rare glimpse of Bella's face, and nearly stumbled at the sight of it. She was grotesquely bloated and pasty-white with glowing ice-blue eyes and black-lips set in a gruesome grin displaying sharp, blood-stained teeth.

Marduk took several deep breaths to steady the slow panic beating against him like an ocean wave on a jagged coastline. He hoped she hadn't been feeding on cells in the Dead Realm. He didn't want her tainted by their inherently dark nature, but he knew he could no longer control her actions.

Despite the tightness in his chest, Marduk smiled at Bella admirably, then nodded his approval at her boldness in showing herself. Bella grinned back and lifted her long fingers to brush away the wild hair framing her bloated face. Marduk had to look away, but he didn't flinch. He didn't want to discourage her newfound bravery. He looked back and forth between Bella's bloated face boldly grinning at him with love and admiration in her glowing hollow eyes, and Lilith's stunningly beautiful face looking at him with respect and affection he'd never seen in her eyes before. Both were anxiously awaiting the first glimpse of the dresses.

Marduk gently placed the bag of dresses on the bed and slowly unzipped a half-inch at a time, then zipped it back up, teasing them both until they began to laugh simultaneously. Bella's laugh was a bit more demonic than Lilith's signature sultry laughter, but Marduk tried his best not to compare them.

Open it, Papa! Open it! Bella squealed and waved her hands in the air.

"Marduk, do not toy with me when it comes to dresses," Lilith laughed, but maintained her composure without demanding anything from him. She wanted to allow him the pleasure of giving the gifts to her.

Lilith was finally beginning to understand what Marduk wanted from her after watching him with Maeve over the silent months when he didn't speak a word to her, or even acknowledge her presence. When he replaced her with Maeve in an unprecedented move that was much too close for comfort, Lilith was certain she'd come as close to losing Marduk as she was going to allow. She began plotting her way back into his good graces by closely observing Maeve's responses to Marduk, and his responses to her in return.

Marduk showered Maeve with gifts, compliments, affection, and romance. They had an easy camaraderie with no conflict, no tension between them. She saw the relationship that should be hers. She saw exactly what kind of romantic devil Marduk, Son of Omega really was, and realized this was exactly what she wanted from him all along. It could have been hers, but she demanded it without earning it, so he withheld it. Instead, Marduk lavished attention and affection on Maeve without reservation, and held back no romantic gesture in giving Maeve his royal treatment.

Lilith finally began to recognize the complexity of Marduk's persona, as well as the power of his position. She saw things in Marduk she never appreciated before, and rekindled old admirations she forgot she loved about him. She watched him sharing his romantic overtures, boyish smiles, genuine laughter, intimate conversations, and passionate love with someone else, unguarded and confident in himself and his relationship. She wanted nothing more than to get back into that circle. Every day, Lilith scratched, clawed, and dug her way back into Marduk's intimate circle, but his barriers were air-tight. She couldn't get a fingernail's edge inside Marduk's fortified parameters until now.

By watching Maeve, Lilith finally understood what Marduk meant by loyalty, or at least what she assumed was loyalty. She was still unclear on the distinction between loyalty and submission, so she erred on the side of submission. She got a taste of life without Marduk on his four-month journey, and she liked that even less than being invisible to him. Her final power play with Maeve came by accident, and Lilith took every advantage of that accident. She declared herself the victor in her battle against Maeve weeks ago, and now that she was back inside Marduk's good graces, she didn't want to risk losing her place again, so Lilith made a definite decision to surrender her war against Marduk for good.

"Will ye wear them for me, my love? I would like to see ye in each one of the dresses. Seven pretty dresses,

Lilith. Eight when ye count the red one." Marduk finally opened the garment bag and a burst of color, frills, lace, silk, satin, chiffon, tulle, and beaded sequins popped out.

Bella let out a loud, shrill screech as she floated toward the dresses. *Pretty, pretty dresses, Papa*! Bella's jaw hung open as she gingerly touch each dress.

Marduk's heart broke at the sight of her rifling through the stack of dresses with wide-eyed awe. He remembered bringing her bags of dresses like this when she was alive. She had the same awestruck look on her face then, but less gruesome than this black-lipped, hollow-eyed visage.

Lilith stared at Marduk with tears in her eyes. She saw Bella rifling through the dresses too, and she knew where Marduk's thoughts were. Lilith realized that she never allowed him to mourn Bella properly, and she never told him that she recognized Bella's spirit. She wasn't certain this was the right time to do that, so she simply allowed Bella to play with the dresses first before diving into them herself.

"Try them on, Lilith," Marduk said as he waved his hand over the bag. He was puzzled by her hesitation.

Lilith broke into soft tears when she looked up at him. "They are stunning, Marduk. All my favorite colors. Thank you, my love, you are so good to me. I love the dresses, I truly do, but… I will let Bella play with the gowns first. She is so enchanted by them, Marduk. As am I," Lilith said sincerely through tears as she watched her dead daughter playing with her new gowns.

Marduk took in a deep breath and slowly made his way toward Lilith. He sat on the bed behind her, wrapping his arms and legs around her, then he pulled her toward him and gently rested his head on her shoulder.

"Ye see her?"

"I recognized her the day we left for the Gathering. Somehow, I always missed it before. But here she is. Our little lass. My little Marduk. Bella is content, my love. Finally…Bella is content." Lilith leaned back against Marduk's chest and cried softly. Marduk cried too.

Marduk and Lilith held each other tenderly and finally mourned their dead daughter together, and for the first time since Princess Arabel died, they both spoke of her in the present tense.

Chapter Fourteen

Caraye and Mia lay together on Mia's bed, holding hands while Mia cried softly. "He's back with Lilith. I lost my chance with him, Caraye. That kiss said it all. He ain't never gonna leave Lilith. The cards were right about that. Lugh's all tangled up with his son. Cain is still a punk. I lost all my romantic devils," Mia sighed heavily.

"You still have Draco," Caraye answered with a smile as she wiped Mia's tears from her cheeks.

"Draco," Mia parroted in a dreamy tone. "Long, tall drink of dark water. He's the most beautiful man I have ever laid these eyes upon. There ain't no denying that, but…I'm kinda scared of him," she chuckled lightly. "Very intense man…Incubus. Whatever he is, he's powerful. He's, I don't know…magical. I'm in awe of him…maybe even a little bit in love with him, and I'm not sure I'm ready for all dat."

"Declan loves him. He says he trusts Draco with his life. Mine too. That says a lot, Mia. He's not a bad guy. I'm sure of it."

"Not that kind of scared, sister-mama. I'm scared of falling into that love pit…alone, with no way to pull myself out. Draco's a handsome, powerful Incubus who can have any Incubian Princess, Queen, or Goddess he wants. He ain't gonna want a raggedy human girl like me."

"Mia, you're Incubian royalty. Declan's Cambion daughter. Besides that…Draco is already smitten with you. He didn't take his eyes off you all night!"

Mia perked up a little and smiled through her tears. "All night?"

Caraye giggled and pulled Mia close to her chest. "All night. He stood there like a giant tree with a beautiful grin on his face, literally glowing when he looked at you. Mia, he's so handsome. If I weren't already married…" Caraye chuckled when Mia squirmed out of her arms and smirked at her.

"Hands off my devils, sister-mama. You got your own."

Caraye burst into giggles and pulled Mia back into her arms. "No worries, Mia. I'm not giving up my sweet devil for nobody. Draco is yours."

"But Marduk…." Mia pouted. "I'll never know what's under that kilt," Mia groaned loudly.

"Declan says he's the King of Love in these weird Colonies. Maybe it's better that you don't know. What's up with Cain? Why are you mad at him?"

"He's with Raven in Dorcha! Back to his old ways. One girl here, another one there. I'm not playing that game again with Finn…Cain. Whatever he's calling himself these days." Mia rolled her eyes and smirked. The person she'd caught glimpses of in the days before he left for Dorcha was nothing like the romantically wicked Finn she knew. Finn seemed to have disappeared, and Cain was re-emerging in full force. Mia had never seen this aloof and coldly calculating persona before, but she knew it wasn't a new persona. It was his old one.

Caraye pulled Mia back into her arms and kissed her soggy cheek. "One good thing about being married to the future King of Gael is that I get all the best gossip before it hits the crystal wires in these parts." Caraye grinned widely. "Raven isn't in Dorcha with Cain. Raven is in Dorcha with Lilith."

"Even worse, Caraye. She's in his mother's back pocket and worming her way back into Cain's front pocket. He's sleeping with her again. I know it."

Caraye laughed and slowly shook her head. "No, Mia…I mean *with* Lilith. Raven and Lilith are lovers."

Mia's eyes lit up and her whole face softened. "Raven and Lilith? Lovers? Are you sure?"

"Declan saw it with his own eyes," Caraye said with a chuckle. "Not the actual act, but you know what I mean. Our little Midnight Raven is smitten with Lilith, not Cain."

"That means the reconciliation between Marduk and Lilith isn't as solid as it appears." Mia grinned crookedly. "Maybe I haven't missed my chance with Marduk after all." Her amber eyes sparkled with hope.

Caraye sighed and groaned. "Well, I guess we know who's at the top of your list. Draco is available and willing. You just found out that Cain isn't cheating…and all you can think about is Marduk's not-so-stable marriage. You're asking for trouble, Mia."

"Sister-mama, ya know how much I love my trouble. Can't resist the blue flame when you're wearing moth wings," Mia said with conviction.

"Have you given up on Lugh?" Caraye pouted slightly. "I want a sister-mama, too." Caraye leaned over and kissed Mia lightly on the lips.

"I ain't giving up on Lugh. He's just on the back burner for now. He's busy with his son, and I can't hold that against him. I admire him for it. If Lugh and I find ourselves all caught up with the messiness of our lives, we'll pick this up again. In the meantime, Mia's gonna dance across this battlefield of love. Who's gonna get Mia first?" She narrowed her eyes and smirked playfully at Caraye.

"Cain's already been there."

"Yeah, and I got my sweet boy from him. He'll always be special to me, Caraye. But I'm not ready to take up another round with him. He's not Finn anymore. He's Cain. I would be a fool to take up with that devil."

"Well…at least he's not messing around with Raven again. He's not cheating, Mia. He's just visiting his mother."

"That doesn't help, Caraye. I heard stories about Cain and his mama from the Servants. Cain has been in love with Lilith since the day he was born. Weird ass freaky mother fucker. Literally." Mia chuckled, but the years of pain that Cain had inflicted upon Mia with his wicked, philandering ways were evident in her eyes, so was her deep love for him.

"Yeah, I heard those rumors too, but…I think he's over it now. Lilith is a sex freak, I hear, but she's not that freaky. She's madly in love with Marduk. That was beyond obvious tonight. Cain's not in Dorcha with Lilith, and definitely not with Raven."

"If he's not in Dorcha with Raven, who the hell is keeping him there? He's got a woman in Dorcha, Caraye. I feel it in every fiber of my being."

Cain rolled over with a loud groan and pulled a lean, long-legged blonde into his arms, then reached for the other one.

"Who's ready for another round?" He grinned widely when both blondes moved in and begin to kiss him while running their hands over his naked body.

"You are truly Marduk's son," Maeve said in a soft voice as she straddled Cain, then began to move seductively against his body that responded immediately.

Despite Marduk's warning, Maeve and Cain were deep into a hot, steamy love affair that became Cain's obsession. Cain was enchanted by all of Marduk's counterfeit Liliths, but Maeve had a hold upon him that he couldn't seem to break, despite the knowledge that she was madly in love with Marduk.

Maeve had no reservations about using Cain to get back into the Lair, especially since Cain agreed to keep their affair a secret. Maeve was confident that Marduk would reclaim her as his First Concubine, maybe even claim her as his Queen when he returned to Dorcha.

Cain didn't tell her that Marduk was already back in Dorcha, in the Lair at this very moment. He wanted Maeve to get caught in his bed. Cain knew Marduk wouldn't take her back if he found out she'd been disloyal. He also knew that Maeve would lean on him when that happened, and he would then have the upper hand in their affair. Getting caught with Maeve would also ensure that Lilith regained her prominent place in Marduk's bed, his life, and at his table. More than anything, Cain wanted Marduk and Lilith back together.

"Aye, Maeve, I learned all my bad habits from Marduk. I have his affinity for blondes as well." Cain flipped Maeve over in one swift move, then thrust deep into her while the other blonde ran her hands and tongue over Cain's body. "Oh, sweet fucking bliss," Cain shouted as he and his blondes moved into a twisted triangle of raw, raunchy, untamed sex that drove them into a wild frenzy of debauchery that almost rivaled Marduk's. Cain grabbed a handful of Maeve's hair and made one final thrust before he finally collapsed over her, then pulled the other blonde up to his mouth for a deep kiss.

"It is good to be home," Cain said as he gently coaxed Maeve between the other blonde's open legs. "Finish her, Maeve. She deserves an orgasm, but I am spent," Cain said in a sultry voice and pointed to his flaccid penis.

Maeve lifted the other blonde's legs above her head and thrust her fingers inside while kissing her clitoris and massaging her breasts. Cain grinned as he watched her moan and buck wildly against Maeve's warm mouth. She screamed as she worked herself into a loud and frenzied orgasm that caught Draco's attention as he casually strolled toward the Dungeon.

Draco was confused by the sounds coming from the concubine room. He'd just walked away from the same sounds in Lilith's suite, and knew Marduk was in there with her. He also knew that the concubines had been sent away from the Lair before they left for the journey to Marbh. He moved closer to the door with a furrowed brow and was about to open it when Animus came around the corner at a frantic pace. Draco moved away from the door quickly, but blushed when he noticed his little brother's attraction to the sounds at the door.

"Are you spying on Marduk, Draco?" Animus grinned and winked, but Draco held a stoic face and crossed his arms over his chest.

"Why are you in the living quarters of the Lair, Animus? Your position is in the Dungeon. Who the fuck is guarding the prisoners?"

Animus stood at attention and turned deadly serious, despite his curious eyes on the door. “Nikos is standing guard, brother. I’d never leave my post if it weren’t serious. Titus is in Dorcha. He needs to see you and Marduk right away. Shall I fetch him?” Animus made a move toward the door of the concubine room, but Draco stopped him.

“Marduk is with Lilith.” He looked back at the door quizzically. “I will fetch him.” Draco took two steps toward Lilith’s suite and turned back to Animus, who was standing at the door with a wide grin and his ear to the door. “If Marduk is with Lilith, then who is making the concubines scream like this?”

“It’s our duty to find out, Draco. Marduk needs to know whose head to take.” Animus’s grin widened as he turned the knob slowly to peek inside. His face turned white at the sight on the bed. He closed the door quickly and looked at Draco. “Holy fuckin hell. Cain has returned with a vengeance.” He shook his head and slowly walked away.

Draco grinned widely, and took lighter steps toward Lilith’s suite. If Cain was in Dorcha with Marduk’s concubines, he knew he had a chance with Mia. Draco held a light swagger as he made his way through the halls of the Lair, then softly knocked on the door.

Draco was still in a dreamy haze when Marduk opened the door holding his unbuckled kilt around his waist. Marduk’s wide grin faded instantly when he saw Draco. He expected Servants with food and wine.

“Whatever it is, hold it until morning, Draco. I will not leave my wife’s bed tonight.” Marduk started to close the door, but Draco held it open.

“My liege, Titus is here. He has an urgent message. It may be about the Red Dragon.”

Marduk's face fell and he shivered visibly. He didn't want to think about his dragons tonight, but he couldn't ignore an urgent call from his only tracker on the frontline. He looked back at Lilith, who was emerging from her dressing room in a scarlet red dress with a bodice delicately beaded in an intricate pattern, and a mermaid silhouette that hugged every curve of her body. He couldn't breathe at the sight of her.

"Come back in ten minutes," Marduk answered, then closed the door on Draco's protests.

Draco sighed and threw back his head with a loud groan, then shuffled back down to the Dungeon in heavy steps.

Titus stood at attention and held out his hand to Draco when he entered the office. "General Draco, it's good to see ye again. Not in jail this time, and with Marduk alive and well."

"Good to see you again too, Titus. What can I do for you, lad." Draco took a bottle of Scotch from the cabinet and three glasses, then sat heavily in his chair with a loud sigh.

"News of the Red Dragon, Draco. Ye're not gonna believe this. Is Marduk joining us?" Titus asked, motioning to the glasses on the desk. "If it's alright with ye, General, I'd like to break this news to ye both at the same time. I have to get back to the frontlines as quickly as possible."

Draco nodded slowly. "Marduk is saying hello to Lilith. He will join us eventually." Draco grinned and poured two drams of Scotch while they waited for Marduk. "I hope you have good news."

Titus drained his Scotch and held out the glass for more. "Not sure if it's good or not, but I do have news. Do me a favor and lock up those fuckin demon hounds before

Marduk gets here. He's not gonna like this," Titus sighed heavily. "Gimme that fuckin bottle. If I'm gonna be eaten by hellhounds tonight, I don't wanna feel it."

Marduk buckled his kilt and let out a long, slow whistle as he approached Lilith with heavy-lidded eyes ripe with love and passion.

"I knew this dress was yours the moment I saw it, but I had no idea ye'd wear it this well, *mo ghrá*." Marduk bit his thick bottom lip as he approached her in an easy swagger that made her heart beat wildly. He wrapped his arms around her waist and spun her around the room in a slow dance, grinning devilishly as he twirled her under his hand like a ballerina. Her court train with black lace inserts swished beautifully around her feet as she made a graceful spin, then stopped for a dramatic pose.

"This gown, Marduk, is truly stunning. Thank you."

"The dress is nothing without ye, my Queen." Marduk gave her a thorough once over from her bare shoulders and full breasts under the scalloped neckline to her slim waist and rounded hips in the gown that sparked his shopping spree to replace the gowns he gave to his concubines. He smiled at the memory of the moment when he saw the dress on a tiny blonde mannequin in the window. In that moment, Marduk realized that Lilith wasn't the only one at fault for the disintegration of their marriage. He'd kept her at arm's length, behind his lines of defense to keep himself from getting hurt by her disloyalty, but more so to keep Lilith from getting stung by his darkness. When the realization hit him, he decided to win her back no matter the cost to his pride. Replacing the dresses was the perfect start to his commitment to mend his marriage.

Marduk had the entire store at his command that day as the shop girls displayed hundreds of dresses in Lilith's size. He bought them all. It was Marduk's last fearless moment of self-confidence in the human colony, before the Red Dragon stabbed and shattered his ego, as well as his body.

Marduk's shoulder was healing, but the damage was extensive. He was going to need months of physical rehabilitation to restore strength and agility in his shoulder and arm. Marduk was afraid that hunt might have been his last. He knew he had to start grooming his replacement, but the thought of it was heavy on his heart. He didn't want to see him disintegrate into the Black Dragon, but humanity pushed his hand. Now they would have to face something even worse than Marduk, Son of Omega, the Romantic Devil.

Marduk pulled Lilith close to him and growled before he bent to kiss her passionately. Lilith responded by arching her back and leaning against his chest while running her hands through his hair. Marduk pulled away slowly and held her at arm's length to peruse the dress one more time.

"I would like to have a gala in the Lair, Lilith. I've been away a long time. The Army deserves a homecoming in Dorcha. And this dress deserves an event." He pulled her closer, then kissed her tenderly while running his hands through her hair with one hand, and unzipping her dress with the other.

"A gala is exactly what we need, Marduk. To welcome you home. To welcome our son home as well. The plans are spinning in my head already." Her eyes were bright with excitement over the prospect of having full charge of the Lair again. Lilith grinned at Marduk like a lazy cat; she knew she was back in power, but she wasn't drunk on that power. She was satisfied just to be back in Marduk's arms.

Marduk's smile faded a little at the mention of Cain. He knew he'd have to deal with the disturbing information he discovered in Marbh, but he wanted to uncover every fact first. Right now, he didn't want to take away from Lilith's obvious happiness. He also had a plan brewing in his head while he pulled Lilith's dress off her shoulders and carried her back to the bed.

"This will be your shining moment, Lilith. The entire world will know ye and I are reconciled." He gently lowered her on the bed and kissed her lips, her cheeks, her neck, her shoulder, then lowered his mouth over her breast. "I have to leave ye for a moment, *mo ghrá*. Will ye be loyal to me?" Marduk whispered against her lips while tenderly running his hands over her body.

"Marduk…look at me," Lilith held his face in her hands and forced him to look directly into her eyes. He was afraid to trust what he saw there, but her tone and demeanor were more genuine than he'd ever seen before. "I know how close I came to losing you; losing us. It is a miracle that we found each other again, my love. I never want to be in that position again. Go. I will be right here, playing with my pretty new dresses. Alone…with Bella." She laughed in her signature sultry sound, but she saw the doubt in his eyes still. "I will be loyal to you, Marduk. Loyal to us. No lads in my bed. I swear it. Only a fool would take a lad into her bed when she has the King," Lilith reiterated Maeve's declaration in a seductive tone while she wrapped her legs around him and pulled him in for a tender kiss.

Marduk shook his head slowly and grinned with raised eyebrows. "I cannot believe my ears. My Lilith pledging loyalty. That's all I have ever wanted from ye, my Queen. Just the two of us." Marduk rested his forehead against hers, and once again had the strange notion that he did die on the Mercuria and found his Heaven. The knocking on the door, however, reminded him again where he was.

"Go. I will be fine," Lilith said softly. "I have ideas for the gala rolling in my head and you are distracting me." She giggled excitedly while Marduk playfully smacked her bottom, then groaned loudly as he crawled out of bed. He pulled on his boots, then slipped into a thin sweater while staring lovingly at Lilith with a pen and paper in her hand, while Bella looked over her shoulders.

"Killian and Jade are at the top of our list. What do you think, Bella? Shall we invite Mia as well?" Lilith asked in a tender voice that made Bella's purring moans resonate loudly as she rested her cheek against Lilith's.

Marduk sighed a deep sigh of contentment as he walked away from the first tender moment he'd ever witnessed between Lilith and Bella. Lilith's first genuine pledge of loyalty didn't leave him unaffected either. Marduk shook his head and looked upward with teary eyes.

"Thank ye, Omega. Ye gave me back my life and more." He grinned and nodded when he clearly heard his father's voice in his head. "I know, I know, Father. I promised to save both yer Crown and yer beloved Krava. And I will, even if it's the last thing I do."

Chapter Fifteen

Krava threw himself heavily onto his bunk with a loud groan, then cast his squinted eyes on Malachi bellowing loudly in the cell across the room.

"Shut the fuck up, Malachi! Marduk was well within his rights. Ye raped Aramanth, ye twisted little beast. Count yer blessings that it was Marduk who shoved his finger in yer arse. I would've shoved my whole hand inside, and still might if ye don't stop yer whining."

"It was more than a finger, Krava! He had pepper salve on that finger! I may never recover!" Malachi sobbed dramatically and curled up in the fetal position with his hand over his belly. "No, no, no…not again! I cannot bear to shite again! My whole belly is on fire! He's feeding me all this food to torture me further! Every bite in my mouth becomes a flaming torch out my arse!" He buried his face in the pillow, then groaned loudly as he ran for the bucket again.

Krava groaned loudly. "No one is forcing ye to eat, ye greedy fuckin weasel! Stop fuckin eatin for a day and maybe yer arse will heal! Bloody fuckin hell, that's disgusting!" Krava wrinkled his nose and called out for Nikos again.

Nikos poked his head in and covered his nose. "For fuck's sake, Malachi! No food for a week. General Krava, ye don't deserve this torture. Come with me." Nikos open the cell door, handcuffed Krava, then ushered him out the door.

"What about me? I need a Physician! And a Servant to empty my bucket!" Malachi yelled out loudly. "I am the King of Críoch! A Prince of Marbh, at the very least! How dare you treat the General of my Army better than me! I demand the respect owed to me!" Malachi yelled out tearfully.

Krava smirked as he passed by Malachi's cell. "Ye're no longer a Prince, Malachi…and ye were never a King. Time to grow up and change yer own diapers, lad."

"You will pay for this, Krava! All of you will pay for this! Marduk more than anyone will pay!" Malachi yelled, then doubled over in pain as another flaming torch shot out into the bucket.

Marduk marched toward his Dungeon with a charmed smile fixed on his face. He was pulled out of his reveries of the last 24 hours with Lilith when he saw Nikos leading Krava away from the prisoner's quarters of the Dungeon. He locked eyes with Krava as he approached.

"Where are ye taking General Krava, Nikos?"

"Away from Malachi. The lad's arse is spewing fire. More torture than is necessary for a General," Nikos replied with a chuckle.

"The lad's still spewing flames?" Marduk laughed wickedly as his shoulders shook. "Send for a Physician, Nikos, and put Malachi on a bland liquid diet. Clear fluids for 48 hours. Take General Krava into the Royal cell." He marched toward him with a mischievous smile. "Anything ye need or want, Krava, just wish it and it is yers."

Krava nodded respectfully. "A bottle of Scotch and a sweet-smelling lass to erase the odor of Malachi from my nose," he chuckled. "Yer night of romance with Malachi was the best justice I've ever known, Marduk." Krava bowed reverently, but couldn't stop grinning.

"Do ye like blondes, brother?" Marduk asked with a wicked grin.

"Blondes, gingers, brunettes. Aye. I like them all."

Marduk threw back his head and laughed loudly. "Ye're a true Omegan, Krava. I have six blonde concubines at yer disposal." He grinned devilishly, then turned deadly serious as he pulled Krava to his fiercely scowling face. "My blonde wife, however, is off-limits. Ye so much as look at her, and ye'll be scratching air where yer balls used to be."

Krava lost his grin as he stared into Marduk's colorless squint. "I rather like my wee balls where they are, Marduk. I'll take any concubine ye send my way, but yer wife is safe." His green-gold eyes shined with both mischief and respect.

Marduk grinned crookedly when he recognized himself as well as Omega in his bastard brother. "Ye're a good lad, Krava. The Royal cell is already stocked with Scotch. Nikos, have Animus dispatch the lasses to my brother straight away." Marduk clapped Krava on the back and pulled him to his chest. "Don't try to outshine yer King with the concubines." Marduk raised one eyebrow. "There's only one Omegan King of the Incubi."

Krava sighed heavily as he watched Marduk march away from him in long strides. "Aye. Only one King," he whispered softly with a smile.

Marduk's marching steps stopped abruptly when he heard the commotion coming from his concubine room.

With a quizzical brow and a tight smile, Marduk opened the door slowly. His jaw dropped open when he saw Cain in bed with his concubines. His face withered into a dark scowl when he recognized Maeve draped over Cain with a simpering smile.

"Those are my blondes!" Marduk said incredulously as he kicked in the door. He gave Maeve a harsh squint as his eyes turned colorless again. She withered under that stare and immediately broke into tears.

Cain's face went from boiling passion to wide-eyed fear in a split second. He tossed Maeve aside and pulled the other blonde up from under the sheets, then jumped out of bed naked. Marduk gave Cain a thorough once over from head to toe, and was impressed by his son's naked body. Cain was built more like him than Marduk knew. He couldn't help the proud grin forming on his lips, despite the circumstance.

"We were just…" Cain ran his hands through his hair, then stopped to laugh at himself. Although he wanted to get caught with Maeve, the reality of it was a bit more unnerving than he imagined. Cain realized he was behaving like a young Prince who'd just been caught with his pants down for the first time.

That fact didn't escape Marduk either. His lips spread into a full grin before going back to a scowl he could hardly hold. That grin made Cain comfortable enough to stand his ground and act like an adult with his father for the first time in his life.

"You did say I could visit them, Marduk," Cain chuckled softly and shook his head as he wrapped his kilt around his waist.

"Aye, but I specifically excluded Maeve from that offer." Marduk gave her another disappointed look of betrayal.

Maeve jumped out of bed and ran to him naked, but Marduk shirked away from her.

"So much for yer loyalty, Maeve." He gently pulled her away from him when she draped herself around his body and cried softly.

"You released me, Marduk. When you went away, you released me. But you are back now, and we can start over again. I will be loyal again, I swear it!" She looked up at him with pleading eyes, but Marduk made a wide swath around her to assess the other blonde in Cain's orgy. He gave her a stern look too, but she posed and smiled seductively, then motioned for him to join her in bed.

Marduk grinned devilishly and gave her a thorough once over with heavy-lidded eyes. He hadn't noticed her full beauty before, nor her boldness, but his interest was sparked now. Especially since he'd caught her in bed with Cain. He wanted to remind her again who the King was, but more than anything, he was fueled by the life-long rivalry with his son for sexual dominance over the blondes in Dorcha. He sent her a fingertip kiss while eyeing her long legs crossed at the ankles. She smiled and arched her back, then held her hand out to him. Marduk walked to the edge of the bed and kissed her hand.

"Hello again, not Maeve."

She raised one eyebrow and smirked. "Erin."

Marduk sucked his teeth and scanned her body again, lingering on her full, round hips. "Erin. I will not forget yer name again, lass." He was tempted to crawl in bed with her, but instead he turned back to Cain holding Maeve around the waist while running his hands through her hair. Maeve couldn't take her eyes off Marduk, scowling at her again with hellfire shooting from his pale green eyes.

"If ye can tear yerself away from my concubines, Cain, I would like to have a word with ye in Draco's office." Marduk turned on his heel and marched out the door. Maeve called out to him and tried to follow, but Marduk ignored her while Cain pulled her back.

"Marduk is back in Lilith's bed. You have no chance, lass."

Marduk didn't slow his fierce, angry stride until he reached Draco's office with a scowl still lingering on his face.

"Titus. Good to see ye again, lad. Is she here? In the Lair?" Marduk tried not to feed the panic rising in his chest, but it was creeping up his spine and tingling the back of his neck. He wasn't ready to face the Red Dragon again.

Titus rubbed his hands over his face and sat forward. "She's not here, but I do have news." Titus loosely spread out a pile of photographs on Draco's desk. "Take a good long look, Marduk. Which one stabbed ye?"

Marduk wrinkled his brow and squinted at the photographs on the desk. He picked up the photo at the top of the pile. "This is the Red Dragon," he said resolutely, then dropped the photo immediately. He didn't want to see her face again.

"Are ye sure, Marduk? Have a look at the others," Titus replied, then handed him the stack of photos.

Marduk groaned as he sat in the chair across from Draco's desk and looked over the photographs in his hand, sliding them back and forth from one hand to the other.

"Are ye drunk, Titus? These photographs are of the same woman," Marduk said with a scoffing grin.

"Look again, Marduk," Titus said quietly.

Marduk held the photos up and carefully scanned the details. His eyes widened as the blood drained from his face suddenly. "How did we miss this? Twins? Mother and daughter? What the fuck are we dealing with, Titus?"

Marduk tossed the photos away, then reached for the bottle of Scotch on Draco's desk. He filled Draco and Titus's glasses, then drank heavily from the bottle while staring off into the distance.

In his mind's eye, he was back in that eerie room, tied to the chair with a knife in his thigh. He shivered and drank another sip of Scotch, then glanced at Draco and winced when he noticed Draco staring strangely at him. Draco had never seen Marduk this affected by a dragon before, but Marduk's dragons had never turned on him before. Marduk held Draco's gaze and tried not to let his fear show, but he couldn't hide it from Draco.

"My liege, Titus and I can handle this," Draco said flatly. "Go back to Lilith. Take a fresh bottle of Scotch with you." Draco smiled genuinely, but his concern was evident.

Marduk wrinkled his brow and pursed his lips as he shook his head. "I'm fine, General Draco." He squared his shoulders and turned back to Titus with a stoic face. "I can tell ye that my assailant has a son. Braedon. That woman is the one who stabbed me. Braedon shot me." Marduk flinched when he thought he felt blood trickling down his leg. He took a swig of Scotch and a deep breath. "Is she the dragon, Titus? Or is it the other lass? Which one is the fuckin Red Dragon? We cannot afford another mistake."

Titus sat forward and picked up a photograph of the elegant redhead. "I'm almost certain she's our Red Dragon. The other is her pawn. She and her son do the dirty work, then she reports to the taller redhead. Her sister, I think," Titus said cautiously.

Marduk furrowed his brow and lit a cigarette. "Ye think? We don't operate on assumptions, Titus. Have ye checked their records?"

"Aye…no. I've tried, Marduk, but I cannot find a single record that connects them, nor one that identifies them. They are anomalies. Our Red Dragons have no records. Not even the son."

Marduk's face fell as he sat back in his chair. "How is that possible? Could they be Lucian's minions?"

Titus shrugged and squirmed a little under Marduk's harsh stare. "That's another possibility I'm looking into."

"How many possibilities are ye looking into, Titus? And why do ye have no conclusions? What the fuck have ye been doing all this time?" Marduk asked with a tight jaw.

"Following her, my liege. I know all her gathering places, her schedule, and everyone she knows. She's got one hell of an entourage. The Red Dragon is more than just one person, Marduk. It's a fuckin cult." Titus pulled out another set of photos and tossed them on the desk. "The elite members of the Red Dragon cult."

Marduk picked up the stack of photos and scanned each face thoroughly. "Take them all down, Titus. First, identify the redheads, then eliminate them. Once ye remove the head of any dragon, the body falls apart.

"Is it possibly to identify them without a DNA sample?" Titus asked while rubbing his bald head. He didn't want to get close enough to the redheads to get DNA from them.

Draco shook his head. "Not if they are anomalies, Titus. We need hair, blood, or saliva. Do what ye must, lad."

Marduk remembered the hair sample he took from his dragon, but couldn't remember where it was. He didn't want to admit that to Draco and Titus. He didn't want to show his weakness, but there was no way to hide the fact that he'd been weakened by this dragon.

Cain sauntered into the room with an easy swagger and a wide grin. He was wearing a black and red kilt and a blood-red shirt that hugged his body like a glove. Marduk's ego was somewhat pricked by Cain's easy swagger.

"Titus? What the fuck are ye doing in Dorcha? What is going on here?" Cain wrinkled his brow as he took Titus's extended hand.

"Ye really don't know? I thought for certain ye recognized me. I used to chase yer skinny arse around the Lair, lad," Titus replied quizzically while shaking his head slowly.

Cain looked back and forth between Titus and Marduk's smirking face, then grinned like a young Prince when the truth dawned on him. "You were watching over me, Father?"

"I had eyes on ye," Marduk replied a bit coldly, and took a swig of Scotch. He was still stinging from the incident with Maeve, but couldn't tear his eyes away from Cain's awestruck face upon learning that he hadn't been abandoned and forgotten.

Cain smiled broadly and attempted to hide the tears stinging his eyes. He squared his shoulders and had to work hard to lift his façade again. He didn't want to appear weak in front of his father. "If you're in Dorcha, who the fuck's running the Mortuary, Titus?"

"No worries about the Mortuary. Lord Dervish is managing the place for ye. Good businessman…for a fuckin human." Titus pulled Cain in for a bear hug. "Good to see ye back in Dorcha, lad."

"Good to be back," Cain said with a deep sigh as the façade fell again. His dreamy smile grated on Marduk's nerves a little. Marduk's eyes turned colorless as he squinted at Cain, who was dressed like him, right down to the boots. He scanned him thoroughly and sucked his teeth arrogantly.

"Have a seat, Cain." Marduk waved his hand toward the chair next to Titus and took another swig from the bottle of Scotch. "Draco, my son is home, and it is time to let him into the fold." Marduk grinned wickedly and glared at Cain. "Today is yer lucky day, lad. I'm going to show ye a day in the life of Marduk, Son of Omega," he said ominously, then handed Cain the bottle of Scotch.

Cain's eyes lit up with obvious interest. "Are you serious? You're going to let me in?" Cain took a long swig of whiskey while eyeing Marduk warily. He wondered if Marduk was toying with him as punishment for the concubines.

Marduk laughed in a deep tone. "Is yer back strong enough to step into yer father's role, Cain?" Marduk's eyes were shooting amber sparks. Cain's were shooting ice.

"I am your son, Marduk. In every possible way." Cain grinned and handed Marduk the bottle. Cain was aware of Marduk's duties as the Dark God. The Elders had prepared him for the role years ago, but Marduk never taught him the specifics. Marduk never let Cain into his inner circle, until now.

"Ye're the son of Marduk, the Romantic Devil. In yer own unique way." Marduk drank a long pull from the bottle. His eyes never left Cain's. "But are ye strong enough to wear the mask of the Black Dragon?"

"The Black Dragon?" Cain sat forward with wide eyes, then gave Marduk the same glare Marduk was giving him now. "Are you playing with me, Marduk?" Cain's heart was in his throat. He'd always been unbearably intrigued by the legends of the Black Dragon, but all he knew of the Black Dragon were the dark and gory legends, and the fact that Marduk was the Black Dragon.

Marduk took another swig of Scotch, then pushed the photographs toward Cain. "I never play when it comes to dragons." He handed the bottle of Scotch to Cain and stood up from his chair. He slipped out of his sweater to reveal the scar on his left shoulder.

Cain's face fell significantly at the sight of Marduk's barely healed injury. He knew something happened to Marduk on this journey, but he didn't know the extent of it until he saw the wide, puckered, and still red scar inches from Marduk's heart.

"The Red Dragon is fierce. But not fierce enough to take down the Black One." Marduk grinned devilishly while his eyes turned colorless.

Cain studied the photographs and felt a jolt of recognition that he couldn't quite place. He looked back at Marduk's scar and took a long sip from the bottle. "This woman did that to you?" His eyes glowed with an angry desire to avenge Marduk's assault.

"The lad shot me. This woman is the mastermind of a ring of dragons." He pointed to a photograph of Braedon, another the tall elegant redhead, then tossed Cain a photograph of Shannon. "The lad's mother did this…" Marduk raised his kilt to show the long, jagged scars on his thighs. He raised the kilt high enough to show the monster as well, and grinned crookedly with one raised eyebrow when Cain's face withered and turned pale at the sight of the monster, the other legend attached to Marduk. So far, neither legend disappointed Cain. Despite the fact that the Black Dragon was wounded, Cain found new respect for Marduk. He'd been viciously and brutally attacked, mortally wounded, but was still here. Still strong enough to bring Cain down to his place in the scheme of the Multiverse by showing him exactly who the King of the Incubi was, and why.

Cain looked away from the monster and the scars with a scowl. He drew his brows together angrily when he looked at the photograph of Braedon.

"Count me in. I will avenge you, Marduk," Cain said in a deep, angry tone.

Marduk's face withered slightly at that evil tone, as well as the wicked gleam in Cain's eyes. He knew he had to get Cain's devil under control before he turned him loose on humanity. But first, he would let him have full rein with this dragon. Marduk knew he was too badly injured to take her on himself right now, and he couldn't risk her getting away again. Marduk also knew that inflicting pain upon females wasn't in his inherent composition. But it was in Cain's.

"Work with Titus to identify her, then bring her here, and she's all yers, Son," Marduk said solemnly, then drank heavily from the bottle of Scotch. Cain's initiation by fire was something he was glad he was going to be able to witness from a safe distance.

"I object to this, Marduk," Draco said quietly.

Marduk scoffed and growled. "Draco, I am in no shape to catch this Dragon. Ye know better than anyone the extent of damage to my body. I cannot take on the task myself, and I cannot leave the Red Dragons in the midst of humanity. It is our duty to capture them."

"Let the Army capture them, Marduk. The trackers. I will do it myself!" Draco said adamantly.

"The Army and the trackers have been at this task for 13 years, to no avail. It must be an Omegan. There are only two of us sanctioned to hunt and kill, Draco. Myself, and my son."

"General Krava is Omegan…a fierce Warrior. I am certain the Elders will give him free passage, Marduk. Let Krava take this commission," Draco pleaded.

"Aye, Krava is a Warrior, but he is a bastard. Only a legitimate Omegan has the right to hunt dragons. It's the law. Besides, Krava's a prisoner. He cannot be released until after his trial. It must be Cain."

"He is not ready!" Draco yelled.

Marduk looked at Draco with a sarcastic grin and shook his head. "He's the Son of Marduk. He was born ready."

"Not for this dragon. She is too fierce! She nearly took you out permanently, Marduk. Cain is not ready for the Red Dragon." Draco sat forward with a scowl. He was prepared to fight tooth and nail against the wicked plot he thought he saw rolling around in Marduk's head. He hoped he was wrong, but the wicked gleam in Marduk's eye spoke volumes.

"Cain has spent his entire life preparing for this, Draco. Since the day he took his first steps, he has been trying to take down the Black Dragon. He is well trained in the art of hunting dragons." Marduk grinned at Cain with squinted eyes and took another long sip of Scotch. "Ye've always wanted to be me, Cain. I'm inclined to let ye be me…this time."

Cain blushed under his father's harsh stare as he realized Marduk was either setting him up for a fall, or testing his composition. Cain was determined to win this battle either way. He wanted to prove himself capable and finally win his father's approval.

"My father is right, Draco. I have been preparing for this moment my whole life." Cain grinned crookedly and held his hand out to Marduk. "I'm ready, Father. Your Red Dragons are no match for the bloodline of Omega."

Marduk sucked his teeth and squinted slightly, but took Cain's hand firmly. He lifted Cain from the chair and pulled him closer. "Let's work together instead of against each other this time."

"Aye, Marduk. Finally. You and I," Cain said with a soft sadness in his eyes. He never loved his father more than he did in this moment, but he knew his lifetime of fighting against him might very well come back to bite him in the neck.

"Lads, I would like to have a word with my son in private," Marduk said in an ominous tone that rattled Cain's confidence. "Take the concubines to General Krava in the Royal cell."

"Not Maeve, Marduk. Please. She is…I know she was yours, Marduk, but…Maeve is special to me. I care deeply for the lass," Cain pleaded.

Marduk shot him a fierce glare through squinted eyes. His lips were tight; his jaw firmly set. "All of them," Marduk reiterated arrogantly. "Except Maeve."

Draco shot him a fierce warning glare tinged with pride. Marduk nodded solemnly to acknowledge the nudge from his conscience. "Titus will be with him every step of the way, Draco. Apart from yerself, General, there's no one I trust more than Titus."

"I am placing myself on this commission as well, my liege." He held up his hand to stop Marduk's protest. "Save your breath, Marduk. I am pulling rank on this." Draco lifted his chin and sighed heavily as he and Titus filed out of the room without looking back.

Marduk grinned at Draco's stiff back prepared to take the sword for Cain. "I expect no less from ye, General."

Marduk glanced back at Cain and held out his hand. Cain reluctantly took Marduk's hand, but his hesitation wasn't an effect of fear, it was steeped in guilt. Cain knew what was coming, and Marduk didn't keep him waiting. He pulled Cain to him roughly, then kissed him softly on the lips as he cupped his face. "Lucian keeps meticulous records. I need to hear yer confession, Cain," he whispered softly.

Cain closed his eyes against the disappointment in Marduk's eyes, then sighed heavily before he leaned in and returned Marduk's soft kiss. "Aye, I worked with Lucian against you, Marduk." He pressed his forehead against Marduk's, and let out a small sob, but held himself in check. He didn't want to appear weak. "This all happened before I was banished. Before Salem's wedding. Thirty years ago, Father. I am not that person anymore."

"And Samuel? What was his involvement?"

Cain groaned and hung his head. "As much as I would like to see the little fucker twisting in the wind, I cannot lie to you, Marduk. I will not begin our new partnership with a lie. Salem is innocent. He had no idea I contracted him to marry Akaia so that Lucian and I could use him as a pawn in the Rebellion. The wicked plot looks a little differently from this side of the glass." Cain paced slowly then turned back to Marduk's stoic face. "Lucian took my son as a pawn instead."

"Lucian took both my sons to use as pawns against me," Marduk replied quietly, but with seething anger.

"I'm sorry, Father." Cain leaned heavily against Marduk's forehead. He wanted to show him the entire scenario, but it was too ugly. He couldn't debase himself that much. "I only wanted you to notice me, Marduk. And you have, finally. I swear my loyalty to you. To the Omegans and our cause. I will never fight against you again, Father." Cain smiled sadly and kissed Marduk's lips lightly again. "I fuckin love you, Marduk. I always have. I only wanted to be your son, but you never let me…please, let me be your son," Cain pleaded sincerely while holding Marduk's face in his hands. In that moment, Cain wanted nothing more than to work side-by-side with his father. It was all he ever really wanted, but Marduk had never given him a chance before. "I will prove myself to you, Marduk. I will die avenging you, if that is what you require."

Marduk growled and pulled Cain's face to his for a fierce kiss on the lips while he cupped his son's face in his massive hands. "I do not require yer death, Son. Only yer loyalty."

"You have it. My unwavering loyalty to you, Marduk. Give me a chance to prove myself to you."

Marduk nodded slowly. "Alright then…another chance, but first…we give a proper goodbye to the last chance ye fucked up so royally." Marduk swallowed hard and drew in a deep breath. "I forgive ye for Bella," he whispered.

Cain's face withered into a tearful grimace as he cried loudly. "I am haunted over it, Marduk. I am so sorry for taking Bella's life. I could offer you a million excuses, but none will ease your pain over it, nor mine. I am sorry, Father. I fucked up. I fucked up badly." Cain leaned heavily on Marduk's shoulder and cried until all his tears were spent.

Marduk never said a word. He couldn't. But he accepted Cain's contrite apology and finally released his bitter anger toward his son. There was, however, still one more prick in his side over Cain's actions against him that needed to be resolved.

Marduk kissed Cain tenderly, then squinted and sucked his teeth as he flipped Cain over on his lap and raised his kilt. He slapped Cain on his naked bottom hard with two loud smacks, then grinned devilishly while eyeing Cain's withered face.

"That's for taking my blonde," Marduk said with a crooked grin.

Cain burst into laughter and curled up on Marduk's lap like a young boy. "I did it for Lilith. She needed an edge to get you out of Maeve's bed and back into hers." He leaned against Marduk's shoulder with a mischievous grin.

Marduk broke into loud laughter while he hugged his son tenderly for the first time in his life. "Yer mother needs no edge to get me into her bed." He ruffled Cain's hair playfully. "Thank ye for the effort, however. First time ye've ever pushed me toward yer mother's bed instead of away from it."

"Finally weaned from Lilith's breast," Cain said in a droll, dramatic tone as he rolled his eyes. "My problem now, is that I'm hooked on Maeve's delicious body, but my heart is still sewn to Mia's. I'm fucked," Cain said sadly, then chuckled as he took a swig of Scotch. "I could use a little advice from the King in balancing the lasses in my life."

"Ye're Omegan, Son. Charm the skirts off yer lasses when they're not looking." Marduk winked. "And keep them in separate wings."

Cain and Marduk clinked their glasses together and laughed like naughty schoolboys. Marduk wanted to pinch himself to see if he was awake and alive. It seemed that he'd either stepped into an alternate universe or had been given a new lease on life. He decided to believe the latter.

"Welcome home, ye twisted little fucker."

"I get the trait from you, Papa."

Marduk's face softened significantly as his chest puffed up with pride for his son for the first time in Cain's life. Then he winced as an image of Salem crossed his mind, and he wondered how he was going to properly love both his sons once Salem was free.

Chapter Sixteen

Marduk rounded the corner of Lilith's hallway with a sly grin and a slight limp. His right thigh ached, but he marched on, ignoring the pain. He felt victorious and renewed after his session with Cain. He gave Cain the same speech Omega gave him thousands of years ago, but he didn't tell Cain about the non-existent lines of protocol for the Black Dragon. He wanted Cain to temper himself first. Cain needed to calibrate with the inherent laws before he took on the full role of the Black Dragon. It wasn't going to be an easy task, but Marduk was determined to turn the Red Dragon over to Cain. Marduk knew he couldn't do it. He couldn't bring himself to face her again, and he couldn't bring himself to hurt a woman, no matter how evil she was. Cain had no qualms whatsoever about doling out pain to women. He was a master of it. What frightened Marduk more than anything was the obvious enjoyment Cain got from inflicting pain upon women. He knew he had to get Cain's devil under control, but not before he captured the Red Dragon. Marduk wanted her to feel the same pain she inflicted upon others, and he needed Cain to be ruthless, merciless, and somewhat savage in his dismantling of the red devil. Her justice would have to be harsh, brutal, and equal to her deeds.

Marduk marched into Lilith's suite with his head full of thoughts about Cain's confession to his involvement with

Lucian. He knew there was more, but he believed Cain would tell him everything in his own time. Marduk had another plan cooking in his head to flush out all the details, but right now, he was at Lilith's door, and his passion overtook his reason. He sauntered into her bedroom and smiled when he saw her sleeping soundly. Alone. He breathed a deep sigh of relief, then crawled in bed beside her with a loud groan as his right thigh cramped up suddenly.

Lilith woke with a start and sat up abruptly, then smiled tenderly and seductively at Marduk. She moved closer to him, but when she saw him gingerly massaging his thigh with a tight grimace, she immediately moved into action.

"Allow me, Marduk." She stretched across him for a bottle of herbed oil on the bedside table, then smiled flirtatiously as she poured the oil into her hands and rubbed them together to warm up the oil.

Marduk growled softly while watching her with heavy-lidded eyes. He bit his bottom lip in a sexy grin when she spread his legs wide, then positioned herself between them. He let out a deep breath as the oil, and Lilith's gentle touch, finally began to ease his pain.

With her usual hint of seduction, Lilith tenderly massaged the warm oil over both scars on his thighs simultaneously. She didn't look at him. She kept her eyes on the scars on his thighs, careful not to push too deeply around the edges that were still a bit red and very tender. Lilith absorbed his pain instantly when she touched him and felt his feverish, cramped muscles.

Marduk's face softened as he watched the tender look of concern on her face as her small hands glided gently over his wounds. She reached for the bottle again, then poured the oil over his shoulder and gingerly massaged around his scar, placing soft kisses along his shoulder and chest, working her way slowly to his grinning lips.

Lilith grinned back playfully as her hands slid farther up his kilt. “May I?”

Marduk nodded once and watched her slowly unbuckle the kilt with delicate moves and tender care around his wounds. Lilith smiled seductively and leaned forward to kiss him softly while she rubbed the oil over her breasts and belly while Marduk ran his hands through her wild, tangled hair.

Lilith moaned softly, then took hold of the monster with both hands before lowering herself over it in slow, precise moves. Marduk pulled her slick body close to his and kissed her tenderly while she moved in tantric movements, swirling her hips gently as she wrapped her legs around his waist.

“I have an idea for our gala,” she whispered against his lips, then ran her tongue across them before closing her mouth over Marduk’s thick lips while moving her hips in a slow swirling motion.

“Am I going to like it?” Marduk asked breathlessly while running his hands over her oiled and perfumed body.

“A Dead Party. Masked, of course,” she purred against his ear and jerked her hips forward, then swirled twice to lift her hips while Marduk pushed all the way inside her.

“In whose honor?” Marduk whispered hoarsely as he gently bit her neck, then her shoulder.

“Yours,” she smiled playfully.

Marduk grinned and shook his head as he jerked inside her in one ferocious move. “I’m not dead, Lilith.”

She matched his jerking swirl, then kissed him sensually. “Minor detail.”

Marduk growled, flipped her over in one move, then thrust into her in another hard jerk. “Is that what my life is to ye, Lilith? A minor detail?” He bit her bottom lip and grabbed a handful of her hair, but his smile was playful.

Lilith laughed in her signature sultry voice. “No, my love. Your death was a minor detail. We will honor your minor death, while celebrating your major life.”

“I like it, *mo ghrá*.” He grinned. “A Dead Party is fitting for us. But let’s not limit the honor to me alone. Everyone will honor their own dead by dressing in the style of the dead they most admire.” He closed his lips over hers, then flipped over on his back again. She once again lowered her hips over the monster in one long, slow and precise move.

“Brilliant idea, Marduk. But…let’s make our Dead Party a little more exciting than that.”

“I’m dying to know the ideas rolling around in yer wicked head, Lilith.” He grinned playfully and kissed her savagely.

“At midnight, the young ones will go away to their own room… then, the adult fun begins.” Lilith grinned impishly, then swirled her hips again, kissing him deeply.

Marduk pulled away and looked at her with squinted eyes and an open jaw. “An orgy? Ye want an orgy for my homecoming celebration?” Marduk’s withered face broke into an incredulous grin, then he laughed so hard he nearly lost his erection, but Lilith moved against him again, and his erection was back. “Bold as fuckin brass. I fuckin love ye, Lilith.”

“A night of debauchery to honor both your life and your death, Marduk. I can think of nothing more fitting to honor you." Lilith laughed along with Marduk, but never stopped swirling her hips over his. He flipped her over again and pushed the monster deep inside while she wrapped her legs around his back and let out a breathy, sultry scream. "There is no better pleasure than you inside me, Marduk. There is no love in the world better than yours."

Marduk shook his head slowly and sucked his teeth with a small hiss. "I'm certain ye've thoroughly tested that theory, my love, so I thank ye, from the bottom of my heart…this cold, black heart that beats only for ye, *mo ghrá gheal,*" he whispered, then bit her bottom lip playfully.

"My love, this very big heart of yours is anything but cold," she said as she cupped his swaying balls and gently massaged them.

Marduk raised one eyebrow and grinned crookedly. "My heart is up here, Lilith."

She laughed in a sultry tone that set his body on fire. "I'm so in love with you, Marduk," she whispered against his ear.

"Are ye bucking for a free pass for the night of the party?" He tightened his lips and growled playfully at her with narrowed eyes.

She grinned and ran her hands through his hair, then rotated her hips gently while pulling him closer for a deep kiss. "It is an orgy." She tugged on his hair when he began to pull away, then wrapped her legs tighter around his back. "You get a pass too, Marduk."

Marduk growled and glared at her. "For fuck's sake, Lilith. We've only been reconciled a day and already ye want a fuckin pass?"

Lilith shrugged. "One night only."

He shook his head slowly, rolled his eyes, then kissed her tenderly. He closed his eyes tightly as he rested his forehead against hers. “No free passes. If I agree to this…ye get a list of three possibilities. Three possible loopholes for one night only.”

“Agreed,” she whispered.

He smiled crookedly against her grinning lips and thrust deeply into her with a low growl until he brought them both to fierce, screaming orgasms that reverberated throughout the suite and down the hallway into the concubine room.

Maeve heard those screams and pulled away from Cain’s kiss. She was very familiar with that sound, as well as the source of it. She looked back at Cain with sad eyes, but Cain was preoccupied with her hair, and fueled by the erotic energy drifting across the entire Lair as he thrust harder into Maeve until she had her own screaming orgasm.

Cain smiled when she closed her eyes, because she looked so much like Lilith in that moment. He growled loudly as his orgasm came in shivering rushes that made his entire body weak.

Marduk and Lilith collapsed against each other at the same time as Cain and Maeve. Marduk pulled Lilith close to his chest and wrapped his arms and legs around her tightly. He smiled tenderly while caressing her, and Lilith arched her back to snuggle closer to him. They lay arm in arm, face to face, studying each other intensely, sharing soft, tender kisses that burned deep in both their hearts.

However, Lilith was anxiously waiting for Marduk’s verdict on her Dead Party orgy. She could hardly contain herself, and fidgeted nervously with his beard and hair. She squirmed and wiggled as she played with her own hair, and ran her fingers across his face while staring at him like an innocent young woman.

Marduk read her body language clearly, but kept her waiting just to watch her in action. He missed her wicked machinations over the years. No other woman stimulated his body, mind, and heart the way Lilith did. He'd spent the last thirty years testing that theory extensively with his numerous counterfeit Liliths coming and going through his Lair. He came to the same conclusion every time. There was only one Lilith.

Lilith finally sat up and rested her elbow on the pillow with one raised eyebrow and a sexy smirk. Marduk groaned and rolled his eyes.

"Name your loopholes, Lilith. But I have the final veto."

"No fair," she giggled softly. "Do I have final veto on yours?"

"Aye. That's fair." He brushed the hair from her face and braced himself for a new list of lovers he was going to have to threaten and torture.

Lilith grinned seductively and looked away while thinking of who she wanted on her list. "Dec…" Marduk wagged his finger and vetoed loudly before she finished. "Am…" Again, Marduk vetoed loudly and laughed wickedly. He knew from her playful grin she was teasing him. He was enjoying this moment, a tender moment with Lilith, finally, without the spikes and razors between them.

She leaned forward for a tender kiss and rubbed her cheek against his soft, silky beard that smelled of sandalwood and citrus. She breathed in the familiar scent and rested her cheek against his.

"Marduk," she whispered in his ear. "Number one on my list."

Marduk smiled devilishly. "Check," he said, and made a check mark in the air. "He is on your list, Lilith. My turn," he grinned.

"You better say my name," she warned playfully, and arched her back to press her breasts against him.

He threw his leg over her body to draw her closer. "Lilith," he whispered softly. "The love of my life."

"Check." She laughed her signature laugh, and Marduk's heart burned at the sound of it. "Shall I go again? Or do you want another turn?"

Marduk realized they were at a crossroads, an impasse that required one of them to jump off the cliff first to see if the other would follow. One of them was going to have to concede defeat in the war. Marduk wanted it to be her.

"Yer turn, Lilith." He held his breath while waiting for her answer.

She looked deep into his eyes as a strong wave of love washed over her. She couldn't think of a single name in that moment, but she wanted her limits clearly defined, nonetheless. She might not act on them, but she wanted to make sure there were no repercussions if she did.

"You did say I could keep Raven," she whispered softly.

Marduk let out his breath all at once. "Aye. I did. Check," he said quietly. "Ye may keep yer skinny lass." Marduk rolled his eyes and groaned. Lilith snuggled closer to him.

"I love you, Marduk. Only you." She ran her hands through his hair and sighed sadly. She wanted to give him her full loyalty, but her body wouldn't cooperate. Marduk read her thoughts and pulled her closer.

"I know, Lilith." He kissed her gently, then pressed his forehead against hers softly. "I love ye too. There's never been another lass in my heart." He smiled sadly and fell back onto the pillow, holding her tightly against his chest.

"Erin," he blurted out with a wicked grin.

Lilith sat up and looked at him with shiny eyes and an open jaw. "Yes! She is the prettiest of all your blondes. I want her too." Lilith smiled and simpered seductively.

Marduk chuckled and made two check marks in the air. "Check and check."

"I thought you would say Maeve," she said quietly with a pout and sad eyes. She was deeply hurt by his affair with Maeve and wanted him to know it.

Marduk once again read her thoughts clearly and let out a long, groaning breath. "Maeve is off my list." He ran his fingertips along Lilith's back, then pulled her closer. Marduk was disappointed that Maeve broke his edict, especially with Cain. But he knew Maeve was a painful complication that would always hurt Lilith. He had her exactly where he wanted her now, and wouldn't risk it even if Maeve had been loyal. He knew he had to send Maeve away from the Lair.

"I do not mean to be petty, but…"

"She will be away in the morning, Lilith. The Queen's chair is yers again. Let me handle Maeve," he said resolutely.

"I have no desire to handle your lover, Marduk."

"Ye're my only lover, Lilith."

Lilith smiled seductively and gently nibbled on his neck. "I would like to have my title back. Queen of Dorcha…but more than that, I want to be your Queen again, Marduk. With an official announcement, of course."

Marduk tightened his arms around her and laughed softly at her request. "I knew ye were angling for something more." He gently cupped her cheeks and growled. "I would like that as well, *mo ghrá*. I want the whole world to know I've taken back my Queen. Officially. Whether the Elders agree or not, I will make the announcement."

Lilith smiled victoriously and couldn't wipe the smile from her face as she lifted her lips to Marduk's.

"No need to look so smug. I still have a loophole." Marduk grinned slyly as an image of Mia crossed his mind.

Lilith snuggled closer and hoped he wouldn't name Mia. She saw the sparks between them, and was more afraid of losing Marduk to Mia than Maeve. Lilith held her breath while waiting for him to name his third loophole, but she couldn't bear the thought of it. She wrapped her legs tighter around him, then began to seduce him again to take his mind off the list of potential lovers.

Marduk growled and grinned wickedly when she straddled him and began to move slowly against the monster. Suddenly, all thoughts of Maeve, Erin, Mia, Cain, and the Red Dragon flew right out of his head. The only thing on Marduk's mind at present was Lilith's hips against his.

Chapter Seventeen

Amon somberly marched toward the Citadel with his chin raised in a splenetic scowl as the Elder Guards bowed reverently to him. He appeared to be in a ferocious mood; he kept his fiery eyes straight ahead and didn't even acknowledge the Guards. But in reality, Amon was a bundle of nerves, and didn't want to be distracted from his talking points playing over and over in his head. He waited in the hallway impatiently while Patrick announced his arrival to the Elders. Amon wasn't in the mood for protocol today, but he knew he was still on a thin line with the Elders and needed to be the balance against Marduk's headstrong defiance.

Patrick opened the door with a big grin and waved Amon in. Amon wrinkled his brow and slumped his shoulders at the sight of the Elders sitting sternly on their thrones. He was hoping for an informal conversation.

"Is Hecaté joining us?" Amon asked as he trudged forward to his crystal chair on the right side of the Elder's stage.

"If she is needed, we will call for her. Sit, Amon. Marduk will be here shortly."

"I asked for a private meeting. Informal. This is not about my brothers."

Knowledge lifted his hand and directed Amon to his chair. "Marduk also wanted a private meeting, and since you are both here…" Knowledge pointed toward the door seconds before Marduk burst in with an angry scowl and hard-set jaw. His scowl faded when he saw Amon. He grinned widely as he prowled forward toward him. He knelt beside Amon's chair and kissed him on the lips with a loud smack.

"I'm glad ye're here, Amon. We'll stand together no matter what they throw at us."

Amon felt whole again with Marduk in the room. He knew he'd have an ally to bolster him if he faltered in his talking points that seemed to have disappeared somewhere in the back of his mind the moment he saw the stern faces of the Elders.

"Aye, Marduk. Just as we planned."

Marduk stood with a loud groan and cracking knees, then limped to his onyx chair on the left side of the Elder's stage.

"Marduk, we are all pleased to see you alive and well. Your incident in New York is currently under review. If you would be so kind as to prepare a brief for us, we will consider the matter at length, and work with you on the judgement of your assailant."

"Draco, Titus, and I have prepared our full statements." He handed a thick dossier to the small Scribe, who shuffled it to the Elders. "I have Amon to thank for saving my miserable life." Marduk grinned and pointed to his right. "I wouldn't have survived without this fuckin beast."

"And Amon would not have survived without you, Marduk. Amon saved more than your miserable life," Truth spoke in an ominous tone as he took the dossier from the Scribe, and rifled through it quickly. "He saved himself, as well as the Dynasty."

Marduk wrinkled his brow and slinked down in his seat. He hadn't even thought about how his death would have affected Amon. He eyed the bottle of Scotch on the table, but it was too early in the meeting to start drinking Scotch. Marduk had every one of his talking points lined up in a neat row. He reached for the wine instead and poured a full glass.

"May I begin?" Marduk asked with as much reverence as he could muster. He drained the glass of wine, then quickly poured another.

The Elders all groaned as they turned their attention to Marduk with stern faces. Marduk grinned and broke into a chuckle.

"Cheer up, fuckers. I'm alive. The least ye could do is smile. Have a fuckin drink. Celebrate Marduk, for fuck's sake." He drained another glass of wine, then rolled his eyes when he noticed their stoic faces. "The Lower Colonies are under our rule again. The Army is firmly established. General Krava is in my prison, but I would like to request a private hearing for him…separate from the other Soldiers. There were extenuating circumstances in his collusion with Lucian, but more importantly…I would like Krava in my Army. Eventually. If we are fair with him, he will be loyal. My son, Cain, is home and behaving himself quite well in Dorcha. Lilith is also on best behavior. My family is reconciled, with a few exceptions, but I am certain those obstacles will be removed quickly." He lit a cigarette, then grinned playfully.

"What are you angling for, Marduk?" Justice asked.

"To begin with…Lilith's title. Lilith is my Queen. She will always be my Queen, and I want to reclaim her as such. I want the entire world to know that she and I are reconciled. I want to crown her publicly, and will do so with or without your permission." Marduk finally reached for the Scotch and took one small sip, then crossed his arms over his chest to assess the Elders.

Justice sighed heavily and cast her eye on her fellow Elders, who looked bored and somewhat annoyed with the direction of this meeting.

Marduk noticed the look as well, and acutely felt the negative vibrations, so he quickly continued his report.

"The Incubi of Críoch are free. Lachlan is my emissary in Marbh. Nahemah is my acting Head of State. She has taken the antidote, but her Army does not know it. She prefers to maintain her fierce reputation." Marduk stopped to chuckle when he finally saw life in the eyes of the Elders.

"Aramanth has been rescued and safely returned to Gael. Lugh has also returned to the Colonies and is ready to take his position in the Revolution, alongside his son, Aaden. Jade and Killian are in full training, and the Dynasty is secure with two Alphan generations in line for the Crown. My family is secure. Mair is secure as well. Brian is my emissary. We do not have *lusus naturae* in Mair, but my Incubi are free. I am working with Brian to establish a firmer government. New laws for my Incubi. The Onyx River is secure, and no one will take either of our Colonies again," Amon said with confidence that made Marduk proud as he smiled and nodded his approval.

"Was there bloodshed in the retaking of Críoch?" Strength asked quietly.

Marduk and Amon both chuckled when they remembered Aramanth's blow to Malachi's nose that spilled the only blood in this battle to rescue the Princess and liberate the Lower Colonies.

"Only a little of Malachi's blood when Aramanth broke his nose. He is alive. In my prison." Marduk stifled his grin and reached for the bottle of Scotch again. He drank heavily from it to avoid the piercing eyes of Justice and Strength boring a hole into his head. He knew they'd witnessed the scene with Malachi in the private bedroom of the Dungeon. He tried hard to keep a straight face to no avail.

"Was there was a line crossed with Malachi?" Strength asked ominously.

Marduk's eyes glowed with mischief as he pulled a face and held his hands up. "Only a tiny bit over the line…a fingertip's worth." He shrugged and held up the tip of one finger with a naughty boy grin.

Justice buried her face in her hands as her shoulders shook uncontrollably, but she couldn't control the laughter that sprang up loudly.

"A fingertip's worth," she repeated in a breathless laugh.

Strength began to laugh too, and the entire body of High Council Elders suddenly lost their decorum and stoicism. The mood of the meeting shifted dramatically as the Elders broke into howling laughter until they were breathless. Marduk's punishment of Malachi for raping Aramanth was mild compared to what they might have done to him, but it was quite effective.

"Aye…let us celebrate the life of Marduk. Pass the bottle of Scotch around. We had it brewed especially for you, Marduk," Knowledge said as he wiped the tears from his eyes. "There are more gift bottles being loaded into both your shuttles as we speak. Welcome home, both of you. And welcome back to life, Marduk. None of us were prepared to lose you." The Elders stood from their thrones, and gathered at the informal table with the easy camaraderie of old friends.

"So, both Mair and Marbh are secure again. Nahemah is cured. Both your families are whole again. Well done, lads," Knowledge said in a jovial tone as he poured a round of Scotch for the table. He held up his glass, and motioned for the others to follow. The Elders raised their glasses to their Heads of State, the Ruling Kings of Tosú-Críoch who just unified the Incubian Colonies once again, without a single death. It was something neither of their fathers had been able to do.

"Amon, Son of Alpha and Marduk, Son of Omega, you have earned your rights to full power again, as well as your Crowns. Marduk…your Gates are opened again…and Lilith's title will again be granted to her… on a trial basis. She will be probationary Queen of Dorcha for… five years, ten years, twenty thousand years…how many years do you want to lord the probation over her, Marduk?" Knowledge chuckled.

Marduk shrugged and smiled dreamily. "I don't want to lord anything over my wife. I love her. I trust her." He took a swig of Scotch, then stared off into the distance as the memories of the last 3000 years tumbled around his head. "On second thought…let's give the probation a hundred years."

Amon stared incredulously at Marduk for a few seconds. "I think you should lord it over her a little longer than that, Marduk. After all she's done…"

"Amon is right…let's double that. Two hundred years of probation," he added quickly with a sly wink toward Amon.

"Done." Knowledge nodded firmly, then waived the floor to Justice.

"We have also decided to open the borders between the Upper and Lower Colonies, but only for the Royal families, and on a trial basis. If the Colonies remain stable, full travel will be restored for all." Justice drank her Scotch in one sip, and the other Elders followed. They clapped loudly and bowed reverently to both Amon and Marduk, then hugged each other in a tight huddle.

Marduk was confused by their actions and looked quizzically at Amon. Amon shrugged and shook his head. He was just as confused by this show of loyalty and reverence.

"We are pleased with these decisions," Amon said quietly, then drank his Scotch.

"As ye know, I'm in no shape to hunt, but the Red Dragon, a vicious cult, must be stopped. I'm sending Cain on this hunt," Marduk said quietly, then drank his Scotch as the room suddenly went silent. The Elders took their seats and turned stoic again.

"Marduk, he will not take the Crown. That right has been stripped from him. He is only here temporarily."

Marduk scowled and poured another glass of Scotch. "I'm not asking for the fuckin Crown. I'm telling ye that my son and I are working together on this hunt, but I'm turning the Red Dragon over to Cain."

"Marduk…was it the Red Dragon who assaulted you?" Amon asked quietly with a horrified look on his face. The Elders leaned forward and waited for that answer as well.

"Aye. I thought I could get around the Gates on this journey. But one of the lead dragons turned the tables on me. In fact, this dragon had me in her sights all along. She tried to lure me in, I followed the trail, but without my Gates, I was at a heavy disadvantage."

"You put yourself at this disadvantage, Marduk," Truth said in an ominous tone.

"I am aware. But this Dragon had to be captured. Identified, at the very least. She has been hunting us. On the trail of both my sons, as well as Declan and possibly Lugh. She knows us. She attacked us. I had to do my duty." Marduk drained his glass of Scotch and filled everyone's glass. "A redheaded lass and her son assaulted me. I initially thought she was the Red Dragon, but I recently discovered that they are merely minions of a larger group, a cartel that follows the head Dragon. She has not been identified yet, but Titus is hot on her trail. Now that the Gates are open, Cain will follow through along with Titus. Ye have to give him safe passage."

Knowledge sighed deeply, then looked at his fellow Elders for a decision. They all nodded their consent, albeit reluctantly. "We will allow it. Control his devil before you send Cain on this hunt, Marduk." Knowledge drained his Scotch and sighed deeply.

Marduk nodded and sucked his teeth. "My other son is heavy on my mind as well. I found evidence in Marbh that proves he acted only under threatening coercion from Lucian. Samuel is innocent in the abduction of Jade and Killian. I want him set free," Marduk said adamantly without looking at Amon. He pulled the journals from his satchel, and placed them on the table. "Everything ye need to know is in these journals. They prove Samuel's innocence."

Amon's face fell significantly at Marduk's announcement. "He is far from innocent, Marduk. I will not agree to his freedom."

"He's my son," Marduk said quietly.

"My son paid the price for his part in Issa's escape. Samuel must pay for his."

Marduk groaned and scratched his beard roughly. "He spent 30 years in Lucian's prison. That is more than enough time behind bars."

Amon scoffed and wrinkled his brow. "He took my daughter's life, Marduk. Thirty years is not enough. I wholeheartedly object."

"Samuel did not take her life, Amon. He gave her a chance to be reborn after the Elders condemned her. If he hadn't taken her through the Gates, ye wouldn't have Caraye. Ye'd have a permanently dead daughter instead." Marduk cast his squinted eyes on Amon, then the Elders.

"Issa is permanently dead, Marduk! Samuel did not save her."

"For fuck's sake, she's living in your Palace, Amon. About to give birth to Declan's Heir. She is alive and well, while my son rots in prison."

"Samuel is alive in that prison. Issa is dead," Amon said matter-of-factly.

Knowledge raised his hand to stop the bickering. "We will review the evidence against Salem, and take his time spent with Lucian into consideration. Until then, we need the two of you united on all fronts. The time for the Revolution is close, and we cannot afford another rift between you." Knowledge poured himself another dram of Scotch, then paced around the room slowly before he drank it. "There are more pressing matters to discuss."

"Hecaté," Marduk and Amon said simultaneously, then looked at each other with strained smiles.

"What is Hecaté's role in all this? How and why was she involved in the Rebellion? Why did she take down her own brothers?" Amon asked.

Truth paced next to Knowledge with a withered brow. "Hecaté acted on our orders in all matters. Hecaté is as much a Hero in the arrest of the Lesser Gods as Declan and Cain."

Marduk's eyes widened significantly as he sat forward. "Hecaté worked for the High Council?"

Knowledge nodded solemnly. "Aye. From the day she married Lucian, Hecaté has been our emissary."

Amon winced as he sat back in his chair heavily. "Does Lucian know this?"

"I imagine he does now," Justice said with a playful grin. "Hecaté is safe. No need to worry about Lucian. He will never see the light of day again."

Marduk scowled as he poured himself another dram of Scotch. He downed it, then slammed the glass down on the desk. "I'm less concerned about Hecaté's safety than Caraye's. Hecaté played a wicked hand with the lass." He glanced sheepishly at Amon whose face softened at Marduk's concern over Caraye. "I want to know for certain that Queen Caraye is safe from Hecaté's machinations."

"I agree with Marduk on these concerns. If Hecaté has nefarious plans for Caraye, I want them squelched immediately," Amon added.

"Hecaté has no nefarious plans for the future Queen. There are no such plans from anyone in Gael. Initially, the plans were wicked, but those plans have all been shelved by decree of the High Council. Hecaté was our emissary on that issue as well," Knowledge said softly.

Marduk's face hardened as he glared at Knowledge. "What the fuck did ye do?"

"Long story short…Aramanth and Lugh concocted a very flawed plan. Hecaté informed us of the plan, and we were prepared to fix the plan and follow through so that

Declan could have Issa as his Queen. Our plans were thwarted by you, Marduk. You did not follow the plan."

"Yer plan was flawed as well, and ye were a little too late. Declan was already in love by the time I reached him." Marduk shrugged nonchalantly and reached for the Scotch. He withered under the harsh eyes of the Elders piercing into him. "I almost died! I have a permanent pass." He grinned playfully and chuckled as he drank from the bottle. "As it stands, all is well. Declan has his bride. The Heir is on the way, and both Caraye and Issa are in Gael." He took another long sip of Scotch, then squirmed at the dead silence in the room as well as the white eyes of the Elders boring into him.

"If you had followed the plan, Marduk, Declan would not have suffered."

"Oh no ye don't. Ye're not laying this upon my back. I didn't promise Declan something I couldn't deliver without taking a life. Ye fuckers did that all on yer own. Declan suffered because ye condemned Issa, then promised to bring her back when ye knew it was impossible. How the hell did ye fuck this up so badly?"

Knowledge marched toward Marduk and took the bottle of Scotch from his hand roughly.

"I was drinking that! I died, for fuck's sake!"

"You are alive and well, Marduk. Your near-death was from your own machinations. You do not have a free pass on your defiant transgressions." Knowledge drank heavily from the bottle despite Temperance's harsh stare. He wrinkled his brow and scowled at her as he took another swig from the bottle.

Marduk slumped down into his chair with a smirk and rolled his eyes. "So much for celebrating Marduk."

Amon chuckled softly and clapped Marduk on the shoulder. “Marduk is right. This falls upon your heads. This is your mistake, and I want assurance that Caraye is safe from all of you, and safe from Hecaté as well. Please have her join us. I would like a word with my sister.”

Marduk jumped from his seat quickly with a loud scraping sound as he drew his chair back. “I will fetch her,” he said as he marched toward the door in long steps. He turned to the Elders with a big grin. “It has been 3000 years since I laid eyes on my intended bride.”

“Marduk! Hecaté is not your concern,” Knowledge called out, but Marduk didn’t stop. He marched out the door and ran right into Patrick. He roughly shoved Patrick away from the door before storming off toward the East Wing with his mind racing with images and thoughts of his youth. He began to sweat at the very idea of seeing Hecaté again, but the excitement of it urged him forward a bit faster.

Marduk stopped dead in his tracks, mid-step, when Hecaté turned the corner and floated effortlessly down the hallway in a stunning lavender and silver sequined gown. Her silver hair hung loose around her shoulders with every strand perfectly arranged to allow an ethereal sheen to bounce off the glowing orbs placed along the walls of the Citadel and land right upon her head. Hecaté appeared to be gliding the hallway through her own silver orb.

Marduk drew in his breath and steadied his knees. He crossed his arms over his chest as he gave her a full body perusal while waiting for her to come to him.

“I have not seen that wicked grin in thousands of years,” she said in a sultry voice as she approached slowly. Her heart pounded loudly at the sight of her first love filling up the entire hallway in a Kingly stance she’d never seen from him before. When she last saw him, Marduk was a lean, wiry, overly cocky lad, hellbent on mischief and mayhem, barely an emerging Duke. Hecaté noted with pleasure that Marduk had grown finely into his own legend, and was every inch a King now. She scanned his long, leonine body and sturdy legs beneath his kilt, then blushed when she remembered what else was under that kilt.

"Ye're more beautiful than I remember, and I remember ye being the most beautiful Princess in all the Colonies," Marduk said as he brushed her cheek in a soft, lingering kiss. He growled in a low, breathy sound, draped his arms around her hips, and lifted her off her feet the way he used to do when she was a young Princess.

Hecaté lowered her chin, then smiled coyly as she scanned Marduk's face slowly, thoroughly, and with obvious affection. "Yet not beautiful enough for you, Marduk." She leaned in to place a soft kiss on his grinning lips.

Marduk gently placed Hecaté on her feet, but kept her in his arms. "That is not true, Hecaté. I was the one not good enough," he whispered against her cheek before resting his forehead against hers. His heart thumped loud enough to hear it himself, and he wanted Hecaté to hear it too, so he pulled her closer to his chest. "Has my brother been good to ye, lass?"

She pulled away reluctantly and winced. "Aye. Lucian has been very good to me. But I have not been good to him. I made a terrible mistake, Marduk." Hecaté sighed heavily. "I betrayed the love of my life."

Marduk ran his fingers through her hair and sighed in sync with her. He replayed her words in his head half a dozen times, hoping to find a deeper meaning, but he clearly saw the face value of Hecaté's words when she stepped away from him with a faraway look in her eyes.

"Ye were loyal to the Elders, and yer Kings. It was a brave thing to do, Hecaté. My wicked brother doesn't deserve yer loyalty, nor yer love," Marduk said in a heavy brogue.

"You are wrong about him, Marduk. He tried to do this by the law, and he did. Granted, he manipulated the circumstances, but…he followed the law. Your laws, Marduk. Do you have any idea how difficult that was for him?" She threw her hands in the air and paced in circles as she glared at Marduk. "Lucian has lived in your shadow all his life. Even in our marriage, he lived under the shadow of Marduk. You took more from him than his spirit could tolerate, and…"

"I took nothing from Lucian. Ye were mine at the time of our love affair, Hecaté. Marbh has always been mine. Lucian took from me."

"I was never yours, Marduk," she spat out.

Marduk's eyes narrowed and his jaw tightened. "Ye're telling me no news," he growled.

"I am my own Queen and always have been. Lucian understood this. Lucian never kept me under his rule."

Marduk raised one eyebrow and crossed his arms over his chest. "And yet ye betrayed him. Don't pretend that my brother is more than he is."

"He is neither more nor less than you, Marduk."

"I disagree. Lucian is far less of an Incubus than I am." Marduk lit a cigarette, then blew the smoke from his nostrils in two heavy streams. "He is disloyal, Hecaté. To his King, his Tribe, his fellow Incubi, humanity. My wicked brother was disloyal to his wife as well."

Hecaté narrowed her eyes angrily and charged back toward Marduk. "You have no cause to talk of disloyalty to a wife! You have never been loyal to anyone but yourself.

You betrayed your own son! As well as your brothers! And let's not forget your disloyalty to your wife, Marduk."

Marduk squinted fiercely at Hecaté's firm stance dripping with disrespect and disdain. "Hold yer tongue, lass, and remember where ye are. Ye're in my fuckin Colony, and my wife and sons are none of yer fuckin business." Marduk's brogue was extra thick as he slipped back into the emotions of his tumultuous youth.

Hecaté took a step back and grinned sarcastically while scanning Marduk's long, lean frame shadowing hers. She knew from his heavy brogue that she'd triggered him. She crossed her arms over her chest and smirked as though she had the world at her feet, and the King of the Incubi by the balls. She was certain she had the upper hand, so she played the best card she had.

"Do you still have a wife and sons, Marduk?"

"Aye, Hecaté. I do. My sons are safely back my Colony, maybe not in good graces yet, but there is time to remedy that. And my wife…my beautiful Queen has never been more gracefully situated in my Lair than she is now. Where is yer husband? Yer children?" Marduk smirked arrogantly when her triumphant grin faded. "Don't concern yerself with my family, Hecaté. Ye were never part of it, aside from being married to my brother. The husband ye betrayed."

"You are the most arrogant, small-minded, and wicked Incubus I have ever known. Do not forget that your own fortune wheel is spinning, Marduk."

Marduk took in another deep breath to compose himself with the grace of a King. He set his jaw firmly and took one step forward. "Let me remind ye, lass, that ye're speaking to yer King. Yer future is in my hands, Hecaté." Marduk took a long drag from his cigarette, then lifted his chin to blow the smoke above her head. He never took his eyes off her.

Hecaté lifted the cigarette from his fingers, took a deep drag, then stepped back with a cocky grin. She dropped the cigarette on the floor and stamped it out with her delicate silk slipper, then held her hands up and waved her fingers gracefully.

"I hold my own future in these hands, Marduk. You forget who you are speaking to as well."

Marduk chuckled in a low tone, then let out a small growl. "Ye don't scare me with yer little magic tricks, Hecaté. I know them all, and I know the remedies." He took another step forward and squinted fiercely. "I also know what ye did to Caraye. She is under my protection now, so call off yer fuckin hounds before I turn my own on ye, Hecaté."

Hecaté chuckled and rolled her eyes. "I know my way around the hounds of hell, Marduk. I weaned the sire myself before I gave him to you."

"That was 3000 years ago, lass. The sire is long gone, and his pups will not know ye. I mean it, Hecaté. Caraye is not to be harmed by yer tricks." He held up his hand when Hecaté's eyes blazed, and she charged at him with tight lips and a spunky attitude that he always admired about her. Still, he wanted to break that part of her spirit every time she revealed it.

"Before ye say another word, it is only fair that I warn ye. Both Akaia and Malachi are in Dorcha, in my Lair. Conall as well." He gloated when her spunk melted, but the bewilderment in her soft, violet eyes melted his angry resolve. "Hecaté…Akaia and Conall are safe. They are both well, and ye're welcome to visit them anytime, lass."

"Marduk...please do not do this to me. Let Akaia and Conall come to the Citadel. It is protocol! Your own laws, Marduk. Queens, Duchesses, and Princesses reside with the Elders. Conall is only a babe…" Hecaté's eyes filled with genuine tears that melted the last of Marduk's hardened resolve.

"Akaia hasn't stopped crying since she arrived. Neither has Conall. I suppose she needs her mother." He smiled genuinely and gave her another thorough once over. Marduk ran his hands through his hair and paced a few steps with a withered brow. "In exchange for yer loyalty to Caraye, and yer solemn vow that she's safe from yer magic, Akaia and Conall will remain with ye in the Citadel until Samuel is free. Do not cross me, Hecaté. If ye do, ye'll find that I rarely play fair with traitors."

Hecaté relaxed her shoulders and stepped lightly toward Marduk. "Thank you, Marduk. I will not cross you, I swear it. I have no desire to hurt Caraye any more than she has already been. Nor Declan. My solemn vow, Marduk. Caraye is safe." She gently placed her hand on Marduk's chest, but pulled away abruptly when she suddenly had the urge to kiss him.

The thought wasn't lost on Marduk, however. He slipped his arm around her waist to pull her toward him, then leaned forward to lightly brush his lips over hers.

"I don't want to fight with ye, Hecaté. Whether we like it or not, and our past be damned, for the rest of our lives we're connected through Samuel and Akaia. For Conall's sake, let's put aside our old deeds," Marduk whispered tenderly.

Hecaté pulled away slowly and nodded firmly. "Truce. Enough fighting amongst our Tribes…and…enough animosity between the two of us," she replied softly with misty eyes.

"Agreed. How did we end up like this? We were inseparable once. We shared love, Hecaté. Deep love," Marduk said in a hoarse whisper that sent chills down Hecaté's spine, but it also sparked her anger again. Despite her great love for Lucian, Hecaté never quite got over the fact that Marduk choose Lilith over her.

"You know exactly how we ended up here, Marduk. Did you come here just to remind me of it?" she replied flippantly.

"No. I came to tell ye that the Elders have summoned ye." He grinned crookedly when he saw the flush on her cheeks. "Amon is here as well."

Hecaté smiled brilliantly, and it was Marduk's turn to feel the warm shiver of emotion run down his spine.

"Amon is here? I am so anxious to see my brother. I have not lain eyes on my darling Amon in thousands of years." She started off toward the Elder's chambers, then stopped suddenly and turned back to Marduk with a curious stare.

"Did you say Malachi was in Dorcha? Marduk, where is Malachi? What have you done with him? He is Lucian's First Son! His only son…" Her eyes clouded over with fear and anguish as she made her way back to Marduk. She knew Malachi abhorred Marduk and wouldn't easily fall under his rule. She shivered again at Marduk's proximity, but held her ground.

Marduk snickered when he thought about his romantic episode with Malachi, but recovered quickly. "Malachi is in Dorcha. In my prison. He is unharmed, so far…but the lad has a wicked stubborn streak my Guards are determined to break."

Hecaté slumped against him and let out a rush of air. Marduk held her up and growled softly when he breathed in her scent of lavender and plumeria.

"Do not harm Malachi to settle your score with Lucian, Marduk. That is beneath the privilege of the Crown. Malachi is innocent."

"He is far from innocent, Hecaté. Malachi abducted Aramanth, and raped her."

"Abducted her? Rape? Oh Marduk…" Hecaté pulled away slowly and held her hand to her mouth. "Is Aramanth alright?" Her violet eyes were flaming with anxiety and confusion. Marduk had little defense against her vulnerability. He stepped forward and held her shoulders to bolster her for the rest of the story.

"Aramanth is fine, but… she is with child," Marduk replied quietly.

"With child? Malachi's child?"

"Aramanth claims that Malachi is not the father, but Malachi is challenging her claim."

"For Aramanth's sake…I hope Malachi is not the child's father. No child should be born of violence." Hecaté wrinkled her brow and brushed away her tears quickly as she pulled away from Marduk. "If the child is Malachi's, I will intervene on Aramanth's behalf," she whispered to herself.

"Ye'll be the child's grandmother, with all the rights afforded that position. Fair warning, however. I will kill the lad myself before I allow him to take Aramanth's child."

Hecaté barely blinked at Marduk's threat. She paced in circles with a wrinkled brow as she contemplated the implications of Malachi's actions. "Why did Malachi do this to Aramanth? To his family? That lad grows more wicked every day." Hecaté threw her hands in the air and let out a soft sob.

"Malachi did this to win the Crown of Críoch. He declared himself the One Victor in the Rebellion, and took Aramanth from the Palace as his prize. Amon and I journeyed to Marbh to rescue Aramanth, and reestablish control of Marbh and Mair. The Colonies are reunited."

"Was anyone harmed in the battle?"

"There was no battle to speak of, Hecaté. Marbh's meager forces were easily taken with the help of Krava, who surrendered himself and his Army before we stepped off the Mercuria. The only bloodshed was when Aramanth broke Malachi's nose with her wee fists. It was a beautiful moment of justice no one will ever forget. Wicked lad ye got there, Hecaté. But he has no stamina in battle. Aramanth took him down in three moves." He laughed wickedly, and lit another cigarette.

"It seems that Malachi is a true Omegan, then. No stamina is an Omegan character flaw, a weakness I have personally witnessed in every one of the Omegan brothers," she spat out as she pulled her train behind her and glided down the hallway toward the Elders' chambers.

Marduk growled and shook his head slowly while watching her hips sway gracefully with each carefully measured step.

"My brother never deserved ye." He took a long drag of his cigarette, then grinned devilishly as he followed those swaying hips.

Hecaté entered the Elder's chambers with a casual familiarity that grated somewhat on Amon's nerves.

"Amon! My dear, sweet brother…I am so happy to see your face!" She daintily glided toward him, and threw her arms around his neck.

Amon smiled despite his anger and hugged her tightly. Hecaté's grace was her most charming feature. No King, Duke, Man, nor God had ever been able to resist Hecaté's graceful, albeit cold, personal charm. She was a work of art in her every movement, with her long, lean hands flowing as though conducting the air around her, molding it into language, into reality, into the very curves of her body. Amon lost all his anger for a moment when she leaned toward him with a brilliant smile.

"I cannot believe my eyes. My beautiful Hecaté. Are you well, sister?" Amon asked sweetly.

"I am well in body…but my heart, Amon. My heart is so heavy." She leaned against his massive chest and cried softly.

Amon's anger resurfaced when he recognized a typical Hecaté move in playing the victim. He tried to squelch his anger again, but in his usual logical manner, he weighed her previous actions against her reaction now, and found that he couldn't trust it completely.

"Hecaté…" Amon held her away from him, and cast her a look of soft compassion mingled with disappointment. "I am sorry your life was disrupted, my dear. But the fact that you have been a double agent in the Rebellion cuts me deeply. Another betrayal from my siblings. I shared everything with you, Hecaté, including my war strategies. I accepted advice and secrets from you. It all feels so disingenuous now." He was also suspicious of the invitation she extended to their brothers at the Banquet, and couldn't help feeling that she implicated them in Jade and Killian's abduction as a means to protect Lucian.

"Amon…I never lied to you. I withheld information, but I never lied to you. Everything I did was to save your Crown. Our father's legacy. The Colonies are reunited now because I risked my own life, my own marriage, Amon. I betrayed myself, but I never betrayed you."

"I still have questions for you, my dear." Amon gave her his most stern look as he motioned for her to sit next to him.

"So do I." Marduk couldn't stop grinned as he took the seat across from her while the Elders circled around her.

"Am I to be interrogated by all of you?"

"You are not under interrogation, Hecaté. We only have a few questions for you. First, is Caraye safe?" Amon asked.

"Of course she is safe, Amon. I saved her life in Marbh. For Declan's sake as well as Jade's. Caraye is well and healthy, is she not?" Hecaté began to squirm a little from Amon's stern face, as well as Marduk's boyish grin across the table. "I gave the Elders my word. Marduk was given my promise as well. Caraye is safe." She lifted her chin, and tried not to look at Marduk's gloating smile, but his eyes bore into her thoroughly, and she couldn't look away from him.

"I will hold you accountable for that promise, sister. If anything happens to Caraye, you will be the first person to answer for it." Amon leaned forward to give her a fierce squint that almost rivaled Marduk's. "Why did you involve Jacey, Mahdi, and Inuus? You clearly knew they were innocent."

"Innocent? None of you are innocent, Amon! You all played wicked hands in the Rebellion. All of you shed blood, and I was not going to let…" Hecaté stopped abruptly, and sat back with tight lips and a furrowed brow.

Marduk sat forward and sucked his teeth with a hissing sound that grated on Hecaté nerves. Not only because his arrogance was so evident in that sound, but because she'd always been unbearably attracted to his arrogance.

"Finish yer sentence, Hecaté. Or shall I finish it for ye?"

"Do not pretend to know what is on my mind, Marduk. You were never able to read me in our youth, and you certainly will not do so after 3000 years away from me." She narrowed her eyes and stared him down without blinking. That move was something Marduk always had to work hard to resist, but he did. Especially now. They held each other's stare without blinking, but not without a blazing fire between them.

"Do not disrespect me, Hecaté. I am yer King." Marduk lit a cigarette without taking his eyes from her, but he covered his quick blink behind the smoke. Hecaté's violet eyes were more beautiful, more savage than he remembered. "Let me remind ye what's at stake, lass. Yer daughter is still in my Lair. So is yer son. Finish yer sentence."

Hecaté broke the stare first when she lowered her eyes, but she sat silent for a full minute before she finally conceded. "My commission was to stop the Rebellion and bring the Rebels to the High Council. I saw my opportunity to finally end this, and I took it. Lucian did not fight the Rebellion alone. The Elders know this. You both know this as well. My brothers are all guilty. Yours as well, Marduk. I did not want Lucian to answer for war crimes alone. Is that what you want to hear?" She tossed her hair over her shoulder and turned away from Marduk with her chin held high.

Knowledge groaned loudly and stepped forward. "Hecaté…who was responsible for abducting the Cambions?"

"Salem." She smirked at Marduk with a raised eyebrow. "He is the one who took Jade and Killian from New Orleans." She gloated at the shock crossing Marduk's face. He stood abruptly, nearly knocking over his chair in the process.

"Who gave Samuel the order to take them?" Marduk spat out through a clenched jaw.

Hecaté tightened her lips, crossed her legs and her arms, then looked off into the distance. She didn't say a word.

"Answer me, Hecaté! Who gave the order to my son to take Jade and Killian from New Orleans? Who was with him in New Orleans? More importantly, why was my son in Marbh in the first fuckin place?"

Amon gently touched Marduk's arm, which calmed him immediately. "Marduk, she is not a prisoner, nor is she on trial," Amon said matter-of-factly. Marduk huffed loudly and took his seat again.

"I ask the Elders to persuade Hecaté to answer the questions," Marduk said in his most reverent tone, but the look in his eyes was anything but reverent.

Truth lightly touched Hecaté's shoulder. That was all the motivation she needed. She opened her mouth and took a deep breath, then looked away from Marduk.

"Lucian gave Salem permission to bring his daughter to Marbh. Malachi took Killian by mistake. You already know why Salem was in Marbh." She shot Marduk a hateful scowl, then cast a contrite look to Amon. "Amon…none of our brothers, nor Seth and Herne, knew that Jade and Killian were in Marbh. It was Lucian's doing, but he did it under the law. He did not break the law. Salem had the right to his daughter."

"There is more to the story than that, Hecaté," Marduk spat out through a clenched jaw. "Samuel was taken to Marbh specifically to be used in Lucian's plot to win his war game. He used Samuel to father Jade, then used him again to abduct Jade as a pawn for the Crown. Lucian meticulously planned and recorded every detail of the last thirty years while he held my son prisoner." Marduk pushed Lucian's journals toward her. "Journal number 666. Pages 13 through 66. Ye'll find Lucian's entire plan meticulously recorded there."

Hecaté nodded slowly, but didn't look at Marduk, Amon, nor the journals. "Lucian's strategy was to trade Jade to the Elders for the Crown of Críoch."

"Did Samuel know the plan?" Amon asked softly. "Did he know Jade was going to be traded for the Crown?"

Hecaté lowered her head and picked at a loose thread on her gown. "No. Salem believed he was saving Jade from the Elders…from the same fate as Issa. But he knew full well the Elders were looking for her. Killian was Malachi's mistake. He thought Killian, as Cain's son, was the mark. Lucian did not hurt them in any way. Jade and Killian were treated with dignity and respect, perhaps even a little love. They were never mistreated."

"Samuel was mistreated," Marduk added.

Knowledge took a seat and motioned for the Elders to join him at table. "We will take all this into account when the trials begin. Although the younger brothers were innocent in the plot to take the Cambions, we must also take their war crimes into account."

"And Samuel? Ye have yer answer…he's innocent. He was held against his will and did not have knowledge of the plot to take the Crown. Moreover, Samuel was gravely harmed and badly mistreated by Lucian, Malachi, and perhaps even Hecaté. I want all charges against him dropped. Including his part in Issa's escape. He paid his debt the same as Declan. Thirty years in Lucian's prison is more than enough."

"We will have an answer for you after every detail has been reviewed," Knowledge replied solemnly.

Marduk grinned and held out his hand to Knowledge. "Fair enough." Marduk was certain the journals as well as Hecaté's testimony was enough to set Samuel free. He held his hand out to Amon and gave him his best wounded puppy look. "Can we agree on this, Amon?"

Amon sighed heavily and took Marduk's hand. "Aye. But Declan will balk. Cain will as well. Are you certain, Marduk, that Samuel is not safer in prison?"

"I agree with Amon on that one," I said in a solemn tone while scanning Samael's face with a withered brow. "Marduk's not thinking clearly. Cain's gonna make Samuel's life miserable, and he's already suffered more than anyone in this mistake of the Gods. Bad call, Marduk."

Samael cocked one eyebrow sarcastically. "Look at you, Lily…turning against your lover boy. Is your crush on Marduk fading?" He chuckled and lit a cigarette.

"No. I'm still in love with him." I took the cigarette from his fingers and smirked arrogantly. "Does that piss you off?"

Samael shrugged and looked away, staring off into the distance. "Not in the least. Love whoever you want, Lily," he replied nonchalantly.

Samael's apparent lack of jealousy, as though he was winding down our relationship to make a smooth escape, knocked the wind right out of me. The very idea of that felt like a spike through my chest, and my sanity seemed to slip farther and farther away from me.

"Bullshit. He's so jealous, he can't sleep at night," Drake said with a chuckle. "But if it means anything to you, Lily. I'm mad jealous of your crush on Marduk."

"I sleep just fine! Lily's infatuation with Marduk is none of my business. None of yours, either, Drake. I have my own infatuations."

Samael's words stung deep. I couldn't look at him, but also couldn't take my eyes from him. The attempt to do both hurt my head fiercely. I buried my face in my hands and groaned fiercely. "This is fucking madness! How is it possible that I'm in love with the Devil?!"

Samael's face lit up, and he crossed the room in two long steps. "You're in love with me?" he whispered softly as he knelt beside me and held my hand gently.

"She said the Devil, Samael!" Drake shouted. "She was referring to Marduk."

"I am the fuckin Devil!"

"In theory," Drake answered quietly.

"I must be insane. Take me back to the fucking hospital. I need a shrink. And a rubber room."

Samael pulled me close to his chest and softly brushed his lips against mine. "Would it help if I told you that I'm in love with you too?"

"Maybe." I shrugged, stuffed a gummy worm in my mouth, then fell to the floor in tears. "This is madness. This is not happening." I sobbed until I couldn't breathe.

"You're breaking the rules, Samael! Just a few weeks ago, she said she loved us both! The Keeper of Scores documented it," Drake interjected. "Where do I fit into the scheme of things, Lily? Am I in your heart?" Drake pleaded as he pulled me to my feet. I suddenly felt sane again at the sound of Drake's voice. I couldn't begin to explain why, but his soothing voice and familiarity were my grounding rods. I could read Drake better than Samael, and was more certain of Drake's affections.

"Drake…of course I love you, but I can't…"

"Can't what, Lily?"

"See you," I replied sheepishly.

"Is my face so important to you? It's possible to love someone without seeing their face. You love Marduk…and you've never seen him."

"Stop begging, Drake. It's beneath you and so fucking sad. You're pathetic, brother. Get off your fucking knees." Samael chuckled as he ducked left. "You lost, Drake. She loves me." His grin faded when his head snapped back, and he hit the floor with a heavy thud.

"Low fuckin blow!" Samael bellowed, then spit out a stream of blood on the floor. "Clean it up." His eyes were shooting black fire when he stood and walked toward me.

I pulled away from Samael when a dark thought suddenly dawned on me. "Are you two in some twisted competition to make me fall in love with you? Are you two playing with me?! Who's the Keeper of Scores? What the hell is going on?"

"It's not a game, Lily…it's not like that at all," Samael answered a little too quickly.

"Don't lie to her, Samael! That's exactly what this is. A competition to win your affections. Only he has the advantage!"

"This time! Last time, you had the advantage, and you blew it!" Samael shouted.

"I did not blow it! You interfered!"

"Stop it!" I yelled. The immediate and complete silence in the room unnerved me and made my head spin. Had I crossed over into total insanity? Were these voices and visions only in my head? Was it possible that I did love Samael? Or was it Drake? Were they the same beings? Were they even real?

I buried my face in my hands as the questions tumbled from my mind, then I began to cry softly as my sanity drifted away. But I couldn't deny the warm touch of two very different and distinct beings attempting to comfort me. I pulled away from them both abruptly.

"If this is nothing more than a competition to see which one of you can get in my bed first, then you both lose! This is the most twisted and evil thing I've ever experienced in my entire life! Samael, you made me believe I was your wife that you loved!"

"You are my wife!" Samael yelled back.

Drake groaned and made an exaggerated gagging sound. "You make me wanna puke, Samael. You're a fucking liar, and they fall for it every time," Drake said in a harsh tone, then walked toward the door. "I have guests to haunt, Lily. Let me know when you come to your senses."

"Drake…don't leave me in limbo like this! I trust you more than I trust Samael."

Drake laughed in a menacing tone as Samael smirked in the direction of the door. Samael pulled me toward him and held me against his chest. "Let me prove to you how much I love you, Lily."

"Now you're really playing unfair, Samael. Lie after lie after lie. She deserves better than this. Better than you," Drake spat out viciously.

“I’m not lying to you, Lily. I do love you. I’ve always loved you. Drake is just jealous because he’s in a subordinate role.”

“Invisible, Samael! Not subordinate!”

“You have to do as I say,” Samael replied arrogantly. “I say shut the fuck up.”

“I don’t take orders from you, you slimy little devil…”

“Stop!” I yelled again, and moved as far away from them as possible. “I don’t know what kind of game the two of you are playing, and to be honest, right now I don’t love either of you! But apparently, I’m stuck with you two until this fucking book is finished! Before we go another step on this journey, Samael, I need an honest answer to one question. Am I really your wife?”

“Yes!” Samael shouted and charged toward me with open arms I desperately wanted to fall into.

“In theory,” Drake added mysteriously.

Chapter Eighteen

Lilith scanned herself thoroughly in the mirror, from her intricately braided hair to her six-inch red stiletto heels. She turned left, right, smoothed her dress over her perfectly rounded hips with a satisfied smile, then carefully slipped her mask over her face. Lilith sighed contentedly, then glanced up at Marduk leaning against the wall with one booted foot crossed over the other and his thick arms crossed over his chest as he watched her every move.

Marduk looked wickedly handsome in a floor-length black coat trimmed with blood-red piping along the outer edges, intricately embroidered along the piping from the stiff collar to the stiff hem. He wore a chained leather kilt with a black front panel and two blood-red panels along each side, and black leather boots that shined like glass. His braided hair was covered with a loose black hood; his black leather mask was intricately sculpted into small dragon scales fitted along his cheekbones, nose, and forehead. The sculpted edges were twisted into stiff, hair-thin leather spikes that fanned out widely into pewter tips, topped by a pair of nine-inch twisted leather horns.

Lilith sauntered toward him with a sexy sway of her hips in her black satin and chiffon gown, heavily beaded and sequined, with a mermaid skirt and a red peek-a-boo court train flowing beautifully behind her. Bella rode the train with wide innocent eyes while dragging another of Lilith's black dresses along the floor. The top of Lilith's boatneck, lace-trimmed neckline fanned into an intricate design of skulls with scalloped and slightly frayed edges. Her arms were covered with black lace that tapered down to stiff points over her hands. Lilith's black lace mask was delicately sculpted into flames with blood-red tips, and one red Ostrich feather at her right temple.

"You look positively wicked, Marduk. I have never seen you look more alluring," Lilith whispered in a sultry voice as she sidled up to him and lifted her face for a kiss.

Marduk lifted his mask, then bent to kiss her tenderly so he wouldn't undo her delicately braided hair, but he wanted nothing more than to pull those braids loose and run his hands through her hair. Lilith wanted to do the same with his braid. They kissed breathlessly, soundlessly, as he pulled her close and ran his hands along her hips, then slowly began to unzip her dress.

Dead Party, Papa! No time to fuck! Bella screamed and pulled her dress closer to her as she tried to fit it around her shoulders.

"She is not your daughter, Lilith," Marduk chuckled. "Nor mine."

Lilith rested her head against his chest and giggled softly. "Bella is right, my love. The guests will be arriving any minute now. No time for love." She kissed him tenderly, then grinned playfully. "I can hardly wait for midnight!" Her eyes sparkled like blue glass in sunlight.

Marduk growled and rolled his eyes, then pulled his mask over his face. "Just remember who's first on your list, Lilith." He held his arm out to her with a crooked grin.

"I have not forgotten my list, Marduk, and you have not completed yours. I still have a veto," she said with a triumphant arch of her neck.

"My third loophole awaits," Marduk said wickedly, and led her out the door.

Lilith pulled on the train of her gown and smiled sweetly at Bella. "Mother's dress does not need more adornment, Bella. Roam free tonight. It is a Dead Party, after all."

Bella jumped off the dress with a scowl, and dragged her own dress behind Lilith and Marduk sauntering regally down the hallways of the darkened Lair, arm-in-arm in matching steps. Bella finally looped the dress around her neck, and grinned gruesomely at the pretty picture she assumed she made in that moment.

Lilith and Marduk stood together in the doorway to assess the transformation of the elegant Dining Hall into a wicked den of deadly sins. The delicate chandelier was replaced with a massive fixture made entirely of human vertebrae and finger bones. The carefully constructed scenes along the back end of the Hall were designed in unique themes, partitioned by paper-thin curtains of human skin stitched together in intricate patterns.

In the left corner, there was a small parlor setting with a dozen satin-lined caskets, wooden coffins lined in layers of leather and lace, and a long row of ancient headstones. The walls were covered with bloody handprints, smears, and splatters. The corners with littered with bones, both human and animal. More than a dozen roughly severed heads with no eyes hung from the ceiling. Each one had a candle carefully inserted in the jawbone, which made the eyeholes glow in soft, amber hues.

The bar in the central scene housed a massive cauldron in the anatomical shape of a heart with a smoking red brew bubbling and pumping from it. A tall wooden table carved with ancient hieroglyphic symbols held dozens of whiskey and wine bottles neatly lined up around crystal glasses and decanters. Hanging from the ceiling were dozens of blood bags filled with thick, blood-red wine laced with small chunks of fruit pulp to simulate blood clots. Along the back wall of the bar, a small fire pit built of human skulls burned brightly with flaming skulls popping loudly from the cracking bones.

The right corner was transformed into a torture chamber with ancient medical slabs, primitive torture devices rusted with dried blood, heavy twisted chains, and meat hooks with a roasted lamb hanging from the middle hook and a row of fire-roasted chickens on each side of the lamb. Lilith's 13 black cats were perched along the walls in small, recessed alcoves. Only their glowing eyes were visible in the dimly-lit room.

Along the East wall was a sadomasochist scene with chains, ropes, whips, paddles, crops, spiked masks, and mannequins in leather bondage suits that looked a little too real in Marduk's opinion. Still, he was intrigued by the spiked bondage rack. His mind was on all the ways he might position one of his loopholes on that rack after midnight.

The West wall held a variety body parts soaked in formaldehyde. Each glass jar was labeled in an ancient script nobody in this generation could read. There was a small table with a crystal ball and a deck of tarot cards in a dark alcove that made Marduk think of Mia. He looked back at the bondage table with a raised eyebrow, one squinted eye, and a small wicked smile when he finally saw his way around all the obstacles of the table.

The buffet tables had 13 human skeletons stuffed with finger foods arranged to look like organs, brains, intestines, lungs, eyeballs, livers, hearts, and racks of beef attached to the ribcage of the skeletons. It was a savage feast that brought an instant smile to Marduk's face.

"Ye've outdone yourself, Lilith. Best Dead Party yet, my love."

"I wanted to impress Killian." Lilith shrugged and took the compliment well, then giggled at Bella dragging the dress into one of the coffins.

Marduk smiled and pulled Lilith closer. "She set herself free."

"She set you free as well. Your back will be lighter now, and no more scars, Marduk," Lilith said with a genuine smile. Marduk nodded sadly. He didn't want to admit how much he missed the weight of Bella, as well as the cuts and scratches. They'd become so much a part of who he was, he had to wonder if his confidence was rattled now because he no longer had a second conscience.

Cain sauntered into the Dining Hall with a wide, boyish grin and stopped dead in his tracks at the sight of Marduk. He tilted his head and shrugged when Marduk lifted his mask to smirk at him. Cain was wearing the same chained leather kilt as Marduk, but with a red front panel and two black side panels. Their masks were nearly identical, but Cain's mask didn't have horns. They both wore black embroidered coats and knee-high leather boots.

"Remember that I'm the one with horns, Lilith," Marduk quipped in a droll tone.

Lilith glided toward Cain and held her cheek against his. "You look so wicked, Cain. Mia will love your costume." She fussed over his hood and smoothed his coat while he stared at her with open adoration, but not lust. He was still madly enchanted by her, but he'd pledged his loyalty to Marduk, and wouldn't cross him under any circumstances now that he'd found a way inside Marduk's circle. He also found a way out of Lilith's grip. Maeve. Maeve was Cain's Lilith. His. Not Marduk's.

Cain cleared his throat and hung his head. He knew tonight was going to reveal more than Mia's attraction to his wicked side. He was prepared for the fallout, but not looking forward to it.

"Mother…Maeve is my date tonight."

Lilith's face fell as her eyes widened. "Maeve? She is not on my guest list. Nor is she on your father's list anymore. She cannot attend!" Lilith said adamantly and looked at Marduk for support. Cain did the same.

"Marduk, do something!"

"Father…"

Marduk groaned and marched forward slowly. "Lilith, let the lad have his fun. He's smitten with Maeve. It is an orgy, after all. We need the concubines." Marduk raised his hands in the air helplessly when Lilith set her hands on her hips angrily. She was surprised at the camaraderie between Marduk and Cain, but more than that, she was all too aware that Marduk still hadn't named his final loophole. She didn't want to give Maeve an inch to work her way between them again. Marduk read her thoughts and pulled her to him gently.

"She's off my list, Lilith. And she has been warned to show ye the respect ye deserve as my wife. My Queen." Marduk wanted to cover all his bases tonight. He wanted to assure Lilith that her place in his life, Lair, heart, table, and bed was secure, but he also wanted to remind her of how easily it could all be lost again. He wanted Cain secure in his position in the Lair as well. Secure enough to take his own concubine, with or without his mother's approval. Deep in the back of Marduk's mind, however, was the small devil screaming in his ear that with Maeve on Cain's list, Mia was fair game.

Lilith huffed loudly and threw her hands up in the air. "If she crosses the line, Marduk, we will have a very real dead party tonight!"

Lilith stormed off toward the dinner table waving her hands in the air, muttering to herself. Both Cain and Marduk growled softly while watching the sway of her hips. Marduk slapped Cain in the gut with the back of his hand.

"She's yer fuckin mother," he said ominously and shot Cain a fierce look before he pulled the mask over his face again, then marched off toward the bar for a bottle of Scotch. Cain followed him in his own long-legged march and caught up to Marduk in three steps.

"I can still admire her." Cain grinned wickedly as he kept pace with Marduk's marching swagger.

Marduk cast him a quick sideways glance and sucked his teeth. Cain read his reaction as disappointment, maybe even disdain. But Marduk was glowing with pride. No one, not even Draco, kept pace with him. For the first time in his life, Marduk saw himself in Cain, and liked what he saw.

"Relax, Marduk. The old Cain is dead. The new Cain has no interest in fucking his mother," Cain chuckled, then passed up Marduk to reach the bar first. He poured them each a dram of Scotch, then handed one to Marduk.

"To the dead," Cain toasted.

Marduk held up his glass and nodded once, then drained his glass. "A word of caution to ye, Son. Maeve is to show yer mother respect as my wife, and she is to keep her distance from me. Maeve is all yers, Cain. Erin, however, is not. It's a loophole night. Erin is mine. And yer mother's." Marduk's squinted eyes shot amber fire through the mask, but he couldn't help grinning at the idea of Erin and Lilith.

Cain hung his head and laughed softly. "You two are the most twisted fuckers I have ever known."

"Ye're telling me no news. Yer mother will never be happy with only one lover. I'm conceding the war to her for the time being. But she will learn that fair is fair. If she keeps her lasses, I keep mine. Except for Maeve. She's off my list. Take Erin off yers." Marduk poured them each another shot of Scotch and held his glass to Cain's.

"Done. I only have eyes for Maeve. And Mia, of course," Cain said dreamily. Marduk smirked and rolled his eyes. Cain was back to being Lilith in his eyes. "Mia's not going to like it."

Marduk tilted his mask back and lit a black cigarette, then blew out the smoke through his nostrils. "Neither will yer wife. Hurit will also be here tonight." Marduk chuckled wickedly when Cain began to squirm.

"I am so dead," he moaned, then drained his glass of Scotch.

"Does Mia know about yer blonde? Or yer wife?" Marduk grinned and licked his lips.

"You're enjoying my discomfort a little too much, Marduk."

"Old habits die hard when ye're eternal." Marduk winked and draped his arm across Cain's shoulder. "Do ye need protection tonight? Shall I dispatch the Army to keep yer lasses in check?" Marduk chuckled.

"It might not be a bad idea. You have no idea what Mia is capable of with her Voodoo. If you happen to see a snake crawling through the Lair tonight. Don't kill it. It'll be me… after Mia's done with me." Cain grinned boyishly, then quickly pulled himself into a manly stance. Marduk noted the shift in his persona, as well as his loss of boyish arrogance that was replaced with manly confidence. He wanted to trust the sincerity of it, but Marduk didn't lie when he said old habits die hard in his kind.

"Maeve and Hurit aren't innocuous either. How much trouble are ye in, Son?"

"None of them know anything about the other, and that's all gonna change tonight. You may yet have use for those coffins," Cain said in a droll tone.

"Ye're the son of Marduk after all. A true Omegan."

"What would you do in my situation, Father?"

"I am the King of the Incubi. I do whatever I please with whoever pleases me." Marduk lifted his chin arrogantly and sipped his Scotch.

Cain admired Marduk's firm resolve, but he knew it was a façade. "I don't have the luxury of being King. What would you advise me to do?" Cain asked with a pleading look.

"Honesty, Cain. Be bold. Be brave. But be honest. I've learned that lasses are strong enough to handle any truth ye throw in their faces. But none of them handle lies very well." He shook his head and growled, then let out one deep chuckle. "Let the lasses know from the start who rules the monster." He grinned crookedly and raised one eyebrow.

"Does Lilith know who rules the monster?" Cain smirked at Marduk staring at Lilith with heavy-lidded eyes glowing with love-sickness.

Marduk smiled brilliantly at Lilith from across the room. She blew him a kiss, then went back to organizing the wine glasses and rearranging the place settings.

"She does now. Only took me 3000 years. There's hope for ye, Son."

Cain laughed softly and threw his arm around Marduk's shoulder. He felt the lifelong tension between them melting into an easy camaraderie that he desperately wanted to cling to.

"Have ye studied the dossier?" Marduk asked while refilling their glasses.

"Aye. She's got quite a record. I had no idea this dragon killed Mia's mother. Maddie. She was a good woman. She liked me, for some strange reason. Mia and Killian were broken after her death." Cain sighed heavily and drained his Scotch. He was the one who held up Killian and Mia after Maddie's murder, and Cain was itching to avenge them as well as Marduk. He was formulating an intricate plan that he was bursting to share with his father. Cain wanted Marduk's approval more than anything, and was ecstatically happy to have this secret project connecting them. It was the first time in his life that he shared secrets with his father.

"I imagine Maddie suffered more than was necessary because of her beliefs and her open practice of them. Avenge her before ye avenge me. I survived." Marduk drank another shot of whiskey, filled two more glasses, then walked toward his first guests with a wide smile.

"Amon! I have never seen ye in black." Marduk handed him a glass of Scotch and clinked his against it. "Ye looked a wee bit evil tonight."

Marduk handed Makawee a glass of wine from the wine tray floating by under the hands of a petite brunette both he and Amon grinned at while watching her swinging hips as she sashayed around them. Makawee giggled and nudged Amon with her elbow. He blushed bright red to match his red mask.

"Welcome to the Onyx Lair, Makawee. Hurit is here tonight as well. She's dressed in native regalia, so ye'll recognize her." He lightly kissed her cheek and lingered to smell her hair, but he managed to maintain polite reverence despite the tingling under his kilt.

Makawee's eyes glowed with a bit of fear, but her excitement at being included in this wicked party was evident even beneath her delicate lace mask.

"Your Lair is magnificent, Marduk. It is the most wicked thing I had ever seen!" Makawee said with a small, nervous giggle, then shivered visibly as she sipped her wine.

Amon chuckled and leaned into Makawee with a gentle kiss on her temple. She was dressed in a black silk gown that hugged her lean torso and fanned out into a flowing skirt that billowed when she walked. She'd never felt so beautiful in her entire life.

Amon wore a black hooded robe with a red leather mask in the shape of a phoenix. Amon was obviously dressed as his grandfather; Marduk was dressed as Omega. Marduk was a bit unnerved that Cain was dressed like him, but he chalked it up to Cain's twisted way of burying his childhood fantasy of killing him. He was, after all, still alive and breathing.

"How did you recognize us, Marduk? We are wearing masks," Amon chuckled.

"Ye're the biggest beast in the room. I would know ye anywhere. Where are yer sons?" He looked behind him and saw Lugh and Aaden bouncing into the room with Killian and Jade behind them. Lugh was also dressed in a black kilt with knee-high black leather boots, and a simple black coat with an intricate leather hood.

Marduk looked around the room at the guest pouring in and noticed more than one guest dressed like him in black kilts and heavy boots. He felt a small shiver run down his spine as he wondered again if he actually survived the incident on the Mercuria.

Lilith glided toward her young guests with open arms and a brilliant smile. “Killian! Welcome to the Onyx Lair! Come, my love, I have so many things to show you. Come along, Jade, Aaden.” Lilith’s smile lit up the entire room as she proudly showed off her caskets and coffins, severed heads, and body parts to the young guests. Marduk watched her closely. He watched all the Dukes in the room watching her as well, and was relieved that she didn’t seem to notice them. She didn’t flirt with Aaden either, but Marduk noted Aaden’s eyes on Jade. He groaned softly before greeting Lugh with an outstretched hand and a furrowed brow.

“Welcome to my Lair, little Lugh. Ye look more familiar than I’m comfortable with,” Marduk said grimly.

“It’s my way of honoring your return to life from the dead realm, Marduk. Ye’re both my favorite dead and my favorite living Incubus,” Lugh said with a mischievous grin as he clapped Marduk on the back.

“More than one of ye had the same thought. I am alive, aren’t I?” Marduk wrinkled his brow quizzically and groaned when more guests entered the Dining Hall in black leather kilts and thick black boots.

“Aye, ye twisted fucker. Ye cheated death. This is our way of honoring ye.”

“To honor a dead King who still lives is more twisted than anything I’ve ever done,” Marduk replied solemnly and lifted his mask higher to kiss Lugh tenderly on the lips. “Let me get ye a drink, lad. Amon, Makawee, make yerselves at home. We have food, wine, lovely lasses, and loads of wicked things to fuel yer chill, Makawee.” Marduk clapped Amon on the back, and noticed his eyes on Lilith. He growled and nudged Amon out of his intense stare. "My wife is stunning tonight, isn't she?" Marduk asked proudly, but with a warning stare that Amon didn't even notice.

"Stunning as usual," Amon replied quietly before he led Makawee to the dining table with his head down. But beneath his mask, he watched Lilith gliding across the room gracefully while his heart pounded in his ears.

Lugh smiled and pulled back his leather hood as he draped his arm across Marduk's shoulder. "Aaden was freaking out a little on the shuttle ride here. He may need a drink too." Lugh chuckled, then waved Aaden over to him.

"Aaden is a fine lad, Lugh. Ye did well with that one." Marduk poured three drams of Scotch, and handed one to Lugh and another to Aaden.

"For fuck's sake, Marduk. This is the most crunk party in the history of parties. Ye got real coffins! And the severed heads look so real! They're fuckin creepy! Wicked cool." Aaden grinned, drank his Scotch in one swallow, then held the glass out for more.

Marduk laughed wickedly as he refilled his glass. "Aaden, ye're more like yer Uncle Marduk than ye know, lad. Ye should consider staying here a while. I have a project ye might be interested in."

Lugh shot Marduk a warning glare, but Marduk grinned devilishly and refilled Lugh glass too.

"Can I tempt ye, Nephew, into re-enlisting with yer son?"

"No. And don't tempt my son, either. He's only a lad, Marduk. Let him grow up, for fuck's sake."

"He's of age. The same age ye were when ye first enlisted, Lugh. I need Alphans on the team." Marduk lit another cigarette and blew the smoke from his nose. "The

Omegans are winning." He raised one eyebrow and took a long drag from his cigarette. He knew Lugh didn't like to lose competitions, and hoped he might rise to the challenge of his bloodline.

"For fuck's sake, are ye gonna tell me what this project is? This is the second time ye mentioned it, Marduk. I'm interested. And I'm an adult, Dad. I make my own decisions."

"Son, ye have no idea who ye're up against here. Marduk is the fuckin devil. He'll chain ye to that rack and make ye believe ye wanna be there. Don't listen to him."

Marduk laughed wickedly and clapped Aaden on the shoulder. "Don't listen to yer dad. He's jealous. Ye'll meet some fine lasses in this project, Aaden. All the sex ye can handle, lad."

"Marduk! No!" Lugh shouted, and pulled Aaden away from Marduk with a withered scowl, but Aaden looked back with shiny eyes and gave Marduk two thumbs up.

Marduk laughed again and lowered his mask, then moved toward Lilith, who was still rearranging the dinner plates. He wrapped his arms around her from behind and leaned in to kiss her neck softly.

"Is that my monster?" She swirled her hips gently against him and leaned her head against his chest.

"Aye, Lilith. Yer monster is alive." He turned her around and grinned seductively. Lilith draped her body against his and threw her arms around his neck.

"Hold that thought until midnight, my love," Lilith whispered seductively.

Marduk smiled and cupped her face. "I have a surprise for ye. At midnight."

Lilith laughed in a sultry voice. "We have been married 3000 years, Marduk. It is hardly a surprise anymore. Always a pleasure, however. But no surprise that your monster and mine ache for each other."

"My surprise is a little different this time. When the Dead Party is over, and the young ones go their separate ways, the King and Queen will also separate. I'll take the Dukes into the black parlor. Ye'll take the Duchesses into the red one. There ye'll find yer surprise." Marduk smiled at her wide-eyed interest and lifted his mask again.

"I cannot wait until midnight. Tell me!" Lilith teased with a brilliant smile.

"Dancers. Handsome lads. They will entertain the Duchesses tonight. The concubines will entertain the Dukes. One hour apart, then we will find each other again in the Maze." Marduk grinned wickedly when Lilith's jaw dropped open and her eyes lit up like diamonds in sunlight.

"You opened the Maze?" Lilith's eyes were bright with mischief.

"Aye. My gift to ye, Lilith. We cannot have a Dead Party without the Maze."

The intricate outdoor garden Maze was a wickedly magnificent addition to the Dead Party, but even more so for the orgy to follow. The Maze provided an exhilarating element for a stalking game and broad coverage for the sex games that followed once the stalkers found their prey.

"Is the hour with the dancers free time?" Lilith asked slyly.

"For fuck's sake, Lilith." Marduk threw back his head and groaned. "Ye can look. Ye can touch. But the dancers cannot touch my wife. They have been warned," Marduk said ominously.

Lilith grinned playfully. “That leaves a wild swath of imagination, Marduk. Looking and touching. And the Maze?” Her eyes shined again and momentarily blinded Marduk. He didn’t see the arrow coming right at him until he was stung.

Marduk kissed her softly on her full cherry lips, then grinned mischievously. “The Maze is the Maze. The first Duke to catch ye, is yers. For one night only.” He growled softly in her ear and rubbed his beard gently across her cheek. “Enjoy yer surprise, my love,” he whispered with a sly grin.

“The Duchesses and I thank you.” Lilith curtsied gracefully, never taking her eyes off Marduk until she spotted an unmasked beauty leading the Duchesses of Críoch toward the Dining Hall. “What is she doing here?” Lilith asked angrily.

Marduk turned to see Hecaté standing in the doorway, in an elegant plum-colored cape, waiting to be greeting by her hosts. “I invited her, Lilith. I invited all the Duchesses of Críoch, and their offspring of reasonable age. Ah, they brought the lad and the redheads.” He grinned crookedly, and looked around for Killian. Marduk motioned toward the girls and Scotch, who looked bored to death already. His eyes lit up, however, when he saw Killian, Jade, and Aaden sprinting toward him.

“I have no objection to your sisters, nor Amon’s. Apart from one,” Lilith answered coldly with a slight pout.

Marduk tried to hide his grin, to no avail, as he gave Hecaté and Delphi thorough head-to-toe scans. He’d always been intrigued by the divergent eccentricities of the Alphan Princesses. No two of them were alike in looks nor mannerisms.

"Hecaté deserves a night of fun, my love. After 3000 years in exile with Lucian, she deserves a night in the Maze more than any of the Duchesses. She's no threat to us, Lilith."

Lilith set her jaw and huffed loudly. "She is a threat to me, Marduk. Have you forgotten the spell she cast on me all those years ago?"

Marduk pulled her close and kissed her temple. "I broke that spell, *mo ghrá gheal*. Hecaté is no match for yer devilish husband."

"Just to be clear…I am vetoing her, before you even ask." Lilith huffed again and smoothed her dress in quick, angry movements. "She will not be your third loophole, Marduk."

Marduk glanced back at Hecaté with squinted eyes and a mysterious smile. "The thought never crossed my mind," he lied, then sauntered toward the Duchesses with Lilith in tow.

"Welcome home, Lucina!" Marduk bellowed, then hugged his rigid, too-thin sister tightly.

"No need to crush me, Marduk. I do not have enough flesh on my body to shield me from your wicked grasp," she balked immediately and pulled away from him.

Marduk was stung by her cold greeting, but not surprised. She was Lucian's twin, and had always been his most loyal ally. The two of them were always allied against Marduk in their youth.

Marduk took in a deep breath and turned to the Alphan sisters. He found much more warmth in their eyes.

"Welcome back to Dorcha, Hecaté. Delphi, ye're stunning in red, lass." Marduk grinned devilishly at Delphi.

"Marduk, Son of Omega you are the most handsome devil I have ever known in all my life," Delphi said in a high-pitched voice that made Marduk chuckle immediately.

"Delphi…ye flatter me, lass. Everyone knows Seth is the most handsome of the Omegan brothers."

"Aye, my Seth is handsome, but he does not have your charm," she replied as she sidled up to Marduk and lightly ran her hand over his kilt.

Marduk didn't even flinch when her hand slipped under his kilt. "Still keeping the charms hanging, Delphi." He winked and bit his lip as he gave Delphi another thorough perusal. "Is Cadenza joining us?" Marduk said as wicked plots of revenge against his brothers began to form in his head. He had to work hard to keep them at bay, especially with Delphi's hand on his thigh, and Hecaté's violet eyes locked on his billowing kilt.

Delphi pulled her hand back and sighed as though bored with the party already. "She is such a prude, Marduk. She goes nowhere without her husband. I, however, am thrilled at the prospect of an evening without Seth standing over my shoulder. Where is the wine?" Delphi asked while scanning the room for the bar. Her eyes lit up when she spotted the heart-shaped cauldron. "Marduk, you are so thoughtful to invite us. Lilith, my dear, how lovely you look tonight! But you always do." She leaned in and air-kissed Lilith with genuine affection. "Let's catch up on our gossip later, Lilith. If you will excuse me, I must inspect that cauldron up close." She casually draped her cape over Marduk's outstretched arm, then flitted off to the bar without looking back.

Lilith cast a smirking glance at Marduk closely watching Delphi walk away. Marduk raised one eyebrow and draped his arms around Lilith's waist. "Veto?"

Lilith sighed heavily, rolled her eyes, and made a small check mark in the air.

Lucina smiled stiffly as she stepped up to Marduk again. "I hope you have enough wine to refill that cauldron, brother. Delphi will drink every drop of it before midnight." She briefly glanced at Lilith, lifting her chin arrogantly. "Lovely to see you again, Lilith." She turned back to Marduk with a cold, calculating eye. "I would like to have a word with you before I am sent back to the Citadel, Marduk. I will speak on my own behalf, not for Magdalia nor Shala. Neither wanted to attend tonight. Magdalia because of the child; Shala because she feels it would be a betrayal to Mahdi to attend a party while he is in prison. Personally, I have no such qualms, and beg you to keep Inuus locked away forever." She smiled a little less stiffly, then rolled her eyes. "But we are all anxious to know your plans for us." Her hardened face softened instantly when she scanned the room and spotted Amon, her first love. "If you will excuse me, I must say hello to an old friend."

Marduk lifted one eyebrow as he watched her glide toward Amon's bright red blush when he spotted Lucina approaching.

Lilith greeting the young guests warmly, pointing out the food tables, but gladly relinquished her hostess duties to Killian and Jade, who were holding court over the young crowd. She smiled genuinely at Killian's obvious comfort in the Lair. She hoped to find a way to keep him in Dorcha. He belonged here, she thought. Her mind filled with her own wicked plots to get Mia and Cain back together. Lilith was determined to get Maeve out of the Lair, no matter what. She would always be a thorn between her and Marduk, and right now, she had enough thorns between them. Lilith huffed loudly when she turned back to see

Marduk locked in a stare with Hecaté, her original nemesis, with a romantic gleam in his eye.

"May I take yer cape, Hecaté?" Marduk asked politely. He knew Lilith was anxious to see Hecaté's gown, as the two of them held titles of best dressed Duchesses of the Colonies for thousands of years. Lilith and Hecaté's stylish flair was widely renowned, so was the competition between them. Neither had the majority consensus on the title, but it never stopped either of them from claiming it.

Hecaté pulled her cape around her shoulders and lifted her chin defiantly. "The Lair is as chilly as ever, Marduk. I would prefer to keep my cape." She glanced at Lilith and gave her a critical appraisal with pursed lips. "Lilith," she nodded reverently, but her disingenuousness was obvious as she gave Lilith a slow, disapproving perusal. "Your dress is…very…black," Hecaté said with a wrinkled nose, then regally glided away from her hosts with stiff shoulders.

Lilith let out another huff of air and held her hands on her hips. "She has not been here five minutes and has already insulted me! Why did you invite her here? This is my party!"

Marduk chuckled and pulled Lilith to his chest. "It's our party, Lilith, and Hecaté is technically correct. Yer dress is very black…which is exactly how I like ye, my love. Except when ye're wearing red." He laughed and growled slightly as he ran his hands over her rounded hips. "Yer dress is magnificent, Lilith. Every eye in the room is on ye, *mo ghrá gheal*…in yer very black dress. Hecaté is jealous of yer beauty. She always has been."

"Well…she should be jealous. I am your wife. Your Queen, Marduk. Something Hecaté could not manage to become, no matter how many tricks she played." Lilith laughed seductively as she pulled Marduk closer for a steamy kiss. “But she should be masked, just like everyone else. I happen to have a few old masks lying around. The old masks will suit your old love well,” Lilith said in a triumphant tone.

Marduk chuckled again and shook his head slowly. “I’ve had only one love my entire life, and Hecaté is not her.”

“Oh? And who might that one love be, Marduk? Am I familiar with this lass who occupies your heart?” Lilith smiled seductively and raised her chin.

“Aye, Lilith. Ye should be very familiar with my one and only love, as much time as ye spend in the mirror.” He raised one eyebrow and leaned down to kiss her tenderly.

“You say the most wickedly romantic things to me.”

Marduk and Lilith held each other tightly as they strolled through the guests, making small talk and offering drinks to their black-clad guests. They were the perfect host and hostess, each staying well within the lines of protocol because they finally found their footing in their love war. Lilith learned that loyalty didn’t mean she had to be restricted. She only had to work within Marduk’s wide perimeters, and put him first in line for her love. Marduk learned that by removing her chains to allow her the freedom to be who she was, she became loyal to him, to them.

It was the same lesson he learned with Bella, who was casually roaming around the room, dragging her black chiffon dress behind her while the guests made a wide swath around the roaming dress, marveling at the animated decoration that added to the wicked allure of Marduk and Lilith’s Dead Party.

Amon, however, found all the allure he needed for this Dead Party in a different moving dress. He sat back at the table with Makawee, sipping Scotch and watching every movement of the dress. He hated himself for it, but she was in his frontal view, his periphery, his sideview, and he even saw her movements behind him in his mind's eye. He tried to focus his attention on Makawee in her silky gown with her hair in an intricate braid laced with blue orchids. He even tried to distract himself with food and conversation, but every time she glided by, Amon's head was turned. And when she laughed, or moved around the room, his mind went right back to the curves inside the skin-tight mermaid silhouette of that very black dress.

Chapter Nineteen

For fuck's sake, the dress is humping me!" Aaden yelled, then pulled the moving dress away from him, but it came right back. "The fuckin dress is alive!" Aaden jumped up from the casket he was lounging in, but again the dress followed him and draped itself over his body.

Killian giggled and gently pulled the hem of the dress. "Stop it, Granny," he whispered.

Dis boy is cute, cute, cute. Granny's getting her some of dat. Maddie whispered back then broke into wicked laughter.

Killian groaned loudly, then pulled the dress to the floor. Aaden still held up his hands to shield himself from the ice-cold hands running over his body.

I don't need da dress, Kill. Y'all can keep da damn dress. Maddie chuckled again and moved closer to Aaden. *Dis boy here is mines.*

Killian groaned again and threw his arms around Aaden's shoulders, then pulled him close to his chest. "It isn't the dress that's alive, Aaden. C'mon. Let me get you outta here before you end up scarred for life." Killian swatted the air around him playfully, then pulled Aaden back into the crowd.

"Behave yourself," he whispered to the air behind him, then breathed a small sigh when he heard Maddie's laughter fading away as the dress began to move slowly in a different direction.

Marduk turned to see the young men struggling with the roaming dress and chuckled in a groaning sound as he marched toward the dress.

"Stop humping the guests, Bella. Ye'll have yer chance in the Maze, lass." When Bella didn't answer, Marduk felt a cold chill run down his spine. "Bella?"

Guess again. Maddie answered in a chuckle, and suddenly appeared inches away from Marduk's face. He stiffened and took in a sharp intake of breath.

"Madeline?"

How you know my name?

"Not my first Dead Party. Welcome to Dorcha. Can I do anything to make ye comfortable, lass?" He looked around the room to make certain no one was listening.

You can catch dat red devil dat killed me.

"I'm on her trail as we speak. What can ye tell me about her?"

I can tell ya everything. But where's the fun in dat?" Maddie laughed eerily, then ran her fingers across Marduk's beard. *Tomorrow…when you not drunk, remind yourself to remember that you already know what's up with da red devil, Marduk.* She tapped him in the middle of his forehead and clicked her tongue. *I thought you was smarter than dis.*

Marduk scowled slightly as he pulled away from Maddie's icy hands, then lit a cigarette. "Madeline, I hate to ask ye this, but I have to. Are ye the Voodoo Priestess who turned my son over to Lucian? Ogoun, as ye call him."

Yep. Dat was me. I didn't know dat son of a bitch wasn't da real thing. He lied to me.

"Did ye hurt my son." Marduk stiffened and took a long drag from his cigarette. Maddie leaned closer and took in a deep breath.

Hell nah. I brought dat poor boy back to life. He was broke in a buncha places. I healed him. He said his Papa was God, and I called the only God I knew. Maddie took in a deep whiff of smoke. *Blow some of dat my way, Marduk. I ain't had a cigarette is 3 years. I was smokin one when dat bitch caught me. Stepped outside for a five-minute smoke, and bam…bitch hit me over da head wit an axe. I believe I was dead before I hit da ground. Ha! Cigarettes did kill me after all. Just not by cancer like everybody said.*

Marduk blew a long stream of smoke from his nostrils toward her and looked around the room again. "Can ye help me bring Lucian to justice? What information do ye have about his role as Ogoun?"

I got everything ya need, Marduk. You help me, I help you. Read da goddamn book Mia and Caraye brought wit 'em. Maddie took in another whiff of smoke. *Dat red hair you been looking for. It's in dat purse ya wear around your waist.*

"It's a sporran, not a purse," Marduk said indignantly, but grinned when the memory came back to him. He knew exactly where that sporran was.

Look like a fucking purse to me. Y'all look silly in dem skirts too, ya know. A man wear pants, not skirts.

"It's a kilt, Madeline. We're Gaelic. We keep the balls hanging."

Mmmm hmmm. I seen what's hanging under dat skilt. Keep dat thing away from my daughter. She ain't never goin' get over dat shit. Maddie laughed then drifted back toward Aaden. *I'm getting me some of dat before the night is over. C'mere, boy. Maddie gonna show ya something y'ain't never seen.*

Marduk hung his head and groaned loudly, but grinned again when he noticed Bella hovering near Declan and Caraye in a dark corner near the caskets and coffins. Bella was watching Declan wrap Caraye into his arms while kissing her softly along her neckline. For a moment, Marduk was reminded of Herne and Cadenza. He rolled his eyes and sauntered toward them.

Declan was also dressed like Marduk, in a black and red kilt, black silk shirt, and a tartan sash pinned to his shoulder with the Omegan brooch. Declan was dressed like a young Marduk. He wore a black dragon mask, similar to Marduk's, but with smaller horns.

Caraye was stunning in a black chiffon and lace gown with a beaded empire waist, off the shoulder scalloped neckline, and a black hood covering her shoulders, neck, and hair. Her delicate lace mask held a single red rosebud at her left temple.

"Ye remind me of my little brother, Declan. He's always in dark corners whispering to his wife, too. Next thing ye know, the two of ye will dress alike and speak to each other in poetry." Marduk sauntered toward them with a playful smirk. "Snap out of it, Nephew. There's more to the world than your wife's lips and thighs." Marduk smiled brilliantly as he pulled up his mask just enough to show an easy, devilish grin.

Caraye was surprised to see him so jovial. She'd never seen a genuine, carefree smile on Marduk's face before. "Handsome devil when he smiles," Caraye whispered to Declan, then held out a graceful hand to Marduk.

Marduk lifted his mask over his forehead and gave Caraye a steamy look while kissing her hand. "Ye're radiant, my dear. Marriage, Declan, and the wee one all agree with ye, lass."

"Aye. My wife glows." Declan leaned in and kissed her tenderly as Bella touched Caraye's face. Caraye gently held her hand to her cheek and smiled at Bella's affections. Caraye knew the spirit was there, but she didn't know who the spirit was until she saw Marduk looking over her shoulder with sad, tender eyes. She knew then. Bella.

Declan told her the sad, twisted story of Bella's murder and Marduk's haunting. She was reluctant to bring it up, but Caraye wanted to find a way to connect with Marduk. He'd held her at arm's length since she arrived in the Colonies, but Caraye was unbearable curious about Declan's dark and savagely handsome uncle whose commanding presence never failed to send the Duchesses and Queens of the Colonies into a fluttering tailspin. Caraye was no exception. Marduk's animalistic sex appeal, coupled with his confident authority, was impossible to ignore or resist. He was Declan's beloved uncle, who he admired and mimicked more often than not, and Caraye wanted to find a way inside Marduk's inner circle, as well as his heart.

"Bella has a beautiful spirit, Marduk. Innocent," Caraye said softly.

Marduk's face withered for a second, then he looked at her with tender eyes. He gently touched Caraye's cheek and recognized a kindred spirit. Caraye saw Bella and apparently loved her. That was all it took for Marduk to open his tight fold and let Caraye inside. He kissed her right cheek while Bella kissed her left. Caraye blushed profusely and smiled sweetly at Marduk, then tilted her head toward

Bella. Marduk heard Bella's soft purring; he wondered if Caraye heard it too.

"Aye, Arabel was innocent." Marduk lowered himself into the coffin across from Declan and Caraye and lay back with crossed ankles while lacing his hands behind his head. "This fuckin party is awesome. My Lilith did well." He grinned as he glanced up at Lilith gliding around the room with Killian and Jade. He was pleasantly surprised to see that she still wasn't flirting with the Dukes and Soldiers. He raised one eyebrow when he saw the haunted dress dancing and swaying in the center of the room.

"Mia's mother is enjoying herself," Marduk chuckled. "She's wearing the dancing dress right now. So, don't blame Bella if she molests your husband, Caraye." He grinned mischievously when he glanced at Caraye's surprised face. She smiled brilliantly when she finally found a kindred connection to Marduk.

Marduk's face flushed and his eyes lit up when he found his way into Caraye's good graces. She'd also held him at arm's length since her arrival. He thought she was afraid of the Incubi, the Colonies, and him. But the glow in her eyes told him everything he needed to know about Caraye. She wasn't afraid of anything in this world. Least of all, him. She seemed right at home amongst kindred spirits who communed with the dead while carrying them on their shoulders.

"Maddie's always been the life of the party. Alive or dead." Caraye's eyes were bright with unshed tears as she watched Maddie dancing in the center of the room with a crowd watching in awe as the animated dress twirled and twisted. "I'm glad she's here with us," Caraye added with a dreamy smile.

Both Declan and Marduk stared at her luminous face with the same shade of love in their eyes. They exchanged glances; Marduk nodded, then held one hand over his heart. Declan understood the gesture to be one of genuine affection and reverence. He once again breathed a deep sigh of relief over his dilemma. Caraye had Marduk's approval, and Marduk was a solid ally who held equal weight with Amon. With both Kings on Caraye's side, no one would dare harm her. Not even the Elders.

Declan broke into a wicked chuckle when he turned to see the dress following Lugh, who was dodging and swatting the dress away from him. "The dress found little Lugh. He's in for the fight of his life, if I remember correctly. I couldn't get her off me for days."

"Where is Mia, by the way? I haven't seen the lass all night," Marduk asked quizzically while leaning his head on his elbows. He scanned the room again, but didn't see her.

"She's well hidden. Nobody has detected Mia yet," Caraye said mysteriously.

Marduk's eyes lit up as he swung his legs over the side of the coffin. "I am intrigued. Is she the lass in the purple mask?" Marduk stretched his neck to get a better look, and nearly fell out of the coffin. He held himself steady with one foot as it toppled over, then leaned back and straightened the coffin with one easy and graceful move. Marduk's powerful move wasn't wasted on Caraye. She let out a rush of air, then giggled softly.

"No. She's better hidden than that." Her electric-blue eyes shined with mischief as she coyly scanned Marduk's long, leonine body that was finely sculpted with the most defined muscle tone Caraye had ever seen. Even Declan's magnificent body paled in comparison. Caraye had to look away quickly. Her hormones were creeping up her spine as well as her thighs.

Declan was mesmerized by the blush creeping up Caraye's cheeks. He didn't really mind the flirtatious repartee with Marduk, though it stung his heart a little. Declan wanted Caraye to fall in love with his Colonies, but not in bed with them. Especially Marduk's bed. No woman, Princess, Duchess, Queen or anything in between ever recovered from Marduk's bed. Declan was very aware of that fact.

"Is she wearing an invisible cloak? I've inspected every female here tonight. None of them are Mia." Marduk let out a wicked chuckle when Declan gave him a fierce glare. "What? I'm the host. I greet all my guests, personally." He raised both eyebrows and grinned like a naughty schoolboy.

Caraye fell in little in love with Marduk at that moment, mostly because she saw Declan in a few thousand years. They had the same wicked grin and naughty boy charm. Judging from Marduk's magnificent body, Caraye knew Declan would only get better with age. She liked what she saw in her future in that moment. Caraye looked from one to the other, and saw the uncanny resemblance in their mannerism that took her breath away. Then a small shiver ran down her spine when she looked at Lilith and saw a different side of her future being played out right before her eyes. She was witnessing the pitfalls of an eternal marriage that she and Declan were sure to fall into. But there was no turning back. Marduk never let Lilith go, and Declan would never let her go, either. She took a deep breath and shivered again, then held her hand to her belly. Another cold chill ran up her spine when she realized that even Rory wasn't hers. Rory was Declan's. She suddenly had an urge to talk to

Mia. She felt oddly out of place surrounded by Incubi and ghosts. She wanted a human perspective, a human touch, but she didn't want to break Mia's cover. Mia set a trap to see which of her potential lovers would spot her first.

"Is she the lass in white? Aye! Mia the White. That's her." Marduk grinned wickedly as he gave the lass in white a thorough head-to-toe perusal, but recognized Hecaté's long, slim figure instead. He gave her another slow and thorough once over, lingering on her hips. He grinned when he thought about the vacant spot on his loophole list. It would be the ultimate blow to Lucian, and would also keep Hecaté under his spell, willing to testify against Lucian if he did his job right, and Marduk always did his jobs right. Fucking and killing. He was a master at both, but took pleasure in only one.

Caraye squinted and sat forward as she also scanned the Duchess in white. There was something familiar about her that made Caraye shiver a third time. She knew it was a bad omen and turned back to Marduk. She drew in her breath, then sighed dreamily at his wide grin and sparkling eyes slowly perusing the mysterious white Duchess.

Marduk glanced back at Caraye and winked with a devilish grin when he caught her staring at him. His mind suddenly began to race with wicked thoughts and plots of revenge for old betrayals.

Caraye's dark thoughts disappeared with Marduk's playful mood and charming smile. "Nope. Guess again," Caraye giggled and Marduk did too. His boyish grin made her heart speed up, and her fears fell away at that exchange between them. Marduk and Declan's charm wasn't something that would wear off with time. She knew that she would love Declan throughout his eternity, even if he became fierce in public, like Marduk. In private, he would still be the charming and boyishly naughty person she loved now.

"Tell me who she is, Caraye. I cannot stand the suspense!" Marduk laughed from his gut, which was more than unusual for him. He scanned the room thoroughly, but Mia was nowhere in sight.

"Leave my daughter alone, Marduk," Declan said in a playfully adamant tone. He was affected by Marduk's playful mood as much as Caraye.

"She's a grown woman, Nephew. And it's a loophole night." Marduk raised one eyebrow and one corner of his mouth.

"Keep your hands off Mia's loopholes, ye twisted fucker." Declan couldn't help laughing at Marduk's excited grin. It was rare to see Marduk without his masks in public.

Marduk jumped out of the coffin and bowed gracefully, then held up his hands. "My hands will not touch her. I swear it." He laughed wickedly while he marched back toward the center of the Dining Hall, determined to find Mia.

He found a counterfeit Lilith instead and marched toward her with an easy swagger. She wore an embellished and beaded bra in various red tones, and a short, tattered silk hip skirt with a tribal belt covered in bells and silver coins. She tinkled when she swayed her hips toward Marduk, gracefully waving a black scarf behind her. She wiggled her hips in a playful dance that sent her bells ringing, and Marduk's kilt billowing.

"Ye've awakened the monster, Erin."

"The monster never sleeps. I have been to many of your orgies, Marduk." She wrapped the scarf around his neck and smiled seductively. "You remembered my name," she whispered softly before pulling him closer for a kiss.

Marduk obliged her with a sensual kiss while running his hands along her skirt and beneath it. He growled softly when he discovered her firm, bare bottom under the skirt.

"Bold as fuckin brass, Erin." Marduk guided her into an alcove and pulled her into a savage kiss that left Erin panting breathlessly when he pulled away from her slowly. "Ye're on my list tonight, lass. My wife would also like to add ye to her list." Marduk cupped a double handful of her bare bottom and growled loudly as his temptation to pull her under his kilt grew.

"Are you inviting me into the private bed chambers of Marduk and Lilith?" Erin asked excitedly. No one had ever been in the same bed with both Marduk and Lilith, at the same time.

Marduk lowered her skirt and pulled away from her with a slight scowl. Although Marduk loved bold lasses, he didn't like it when they overstepped their boundaries and assumed something more than what he was offering.

"I'm inviting ye into my bed, Erin. My wife would like ye to be in hers as well. If my wife wants us both in her bed at the same time, I'm willing to oblige her. But that will be her decision. Not mine. Not yers. I will warn ye, lass. Lilith is my Queen. My only Queen. Lilith will never be replaced. Respect her. Respect our marriage, and do not cross the lines between me and my wife." He paused and gave her a slow body scan, then narrowed his eyes at her and sucked his teeth with a slight hiss. "I demand loyalty, Erin. If ye're in my bed, no other lads will be in yers. Including my son," he said in a stern voice that sent shivers up Erin's spine. His eyes were the palest shade of green she'd ever seen, piercing a hole right through her in this moment. Erin knew she was about to make the deal of a lifetime, the proposition she'd been waiting to hear for nearly ten years to the day of her first week of debauchery in the Onyx Lair. She became a standard fixture at Marduk's orgies, but he'd never taken notice of her until now.

"Aye, Marduk. I am your loyal concubine. Lilith's as well." Erin curtsied solemnly, then grinned seductively as she made her way down to Marduk's kilt and lifted it slowly, but Lilith came around the corner of the alcove with her hands on her hips and her brows furrowed.

Marduk grinned devilishly. "Loophole, Lilith." He lifted Erin with one hand, then raised her tattered red skirt to reveal her bare bottom. "For both of us."

Lilith's eyes wandered over Erin's bare bits slowly, appreciatively, but she didn't like her in Marduk's arms, nor Marduk's hands running over her bare skin. She sauntered toward them with a sexy sway of her hips and a tight smile. Marduk's grin faded when he noticed her displeasure. He pulled away from Erin and marched toward Lilith with a wrinkled brow.

"What's the matter, my love? Ye didn't veto Erin. I secured her for both of us." He paused to assess her reaction and was surprised by what he saw. "Are ye jealous, Lilith?" Marduk grinned like a just fed cat as he took her in his arms.

"I am not sure I like this, Marduk. It reminds me of the silent years, when we were so far apart. I do not want to go back there." She let out a heavy breath and leaned her head against his chest.

Marduk held her tighter against his chest and ran his hands along her back. "*Mo ghrá*, we will never go back there." He kissed her tenderly, then grinned devilishly at her worried frown. "She's been warned that ye're my Queen, and she is to show ye the respect ye deserve as such. No one will replace ye, Lilith. No one." Marduk smiled boyishly as he placed a tender kiss on her tight lips. “Ye asked for this, lass. Live with yer decision.” Marduk playfully smacked her bottom, then walked away from his blondes to continue his search for Mia.

He turned the corner and ran right into Maeve, staring up at him with sad, teary eyes and pouty lips. Marduk’s firm resolve to ignore her melted instantly. His greatest weakness was a crying female. He simply couldn’t ignore her any longer. He opened his arms and enveloped her into them gently.

“Marduk, I am so sorry… Please forgive me, Marduk…please,” she pleaded.

Marduk winced and brushed the tears from her eyes with his thumbs, then pulled her into a smaller alcove. “Maeve…I don’t want to hurt ye, lass. I care for ye…very much. Ye and I shared a beautiful season together, but… it’s over now.”

Maeve began to sob loudly. “My father will not take me back, and I cannot marry now that I have been your concubine…I am ruined.”

Marduk groaned loudly and hugged her tighter. “It’s not as bad as all that.” He smiled genuinely and kissed her temple, then looked around quickly to make sure Lilith wasn’t around. “Cain is quite smitten with ye, lass. He wants ye as his concubine, and I’ve given him free rein to pursue that goal… however…ye cannot remain in the Lair, Maeve.”

“Where will I go?” she sobbed. “I have no place to live except the gardens of Dorcha with no roof over my head. Please, Marduk…I learned my lesson. I will be loyal to you. Please do not throw me away.”

Marduk’s heart melted as guilt overtook him. He knew he’d used Maeve for his own end game with Lilith, and knew he had to make amends for that now. "Maeve, my beautiful little lass…don't cry. I will take care of ye. Ye served yer King well, Maeve, and I will provide ye a home of yer own. A household staff…and a pension so that ye no longer have to rely upon yer father, nor Cain…nor me."

"But I want you, Marduk…I want what we once had. I was fooled by Cain. He swore to me that you gave us permission…I would have never even kissed him otherwise."

"Maeve, no matter what Cain may have told ye, I warned ye, lass…I warned ye that I would not tolerate disloyalty. In no uncertain terms, I told ye…no lads in yer bed if ye want to remain in mine. Ye broke my trust, Maeve. That's an unpardonable offense in my eyes," Marduk said softly, but in a stern voice that left no room for interpretation.

"Can you not find it in your heart to forgive me? I love you, Marduk. I hoped I would be your Queen," she sobbed and clung to him harder.

Marduk hung his head and gently peeled her arms from his neck. "Maeve…stop. Get ahold of yourself, lass. I am sorry that ye were hurt from our affair. I was hurt as well." He winced and scowled slightly. "But all that is beside the point. The point is…my son loves ye, but my wife hates ye. They both win. Ye and I are done, lass. No, no, no…dry those tears, Maeve," Marduk offered in a soothing voice. "Ye won't be left in the cold without a roof over yer head, I swear it."

"I love you, Marduk," Maeve sobbed loudly. "Cain loves me, aye, but he will never marry me."

"I am offering ye an opportunity to take care of yerself without marriage. Ye'll be free, Maeve. Ye'll have yer own home, yer own allowance, and ye'll be free to take any lover ye want…except me. I am no longer available. Take me off yer list and out of yer heart. Give that love to my son instead. Better still…give the love to yerself. Ye deserve love, Maeve. But I cannot give ye that. I love my wife. Lilith will always be my Queen. My only Queen."

Maeve cried softly against his chest while Marduk held her silently.

"I am so very sorry for what I have done, Marduk."

"I know, Maeve. I'm sorry as well." He smiled and brushed the hair from her face. "Ye and I had loads of fun together, lass. Ye'll always be special to me, but…my wife is alone in my heart. She's…everything to me, Maeve. I cannot live without her, and no one is capable of replacing Lilith in my life. Take the gift I am offering ye, Maeve."

Maeve nodded slowly. She was reluctant to agree, but she knew this was the best offer she could hope for. "I would rather have you than all the lads in Tosú-Críoch and all the houses here as well…but I will accept your gift because I have no choice," she replied tearfully.

"There's a good lass. I will provide well for ye, Maeve…and…" he pulled her close to his chest and lowered his mouth over hers tenderly. "Thank ye, Maeve. Ye were the most loving, kind, and beautiful concubine I've ever had. Ye restored my old black heart when it was in pieces." He smiled sadly and kissed her forehead softly. "I do care for ye, Maeve. We had our own brand of love, but I am in love Lilith. I love Cain as well. Make him happy, if it makes ye happy," he whispered hoarsely as he ran his hands through her hair.

Maeve wiped away her tears and nodded solemnly. "Aye, my liege. I will do as ye command."

Marduk groaned and held her at arm's length. "I have only one command, Maeve. Live as ye choose, not as ye're commanded. Alright, lass? Can we step past this?"

Maeve nodded slowly and sadly, but still clung to his arm.

Marduk leaned in for another tender kiss. "I will have General Draco make arrangements for ye straight away. Ye'll not spend a single night without a roof over your head."

"Thank you, Marduk. You are a great King." She bowed reverently and tried to smile, but her grief over losing Marduk was too strong. She cried softly as Marduk turned his back on her and marched back toward the crowd.

"I will never love another the way I loved you, Marduk," she whispered to herself, then jumped with a start when she felt a hand on her shoulder. She turned to Cain's ice blue eyes staring lovingly into hers. He pulled her into a small alcove behind the sadomasochist stage.

"Maeve…I know I will never measure up to my father in your eyes, but…I want you to know that I love you the way Marduk loves Lilith. I want ye for my own, Maeve."

Maeve melted against Cain's chest and began to sob softly. "Even though I am in love with your father?"

Cain sighed deeply and ran his hands through her hair softly. "In time, my love, that will change. Will you give me a chance to show you how much I love you?"

"If…if you marry me, I might be persuaded to change my heart. But I will not marry you unless I am your one and only, Cain."

Cain hung his head and winced. "Uh…well…about that, Maeve…" he began.

Chapter Twenty

Marduk breathed a sigh of relief as he marched away from Maeve toward the torture chamber in long, heavy steps, then shivered at the remembrance of Omega's primitive laboratory. He groaned sadly when he saw the lamb and chickens hanging from the meat hooks, half-eaten, with legs, wings, and chunks of flesh torn from each one. He ripped off a piece of the lamb meat, but couldn't bring himself to eat it. He tried to put it back on the lamb, but the chunk of meat fell to the floor, and Lilith's 13 black cats jumped down from their perches to fight for the prize. Marduk shook his head and groaned again, then pulled more chunks from the lamb for the cats. He scowled and patted the lamb on the hip, then wiped his greasy hand on the cats. He jumped slightly when he heard a woman's soft laughter behind him, but he recognized the laugh and turned with a devilish grin.

"Are ye enjoying the party, Hecaté?" The twinkle in his eye was impossible to miss as he slowly scanned her body appreciatively.

She shrugged and rolled her eyes. "It is not my taste, Marduk. Too dark. Not enough conversation. Everyone is led by the smell of sex in the air."

"Precisely the point, Hecaté. It's Dorcha. The stately pleasure dome where sin is not only allowed, but encouraged." He winked and grinned.

"Your Dead Party is exciting, even without stimulating conversation. Especially watching you in the dark corners of the Lair comforting crying blondes. That was a very familiar scene, but this… watching you so lovingly caress the wee lamb. Is there more to that story?" Hecaté asked with a wicked grin. "Has Lilith driven you to whoring…and bestiality?"

Marduk grinned mysteriously and took one step closer to her. "I'm the beast, Hecaté, as ye well know. But I prefer naked skin to fur."

"Omegans are notorious beasts. You are still the King of them, I see." She tossed her hair over shoulder, then sipped her wine delicately.

"When I scanned ye from across the room, I thought your gown was white. Up close I see it is as silver as your hair, Hecaté." He took another step closer and pulled her hair back over her shoulder, then growled softly while draping it over her breast. "Ye're dressed as your mother, Aradia."

Hecaté nodded and winced. "Aye. I miss my mother terribly." She took another sip of wine and sighed heavily. "So, you have been scanning me from across the room?" She smiled coyly and lowered her lashes flirtatiously.

Marduk sucked his teeth, then grinned boyishly. "Aye." He leaned down to kiss the corner of her mouth softly. She drew in her breath and stepped back.

"I am your brother's wife." Hecaté raised her chin as she crossed her delicate arms beneath her breasts. "It is inappropriate for you to ogle me."

Marduk scanned her full breasts and grinned. "Don't flatter yourself, Hecaté. I said I scanned ye. I didn't ogle ye."

Marduk blew her an air kiss, then made his way past her toward the sadomasochist stage. He grinned and raised one eyebrow when he approached the bondage table, and his after-midnight plans flooded his mind again.

At the moment, Erin was in his mind's eye. He barely remembered her at his orgies, so he wanted to make this a night neither would forget.

Marduk walked past several couples locked in passionate embraces, and the sexual tension in the air turned up several notches as Marduk made his way through the crowds. He suddenly stopped, mid-step, and squared his shoulders when he felt the hair on the back of his neck bristle suddenly. He turned slowly toward the stage while his entire body shivered, then he broke into a wide grin when he saw one of the leather-clad mannequins lift a corner of her mouth, then shift her eyes to his.

"Mia Leblanc. Boldest fuckin lass I've ever seen." He slowly made his way to her at the back wall with heavy-lidded eyes and a confident grin. Mia finally relaxed her pose, tilted back her head, and stretched her shoulders before crossing her arms over her chest.

"I was beginning to think no one would find me." Mia flashed a brilliant smile and took one step forward. "I've been here for hours. I know all the good gossip," she chuckled, and held a sexy pose in her skin-tight, full-body dominatrix suit with a leather and lace corset that barely covered her full, round breasts. Her waistline was cinched with delicate chains and a skinny belt that held a pair of handcuffs and a small crop. Beneath the fitted corset, black leather pants clung to her rounded hips and shapely legs all the way down to her bright red 7-inch spiked heels. Her arms and hands were covered with black leather gloves sporting 13-inch leather whips at each fingertip. Her black mask had cat-like eyeholes, and two bejeweled horns above her temples.

Marduk slowly and meticulously took in every inch of her. He clearly saw every curve and dip of her body under the leather suit. When he looked up into her eyes again with heavy-lidded admiration and undisguised passion, Mia finally exhaled and took a step forward.

"I've been looking for ye all night, Mia," Marduk said in a hoarse voice as he approached her in a slow, panther-like strut.

"You found me. Or maybe I found you." Mia smiled seductively and took another step toward Marduk.

He stopped walking and waited for her to come to him. Mia did the same. She was determined to hold her own against Marduk's romantic charms. Mia knew she would be swallowed whole if she gave Marduk an inch of power over her. They stood firmly at this impasse and both held their ground.

"I know about Cain's wife. And his new girlfriend. He took Blondie into the gossip alcove to tell her about me…and the wife." Mia shrugged and smirked. "He'll never change."

Mia took another step forward and attempted to walk past Marduk, but he reached out and touched the back of her hand lightly. Even through the glove, Mia felt the heat of his touch. It was enough to make her stop, but she didn't look at him. She lifted her chin and walked past him without saying another word.

Marduk turned to watch her walk away. He grinned devilishly at her curvy backside and long legs strutting so elegantly in her leather body suit. He took a deep breath and followed those red heels. Marduk caught up to Mia in three steps, and pulled her away from the crowd into a dark, arched alcove lit by amber candles. He held her by the shoulders and looked deep into her eyes. He noted the passion brimming the edges of her cheekbones, the fire simmering in her eyes. He wanted to kiss her. He leaned in a half inch, but stopped and pulled away slowly when he recalled the words he'd just spoken to Maeve.

"My son loves ye, Mia. He told me so before I left on the Mercuria. The blonde is my fault. I introduced them in an attempt to bond with my son, and… he's under her spell for the time being. I'm sorry, Mia. Cain, like his mother, has no idea what it means to be loyal in love. Ye deserve better, lass. My advice to ye is to move on. But be fair, Mia. Ye can't hold nature against someone. Passion is natural, and something the Incubi do not apologize for. I'm learning this the hard way with my wife." Marduk smiled sadly and lightly brushed his fingertips across her cheek. His eyes were full of regret. He wanted Mia badly, but he couldn't hurt her more. She was already stinging from Cain's duplicity. He also knew that the passion he felt so strongly for Mia might be the final shovel of dirt on his marriage that he was determined to dig up from six feet under. He couldn't give up Lilith, and he couldn't give Mia what she wanted, loyalty. Marduk stepped back and resigned to take Mia out of his thoughts and off his list.

"He played me again, Marduk. I almost fell for it. But I didn't. Not this time. I knew there was another woman here, but I didn't know he had wife too."

"Samuel's mother. Hurit. She was a pawn in his game against me years ago. He's changed in many ways, Mia. But he'll always be Lilith's son when it comes to love. Move forward, Mia." Marduk leaned in and kissed her forehead tenderly. "I am grateful that ye and Killian are here. The two of ye are family, no matter what. Mia, I love my son, but he doesn't deserve ye." He smiled tenderly and leaned his forehead against hers, then walked away in heavy steps.

Mia stepped out of the alcove and watched him march toward Lilith. He twirled her around the dance floor with a dreamy, romantic grin on his face. Lilith glowed under Marduk's attention as she draped herself against his body seductively. Mia sighed loudly, then turned around to see Draco standing across the hallway, staring at her with a disapproving glare and his arms crossed tightly over his chest. He witnessed Marduk emerging from the alcove, and Mia following, with her heart on her sleeve. Draco blinked once, then looked away as he lowered his mask and stormed away from her in heavy steps.

"What? I didn't do anything," she said to herself. "This party blows. Where's Caraye?" Mia stormed across the room in her own heavy steps. She found Declan and Caraye still huddled together in the same arched alcove, kissing and holding each other up like brush strokes in a masterpiece, fingers and arms laced together to create the perfect frame of an exalted image of love.

"Break it up, y'all. Mia's been outed," she said sarcastically, then threw herself heavily into the coffin Marduk had just been lying in. She sighed loudly as she angrily twisted the leather strips on her fingertips that she suddenly wanted to use on Cain and his blonde girlfriend.

"Who found you? Lugh?" Caraye asked excitedly, then looked around the room for Lugh. She hoped to catch his eye to call him over to join them, but his eyes were on Aaden, who was following Jade around the room while Lilith and Marduk held Killian's attention in a friendly conversation.

"Marduk," Mia answered quietly.

"Oh no," Caraye answered back. "Are you okay?"

"Did he act inappropriately, Mia?" Declan asked while standing abruptly. He was ready to confront Marduk or whoever made Mia look so sad.

"Marduk only has eyes for Lilith. It's ya new best friend, Daddy," she said in her best New Orleans sarcasm. "Cain. He has a girlfriend. Concubine Barbie. He's always had a thing for Barbie dolls." Mia rolled her eyes and huffed loudly. "Marduk was just trying to explain the passionate nature of the Incubi. He was a perfect gentleman while explaining Cain's new girlfriend, and…his wife." Mia rolled her eyes and sighed again.

Caraye's jaw dropped. "His wife? When did this happen? Who is she?" Caraye turned to Declan with an accusatory scowl. She was certain Declan knew about Cain's wife, but kept the secret from her, as well as Mia, to protect Cain.

Declan squirmed and shifted on his heels, then held his hands up in surrender. "She's not actually his wife. He claimed her son and called her his wife, but he never officially married her. Hurit is Salem's mother," Declan answered in a tired voice.

"You knew all along and didn't tell us?! And now you're defending him!" Caraye yelled as she walked toward Mia. She cast a harsh look at Declan, then threw her arms around Mia and held her head against her chest.

"I'm not defending him, Caraye. What Cain did was wrong, but give him a break, for fuck's sake. He's had a very difficult life, and he's trying to change."

Mia pulled away from Caraye, and shot Declan a fierce scowl. "He ain't trying very hard, Declan! You are defending him! I can't believe this. You knew he had a wife and you didn't tell me!"

"She's not his wife!" Declan reiterated.

"But you knew about her!" Caraye yelled.

"Did you know about the concubine, too? The new girlfriend?" Mia asked angrily.

"I…may have… heard a rumor." Declan held his hands up and opened his mouth to defend himself further, but both Caraye and Mia were glaring at him angrily. "For fuck's sake, I need a drink."

Declan shuffled toward the bar angrily, narrowly missing Hecaté as she ducked into the dark alcove. She breathed a sigh of relief until she felt a cold hand on her shoulder.

You dead too?

"Dammit, Maddie…you nearly scared me to death! What are you doing in Dorcha?"

Looking over her like I promised. Is you ever gon tell her da truth?

"No. She'll hate me."

Dey don't keep secrets round here, sister. She gon find out, and she gon hate ya anyway. Seem to me you better off telling her yourself 'fore she hear it from somebody else.

"Why are you staring at my wife, Hecaté?"

Hecaté turned to Declan's angry scowl and winced visibly. "I was simply admiring her gown, Declan. I am quite obsessed with the fashions of Earth. Your beautiful wife wears that gown well," she replied absently.

"I will only warn ye once, Hecaté. Leave my wife alone."

Hecaté huffed loudly and crossed her arms over her chest. "Do not forget what I did for you in Marbh, lad. Without me…you would have no wife. No child either."

Declan marched toward her angrily. "I would have found her and saved her even without your machinations,

Hecaté. My wife is none of your concern. Stay away from her." Declan spat out, then marched away in heavy steps.

Hecaté opened her mouth to tell Declan the entire truth, but Maddie draped her cold hand over her mouth.

Not him, ya fool. Tell her first.

"I cannot do that, Maddie."

The truth gon set ya free. It'll set her free too.

Hecaté smirked and shot Maddie a harsh look. "That's exactly what I am trying to avoid."

You fixin to lose it all, girl.

"Go away, Maddie. I do not take advice from you."

Ya never did. Have it your way, but Imma say I told ya so. You can bet on dat.

Hecate slipped deeper into the alcove after Maddie floated away from her, but her words lingered. "Despite everything you have suffered…I am truly happy you found your way to Gael," she whispered to herself. "I hope you never discover the entire truth, but if you do…please forgive me."

Declan was still scowling when he spotted Draco at the bar wearing his own angry scowl as he glared at Marduk's back. Draco looked wicked in his black leather kilt, black turtleneck, thigh-length cashmere jacket, and black boots that shined like glass. He wore a black leather mask with dragon scales covering his cheeks and forehead, but the angry glint in his eyes was evident through the mask.

"Ye're bordering on Treason with that look, Draco. What did Marduk do now?" Declan asked while he poured them each a glass of Scotch.

"The same thing he always does. Putting his hand up every fucking skirt in the Colonies." Draco shot back his Scotch and poured another.

Declan looked at Marduk hanging onto Lilith's hips as though they were his lifeline and chuckled softly. "Marduk has all his hands up Lilith's skirt tonight. Who are ye talking about?"

"Your daughter. I saw them in the alcove. She will get hurt, Declan."

Declan clapped Draco on the back and smiled boyishly. "Ye're wrong, Draco. Marduk was playing the dutiful father in the alcove with Mia. Explaining Cain's wife as well as his new lover. Mia said he was quite the gentleman." Declan lifted his Scotch to Draco's wide eyes, then drank it all at once.

"Marduk was not making love to her in the alcove?" Draco asked hopefully.

"Aye. He was not."

Draco broke into a wide grin; his eyes went from bitter anger to absolute adoration when he caught Marduk's attention. Marduk nodded and grinned at Draco as he pulled Lilith closer to him.

"I misjudged him. And Mia." Draco drank his Scotch, then refilled his and Declan's glasses.

"Come with me, Draco. My lasses are angry with me. I think ye might be the balm for this situation."

Draco happily followed Declan with a wide grin. He grabbed a glass of wine for Mia; Declan grabbed a glass of ginger ale for Caraye. The two of them slowly approached the sullen women with sheepish grins.

"I brought a shield, so the two of ye won't gang up on me again." Declan gave Caraye his best puppy dog eyes as he held out the glass of ginger ale to her with a contrite smile. She rolled her eyes and took the glass from his hand.

"Only because Rory's thirsty. You're still in trouble, but you're just so cute in that kilt." Caraye smiled sadly while Declan approached her slowly and draped his arms around her gently.

"I'm sorry I didn't tell ye, Caraye, but it wasn't my secret to tell." He sighed heavily and buried his face in her hair. "Let's keep our pact, my love. No interference in Mia's love life."

Caraye pulled away and gave him a playfully fierce look with one raised eyebrow. "You brought Draco to her. You already broke the pact."

Declan blushed and grinned like a little boy. "He looked so sad. He needed cheering up." He kissed her cheek and assessed her mood thoroughly. She was still a little distant, which made Declan nervous. He knew there was an orgy planned after midnight, and he didn't want to be at odds with his wife when it began. His plan was to stay at her side the entire time to keep her from being caught by another Duke in the Maze. He knew the rules of the game. The first King or Duke to catch the masked Queens and Duchesses in the Maze had a free pass for the night with his prize. Marduk's strict policies for the Maze Game participants was that no one would be held accountable for the sex games that occurred in the Maze, no one unmasked during the orgy, and the identity of the secret lovers remained a mystery for eternity.

Declan also knew that as King of the Incubi, Marduk had the first run through the Maze and his pick of the Duchesses. He hoped Marduk wouldn't take revenge on him tonight for the 42-day affair with Lilith.

Draco held out the wine glass to Mia with a sheepish smile. She raised one eyebrow sarcastically and took the Scotch from his hand instead. She drank it in one shot, handed it back to him, then took the wine glass. Draco chuckled as he sat next to her in the coffin. He wanted to apologize, but he wasn't sure where to begin. Mia had him rattled; he could barely breathe.

"What you saw in the alcove wasn't what you think. Marduk was only apologizing for Cain," Mia said in a slightly huffy tone.

"Aye. Declan told me. I always assume the worst with Marduk." Draco sighed while eyeing Mia in a sideways glance. "I should not have jumped to conclusions."

"You have no right to jump to conclusions about me, Draco. You have no claims on me," Mia said a bit too harshly. She was stinging from Cain's games as well as Marduk's unwavering attention to Lilith. She'd observed him all night and knew Marduk was never going to give up Lilith. He might take other lovers, but Lilith would always be his Queen. Mia wasn't interested in being a concubine or side girl.

"I do not need a claim on you to care about you, Mia," Draco said softly, and Mia's angry façade faded. She leaned in toward Draco and smiled brilliantly.

"Thanks for the wine…and the Scotch. I really needed a drink. I've been standing on that stage for hours."

"I know. I spotted you the moment I walked in the door." Draco grinned and leaned slightly toward Mia to smell her hair. He blushed when she caught him sniffing the air around her.

"Pineapple and Lemon Verbena," she whispered with a sly smile. "Why didn't you say something when you spotted me?" Mia thought Marduk found her first, but Draco spotted her before anyone.

"The sight of you standing there so bold and brave, as still as the dead, was the most beautiful thing I have ever seen in my life. I could not bring myself to disturb the work of art you were."

Mia's smile lit up the corner of the room brilliantly, and her resonating laughter caught Marduk's attention. He grinned slowly as it suddenly dawned on him that Mia was the reason Draco was in a dreamy haze since Declan's wedding. He also saw a way out of his attraction to Mia. Marduk would never cross the line of loyalty to Draco, who'd finally found his lass with color in her cheeks. He breathed a romantic sigh as he began to weave a love spell for his faithful companion, his conscience, his General, his most trusted friend who'd never shown a moment of disloyalty to him.

Just then, the coffin tilted over, and Mia started to fall, but Draco caught her with one hand and held up the coffin in the other. Mia took in a sharp intake of breath at Draco's proximity, as well as his strong arm around her waist.

Draco didn't know where he suddenly found the courage to lean forward and kiss Mia with all the passion he'd been holding back all night while watching her on the sadomasochist stage in her skin-tight leather and lace bondage suit, but he was pleasantly surprised when she kissed him back with as much ferocity.

Marduk raised both eyebrows and grinned devilishly, then pulled Lilith into his arms. She looked up and saw Draco locked in a kiss with a mystery woman.

"Marduk! Draco has found a lass!" Her eyes were bright with romance.

Marduk leaned down to kiss her tenderly, then cupped her chin in his hands. "Draco found Mia." He laughed in a low tone when Lilith's eyes lit up further. She looked like an innocent young Princess in that moment.

Marduk could hardly breathe at the beauty of genuine emotion crossing her face.

"This is perfect, Marduk. How did we not see this before? Mia and Draco. I like it." She cast a mischievous glance at Marduk. His lost his breathe again, because he loved the naughty lass she just morphed into as well.

"I rather like it myself, Lilith. Draco has been asking for a lass from his own Tribe for many years. There she is." Marduk sipped his Scotch and chuckled softly. Lilith did too.

"This means that Cain and Mia will not reconcile, but Draco deserves a love of his own. Cain has Maeve," she groaned and rolled her eyes toward Cain leading Maeve around the room with a lovesick grin. "Let's help Draco along, my love." Lilith snuggled under Marduk's arm and rested her head against his chest as he pulled her closer.

"Ye're reading my mind, *mo ghrá*. I've already begun," Marduk said proudly.

"My romantic devil. I am so in love with you, Marduk," she said in an honest, breathless whisper.

Marduk leaned his forehead against hers and closed his eyes while he waited for his heartbeat to slow to normal. He brushed his lips against hers lightly, then breathed a huge sigh of relief. He waited hundreds of years to hear her say those words again without an ulterior motive.

"I have never been more in love with ye, Lilith."

"I look forward to weaving a love spell together with you." She smiled at him with love and adoration overflowing from her eyes.

Marduk wrinkled his brow and chuckled. "I cannot recall a single time in the history of our marriage when ye and I worked together. I like it. Play the game of love with me, *mo ghrá gheal*." Marduk leaned down and kissed her tenderly, then melted into her body. Lilith held her head against his chest and purred softly.

"For Draco. And for Mia." Lilith smiled sweetly, but in the back of her mind, she knew that Draco might be the only one to douse Marduk's obvious attraction to Mia, and Lilith wasn't going to let any lass get between her and Marduk ever again.

Marduk ran his hands along her hips, and suddenly wanted to call off the orgy. He didn't want another woman. He only wanted Lilith, and he was terrified that she'd find another lover tonight. But Marduk didn't want to douse Lilith's obvious excitement over the dancers and the Maze. He resigned himself to the night ahead, and wouldn't hold any actions against her as the rules of his game directed.

"Five minutes to midnight, Lilith," Marduk whispered, then growled against her grinning lips.

Chapter Twenty-One

Lilith huffed loudly when the dancers twirled and sashayed into the room, swaying their hips in silky skirts lined with tinkling bells. Their full breasts were overflowing from their tight, bejeweled bras as they shimmied their shoulders in the faces of the grinning Duchesses.

"Marduk said we would have lads! These are not lads." Lilith crossed her arms over her chest and pouted. "Marduk is wicked," she huffed.

Mia chuckled and leaned in toward Lilith. "Look again, Lilith. See that shadow under the skirts? Those are definitely lads." Mia grinned mischievously from behind her mask and settled in for the show.

Lilith's jaw dropped as she let out a squeal of delight. "They are lads! With breasts! Marduk is wicked!" Lilith leaned forward with wide, shiny eyes full of mischief. She was fascinated by the half-male, half-female dancers that she saw as ideal lovers. She caught the eye of Candy immediately and smiled seductively. Candy gasped when she scanned Lilith's perfectly sculpted cheekbones and full cherry lips. She smiled back and blew a kiss to Lilith.

Both fell a little in love with the look in each other's eyes. It was the first time Candy was truly appreciated for her uniqueness and her beauty as both male and female. Even though Lucian adored her, he still paraded her around like a prized freak, and he never looked at her the way Lilith was looking at her right now. Candy sighed dreamily and sent a mental note of thanks to Marduk. Lilith did too.

Delphi stumbled toward Lilith, incoherently yelling a stream of drunken mumbles and curses as she tripped and fell on the pillow beside Lilith. She laughed maniacally as her legs flew up in the air and her gown rose up to her waistline, but she managed to hold onto her wine glass and bottle. She pulled herself up into a sitting position, then draped her arm over Lilith's shoulder and poured a glass of wine for her, then refilled her own. "Lilith, you are the luckiest fuckin Queen in the whole of the fuckin Colonies! Seth would never allow me to do something like this. I must say, lass. I am green with envy!"

Lilith moved a bit closer to Delphi and chuckled with her in easy camaraderie. "Are you certain it is envy and not wine that has you green around the gills?" Lilith laughed.

Delphi let out a shrieking cackle and moved closer to the Lilith. "You are a treasure, Lilith! Hecaté and the other bitches hate you, but I never did. They hated me as well, but I welcomed their scorn. Their tight lips and even tighter cunts dripping with disdain for me and my wine was the only form of entertainment I had in Marbh."

Lilith chuckled and pulled Delphi in for a kiss on the cheek. "I heard rumors of Hecaté's too small cunt…so it is true then?"

"So very true, Lilith. The rumors are that she cannot even piss from it, and that's why her hair is silver!"

The two of them huddled together in cackling laughter that rang out above the bawdy whistles and yells of the Duchesses trying to grope the dancers.

"You and I should be friends, Lilith. We are too much alike to not be friends," Delphi said in a slur as she aimed her wine glass toward her mouth.

Lilith smiled as the idea rolled around in her head and she politely guided Delphi's hand closer to her mouth. "I actually agree with you, Delphi. It would be nice to have a friend. I have never had a female friend before."

Delphi finally found her mouth and slurped her wine noisily, then raised her glass to Lilith. "To friendship…but I must tell you, lass. I am lusting after your dancing lad there… and maybe even your husband a wee bit. But right now, your blonde lad with the swinging cock and bouncy breasts has me drooling…and not only from my mouth." Delphi screamed out a howling laugh that nearly knocked her over again.

Lilith laughed loudly and hooked her arm with Delphi's to hold her up. "We could be sisters," Lilith replied. "Aye, be my friend, Delphi. I will see to it that you have loads of fun in Dorcha. I cannot imagine how boring it must have been for you in Marbh, under Hecaté's rule."

Delphi groaned and drained her wine glass, then tossed it aside and drank straight from the bottle. "I prayed for death every fuckin day, but it never came for me. Wine was my salvation, Lilith. It was my only tether to sanity in Marbh. You have no idea how tightly Hecaté ruled over us. I never want to be under the thumb of prudish snobbery again." She took a long pull from the bottle of wine and handed it to Lilith. "How prudish are you? Do you allow Marduk to have lovers?" Delphi asked with a playful grin and handed the bottle to Lilith.

Lilith laughed excitedly and drank from the bottle. "Prudish is not a word I would ever assign to myself, nor Marduk. He and I have never restricted each other sexually.

We have an open marriage…but only until sunrise. After that, the doors of opportunity will shut for both of us. Delphi…" Lilith said in a more serious tone. "It is a loophole night tonight, and Hecaté must not get her hands under my husband's kilt." Lilith winked, then grabbed the edge of Candy's skirt and pulled her closer.

Delphi took the bottle from Lilith's hand and sighed heavily as she and Lilith both began to seduce Candy. "Best friends share, do they not?" Delphi asked in a high-pitched, drunken giggle.

Caraye and Mia were giggling like schoolgirls as the dancers moved closer and closer into the circle of Duchesses. Caraye blushed and tried to look away, but she couldn't take her eyes away from the beautiful she-males twirling and tinkling around the room. She'd seen exotic dancers many times in New Orleans, but these dancers were more beautiful than any she'd ever seen. This was the most wanton thrill Caraye ever had in her life. She loved that the Incubi explored sexual pleasures without repercussion or shame. Caraye had no idea of the sexual exploration that was about to come in the Maze, however.

"Mia! They are magnificent! Look at those bodies. Absolute perfection. I can't look away. I think Rory is looking too!" She giggled and leaned against Mia.

"If he's anything like his daddy, he's looking," Mia chuckled. "Damn. Look at the one in red. Oooo! That's the biggest penis I've ever seen, and she ain't even excited yet." Mia pointed toward Candy and fanned herself while Caraye squealed and tilted her head to the right to get a better look.

"Do you have a dollar?" Caraye asked Mia.

Mia smirked and clucked her tongue. "Girl, they don't use money here. What you want money for anyway?"

Caraye giggled and clapped her hands excitedly when one of the dancers moved in closer to her. "I need an excuse to stick my hand in the skirts."

"Sister-mama, just go on and touch if you want to. Declan will never know."

Caraye squealed with delight as she reached inside the skirt of the dancer in front of her, but she pulled her hand back immediately. "I feel guilty."

Mia grinned and nudged her aside. "I ain't got nobody waiting on me in the next room. Move over," Mia yelled.

Hecaté sat in the back corner with her arms crossed over her chest, glaring hard at the dancers with tight lips and squinted eyes.

"You are evil, Marduk. To flaunt Lucian's whores in my face. Now I know why you invited me. You want to turn me against Lucian." Hecaté let out a heavy puff of air and looked away from Candy. "You forget who you are dealing with. You think you know me, but I was only a young Princess when we last dabbled in magic together. I am no longer a Princess."

Hecaté grinned wickedly when she glanced at Lilith and Delphi touching Candy's breasts and running their hands over her thighs with a seductive smile. "You have your own disloyal devil, Marduk, Son of Omega. Perhaps I will stoke your devil's fires with my little magic tricks." Hecaté pulled her cape around her shoulders, then left the room quietly with her head held high.

All the other Duchesses yelled and laughed in bawdy voices, even Makawee and Hurit, who were shouting out native yells while they blushed and giggled like young girls.

The noise carried over to the King's room where Declan, Lugh, Amon, Cain, and Marduk all leaned far to the left in perfect synchronized timing with their heads tilted.

"How the fuck does she do that?" Declan asked in a high-pitched voice as he eyed Erin sliding upside down on the pole with one leg outstretched, exposing her entire naked bottom. She winked at Marduk and pulled herself upright before unclasping the front of her bra.

"Ohhhh fuck…" Marduk said under his breath as her full breasts popped out and bounced when she shimmied her shoulders. "Did ye see that?" Marduk asked with a wide, wicked grin as he settled back on the pillows to watch the show.

Cain leaned back next to his father and grinned at him devilishly.

"Aye, I saw it. I am Omegan, Marduk," Cain said with a huge grin as he leaned closer to his father with a proud glint in his eyes.

"I love bouncy blondes," Marduk replied breathlessly, then threw his arms around Cain's neck to pull him in for a kiss. "I want to introduce ye to the new blondes later tonight."

Cain's eyes lit up with interest. "New blondes? My interest is piqued, Marduk."

"They're very special. Very lovely lasses who are not to be mistreated or ridiculed."

"I would never ridicule a blonde lass, Marduk. I'm your son." Cain winked, then turned his attention back to Maeve who was staring at Marduk with sad eyes. Marduk smiled stiffly before he looked away from her.

"These blondes are both lad and lass," Marduk said more seriously.

"There are blondes in Dorcha that are both lad and lass? May I have them, Father?" Cain's eyes were bright with curiosity and excitement as he grinned and blushed.

Marduk wrinkled his brow. "Is that your taste, Son?"

"It's no secret that I'm bisexual, Marduk. I've never hidden that fact from you."

"Aye, and I've never faulted ye for it. I have no aversion to same-gender sex." He smiled genuinely at Cain. "There is no condemnation for homosexuality in the Colonies, Cain. That's human stuff."

"So…that isn't the reason why you and I never bonded all these years?"

Marduk's face withered into a playful smirk. "Son…of all the fuckin things ye did in your lifetime, having sex with lads is the last thing I would hold against ye. Ye were a snotty, whiny brat in love with my wife. That's why I never bonded with ye."

Cain hung his head and sighed heavily. "Plus…what I did to Arabel."

Marduk took a deep breath and draped his arm around Cain's shoulder. He lightly kissed Cain on the temple and sighed with sad contentment.

"It's past, Cain. We settled all that. There's nothing either of us can do to bring Bella back. Holding anger against ye for her death only perpetuates the tragedy…and my grief. And if the truth were told, I've had Bella with me all along."

"Aye. I see Bella's spirit everywhere in this Lair. I've tried to talk to her. To tell her…" Cain choked up and swallowed hard. "I want to apologize, but Bella ignores me when I try."

Marduk sighed noisily. "This is too fuckin heavy for tonight, but let me leave ye with one thought to ponder.

Bella does not forgive easily. She never did. She's my child from core to skin." Marduk chuckled. "Earn her forgiveness. Ye've earned mine."

Cain draped his arm around Marduk and smiled genuinely. "Am I dreaming?"

Marduk sent an air kiss to Erin before he turned back to Cain. "I never thought ye and I would have this opportunity, this moment to finally put everything behind us, even Bella's death, but here we are. Let's not fuck it up, eh?"

"Not a chance, Marduk. I waited my whole life for this moment between us." Cain's eyes misted over, but he cleared his throat and looked away. He didn't want Marduk to see his tears.

"Cain…it's okay to cry. I cry all the time. The romantic curse of the Omegans. We cry like babies." He shook his head slowly and ruffled Cain's hair as he chuckled softly.

"I don't want you to think I'm weak. I'm not."

"Why would I think that? Because ye like lads? That doesn't make ye any less of an Incubus, Duke, Prince, nor Man. Sexual orientation doesn't define ye. Actions do."

"That does not help," Cain said sadly, slowly enunciating each word. "My actions haven't always been stellar. I don't want them to define me either. I may never live down my past."

"No one does, Son. But it's those unstellar actions that makes us grow wise enough to change yourselves. As long as ye're alive, there's opportunity to change."

"Only if others let you change."

"True change comes with or without the approval of others, Cain. Everyone will have an opinion of ye. Those opinions are only important to the beholder, and have nothing to do with who ye are." He paused to grin seductively at Erin, and blew her another fingertip kiss. "She's got the roundest arse I've ever seen."

Cain chuckled wickedly. "I agree with you there. Best ass in Dorcha." Cain growled and crossed his ankles like Marduk. "So, when do I get to meet the new blondes?"

"Tonight. They're entertaining the Duchesses at the moment, but they've been invited into the Maze. The Dukes are in for quite a few surprises tonight." Marduk grinned devilishly.

"How fuckin twisted! I love it! That alone is worth the price of admission into the Maze," Cain said proudly with a wide grin. Marduk saw another small glimpse of himself in Cain and leaned a little closer to him.

"The new blondes are neither concubine nor slave in Dorcha. They are free. Let me warn ye, Cain, no one is immune to my wrath if any of them are mistreated. Especially Candy. She's special to me." Marduk pulled away slightly and looked deep into Cain's eyes to assess him. He liked what he saw. He saw an honest reaction, an honest emotion. Love. "Candy? She's in Dorcha?" Cain's face lit up, then he blushed again when Marduk turned smiling eyes to him. This was exactly what Marduk hoped for that night he discovered Candy's secret and decided to bring her to Dorcha. Still, he wanted Cain's full confession to his collusion with Lucian, and would dangle the new blondes as bait if he had to. He had to, so he did.

"Aye, she's in Dorcha. Ye know her, Cain?" Marduk raised one eyebrow and held a tight jaw.

"I met her with Lucian…many years ago. Is she your lover, Marduk?" Cain asked in a child-like voice. He hoped he'd found another connection to Marduk, but his affections for Candy were powerful and he didn't want to share her with his father. He breathed a sigh of relief when Marduk shook his head.

"No. She's not my taste, but I care for her, nonetheless," Marduk answered solemnly, then glanced sideways at Cain with squinted eyes. "Ye met Candy during your love affair with Lucian?" Marduk asked quietly.

"You know about that?" Cain drew in his breath and looked away from Marduk's sternly squinted eyes. "I hoped you'd never find out." Cain's eyes stung with tears.

Marduk leaned toward him and lifted Cain's chin. "I do not hold this against ye, Cain. I know how long ago it was. I only want to know one thing. Were ye forced into Lucian's bed?"

Cain shook his head wrinkled his brow. He hated that Marduk knew about his affair with Lucian. This wasn't something he would easily live down in Marduk's eyes. "I was not. And he wasn't my first male lover," Cain replied softly. "Candy was the link between us, so to speak." Cain blushed and lowered his eyes. "I loved Candy. Lucian was nothing to me. It was a drunken mistake…once…maybe twice. There was an affair between Lucian and I, but not love. My love was reserved for Candy.

"That's all I needed to know. If mutual consent was given, that's all that matters. But I still have questions. When was the last time ye colluded with Lucian? Do not lie to me, Son. I know everything."

"Then you know that I haven't seen Lucian since I was banished…except at the Banquet."

"Did ye have a hand in Lucian taking Samuel?"

"Only in arranging the marriage with Akaia before he met Issa. But I had no hand in Lucian taking him after his fall from grace. I had no idea Salem was involved with Lucian until they took my son."

"Are ye still plotting against me, Cain? With Lucian?"

"I am not. But I'll happily plot with you, against Lucian." Cain replied sincerely with tears in his eyes and more than a little guilt.

Marduk found the truth in the honestly contrite and penitent look in Cain's ice-blue eyes. Marduk smiled genuinely and held out his hand. Cain took it immediately.

"Tomorrow we discuss the Rebellion. Tonight is for pleasure." Marduk leaned back further and leaned his shoulder against Cain's. "Thank ye for your honesty, Son. It means more to me than ye'll ever know."

"Your forgiveness and your acceptance, Father, of who and what I am…nothing means more to me than that. It's all I've ever wanted." Cain sighed heavily as the last of his secrets lifted off his shoulders. But there was still one very large demon hovering over him, and even the 13 nearly-naked blondes twirling and tinkling around the room couldn't ease the burden of his unnatural attraction to his mother.

Declan and Lugh sat forward with wide eyes and open jaws while they ogled the dancers writhing and wriggling their hips in so many directions, they didn't know where to look.

"This is the best fuckin party in Marduk's long history of fuckin parties," Declan said with a wide grin.

"Aye, brother. These lasses are a sight for my sore eyes. I love my Maggie, but 13 naked blondes in one room is easing the pain of losing her," Lugh chuckled and clapped Declan on the shoulder.

"My wife's gonna get a load of love tonight." Declan grinned crookedly and leaned closer to Lugh. "Look at that! Did ye see what that lass did with the cheeks of her arse? Oh, I can hardly wait for the fuckin Maze."

"I like the one in red. I'm claiming that lass tonight." Lugh said as he eyed Erin with heavy-lidded eyes full of lust he hadn't felt in a long time. "I've never seen such a firm bottom in all my life." Lugh sucked in his breath and growled slightly.

"Aye, brother. That's a ripe peach of an arse, but ye might want to choose another. I saw her with Marduk earlier tonight. From the looks of that kiss I witnessed, she's in Marduk's sight as well, little Lugh. Find another blonde to lust after."

"It's the Maze, Declan. Free rides for everyone tonight. I'm staking a claim on Marduk's prized lass," Lugh said with a wicked gleam in his eyes as he stretched out his long legs and sipped his Scotch.

"Tangling with Marduk's lasses breeds a heavy fate, Lugh. Find another lass." Declan shook his head, then grinned widely at a golden blonde shaking her bells in his face. "Like this one. If I weren't a newlywed…" Declan's eyes lit up as she got closer. He sat on his hands to keep them off her naked breasts.

"They're all stunning beauties, Declan. But I'm taking the lass in red tonight." Lugh lifted his chin toward Erin with a wicked gleam in his eyes. Lugh grinned like a naughty boy when he glanced at Marduk and winked. Marduk squinted fiercely, then broke into a wide grin at the excitement he saw in Lugh's eyes. He wanted to bring Lugh back into the Incubian lifestyle after so many years of restriction as a man, even at the expense of his prized concubine.

Lugh finally caught Erin's eye and grinned devilishly when her eyes widened with interest and she moved toward him like steel to magnet. She shimmied her hips in his direction, then pulled his head between her breasts. Lugh let out a loud yell and pulled her closer. Erin began a slow, sensuous lap dance that had Lugh's cheeks bright red.

Marduk growled when he noticed the exchange between Lugh and Erin, then rolled his eyes toward another blonde dancing beside Maeve. She was staring at Marduk with open lust, and blew him an air kiss right before she unclasped her bejeweled bra and stepped forward. Marduk sucked in his breath and leaned toward Cain.

"Who is the lass in green?"

"Gwendolyn. She's a fine ride, Marduk," Cain said dreamily as he scanned her body.

"Have ye fucked all my concubines?" Marduk asked with a withered face, then turned back to Gwendolyn with a sexy grin when Cain nodded and chuckled.

"Aye. Every single one. Many times." Cain chuckled wickedly when Marduk squinted at him with a hard-set jaw. "Somebody had to look after the blondes while you were away, Marduk." Cain winked and grinned like a naughty schoolboy.

Marduk growled again and shook his head slowly. "I have been away too long. Time to reacquaint myself with my concubines and remind them who is King." Marduk blew Gwendolyn a fingertip kiss, then motioned for the girls to move closer to the Kings and Dukes.

Amon held his hands over his eyes, but he wasn't fooling anyone. He was watching the long legs and naked breasts flying around the room from beneath his hand with a silly grin and blushing cheeks. He finally lifted his hand when two of the blondes moved closer and wiggled their hips seductively on either side of him. His cheeks were bright red, but he couldn't stop smiling. He didn't touch them, but he watched every move they made.

Marduk nudged Declan, then nodded toward Amon. "Yer father is enjoying the show more than all of us." Then he reached out his hand to pull Gwendolyn down to him for a deep kiss. He growled seductively before he released her, then turned back to Declan, who was grinning and shaking his head at Amon's blushing cheeks and shiny eyes as the dancers ran their hands through his hair.

"I have never seen Amon in lust," Declan said.

"Oh, I have, Nephew. Many times. Amon hasn't always been unwavering. The two of us had more than our share of lasses in our days as young Princes. Amon was known as a beast in the bedroom. But Makawee has tamed him." Marduk caught Amon's eye, lifted his glass to him, and grinning wickedly.

Amon sat back with a cool smile on his face as the blush began to fade. He was thoroughly enjoying the attention from the blondes in each of his long arms.

"Only the fuckin devil can tempt Amon into an orgy," Declan replied as he shook his head slowly.

"The orgy hasn't yet begun, Declan. Amon declined to participate in the Maze. This is his breaking point. I will tempt him no further."

"I'm a bit concerned about the Maze as well, Marduk. I'm declining along with my father. My wife is pregnant, for fuck's sake."

"Oh no ye don't, Declan. Ye're not declining. Your wife will survive a night of sin. Amon is the only one exempt from the affair," Marduk said adamantly.

"I don't want my wife caught in your web of debauchery, Marduk. She's not like us. She doesn't know the way of the Incubi."

“It’s time she learns, Declan. She’ll be here a very long time. She should know what is acceptable, and what is not. I will not dismiss ye from the Maze.” Marduk held Declan’s gaze and didn’t bat an eye. “Don’t look at me like that, Declan. Ye owe me. Ye fucked my wife.” Marduk squinted and sucked his teeth with a small hissing sound as he glared at Declan with emotionless, colorless eyes.

Declan’s heart fell to his stomach.

Jade, Killian, and Aaden passed around a bottle of Marduk’s prized whiskey, giggling as the alcohol went to their heads. They snuggled together on a plush casket with Jade in the middle. Aaden wanted to kiss her, but he didn’t want to interfere with Killian’s prior claim as Jade’s date. Still, he couldn’t take his eyes from her.

Madeira and Sherry fidgeting anxiously across from them in a wooden coffin. The redheads sighed together in bored tones as they read each other’s minds, then raced each other to the bar, grabbing two bottles of wine before they giggled their way down the hallway toward the Queen’s den.

“Do not let Madeira get carried away, Sherry. You know wine goes straight to her empty head,” Scotch called out sarcastically from the casket he was sprawled out in, holding his own bottle of Scotch. He carefully eyed Jade and her suitors, then smirked wickedly when he easily read the love triangle. He had a sudden urge for a share of the attention and dove into a wicked game he hoped Jade would rise to.

“Princess Jade, you are the most beautiful lass in the room,” Scotch said in a droll tone.

Jade rolled her eyes and shot him a disenchanted glare. “Thanks, Scottie. That means so much, given that I’m the only lass left in the room.”

“Don’t be jealous of my sisters. Your lads hardly noticed them all night.” Scotch narrowed his eyes and shot her a teasing glare in return. “Both are fawning all over you in synchronized drools. Count your blessings. Two of the three lads in the room are in love with you.” Scotch curled up his lip in disdain, but the spark in his eye was evident. He got a burst of pleasure at Killian’s crestfallen face and was just about to dig his claws into Killian’s flesh when another loud wave of laughter and high-pitched screams floated down the hallway, breaking the tension in the room.

“What are they doing in there?” Aaden asked with a withered brow. “They’re yellin’ like bolloxed bogtrotters.”

“What?” Jade giggled uncontrollably. “That’s the most Irish thing I’ve heard you say,” she slurred, chuckled, and sipped the Scotch again. “I love Irish slang, even though I have no idea what half of it means.”

Aaden giggled and leaned toward Jade. “It’s means drunk country folk.”

Killian burst into laughter and leaned closer to Jade too. She reached up both hands and touched Aaden and Killian’s faces tenderly, but she held Aaden’s gaze. She was mesmerized by his sea-green eyes and bow-shaped lips, poised in a perpetual smile. She had to work hard to pull away from him, but Killian was pulling on her arm.

“Judging from the concubines I saw here tonight, I’d say they’re all getting fucked right about now,” Scotch added with a sly grin. “Those are definitely sex screams.” He took a long, slow pull of Scotch and growled slightly.

“I wonder what my mom is screaming about. Declan’s not in the room with her.” Jade giggled again and took a sip from the bottle of whiskey, then coughed as it burned her throat. "This stuff is awful." She handed the bottle to Aaden. He bit his lip, then grinned at Jade's withered face and flushed cheeks. He drank a long sip, then handed the bottle to Scotch.

Scotch grinned crookedly and drank the rest of the bottle in three big gulps, swallowing without hesitation. He grinned and handed the half-full bottle he'd been hoarding to Killian, then tossed the empty one on the floor.

Killian took a gulp and began to cough and gag. "It's like drinking fire," he choked out as he handed the bottle to Aaden.

"Ye're only half Irish. Ye gotta be a true Gaelic to drink Scotch from the bottle. Like Marduk. That fucker drinks it like water. Never gets drunk. That's a real Gaelic King," Aaden said with dreamy eyes as he heard Marduk's yell. He recognized it above all the other yelling and laughter coming from both sides of the hallway.

"They're acting like teenagers," Jade said with a chuckle.

"We're teenagers, Jade, and we're not acting like that. They're acting like drunk adults," Killian replied in a slightly drunken slur. He leaned in closer to Jade and ran his hands along her thigh, but stopped when he felt Maddie's hand on his shoulder.

Y'ain't in no shape to be making love to dat girl, Kill. And if I can't have Blondie, you can't have da Princess.

Killian pulled away immediately and jumped out of the casket to pull several blood bags full of wine from the ceiling, then picked at the food in the skeletons. Scotch jumped out of his coffin to follow Killian.

Aaden took the opportunity to plant a quick but thorough kiss on Jade's lips.

"I wanted to do that all night," he whispered.

She drew in her breath as her stomach tightened. Maddie saw the exchange and growled slightly before she moved in toward Aaden. He jumped at her ice-cold touch and nearly knocked Jade out of the casket, but Aaden caught her right as the casket flipped over. They landed on the floor in each other's arms squealing with laughter.

Killian dropped his blood bags and ran to flip the casket over. He winced at the sharp sting of the two of them giggling and holding each other intimately. The affection in Jade's eyes when she looked at Aaden felt like shards of glass exploding in Killian's gut. Scotch stood with his arms crossed over his chest with a small, wicked smile on his lips and moved a little closer to Killian.

"You guys okay?" Killian asked as he pulled Jade from the floor and wrapped his arms around her waist.

"That was wicked! Turning over in my casket while I'm still alive. Cool as fuck." Jade giggled uncontrollably, and lay her head against Killian's chest. The whiskey was going to her head, so was the romantic and heavily erotic vibrations in the Lair. "Thanks for rescuing us."

"Dude, what the fuck is touching me?" Aaden jumped again, then moved closer to Jade and Killian. "Let's get the fuck outta here and explore this wicked place."

Scotch's eyes lit up as he motioned them forward. "Follow me, humans. This was my father's childhood home. He told me about the scariest places in the Lair, and I'm dying to see them all."

Aaden's eyes were bright with mischief. Jade's were too. Killian balked at the idea, but followed Scotch as he led the way out of the room into the twisting, winding maze of halls.

As soon as they turned the darkest corner of the Lair, Jade spotted Raven wandering aimlessly through the darkness.

"Raven!" Jade squealed as she ran toward her with open arms. The two girls giggled and hugged each other tightly, both talking at once. "I haven't seen you since the wedding, and I miss you so much. Why haven't you come back to Gael?"

"Finn brought me here, and I didn't have a way to get back. I've been stuck in this fucking place with no one but Lilith to talk to for months. I'm so ready to go back home, or back to Gael, at least," Raven said in a dramatic huff.

Aaden squinted his eyes and smiled curiously as he moved toward the girls locked in an embrace and a jumbled conversation.

"Siobhan? Is that you? For fuck's sake! It is you! What are ye doing here, lass?"

Raven eyes widened when she saw a familiar face from home. Not New Orleans, not Manhattan, but Bethel Woods from her happy youth with her grandfather.

"Aaden Eamon? What the fuck are you doing here?" Raven asked with wide eyes as she ran into Aaden's arms.

"I haven't seen ye in years, Siobhan. How did ye get here?" He hugged her tightly and twirled her around gracefully.

"Damned if I know. I boarded a yacht, and the next thing I know, I'm in this fucking nightmare. What are you doing here?" She punched Aaden in the arm and laughed from the gut for the first time since she arrived in the Colonies. "Fuckin Aaden Eamon! Dude, you're the last person I expected to find here. How the fuck did you end up here?"

"My dad. Apparently, this is his home territory. I'm still fucked in the head about the whole thing. Even more so finding you here." Aaden said as he lifted Raven again with a loud groan. "Good to see a face from home, lass."

"You two know each other?" Killian said with a little too much hope in his voice as he watched the affectionate exchange between them.

"Aaden and I have known each other most of our lives. We both grew up in Bethel Woods. Haven't seen this fucker since middle school. How do you know Jade and Killian?"

"Long story, Shiv."

Scotch stepped up with a romantic gleam in his eyes as he took Raven's hand in his. "Scotch, Son of Seth." He lifted her hand to his lips and flashed a sparkling smile as his green eyes turned nearly white. "You, Princess, are the most beautiful lass I have seen since I arrived here."

Raven was immediately drawn to Scotch, despite his overwhelming and disingenuous charm, but she wasn't about to let him know it yet.

"Raven. Nobody's daughter." She lifted her chin and pulled her hand from Scotch's.

Aaden took note of the exchange and took a protective stance over Raven as he guided her down the hallway. "C'mon. We're gonna explore this wicked cool place. We can catch up along the way." Aaden threw his arms around Raven's shoulders and grinned at his first love, his middle school sweetheart, and the first girl to break his heart.

Jade felt the sting of the arrow pierce right through her heart at the sight of Aaden's arm around Raven's waist, as well as the gleam of romantic affection in both their eyes.

"Alright Scottie, show us the scariest room in the Lair," Killian said with a wide grin as he pulled Jade closer to his side.

"The scariest room is Marduk's bedroom judging from the screams I hear coming from there." Raven piped in.

"Aye, I imagine the screams of Marduk's concubines are legendary in Dorcha. But his bedroom is far from the scariest room in the Lair. Hold onto your balls, lads. We're going to the Dungeon."

Chapter Twenty-Two

Marduk proudly strolled back and forth in front of the Dukes lined in a sloppy formation with slumped shoulders and downcast eyes. No one wanted to catch Marduk's attention as he contemplated which Duke to pick for his game. As the King of the Incubi, Marduk had first run through the Maze, first pick of the Queens and Duchesses, and first choice of kilts to exchange with the Dukes. He also picked the order of the Dukes to go through the Maze.

Marduk's Maze game required every Duke to exchange kilts to confuse the Duchesses in the hunt. No one was to unmask, and each Duke was given matching black leather masks for the game. The intricately carved dragon scale masks covered the entire face, except the lips. The eyes were covered with black mesh, and each mask had small curved horns made of bone, painted red.

The Duchesses remained in their own gowns and masks, and had no idea the Dukes exchanged costumes before the game began. The idea of being chosen and chased added to the excitement all night long as the Duchesses flirted and vied for the attention of the Duke or King they hoped would catch them in the midnight Maze. Most of the Duchesses were hoping to be caught by Marduk. None of the Dukes, however, wanted to be caught by him. Whoever he exchanged kilts with would lose the Duchess they'd been eyeing all night, or worse, a wife.

Marduk grinned widely when he finally stopped pacing and waved one hand across the line of red-faced Dukes.

"Drop yer kilts. All of ye."

"Oh come on, Marduk…not again," the Dukes balked. They were mortified at having to strip in front of everyone, but Marduk was insistent.

"I am yer King! Drop yer fuckin kilts. I want to see all of yer naked arses," Marduk commanded with a mischievous grin. He knew that more than half the Dukes in this room had crossed Lilith's threshold, and he was anxious to size up his competition.

"The biggest among ye is my target." Marduk sucked his teeth arrogantly as he marched back and forth slowly with heavy boot steps that echoed in the arched holding room tucked away in the northernmost section of the Maze. The Duchesses were waiting on the southern tip of the Maze for Marduk to release them.

The Dukes shivered at Marduk's ferocity, still a collective groan waved through the line as they reluctantly stripped off their kilts. Declan was especially concerned when he saw Marduk's squinted eyes on him as he stripped off his shirt, then unbuckled his kilt and let it drop to the floor.

Marduk scanned each of his competitors thoroughly as he paced back and forth in front of them, measuring each one against the other. He was pleased to see that no one measured up to him, not even Declan, Lilith's favorite lover.

"Some of ye are more susceptible to the chilled night air than others," he chuckled as he strolled past a pair of handsome young Dukes who had been edging towards Lilith all night. "None of ye measure up to the Royal Dukes. My son and nephews have ye all beat." He grinned devilishly and winked at Cain who swelled up with pride at his father's twisted compliment.

Marduk took his place at the front of the line again, stripped off his floor-length jacket and slowly unbuttoned his shirt. He tossed the shirt on the floor, then unbuckled his black leather kilt and let it drop to the floor noisily.

"However… I am still the undisputed King of the Incubi. Never susceptible to a chill," he said a little arrogantly as the Dukes stared red-faced at the monster. He held his hands out and bowed to his audience with a wide grin.

One Duke started to clap slowly as he rolled his eyes. "We have all seen the monster before, Marduk. Must you humiliate us every fuckin time?"

Marduk shot him a fierce squint, and began to stroll toward him slowly without saying a word. His eyes said it all.

The Duke stopped clapping immediately and shook his head vehemently. "I am not interested in an up-close inspection, Marduk. Ye're the fuckin King." He bowed reverently. "Save it for the Duchesses at the South end of the Maze."

Marduk chuckled as he picked up his kilt from the floor. He hesitated a split second, then walked toward Declan, Lugh, and Cain with a mischievous grinning smirk. He stopped in front of Cain first and smiled proudly.

"More like your father every year of your life." He winked, then turned toward Lugh and wrinkled his brow.

"More like your father every day of your life," he said in a droll tone.

Lugh squared his shoulders and balled up his fists, but Marduk's face turned stoic; his eyes, colorless. Lugh backed down, but not before he gave Marduk a harsh glare as an obvious rise to Marduk's challenge. Marduk turned from Lugh toward Declan with a twinkle in his eye. He slowly scanned Declan's body, and couldn't help the grin forming at the corners of his mouth, but his squinted eyes were shooting amber fire when he met Declan's eyes. He broke into a wide grin as he shoved his kilt into Declan's chest.

"Congratulations, Declan. Ye're my target. Ye're second in line. Cain, then little Lugh." Marduk chuckled and winked at Lugh who squinted and set his jaw harshly. Lugh knew he outranked Cain in this competition, and the added insult of calling him by his childhood nickname stung deeply.

Declan was stung more than anyone in the line, however, and the sinking feeling in his gut made his knees weak. Marduk sucked his teeth arrogantly as Declan picked up his own kilt, shirt, and sash from the floor and handed them to Marduk hesitantly.

"Not my wife, Marduk. Please…not my bride," Declan pleaded.

Marduk squinted and raised one eyebrow slightly. "Forty-two fuckin days, Declan," he said ominously. "Tonight, we settle that score." Marduk's face hardened as he lifted his chin and wrapped Declan's kilt around his waist.

Declan groaned as Marduk sent the signal to release the Duchesses, then lined up the Dukes in order to oversee the exchange of kilts.

Marduk turned once more to Declan, staring hard with a wicked, mischievous gleam in his eye. He winked, then blew him an air kiss before he pulled his mask over his face and hair, then marched out of the holding room into the Maze, proudly wearing Declan's kilt.

Marduk strolled casually through the Maze with a confident smile. He knew exactly who he was hunting, and ignored the Duchesses peeking from behind the hedges and the grassy alcoves calling out to him.

Marduk stopped in his tracks when he saw Caraye coming towards him with a wide smile. His heart sped up involuntarily when she walked right into his arms.

"There you are," Caraye whispered as she glided closer and pulled him in for a kiss. She was surprised by the savage intensity of his kiss. Declan had never kissed her like this before. Caraye responded by arching her back and pressing her breasts against him. "I watched she-male dancers, and I am so turned on right now. Did I mention how sexy you are in that kilt?" Caraye ran her hand over the kilt, then reached her hand under it. She immediately drew in her breath sharply and pulled her hand away as though she'd been burned. She tried to break free from Marduk's grasp, but Marduk held her tightly in his arms.

"Surprise."

"Marduk?" Caraye asked with trepidation when she recognized his voice.

"The game is designed to keep the Dukes a mystery, lass. I wouldn't want to spoil the fun for ye." He laughed wickedly and ran his hand along her spine, then growly softly when he kissed her tenderly on her lips.

"I can't do this to Declan," Caraye whispered. She blushed when she realized that in this moment, she wanted to. Her spine was tingling from Marduk's hand, and the heat coming from his body was impossible to ignore. She was also intrigued by the surprise she found under that kilt, and had to work hard to resist Marduk's growing charm under the kilt.

"Neither can I, lass," he whispered against her cheek. "As beautiful as ye are, I cannot take ye from my nephew. I couldn't allow anyone else to take ye from him either." He kissed the tip of her nose and smiled sweetly at Caraye. "Ye're not my target, Queen Caraye." Marduk made a grand, sweeping bow. "Ye'll find your husband five rows over, to the left. He's the next Duke to enter the Maze, and he's wearing my kilt." He held one finger over her lips. "Shhh…secret of the game." He chuckled and cupped her face gently. "Caraye…your loyalty to Declan is admirable. I hope ye will maintain that loyalty throughout your eternity. Declan is all heart, lass. And that heart belongs to ye alone. But ye should know that Declan has a hard task ahead of him. He will need ye to stand as strong and faithful as ye are now, especially when his burden is heavy and dark. Love him through it, Caraye. Be his conscience, but never his judge." Marduk kissed her again, tenderly, then flashed a charming smile as he moved aside to allow her to pass.

"Thank you, Marduk. I will take your words to heart. Five rows over?"

"To the left." He grinned again, and watched her walk away with his hand over his heart. He turned to see his target coming down the path with a sexy sway of her rounded hips. He sucked his teeth and hid in the alcove to watch her from the shadows, then pushed the button to send a signal for the next Duke to come into the Maze.

Declan ran out of the holding room as soon the signal light flashed and the doors unlocked. He stopped short with a deep sigh when he saw Caraye rounding the corner. He lifted his mask to reveal himself when he saw the look of confusion on her face.

"I was afraid Marduk would catch ye before I did."

"He did." She glided toward him gracefully and fell into his arms easily.

Declan's face fell, and his eyes teared up. "Did he molest ye?"

Caraye laughed and threw her arms around Declan. "He didn't. But I molested him. I thought he was you…until I reached my hand under the kilt and got the surprise of my life." She laughed and blushed again. "Marduk is more romantic than I ever knew. He told me where to find you. He said you'd be dressed in his kilt, but…this isn't Marduk's kilt."

"Aye. I switched at the last minute. I think I was the only Duke in the room who didn't want to be in Marduk's kilt. The Duchesses will be all over that leather," Declan chuckled. "Fuckin Marduk is trying to tempt us into debauchery." Declan set his jaw hard and fumed at Marduk's ploy.

"I think he was trying to protect us…from something we'd all regret later. He gave me a beautiful speech on loyalty, and I kinda love him for that, Declan." She giggled and leaned in for a kiss.

"Protect us? How the fuck is he protecting us by wearing my kilt and tempting my wife?"

"Declan…he said he didn't want anyone to come between us. He led me right to you. Five rows over to the left, he said. He even told me what you'd be wearing. He was keeping us from temptation," Caraye said softly.

Declan hung his head when he saw the full scheme of Marduk's machinations. He chose Declan's kilt so Caraye would recognize him and he could direct her path.

By choosing Declan to go through the Maze second, no other Duke would have the opportunity to catch Caraye. A strong wave of guilt washed over him for misjudging Marduk, and for his betrayal all those years ago. The 42-day affair with Lilith was Declan's deepest regret in life, but never had it weighed heavier on his shoulders than right now. Marduk had the perfect opportunity to take revenge, but he showed love and mercy instead. Declan vowed to make it up to Marduk somehow as he leaned his forehead against Caraye's.

"I am forever in my uncle's debt." Declan kissed her passionately and hoped the response he received in return wasn't due to Caraye's brief encounter with the monster.

"I'm so horny after watching those exotic dancers. They were both male and female! Beautiful creatures, Declan. Take me into the nearest alcove and fuck me senseless," she whispered against his cheek.

Declan grinned widely and pulled the mask over his face again. "Ye should've seen our dancers. Those lasses were so limber! Lugh was smitten by one of them." Declan's full lips spread into a wide grin under the wicked mask that sent a jolt of erotic energy up Caraye's thighs as he led her into a private alcove. Declan noticed the look in her eye and unzipped her dress with one hand, then pushed the button to signal the next Duke to enter the Maze with the other hand.

When the lights flashed again, and the doors unlocked, Cain turned to Lugh with a wink and a boyish grin. "We both know it's a tie between us…maybe you're a little ahead. Half-inch or so. C'mon, Lugh. Let's break the rules and go together."

"Aye. I'm all about breaking rules tonight." Lugh grinned widely, and bounced his steps as he and Cain marched through the doors together. Lugh went left while Cain went right. Both had a specific target in mind.

Cain stopped short when he saw what he wanted gliding around the curve of the Maze, then set out toward her in long steps and a wicked grin.

"Finally mine," he whispered.

Lugh saw his target too, but was distracted by the shadow of another Duke stalking her. He was puzzled by this stray Duke. No one else should be in the Maze without a partner.

"For fuck's sake. Cain already pushed his button," he whispered in a huff. He pushed his own button to open the doors, then ducked into a shortcut in the hedges and doubled back toward his target in long steps.

Lilith glided forward in slow, precise steps. She stopped suddenly and grinned when she felt a strong wave of energy behind her. She knew she'd been caught. She turned and took in a long rush of air when she recognized the kilt her mystery lover was wearing. She scanned his body thoroughly, smiled seductively, then held out her hand to him. He reached her in three long steps. She was out of her dress before he caught up to her.

Declan and Caraye were deep in the throes of passion as Declan flipped over on his back and allowed her to ride him hard and fast. She screamed out loudly and tossed her head back as the wave of the most intense orgasm she'd ever had pulsed over her entire body. In Caraye's mind, she saw the she-male dancers, but the most prominent image in her mind was the monstrous surprise she found earlier under Marduk's kilt. Declan didn't care what drove her to such intense passion. He was grateful that she was spending her passion on him.

Lilith and her Duke were locked in a passionate embrace as he lowered her into the sofa in the alcove and kissed her body slowly, sensually.

"You were on my mind all night. I wanted no one else but Lilith," he said in a hoarse whisper.

"Marduk must never know," she whispered back in a sultry voice as she wrapped her long legs around his back and arched her hips forward.

"No one will know but you and I," he replied with a heavy heart, but roughly pulled Lilith closer to him, and began to make fierce love to her. Lilith responded by meeting him thrust for thrust, then screamed in the height of her pleasure. He growled and pushed deeper as he clamped his lips over her mouth gently.

"The entire world will know if you keep that up, Lilith," he whispered.

Lilith collapsed breathlessly against her mystery lover and smiled seductively. "The screams only add to the game. Everyone loves a loud orgasmic scream," she whispered breathlessly, then reached out to remove his mask.

"No unmasking," he growled.

She grinned and pulled her hand away, then bit her lip as she pulled him closer for another kiss. "My husband is fierce…he will have your head for this." Lilith teased as her breathing came in short staccato breaths.

"I will never tell him," he whispered against her lips as he pushed all the way inside and spilled himself into her in hot waves that drove Lilith to madness as she bucked against him wildly in her own fiery orgasm, bellowing loud enough to capture the attention of Mia as she anxiously slinked through the Maze with a heavy feeling of excitement mixed with dread. She was afraid of being caught, but more afraid of not being caught by the object of her desire. She took in a sharp breath when a tall figure stepped out of the shadows in the middle of her path. She stopped dead in her tracks, and watched her mystery lover come toward her in a slow panther-like strut. She was mesmerized by the swinging of his black leather kilt as he marched toward her with long, lean legs.

"You have been caught, Princess Mia," he whispered in her ear as he led her to a secret alcove and ran his hands over her breasts and hips. Mia didn't bother fighting. She found exactly what she'd been hoping for since the first night she landed in Gael.

"Can I get you anything, Lily? A cup of tea? Coffee? Gummy worms?" Samael asked as he quietly approached my desk. I hadn't spoken a word to either Samael or Drake all afternoon. I silently typed the story as they dictated, without personal commentary or questions for the first time since we started this project.

I shook my head and stretched out my fingers. "I need fresh air. I'm going for a walk," I replied as I sidestepped Samael. "Alone."

"It might be chilly. Take a jacket with you," Drake said as I approached the door.

"We're not in New York, Drake. It's hotter than hell in New Orleans."

"Can I come with you? I kind of miss the heat of Hell." Samael chuckled in an attempt to lighten the mood. It wasn't working, however. His voice grated on my nerves badly. I was sick of hearing it.

"No. I need a minute to myself. Don't follow me." I walked out the door, but knew both of them were on my heels. I rolled my eyes and sprinted toward the gazebo where Louise was pruning her rose bushes with an anxious scowl on her face.

"Hey Louise. Can I help with that?"

She jumped when she heard my voice and struggled to get on her feet. "Nah, these are my babies. I tend to them when I'm anxious," she answered sadly, then began to back away from me.

"What's the matter? Business is thriving. You've got your ghosts back. What are you anxious about?"

"Well, for starters…you in my face. Back away, Lily. I don't like it when people sneak up on me. Plus, I got a bunch of rowdy college kids booked for the weekend. I ain't looking forward to it. This place ain't set up to entertain that crew."

"I've got an idea," I said a little too loudly. Louise took two steps back and held up her pruning shears like a weapon. I looked behind me and chalked up her antsy behavior to Samael and Drake behind me. "Back off," I whispered over my shoulder.

"What the hell is wrong with you, Lily?"

"Wasps," I replied and swatted the air around me. "Can you make a maze from the rose bushes?" I chuckled.

"A what?" Louise asked with a withered face.

"A maze. You know…a series of paths with only one opening at each end. You block off some of the paths, so people get lost. Kind of. You have to retrace your steps until you find the right path to get out of it."

"Girl, you ain't right in the head. A bunch of college boys ain't gonna wanna play in that."

"They might if…."

"If what?" Louise put her meaty hands on her hips and pursed her lips.

"If the girls go through one end…and the guys enter through the other, and they stalk each other until they meet in the middle."

Louise stared at me like I'd just lost my mind, then a slow smile spread across her fleshy cheeks. "Lily, you got a wicked mind for a crazy person. I kinda like it. Will cardboard do? Can you build the mazey thing from cardboard boxes?" Louise's eyes were bright with mischief all of a sudden, but she turned antsy again and shooed me away with her meaty hands and the pruning shears when I stepped forward. "I'm going into the city to meet…some people." She wrinkled her brow curiously and waved her hands nervously. "You stay here and build that maze. That shed in the back of the pool house got all the boxes you need." Louise shouted as she waddled off toward her car. "Don't eat me out of house and home while I'm gone!"

I sighed heavily when I realized I'd just made more work for myself, but at least this work didn't require Samael's voice in my ear all day long. I grinned as I watch Louise's car speed off down the long driveway, then jumped with a start when I felt Samael's hand on my shoulder.

"Drake and I will build the maze, Lily. We owe you that much. Take a break; jump into the pool while Louise is gone."

"Can you guys make a maze as wicked as Marduk's?"

"Are you kidding me? Drake and I are intimately acquainted with the Maze of Dorcha. We built it." He winked. "No worries, lass. We'll make this a night those college kids will never forget."

Suddenly, the weight of our earlier argument lifted from my shoulders, and I was happy to have my ghost muses at my side. The idea of actually witnessing a Maze Game had me as giddy as a school girl.

"I'd like to attend one of those real Maze parties one day," I said excitedly. "In Dorcha."

"You've already attended one or two of them, Lily," Samael said in an emotionless tone.

"Did I behave?"

"Nobody behaves in the Maze. It's designed for misbehaving," Samael said in a droll tone.

"A stalking game in a Maze with sexy devils in kilts. Be still my heart," I sighed romantically. "I hope I misbehaved with Marduk."

"Are ye still hung up on Marduk?" Samael huffed and shook his head while walking toward the pool house.

"How can I not be hung up on him. He's so freaking sexy. Wicked. Romantic. Devil," I said breathlessly and melted into a poolside chair with a heavy sigh. I groaned when Drake placed my laptop on the table beside me, but I picked it up anyway. "Alright, back to the story. Who caught Mia? And Lilith? Please tell it wasn't Cain. That's twisted!"

Samael chuckled as he sauntered toward the shed. "What happens in the Maze stays in the Maze, Lily."

"Yeah, but you'll tell me, right?"

"Nope," he said adamantly.

"I'm not writing another word until you tell me who Marduk's target was. Was it Hecaté? Oooo that would make a good storyline!"

"You're not writing a storyline, Lily. You're writing things exactly as they occurred." Drake interjected as boxes began to fly out of the shed.

"Then tell me what happened! If I'm writing this story, I need to know who's with who in the Maze! There're only three possibilities for Lilith…Cain, Marduk, or Lugh. They were the only Dukes stalking the Maze at that time."

"You forgot someone, Lily. There were four possibilities," Samael said with a mysterious grin.

Chapter Twenty-Three

Aaden drew in a deep breath when Scotch opened the door to the Dungeon and swept his hand across the threshold. Aaden was mesmerized by the medical instruments as well as the pristine medical slab with black leather straps hanging above them. He also noted the chains and other instruments of torture along the walls, as well as draining tubes, bone saws, and knives beneath the slab.

"What the fuck is this? A surgery room? A torture chamber?" Aaden slowly and lightly stepped around the room as though he were afraid something might jump out at him any moment. "Marduk's twisted."

"Whoa, this is creepy." Killian said as he examined a shiny, brilliantly clean scalpel. He dropped it and shivered, then walked toward the medical books lining the shelves along with body parts in jars. "I think he's a doctor."

Scotch laughed under his breath and quietly surveyed Marduk's private Dungeon room for the first time. This was the same room his grandfather, Omega, used for his work as the Black Dragon. Scotch had heard stories about this room all his life, and it didn't disappoint.

Jade stepped in behind Killian and Aaden; Raven kept watch in the hallway. Jade's jaw dropped open as she looked around the curious Dungeon with hundreds of herbs and oils in jars and bottles locked in a glass cabinet.

"Raven, you gotta see this," Jade called out. "Look at all this magical stuff!"

"He's a doctor alright…a fuckin witch doctor," Aaden said playfully and grinned at Jade with a sexy spark in his eye. He wanted to kiss her again, and fought hard to stop himself, but he reached out a fist. Jade fist-bumped him and bit her lip when he smiled. Her entire body vibrated from Aaden's simple touch.

Scotch circled back and poked his head out the door at Raven. "Come inside, lass. You're safe with me." He winked and held out his hand.

Raven got a cold chill down her spine at the thought of entering those doors, but the energy in the dark hallway was more terrifying than the Dungeon at the moment. She ducked into the room with her shoulders hunched while rubbing her arms against the cold chill.

"This is way too creepy for me. Let's get outta here, guys. If we get caught…"

Scotch scoffed and made a groaning sound. "Fucking humans. You're fine. You're with me. I am Omegan and I have every right to be in this room."

Raven groaned in a loud huff and pulled away from Scotch. "I hate this place," she spat out.

He smirked and rolled his eyes, then moved toward Killian in long, slow strides. "Who is that lass? How do you know her, Killian?"

"She's my friend from New Orleans…my home city on Earth. Raven came here with the rescue team."

"Rescue team?"

Killian nodded. "Yeah, the people who came to save us from Lucian and your dad," he answered dryly.

Scotch groaned and rolled his eyes again. "My father had no part in Lucian's scheme, Killian. My father hates

Lucian. They are mortal enemies. My mother says it has something to do with Hecaté, but no one knows the whole story. I swear to you, Killian. My father is innocent in whatever plot Lucian cooked up to abduct you and Jade."

Killian nodded slowly and draped his arms across Scotch's shoulder. "Come to think of it, I never saw your father the whole time I was in Marbh, until the Banquet. Lucian was the mastermind of it all."

"Regardless…you and Jade are here now, and it doesn't look like either of you suffered much. I mean…look at the entire picture, Killian. You would have never known Marduk if Lucian hadn't taken you from your home city. As it stands…you are now in line for the Crown."

"I would rather be in the French Quarter than here…in line for a Crown I know nothing about."

Scotch chuckled and shook his head. "Humans." He rolled his eyes and groaned. "Everyone in the family is dying to get their hands on that Crown, and you act like it's a burden.

"It is a burden, Scottie," Killian replied softly.

Aaden bounced across the room and pulled Raven close to his chest. "Don't be afraid, Shiv. I'll protect ye."

Raven pulled away from Aaden too. "Like you did when I was dragged away from Bethel Woods?" She shot him a harsh glare.

"Siobhan…I was just a kid. I couldn't do anything. He was your dad, for fuck's sake. Even your grandfather couldn't stop him. C'mon, we settled this years ago in that fuckin marathon text." He pulled his phone out of his pocket and grimaced. "Phones don't work here, but I still have the text…I'll show you as soon as I get a signal, but ye said these exact words, 'I fuckin forgive ye, ye Irish fuckin mule.' You can't take it back once ye press send." He kissed her cheek and grinned widely, then scanned her face thoroughly.

"It still stings." She hit him in the gut with a backhanded slap. "And it's Raven now. I don't want to be connected to them anymore."

"Ye still have the O'Connor swing, lass. Ye're connected…Raven." He rolled his eyes and smirked.

"It fits my new life in New Orleans." Raven narrowed her eyes and smirked. "My life was shit before New Orleans."

Raven pulled away and walked around the room with a sour face. Killian reluctantly walked toward her and draped his arms around her from behind.

"Are you okay, Raven? You're not still stinging over my dad, are you? You're better off without him."

Raven melted into Killian's arms and sighed heavily. For the first time in months, Raven felt a solid sense of self with Killian nearby. Killian was one of the first people she met in New Orleans, her co-worker in the Temple of Ogoun for years, and the person who introduced her to Cain. Killian knew more about Raven than she knew about herself, and the same applied in reverse. Raven was the person Killian poured his heart out to whenever he was troubled.

"I know I'm better off without his bullshit, Killian. He's got so many women in his bed, it ain't even funny. He doesn't see me, Kill. I'm stuck in this weird fucking place because of him, and I don't even exist to him anymore. Marduk has been nicer to me than Finn…Cain. Whatever."

"Yeah…I did warn you about that, Rave. My dad has no sense of loyalty in matters of love. Women. Men. They all love him…and he takes advantage of that every moment of every day. Move on, girl." Killian tousled her hair and grinned playfully, then cast his eye toward Aaden in a blushing conversation with Jade across the room. He could feel the heat between them from where he stood.

Raven noticed his glance toward Aaden, but not the jealousy apparently.

"Aaden? Nah, man…Aaden was, like, the first boy I kissed, and he's super cool. He really is. But I was 13. He was 12. The crush lasted for, like…a week. But the friendship stayed. Nah, man, there's nothing between Aaden and me," Raven said adamantly.

Killian sighed with a light groan and looked away from Jade and Aaden huddled together near a shelf with dozens of herbal concoctions, giggling and whispering softly.

Jade leaned closer to Aaden with a wide smile. She was feeling bold from the whiskey. "So…you and Raven were an item?"

Aaden's grin faded slightly. "Long time ago, Jade. We were just kids."

"Well, neither of you are kids now," she said sadly. "I assume you guys will pick where you left off." She blushed when she realized her fishing scheme was blatantly obvious.

Aaden grinned when he caught on to Jade's questions. She was jealous, and wanted to know where she stood with him. Aaden's chest burned with excitement. This was the opening he'd been waiting for. He leaned closer and brushed the hair from her cheek, tucking it behind her ear gently, then winced painfully at the spark of love he felt from touching her.

"Not a chance," Aaden answered. "I'm interested in someone else."

Jade drew in her breath and shivered slightly from the look in Aaden's eyes. In that moment, Jade fell in love with Aaden. It broke her heart, because she knew Killian would get hurt, but more importantly, she knew she and Aaden were blood-related. It was an impossible love, but it was love, and it had a momentum of its own that no one could stop. Jade made a conscious decision to keep the truth from Aaden, but it sat badly in her gut.

Scotch sidled up to Killian and Raven with a friendly smile and a sheepish grin. "So what do you humans think about this Dungeon. It's the Devil's work room. The Black Dragon's Lair." He winked at Killian and grinned when Killian's cheeks paled. "You didn't know Marduk was the Devil?" Scotch asked in a droll tone with a charming grin.

"Yeah, kinda…but…I don't really know what that means. I think of him as the Dark God rather than the Devil, and I never heard of the Black Dragon."

Scotch's face softened as he moved closer to Killian. "Legends say he's the Sword of Justice. He kills only the worst of humanity. Sometimes he tortures evil humans to rehabilitate them. My grandfather, Omega…your great grandfather, Killian, was a fierce and wicked Dark God. They say he enjoyed his work at lot. He loved the blood and guts of it. Marduk is a cunt by comparison." Scotch paused to laugh and take a sip of wine from the blood bag, then handed it to Killian. "Rumor is that Marduk cries when he dismantles the incorrigible dead. Are you gonna be that kind of Black Dragon? Or a warrior like Omega when the Crown is passed to you?" Scotch asked in an ominous tone that rattled Killian sober all of a sudden. The weight of those words settled powerfully on Killian's shoulders and he couldn't breathe.

"I'm not staying here long enough to inherit the Crown. I'm going back to New Orleans as soon as possible. The Crown is all yours, Scottie." Killian replied adamantly.

Scotch grinned. "I've wanted that Crown all my life, but my father isn't the Heir. Yours is."

Killian's knees buckled slightly at Scotch's words and Killian suddenly wanted to wake from this dream and find himself back in the French Quarter. He sat heavily in a chair and stared off into the distance. He didn't even notice Jade and Aaden moving closer and closer to each other as they strolled through the Dungeon hand-in-hand.

Raven walked away from Killian and Scotch with slumped shoulders for reasons she couldn't explain. She felt so far removed from everyone here, including herself. She sat heavily in Marduk's chair behind a thick black desk, pouting and sighing heavily over and over until something on the desk caught her attention. She lifted a stack of papers and picked up a pile of photographs beneath it. Her eyes widened when she recognized the faces in the photos.

"What the fuck are you guys doing in here?" A loud voice came from the doorway, and everyone turned toward Cain with a furrowed and anxious brow. "Killian, Marduk will have your head for this. Get out, right now before he sees you. The Maze Game is over, and everyone is coming back inside. Go!" He waved his hands and Jade, Killian, Scotch, and Aaden filed out of the room quickly. Raven stayed behind. She glared angrily at Cain and held up the photographs.

"You care to explain to me why Marduk has pictures of my family?"

Cain's face fell as he rushed to the desk to take the photos from Raven's hands. "For fuck's sake, I knew I recognized that face. I just couldn't place it. Six. I'll be damned." Cain paced while thoroughly examining the photographs. "Who's the guy? And the other redhead."

"My aunt. She's a fucking wicked bitch. I hate her. She acts like a pious do-gooder, but I've seen her collections of weapons. Really off the wall shit. I always had a feeling she was a serial killer or something. She's got the personality for it. The guy is my stepbrother. Braedon is kinda slow. Mentally challenged. He's innocent in a weird way. Believes everything Six tells him, but I've seen him butchering animals. Freak. The whole fucking family is freaky. Now you know why I left Hell's Kitchen the day my dad died. I'm still not convinced that Six didn't kill him. Why do you have pictures of them, Finn?" She asked curiously with a withered brow. "Are you stalking my family?"

"I can't explain everything, Raven. Not now. But I need your help. Come with me."

"Oh, now that you need my help, you suddenly remember I'm alive. Or dead. Not sure which anymore, but I'm still fucking here! I'm not invisible, though you treat me like I am! I followed you here, Finn! To help you survive! Then as soon as we got here…you dumped me into your mother's bed." Raven groaned and wrinkled her brow. "Just saying that aloud makes me sick to my stomach, it's so fucking twisted. Fuck you, Finn. I'm not helping you. I wanna go home."

Raven stormed out of the Dungeon and ran right into Marduk's chest. He glared at her sternly with one raised eyebrow.

"I'm sorry that ye're unhappy here, lass. I'll see ye home, if that's what ye really want. But right now, I need your help. It is a matter of life and death, Raven." Marduk lit up a cigarette and walked forward as she walked backwards into the Dungeon with wide eyes. As soon as they were both inside the doorway, Marduk slammed the door and locked it.

"Tell me everything about your stepmother," he said ominously.

Jade, Killian, and Aaden ran back into the dining hall just as the Dukes and Duchesses were filing in with bawdy smiles and loud voices. Scotch was lost somewhere in the shuffle. Aaden looked back over his shoulder and wrinkled his brow when he didn't see Raven either.

"Where's Shiv? Did she get out? Is she with Scotch?" He started back toward the Dungeon, but Killian stopped him.

"She's with my dad. Give them a minute. She and my dad…they were, like, together… as a thing, ya know, and the breakup was bad. She followed my dad here. That's how Raven ended up in Dorcha."

"Siobhan was involved with your dad? The Vampire? He's fucking ancient! She's only a wee lass, for fuck's sake. The same age as me. How twisted are these fuckin Incubi people?" Aaden's face crumpled into confusion as he looked back and forth between Killian and Jade.

"You have no clue. I have no clue to that answer either, Jade said sadly. "He won't hurt her. Raven's in no danger from Cain."

Aaden relaxed at Jade's soft tone and the tenderness in her eyes. He lifted his hand to touch her face, but he noticed Killian's quick move toward her, and dropped his hand.

"I'm gonna go find my dad," Aaden mumbled, then walked away with slumped shoulders and heavy steps. Jade's eyes followed him as she sighed dreamily.

"Are you in love with him, Jade?" Killian asked quietly while crossing his arms over his chest. The whiskey made him bold, and he suddenly wished he had the bottle now as he waited for Jade's answer.

"No. Don't be silly." Jade heard her own insincerity in her statement and couldn't look at Killian.

"Be straight with me, Jade. After everything we've been through, don't lie to me now." Killian awkwardly shifted his feet and shoulders. He couldn't look at Jade either.

"Killian…I'm…attracted to him. I can't help it. But no. I'm not in love with him."

Killian winced as he shuffled his feet. He couldn't look at Jade when he asked the next question. "Are you in love with me?"

Jade let out a huge rush of air, then slowly shrugged her shoulders. "I don't know, Killian. I'm so confused." Jade's eyes were misty and somewhat tortured. She didn't want to hurt Killian. She did love him, but she couldn't deny her overwhelming attraction to Aaden. She had to explore it further to determine whether she was in love with anyone.

Killian's shoulders slumped as he uncrossed his arms slowly. "If you don't know by now, then the answer is no. I'm stepping away while you figure it out."

Jade's face fell as she reached for Killian's hand, but he shirked away from her grasp.

"Killian…wait…what does that mean? Stepping away? Be straight with me…please."

"Means I'm walking away from you until you figure out which one of us you're in love with." Killian marched away from her with his arms held stiffly at his side. He went straight to the bar and poured himself a Scotch.

Jade groaned loudly as she set out toward Declan and Caraye. "Mom, I need to talk to you," she said with a withered face.

"What's the matter, Kitten?" Caraye asked as she pulled Jade into an alcove and sat her down on the sofa. Caraye pulled the curtains closed, then braced herself for the conversation she knew was coming.

"Killian…and Aaden. I love them both…well maybe not love, but…I have feelings for Aaden, and you know how I feel about Killian. What do I do, Mom? How do I choose between the two?"

Caraye smiled and pulled Jade closer into her arms to comfort her. Jade stiffened as usual and pulled away before Caraye smothered her. Caraye stung a little at her icy rejection of affection, but she knew this was her Jade, the real Jade, not the morphing persona Jade was becoming through her experience in the Colonies. Caraye faced it stoically, logically, giving Jade her distance to stew in her own bubble.

"Jade, you're young. You don't need to decide this now. Take your time. Spend time with both of them. I know Killian will be hurt, but better to be honest from the beginning. You guys should explore your feelings now, before you get into a serious relationship. Or marriage."

"I would like nothing better than to spend time with both of 'em. But that's not how things are done here. People faithfully hook-up for eternity in this place. I'm not ready to marry either of them. I just…want to explore this love thing." Jade smirked and rolled her eyes, then slumped her shoulders.

Caraye let out a small chuckle. She'd just witnessed how the Incubi maintained eternal marriages that were anything but faithful. Luckily, she and Declan were spared tonight, but Caraye knew one day they might cross those lines in one of the many sex games the Incubi played. She was tempted almost beyond her limits tonight just by one savage kiss from Marduk. Caraye blushed and let out a whoosh of air at the memory of it.

"You don't have to marry anyone, Jade. Look at Aramanth. She never played by the rules. You have time to explore this 'love thing' from every angle, and with whoever you choose. When you finally do make your decision, you'll feel good about it. You'll have no doubts. No regrets. Move forward, Jade. Go forth and explore…" Caraye chuckled and waved her slim hand across the air.

Jade smiled, but her sadness was palpable. "I already regret hurting Killian. He knows I like Aaden, and I think he just broke up with me." Jade huffed loudly and ran her hands through her hair. "Mia's gonna hate me."

Mia poked her head through the curtain at that moment with a wide, dreamy grin on her face. "Declan told me where to find y'all. Sister-mama, I gotta talk to ya. Will ya excuse us for a minute, Jade?"

Jade looked up at Mia and smiled sadly. "Come in, Mia, I have to tell you something."

Mia stepped inside with a worried look on her face. "What's the matter, baby?"

"I think Killian and I just broke up. I'm not sure." Jade threw her hands in the air as tears flowed down her cheeks.

Mia's face wrinkled slightly. "Because of Lugh's son?"

Jade's eyes widened as she nodded slowly. "How did you know?"

"Sweetie, I've seen the sparks between y'all. I guess Killian finally saw them, too," Mia said softly and held Jade's hand.

Jade bounced her entire upper body in a nod, and wiped her tears firmly. "I don't wanna hurt anybody, Mia. I'm sorry I feel this way about Aaden, but…I do, and I can't deny it any longer. I can't hide it."

Mia smirked playfully and nodded stiffly. "Oh no, girl, you can't hide dis. It's too damn strong." She chuckled. "Everybody knows, so you now you have to go on and live it, honey. Be true to the oneself you are, Jade. Jade gotta be first in Jade's life…you can't live to please others. Not even Killian. I know you guys love each other, but you're too young to be tied down. As limited as your options are in this place, y'all both need to know what those options are. All of 'em." Mia smiled sadly. She didn't want to see Killian heartbroken, but she could plainly see Jade's confusion was going to hurt him worse in the long run. "It's better to step back now rather than later, baby."

"You're not mad at me?" Jade asked in a little girl voice that made Mia smile.

"Baby girl… I could never be mad at you. I'm Killian's mama, and of course I'm pulling for y'all, but not if this is gonna hurt one or both of you somewhere down the line. Killian's a smart young man. He'll come around and see this is best for everyone. Take your time, Jade. Figure it out while you can. Before things get too serious." Mia kissed Jade's forehead and grinned crookedly. "Now run along, child. I need to talk to ya mama." Mia laughed excitedly.

Jade perked up somewhat as she stepped lightly into the Dining Hall and immediately locked eyes with Aaden from across the room. He tilted his head toward the doors leading to the courtyard. Jade nodded with a sly smile.

Killian caught the exchange from across the room, and groaned loudly as he drank straight from the bottle of whiskey while watching Jade and Aaden sneak out of the Lair into the garden.

"Sister-mama, I just rode to heaven on the devil's kilt." Mia melted into the chair, and let out a breathy sigh with wide, dreamy eyes. "Dat maze is da bomb."

"Which devil? This place is full of kilted devils tonight," Caraye asked excitedly.

"The one and only. Marduk." She grinned and closed her eyes. "I have never experienced anything like that in my entire life. I know why he's King."

"The guys were masked. How do you know for certain it was Marduk?" Caraye asked suspiciously.

"I recognized that kilt. He's the only one wearing that black and red leather kilt. He wore it well tonight." She grinned and lifted her shoulders while she sighed dreamily.

Caraye's face fell as she leaned back in the chair. "Mia…Marduk wasn't wearing that kilt. He was wearing Declan's kilt."

"What?" Mia's face withered as she sat up abruptly. "Why was he wearing Declan's kilt?"

"It's a secret we're not supposed to know. Declan and Marduk exchanged kilts. Don't ask me why."

Mia's face withered into a horrified grimace, and she let out a small whimper. "No…Caraye…the devil in the Maze was wearing Marduk's kilt. Did I just…?"

Caraye shook her head quickly to allay Mia's fears. "No, no. Declan exchanged Marduk's kilt with someone else…he didn't say who, but Marduk was in Declan's kilt, and I was with Declan. The night wasn't that twisted, Mia."

Mia exhaled as she fanned her face quickly. "This is enough to make me catch a heart attack. Then who the fuck did I just…?"

Lugh walked around the Dining Hall with a wide grin and a light step as he searched the room for Aaden. He spotted Killian at the bar, and was confused by his sullen demeanor, as well as the bottle of Marduk's best Scotch in his hand.

"Are ye alright, Killian? Ye're hitting that whiskey pretty hard, lad. Where's your lass?"

Killian took another swig, coughed, then looked at Lugh with sad eyes. "In the garden. With Aaden." Killian smirked and rolled his eyes, then lifted the bottle to his mouth again, but Lugh took it from his hands.

"Ye've had enough Scotch for the night, lad." Lugh clapped Killian on the back, then held him up when he nearly fell over. "For fuck's sake, Killian. Let me get ye outside for some air." Lugh threw his arm around Killian and lifted him from the chair. Killian's knees buckled as he leaned heavily on Lugh.

"I don't wanna go outside. They're out there. Can you show me where my room is?" Killian asked with a groan. "I think I'm gonna puke."

Lugh wasted no time in walking Killian out of the Dining Hall, toward the guest suites. He paused when he saw Marduk coming down the hallway in long steps with a heavy scowl.

"What's the matter with Killian?" Marduk asked in an alarming tone as he sprinted to Killian's side.

"Ye left your Scotch unguarded. The lad tried to drink his sorrows away."

Lugh and Marduk led Killian down the hallway into a guest room. They eased him into the bed, pulled off his boots, then tucked him under the covers.

"I gotta puke," Killian choked out.

Marduk was right beside him with a porcelain bowl just in the nick of time. He shook his head slowly and chuckled softly as he brushed Killian's hair from his face.

"Fetch a wet towel, little Lugh."

"Stop calling me little Lugh. I'm not little, as ye well know," Lugh spat out as he grabbed a cloth and dipped it in ice-cold water.

"We call ye little Lugh because ye're named after Phoenix's father. Ye're the second Lugh." Marduk grinned devilishly. "Are ye still stinging because I chose Cain over ye in the Maze game?"

"Ye know I beat Cain in that competition. And ye humiliated me in front of all the Dukes." Lugh angrily tossed the towel at Marduk.

Marduk grinned widely as he caught it mid-air. "If ye want to avenge yourself, re-enlist in the Cambion Project. I still need an Alphan."

"Ye never stop, Marduk. Rotten to the fuckin core." Lugh scowled fiercely at Marduk's stoic face and squinted eyes.

"Ye've been on Earth too long. Ye're thinking like a fuckin human." Marduk scowled back at him, then relaxed his face with a heavy groan. "My son has been beaten down his entire life. Mostly by me, Lugh." Marduk sighed while running the towel across Killian's face. "We're finding our way back to each other, and I wanted to give him a nod of approval. He has less confidence than ye and Declan have. I knew ye could take the joke better." Marduk grinned devilishly when Lugh's scowl deepened. "I didn't mean to insult ye. Ye know I love ye, Lugh. It's in my nature to tease those I love." He threw his hands in the air as he walked toward Lugh with a contrite smile. "If the truth were told, ye beat Declan as well. By a quarter inch or so." He held Lugh by the shoulders, and pulled him in for a tender kiss on the lips. "But I wanted to protect Caraye, so I gave Declan first place."

"Ye didn't do it to take advantage of his wife?" Lugh asked quizzically.

Marduk chuckled and walked back to Killian moaning on the bed, then wiped his face again with the cold towel. "Of course not. I wanted to make sure they found each other, before anyone else found her."

Lugh's jaw dropped open. "Did ye grow a conscience when ye died? Or a fuckin heart?"

Marduk laughed in a deep tone. "I've always had both, Lugh. But only on rare occasions do I use both at the same time." He winked again, then turned his attention back to Killian. "Why is the lad drinking his sorrows away. He's too young to have sorrows this deep."

"Jade and Aaden. I think romance is brewing between them. I don't like it."

Marduk sucked in a deep breath, then let it out in a huff. "Fuck. His first heartbreak." Marduk scanned Killian's face and smiled as a wave of love washed over him. He wanted to do something to help him, but he knew this love triangle would have to play itself out as scripted by Jade's heart. He'd likely make things worse by trying to force it.

"Aaden doesn't know that he and Jade are blood related. This will open up a nasty can of worms, Marduk."

"The only way through this is with honesty, Lugh. Ye should tell him before someone else does." Marduk groaned as he stood up and his bones cracked. "Unless ye want me to talk to him for ye."

Lugh shook his head. "This has to come from me. Otherwise he'll never forgive me."

"I don't envy ye that task, little Lugh." Marduk scowled slightly, then his face lit up. "Did ye catch a Duchess tonight?" He grinned wickedly with raised eyebrows.

Lugh blushed profusely and nodded. "Aye," he replied softly. "Don't ask me who. I don't fuck and tell." Lugh smiled tightly and looked away from Marduk.

"I'll tell ye mine, if ye tell me yours," Marduk said in playful tone.

Lugh shook his head again, then started toward the door in long steps. "I'll fetch Killian's mother."

"Did ye say catch? Or fetch?" Marduk called out to Lugh's retreating back while laughing softly.

"Very funny, Marduk," Lugh said sullenly.

"I thought so, too." Marduk grinned and shrugged, then sat on the bed next to Killian while running the cold towel across his face. "Poor lad. I need to teach ye how to hold both your liquor and your lasses. Ye've got to live up to the Omegan name, Killian." He placed a tender kiss on Killian's forehead, and smoothed his furrowed brow gently.

Killian was passed out for the most part, but he was softly moaning Jade's name.

Jade and Aaden smiled shyly at each other as he led her toward the rose covered hedges. He reached for her hand and smiled when she didn't pull away.

"I'm still in absolute awe of the night sky," Aaden said quietly. "I've never really been a stargazer until I came here." Aaden smiled shyly at Jade. He'd never felt awkward with a girl before, but he'd never felt this strongly about a girl before. Aaden's head was swimming with romantic ideas, but he knew her circumstances were precarious at the moment, and he didn't want to move too quickly.

Jade blushed and shifted awkwardly. "This is my first time in Dorcha. The sky looks a little different here. I think I like this better than the view in Gael. It's pretty amazing, and this garden is beautiful. It's like a maze or something."

"Wanna explore it?" Aaden asked with a grin.

"Why not?" Jade answered firmly and looked back over her shoulder at the Onyx Lair before she followed Aaden into the Maze, made of dark green shrubs and thick trunks covered in lichens and green moss, 7 feet high, and blooming with Ghost Orchids that glowed against the moonlight. Hundreds of giant moths, in a wide variety of brown, red, orange, and white, flitted about the flowers, dancing from alcove to alcove. Jade and Aaden were immediately caught up in the romance of it, especially with the sexually charged energy lingering in the air after Marduk's contribution to the Dead Party.

"Jade, I know ye and Killian have been through some difficult times together, and he was your hero in all that mess with your father. I know ye love him…but…I see in your eyes that there's room for me in your heart as well. Am I wrong?"

Jade let out a soft, lingering breath and stepped closer to Aaden. "You're not wrong, Aaden. I do like you, a lot. I guess it's no secret…I have a crush on you.

Aaden grinned and a slow blush crept up his cheeks. "I'm kinda crushing on you too, Jade." He held his hands to his face and chuckled. "My damn cheeks are on fire. I'm so embarrassed." He gave her a shy look and held her gaze when she drew in her breath. "Seriously though…I like you. I wanna spent some time with you. Just you. Just me."

Jade melted into Aaden's arms and shivered as a wave of passion ran down her spine. "I want that too, but…Killian. How do we…? Where do we start, Aaden? It's gonna hurt Killian, and that's not sitting well in my gut."

Aaden wrapped her in his arms and smiled sadly. "I don't want to hurt him either. Truth is, I really like Killian. He's a good guy and I want to be his friend, but…" He lifted his eyes toward the sky and huffed loudly. "I can't deny this thing between us, Jade. I can't walk away from you."

Jade grinned and blushed. "I'm not mad at that."

Aaden grinned widely and leaned down for a tender kiss that Jade responded to with breathless passion. Aaden gently sucked her top lip and held it, then opened his mouth over hers in a deep kiss that sent them both reeling with heady passion. When they finally pulled apart, they breathed each other's breath while their hearts pulsed in synchronized beats.

"I can't walk away from you either, Aaden," Jade whispered in reply and pulled Aaden in for a savage kiss that surprised her. She had no idea she could feel this much passion.

"I'm not mad at that at all," Aaden echoed her earlier sentiments. They fell into laughter as they tumbled onto the nearest sofa with their arms and legs entwined.

"I had no idea my body could feel this way," Jade whispered breathlessly as she ran her hands through Aaden's silky waves. "It's a little scary because…" Jade began shyly. Aaden's glistening eyes stopped her. She suddenly didn't want to protect her virginity as fiercely as she always had.

"I won't cross your lines, Jade." Aaden whispered against her cheek. "Just tell me when to stop," he whispered.

"I…I want to explore, Aaden. Just a little..."

Aaden broke into a cocky grin as his hands and mouth began a free roam over Jade's body. Her entire body was on fire as she closed her eyes and arched seductively under Aaden's warm hands and mouth. She stared into his sea-green eyes and didn't balk when he unzipped her dress and ran his hands over her naked skin. She pulled open his shirt and pressed her naked breasts against Aaden's chest, then easily pushed Killian's face from her mind's eye as she wrapped her arms around Aaden's neck to pull him closer to her. She gasped loudly when Aaden's warm mouth covered her breast and his tongue flicked across her nipple.

"Aaden…stop," she whispered softly.

Aaden immediately stopped and lifted his hands from Jade's body, holding them up clearly. His eyes were wide with concern. "Did I frighten ye, Jade? I didn't mean to…I'm sorry, lass." He sat up and helped her up, then zipped her dress quickly, careful not to touch her inappropriately. “Ye okay?”

“Yeah…it’s just…I’m…maybe a little scared. Overwhelmed, actually. I’m a virgin, Aaden,” she said softly and braced herself for his response.

“I assumed as much.” He grinned shyly and draped his jacket over her shoulders. “It’s not easy balancing virginity and natural passions. It is overwhelming, especially if ye have no idea what to expect. Just know that I’m not going anywhere, Jade. Whether we make love or not, I’m sticking around. I’m not a boy. I’m a man. I’m not a virgin, but I respect your virginity and your boundaries, and I’ll address them like a man,” Aaden said sincerely as his cheeks flushed red, then he smiled crookedly and leaned against her. “Ye’re safe with me, lass.”

Jade bit her lip, then gave Aaden a steamy kiss. “I’m not opposed to a little more exploration. Maybe just a little slower.”

Aaden grinned and draped his arms across her shoulders and leaned in closer. “I can do slow…I’m a master at slow. My brothers call me the slug,” he teased with a wide smile and pulled her closer. “I’m in no hurry, Jade. I just wanna be near ye.”

Jade rested her head against his chest and melted into his body. She was amazed at how well they fit together without even trying. “This feels so right, Aaden. I care deeply for Killian, but I’ve never felt more complete than I do in this moment, in your arms. Does that freak you out?”

Aaden pulled her closer and shivered with unbridled passion and a new emotion he’d never felt before coursing through his entire body. “Not a bit.”

Mia charged into Killian's suite with Declan in tow, wearing a worried, frazzled brow. Her heart sped up at the sight of Marduk dressed in his black and red leather kilt. She was more confused than ever. She wanted to believe that it was Marduk she'd made love with, but Marduk barely looked at her. His attention was on Killian until Mia took over Killian's care, then he turned his attention to Declan.

"Did ye find your wife?" Marduk grinned widely and held his arms out to Declan. Declan threw his arms around Marduk and pulled him to his chest.

"Aye. Thanks to ye, Uncle. I don't know what to say…except…I'm eternally grateful. And highly ashamed of myself for betraying ye all those years ago." Declan hung his head, then looked back up at Marduk with sad eyes full of regret and love. "Ye're a better King than I can ever hope to be."

"Ahhh, don't go getting all mushy on me, Declan. I did it for Caraye. Her first game and all. We don't want to scare the lass away so soon after her arrival." Marduk leaned in and kissed Declan's lips tenderly. "The score for the 42-day affair is settled. I kissed your wife." Marduk shrugged and grinned devilishly. "With tongue. Twice. Maybe three times," Marduk chuckled wickedly.

"Ye can kiss my wife as often as ye want. She's a little in love with ye." Declan grinned sheepishly. Marduk puffed up in pride.

"All the lasses are." He waved his hands in the air, and glanced at Mia. He growled slightly when she bent over to run the cold towel across Killian's face.

"Ye surprised me, Marduk. I thought…" Declan stopped short of saying it, as though speaking the words might make them come true.

"Ye thought I would fuck your wife? That's fucked up, Declan." Marduk grinned and pulled Declan in for a bear hug. "I love ye too much to hurt ye that way." Marduk lowered his eyes and groaned. "She's so innocent. Lilith was far from it when ye had your affair. I couldn't stand by and let your wife become corrupted the way mine was all those years ago when Lilith first went through the Maze. I don't want your life to become mine, Declan."

Declan groaned slightly. "But my life will become yours one day, Marduk. I hope my wife can adjust. She thought she was marrying God. She married the Devil too."

"Not if I can help it, Declan. As fierce as ye are, ye're not the Black Dragon. Ye're not Omegan," he sighed heavily. "But Cain is." Marduk closed his eyes tightly and hung his head.

"If the Elders would allow him to stay in Dorcha…" Declan let his words hang in the air.

"I will make this right for ye, Declan. All in the name of love." Marduk kissed Declan again then tousled his hair. "Ye're a good lad. Let's keep ye that way." Marduk looked back at Mia and scanned her body thoroughly.

"Killian will be fine in the morning, but someone should watch over him for another hour or so, until most of the Scotch is in that bowl." He shook his head slowly, winked at Mia, then marched out the room into the Dining Hall toward Lilith.

"*Mo ghrá gheal*! Ye're the most beautiful lass in the entire Lair." He kissed her fiercely and ran his hands along her waist down to her hips. "I take it from that wee wicked smile, ye caught a horny Duke tonight." Marduk smirked and rolled his eyes.

Lilith smiled slyly. "A horny Duke caught me." She stood up on her tiptoes and kissed him tenderly.

Marduk smiled and held her in his arms tightly. "I caught a feisty lass. Or two. Or was it three?" He laughed softly, then twirled her around the room as the musicians began a slow tune.

Erin smiled seductively at Marduk when she caught his eye over Lilith's shoulder. He blew her a fingertip kiss, and grinned with an equally seductive look on his face. His sexy grin faded when he spotted Hecaté gliding in circles around the heart cauldron. She dipped her finger in the steaming wine, and lifted it to her mouth with a sly grin. Marduk scanned her hips swaying as she circled the cauldron three times, then lifted her eyes to him in an intense stare. He growled slightly before looking away, then immediately caught Delphi's flirtatious eye. She began a slow sensual glide across the room as she draped her hair over her shoulders seductively. Marduk winked and lifted one corner of his mouth as he watched her hips swaying in exaggerated dance-like moves that had more than one Duke following her around the room.

Lilith caught Amon's eyes from across the room and held his gaze tenderly. Amon blushed and hung his head, then slowly made his way back to his suite where Makawee had been patiently waiting for him since midnight.

Marduk caught sight of Amon's back as he shuffled across the room toward the door. "What is Amon doing here? And in a kilt, no less. I thought he retired to his suite with Makawee hours ago."

"Amon? I haven't seen him since midnight," Lilith said in a lilting tone that Marduk immediately knew was disingenuous. He pulled away from Lilith and looked deep into her eyes. She looked away for a minute, then smiled sweetly at Marduk. "Did I thank you properly for my surprise? The dancers were a wicked twist to the night. All the Duchesses loved them. Caraye called them she-males. Fitting name. They were so beautiful, Marduk. Will they be staying in Dorcha?"

"Aye. But not as concubines or slaves. They are free, and they are not to be used. They are to be cherished and loved. Appreciated for their uniqueness, but never ridiculed nor judged. Cain staked a claim on one of them." Marduk again smirked and rolled his eyes, but laughed softly against Lilith's cheek.

"That might be a very good arrangement for the lads. Lads or lasses? Which do they prefer?"

"Lasses. They are female in spirit."

"As Cain's concubines, the lasses will never be mistreated by our society. Our son may be a wee bit wicked, but he loves his concubines." Lilith glanced over at Cain who smiled like a just-fed cat while raising his glass. He squinted as he laughed wickedly and drank his glass of Scotch.

"Finally," Cain whispered to himself. "The stage is set."

Lilith grinned playfully at Cain then turned back to Marduk. "Thank you for letting me off my chains tonight." She giggled and held her head against his chest. "I am happier than I have been in a very long time."

"Is it me that made ye happy, Lilith? Or the Duke who caught ye in the maze?" He grinned wickedly and kissed her tenderly. Lilith shrugged her shoulders and smiled seductively.

"Both," she answered honestly and kissed Marduk's thick, wine-stained lips.

Marduk wrinkled his brow and pulled her closer. The image of Amon sneaking away from the party was burning a hole in his head and gnawing in his gut.

Something was suspicious about that, but he didn't want to think of the possible implications of Amon skulking away from the orgy with his head hanging low.

"Ye planned the perfect party, Lilith. I have never been more proud of ye, lass. The most wicked Dead Party I have ever attended. Yer shining moment was brilliant, *mo ghrá*." He leaned in with a sexy growl and bit his bottom lip before grabbing a handful of her hair and kissing her with tender passion.

Lilith melted under Marduk's hands and her head began to spin as he opened his lips over hers savagely. The entire room went silent in that moment while the erotic air waved across the room, and all eyes were on Lilith and Marduk.

Hecaté closed her eyes and hung her head as the memory of Marduk's kisses filled her head. Then an image of her golden-haired husband flashed and her knees buckled. She fell softly into the coffin behind her, then buried her face in her hands.

"I hope you can forgive me, Lucian."

Delphi narrowed her eyes and drained another glass of wine as she watched Marduk seducing Lilith. "I married the wrong brother," she whispered under her breath.

Scotch watched his mother's lustful display and narrowed his eyes while glaring at Marduk from across the room, then he slowly marched toward Delphi and gently nudged her out of her reverie with a fresh bottle of wine.

"Have you forgotten that my father is rotting in prison?"

Delphi wrinkled her brow and pulled the bottle from Scotch's grip. "How can I possible forget, Scotch, when you remind me of it every single day?" She sighed heavily, then grinned. “Cheer up, lad. Perhaps you will get a new father soon.” Delphi winked.

Scotch rolled his eyes. “Please do not make fools of us, Delphi.”

“Scotch, my darlin son…you may have your father’s stance, his eyes, his smile, and one day, his fortune, but you are not your father. You have no right to scold me. That is your father’s job,” she said with a stoic face. “Gather your sisters and see them safely to our suite. Mother would like some alone time,” Delphi said in her most authoritative voice.

Scotch grinned at her and wanted so badly to tell her that even at her most stern, she still sounded like a cross child. Instead, he leaned forward and kissed her cheeks the same way he’d witnessed his father do hundreds of times.

“Aye, Mother. I’ll see the lasses safely to bed. Shall I come back for you later?”

Delphi nodded. “If I am not back in the suite in an hour, it may be a good idea to come fetch me.”

“I will search every corner, chair, couch, coffin, casket, cauldron, and cock until I find you, Mother,” Scotch said in a droll voice.

“Thank you, Scottie. You are my favorite son.”

“I’m your only son, Delphi.”

Delphi raised her hands and smiled crookedly. “I knew I could never do better than you, my love. So I never tried for another son.” She air-kissed Scotch, then went right back to watching Marduk twirling Lilith around the dance floor while his hands roamed her entire body of curves.

Jade and Aaden leaned into each other in the opposite corner, watching the passionate display between the King and Queen of Dorcha. Aaden laced his fingers in Jade’s hair and pulled her toward him in a deep kiss that

Jade melted into as she draped her arms around his neck and pressed her body against his. Marduk noticed them across the room and doubled over like he'd been hit in the gut.

"As wicked and lovely as our party was, my love, there was a tragedy. Killian and Jade. Dorcha might be too much for the lad. I think he should stay in Gael. He's safer there."

"But Killian is ours, Marduk. He is Omegan. He should live with us in Dorcha."

"He is Alphan as well. He cannot fight for Jade in Dorcha."

"Why does he have to fight for her? They are in love."

Marduk smirked sarcastically at her. "Ye and I are in love as well, Lilith. Yet I fight for ye every day of my life." Marduk growled and pulled her closer while scanning her face.

"Those days are behind us, Marduk." Lilith's eyes were full of love as she gazed up at him wondrously, but Marduk saw something else in her eyes that gripped his heart. He saw guilt.

"Aye, my love. Let's bury our swords." He grinned crookedly. "Not in each other's backs this time."

"My thorn is still in your back, my sweet, savage lover," Lilith whispered in a sultry tone that made Marduk shiver slightly.

He sucked his teeth and shook his head slowly. "I am aware of the fuckin thorn, Lilith."

She grinned playfully and chalked up her victory with Marduk in what she hoped was the final battle between them. Lilith knew that thorn was her ace in the hole. It was her not-so-secret weapon that ensured her place in Marduk's heart and bed for eternity.

Marduk scanned the room for a distraction from Lilith's triumphant look. He stopped when he caught Gwendolyn's eye. She was draped seductively over the bondage table with a sexy grin and smiling eyes. He grinned devilishly with one raised eyebrow.

"Are we still in the game, Lilith?"

"I would like to call it a night," Lilith said softly. "Take me to bed, Marduk. I want more." She laced her fingers in his hair and pulled him to her for a deep kiss.

"I still have loopholes, my love," he laughed softly, and never took his eyes from Lilith's flushed cheeks and shiny eyes.

"You might find my loopholes to your liking."

"Ye have the best loopholes in all of Dorcha, *mo ghrá gheal*. Aye. Let's go to bed. Just ye and I, Lilith." Marduk was pleasantly surprised when she nodded vigorously and draped herself against his body as though he were a lifeline.

"Just the two of us from now on, Marduk. I would like the close the open doors of our marriage."

"Do ye really mean that, Lilith?"

"I do mean it. I do not want anyone else but you. I will give up all my lovers. Even Raven…if you give up the blondes."

Marduk's face withered slightly. "All of them?"

Lilith laughed sweetly and ran her hands through his silky beard.

"All the blondes except one. Me."

Marduk groaned as he scanned the room for all the blondes he wanted to remind who was King before committing to monogamy again, but instead of the blondes, he saw a room full of Lilith's former lovers scanning her body with open lust.

"Aye. I will give them up." He kissed her softly. "But if ye betray me again, Lilith, there will be nothing left between us." He raised his eyebrows and set a stern jaw. "Do I need to keep the blondes nearby?" Marduk asked ominously.

Lilith wrinkled her brow and scanned the room. She saw all the concubines and Duchesses, including Hecaté and Delphi, trying to get Marduk's attention. She didn't even see her former lovers lusting after her. She only saw the hungry, half-naked blondes circling Marduk as they waited for her to fall out of favor again.

"No. Send them far, far away, Marduk."

"Amon?!" I asked with an open jaw and wide eyes full of disappointment. "How could he do that to Marduk? To Makawee? No, no, no, Samael…we can't corrupt Amon! He's…he's all there is of good."

"Neither the writer nor the narrators can change what happened, Lily."

"But…he's in love with Makawee. She's going to be devastated. Marduk is going to kill him! What'll happen to the world if the Gods kill each other?"

"The Gods have children, Lily. No one can kill the Gods. Not even the Gods themselves," Drake added. "But once again, you are jumping ahead in the story…and jumping to conclusions. No one said Amon betrayed Marduk."

"So he didn't have sex with Lilith?"

"I didn't say that either. What happens in the Maze…"

“Uh-uh…no way are you guys leaving me out of the loop. I refuse to write another word until I find out who was with who in the Maze.” This event seemed more significant to me than anything I’d written so far. I had to know if this was the event that sparked the animosity between God and the Devil.

“If you stop writing, Lily, you’ll never discover the truth.”

I paused, taking in the decadent noise of the Maze game going on right outside my cabin. The guys were yelling like wolves as the girls squealed with delight. There was something very familiar about these sounds. I suddenly had a flash of something that was very close to a memory, a moment of déjà vu that sent a chill down my spine. I clearly saw Marduk in a black and red kilt, but the setting wasn’t the Maze. It wasn’t even in Dorcha, and there were no happy squeals of delight. I suddenly couldn’t breathe, as a buzzing sound began to whirl in my ear, and I knew something was about to happen. I tiptoed back to my desk with a wary eye on the door as the buzzing grew louder and louder.

“Gimme the bag of gummies and tell me about Marduk. No lies, Samael.”

“For fuck’s sake, Lily. With all the revelations and new conflicts in the story, all you want to know is who Marduk fucked in the Maze?”

“Not just Marduk. I wanna know all the hookups,” I said quietly, but my panic at the sounds outside my door was creeping up my spine and I suddenly had the urge to run.

“What happens in the Maze stays in the Maze,” Samael and Drake said simultaneously. “Mostly,” Samael added and grinned wickedly.

Drake startled me when he dropped a pack of cigarettes on my desk. “Get comfortable, Lily. Another night of revelations is about to begin.”

I lit up the cigarette and sat back with a heavy sigh as more memories hit me square in the face. Everything became as clear as crystal and I suddenly knew who Samael and Drake were. I knew who I was as well. I turned to Samael with tears in my eyes and backed into the farthest corner of the cabin.

“Why did you leave me?”

Before Samael could answer, the playful squeals turned to violent yelling and banging on my cabin door. I jumped with a loud, sharp scream as a dozen men burst into my cabin along with Louise and a blurry, shadowed figure in a navy-blue skirt and clicking red-soled heels that sent me into a panic.

“That’s her,” the woman said in a bored tone and pointed to me as the men moved in quickly. “When are you going to grow up, Lillian? I am sick to death of your games.”

I began to sob loudly when I recognized the voice and felt the sting of the needle in my arm. All the memories and revelations that had surfaced earlier buried themselves deep in my psyche again. Nothing was familiar, and every was familiar. Being in the middle of that whirlwind sent me into the dark abyss, as the voices faded, and I fell into a deep sleep.

Chapter Twenty-Four

Marduk paced the floor of his private office slowly, and finally gave in to his limp. He groaned loudly when the muscles in his right thigh cramped, and he gingerly lowered himself into a chair. He growled fiercely when his shoulder stiffened, and a jolt of pain ran the entire length of his left side. He rubbed his face with both hands, wrapped his hair into a bun, and reached for the bottle of Scotch on the desk.

"This cannot be a coincidence." He drank heavily from the bottle of Scotch, then reached for the vial of herbed oil on the shelf. He poured a heavy layer of the oil on his right thigh. "Is the skinny lass a mole for the Red Dragon? Fuck. She came here with Cain."

Marduk rubbed his thigh harder, groaning loudly at the pain as he dug his fingers deep into the muscle to relax the cramp. He doubled over in pain and hated himself for the tears that surfaced. He didn't want to give into the pain even though he was alone. It was easy to ignore it in front of others. Marduk was accustomed to wearing a mask to hide his emotions in public, but he didn't know how to fool himself into believing he was alright. He growled beneath his breath as he stretched out his shoulder and felt it pop. He cringed at the sound, but more so at the burning pain.

Marduk's entire body tensed up when he suddenly felt a presence behind him. The hair on his neck bristled as he took in a deep breath, shivered visibly, then took a long, hard pull from the bottle of Scotch. He started to sweat immediately and jumped out of the chair when he felt the massive hand on his shoulder. He turned slowly with wide, teary eyes and held out the bottle to the colossal hooded figure standing behind the chair he'd just been sitting in.

"That was your mother's brew, Marduk. Not mine," Omega said in a deep voice that sent another shiver down Marduk's spine.

Marduk drained the rest of the Scotch, then slowly limped to the cabinet for a bottle of pomegranate wine and another of Scotch. He handed the wine to Omega, who stood stoically as he slowly scanned Marduk's body from beneath his black hood. His eyes were shooting amber sparks.

"Is it my time, Father? Is that why ye're here?" Marduk managed to hold a solid march toward the sitting area, then motioned for Omega to join him.

Omega's steps were heavy with a thumping sound that made Marduk's head ache. Omega lowered himself into the chair across from Marduk and opened the bottle of wine.

"You know why I am here, Marduk. Do not play the fool with me." Omega poured himself a full goblet of wine and sat back regally while Marduk drank straight from the bottle with slumped shoulders.

"Krava. Ye want to make sure I don't abuse yer favorite son," Marduk said like a petulant child who'd just been reprimanded. He took a long pull of Scotch and waited for Omega's answer.

Omega didn't make a sound as he stared at Marduk from beneath the hood with piercing and fiery eyes.

"Don't deny it, Father. Everyone knows Krava was yer golden child. Ye would've put the Crown on his head if he were legitimate."

Omega sighed heavily and drank noisily from his wine goblet. “Do not be so foolishly dramatic, Marduk. The Crown was always yours as my First Son. Legitimate or otherwise.”

Marduk smirked at his father and sucked his teeth arrogantly. “Ye don’t deny his prominent place in yer heart.”

“I do not, and will not. Is that why you sent him away, Marduk? Because you believed I loved him more than you?”

Marduk squirmed in his chair and shifted his shoulders. “No. Believe it or not, I love yer favorite son too, Father. I sent Krava away to keep him from harm.”

“You failed in that, Marduk. Do not fail me again,” Omega said ominously before he drained his wine goblet, then refilled it. “I am not here to discuss my son. I am here to discuss yours.”

“Cain.” Marduk took another long sip of Scotch, then let out a loud groan. “Is he behind my assault? Is he plotting against me?” Marduk’s face withered in anguish. He couldn’t bear the thought of Cain betraying him again.

“Cain is not your enemy, Marduk. He is your son.”

“But is he loyal to me?”

“What does your mind tell you?”

“My mind tells me it is no coincidence that the redhead who has been hunting us has a stepdaughter in my Lair. Brought here by my son. There is something amiss. That’s what my mind tells me.”

“What does your heart tell you?”

“My heart tells me it will break if my son betrays me again. If my son was behind my attack, I may never recover from that blow.” Marduk drank another long pull of Scotch, then looked at his father with tender eyes filled more vulnerability than he wanted to show.

"So, both your heart and your mind believes your son has betrayed you. Can you and your son recover from that, even if he is guilty? And what if he is innocent?"

"If he is innocent, I will reconcile with my son. If he is guilty…I will reconcile with that as well."

"Cain cannot be lost, Marduk. If your son is lost, my Crown is lost." Omega sipped his wine while eyeing Marduk critically. "You have been gravely injured, and cannot perform your duties. Whether it is temporary or permanent, whether he is guilty or innocent, your son must be prepared to carry on as the Black Dragon. It is your duty, Marduk, to teach your son the proper way to hunt, catch, dismantle, and annihilate the dragons of this world."

"Aye. I know. It breaks my fuckin heart. I have kept him at arm's length his entire life because I didn't want him tainted by the dark deeds of the Black Dragon." Marduk took a long pull from the bottle and sighed heavily. "Now I have to teach him all the things I tried to hide from him…in my attempt to keep him innocent." Marduk groaned and shook his head.

"Innocent? Marduk, all your efforts were a waste of precious time. Cain was born wicked. You should have nurtured and tempered his Omegan spirit."

Marduk grinned widely as he recalled his recent camaraderie with Cain. "Aye. He's definitely Omegan. It took 3000 years, but I have come to love that little fucker." Marduk sipped from the bottle and pulled out two cigarettes from a silver box. He handed one to Omega who lit it with his fingertip, then leaned in and lit Marduk's.

Marduk grinned like a young Prince as he blew the smoke from his nostrils. "I forgot ye could do that."

"You can do it too, Marduk." Omega smiled gruesomely beneath his hood. "The secret is brimstone. Fire and brimstone are two of our best advantages when dealing with humanity." Omega chuckled in a deep tone. "They expect it from us, and both scare the hell out of them."

"I never knew that. Who says an old dog can't learn a new trick?" He chuckled. "Thanks for the tip, Papa. Humanity is killing me, and I need a new weapon." Marduk said quietly with a heavy sigh.

Omega sucked his teeth and refilled his wine glass. "I miss being here with you and the lads, Marduk. But I do not miss the work." He drained his glass of wine, then reached for the bottle again while eyeing Marduk carefully. "You look more like my father as each year passes. You have grown into a handsome devil. A true King, Marduk." Omega raised his wine goblet in salute, then flashed a stern glare from beneath his hood. "But your wicked proclivities grow more like your mother's each and every day. You have the romantic curse."

Marduk laughed and relaxed finally. "The monster is not a curse. The monster is my greatest blessing." He grinned devilishly as his eyes turned colorless. "Haven't met a lass yet who didn't appreciate the monster."

Omega chuckled and sipped his wine. "The monster is inherited from me. But your inability to control your monster…that is your mother."

"Aye. I remember. My wife is the same. Do ye have an antidote for Lilith's raging lust? It is out of control." Marduk laughed again and sipped the Scotch.

"The monster, Marduk. There is your antidote. If you used it more often on your wife, she might be cured." Omega blew two long streams of smoke from his nostrils.

Marduk nearly choked on his Scotch as he laughed from his gut and coughed hard. “I also forgot yer wicked sense of humor. It is good to see ye, Papa. But not if it is my time. I need more time,” Marduk said with a boyish grin.

“It is not your time, Marduk. The world of the dead is not ready for the Son of Omega and Danu. We need a hundred thousand years or so to prepare enough Scotch for your eternity.” Omega chuckled again, then touched Marduk’s left shoulder with one hand, and his right thigh with the other. Marduk cringed as red-hot flames shot through his body in wave after pulsing wave, then the pain suddenly stopped. He finally exhaled and touched Omega’s hand resting on his shoulder.

“The pain was unbearable today. Thank ye.” He hung his head and winced. He hated appearing weak in front of Omega, who never flinched in pain a day in his life.

“You will recover, Son, but you may never be as you were.” Omega sighed deeply and ran his hand over Marduk’s left thigh. Marduk winced in pain again, but sat perfectly still as the fire ran the entire length of his leg. “We have little defense against humanity’s new weapons.”

“Aye. That fuckin gun was the devil itself.” He sipped the Scotch again and wrinkled his brow. “But it’s the knife that haunts me still.”

“Your blood phobia?”

“Aye. That fuckin phobia.” Marduk nodded and looked away from Omega. “Surely there is something I can do to restore my body.”

“Time, Marduk. Even the Incubi need time to recover from such a blow. This dragon did a disservice to you. To humanity as well. Humanity will face something far worse in your son.”

Marduk groaned loudly and took another sip of Scotch. "They are unaware that their Gods have children to replace them. They cannot kill us, though they try every fuckin day. It's exhausting."

Omega groaned and took a huge gulp of his wine. "I remember." He eyed Marduk critically once again.

Marduk withered and began to sweat under his father's stern eyes. He held his breath when Omega sat forward, poised for a speech.

"I am proud of you, Marduk. You have handled your duties well. I had my doubts. You were much too romantic as a young Prince, but you have found your balance. You follow your conscience well."

Marduk's eyes teared up at his father's compliment. He took a long swig of Scotch and cleared his throat, then sat forward. "Draco is the best conscience a devil could ask for. He has never failed me. Not even with the Red Dragon. I was the failure in that fiasco." Marduk sighed heavily and took another long swig of Scotch.

"In more ways than one, Marduk." Omega sipped his wine and groaned loudly. "The boy is your Cambion."

Marduk's jaw hung open as his eyes widened. "Braedon is mine? How?" He let out a long low growl when he finally recognized the face of the woman who attacked him.

"The mother has your blood as well," Omega said ominously and with more than a hint of disappointment.

"That is impossible." Marduk said absently and took another long pull from the bottle of Scotch with a faraway look in his eyes. "For fuck's sake, I failed at my own Project? How did I miss it? I never fail to recognize my own."

"You failed to recognize more than a Cambion, Marduk," Omega answered sternly. His eyes were fixed on Marduk while he waited for him to see the worst flaw in this fiasco.

Marduk sat forward with a wrinkled brow. "Is there more?"

"Aye." Omega took a long drag of his cigarette.

"Are ye going to make me guess? What else did I fuckin miss?" Marduk asked with a playful grin.

"I am not your conscience." Omega sat back and sipped his wine without taking his eyes from Marduk.

Marduk shook his head slowly and let out a long rush of air. "My conscience will not let me take their lives now."

"They are expendable, Marduk. They tried to kill you."

"It seems to be an epidemic amongst my sons. Why the fuck are they in such a hurry to take my place? It is no paradise to carry these burdens."

"Regardless of your relationship to the Cambions, they must be caught. All of them. They must all be dismantled. I will do it myself, if I must. But I would prefer that Cain prove himself to the Elders. Let your son hunt these dragons. It is his duty. Take him under your wing. If he is innocent, you will have regained your son. If he is guilty, find it within you to forgive him. Turn him around, and you will have regained my Crown." Omega sipped his wine and took a long, laborious drag of his cigarette. "He needs a conscience, Marduk. That is your duty."

Marduk shook his head. "I cannot be both his conscience and his devil."

Omega nodded. "You can be neither his conscience nor his devil. You are his father. His teacher. I would advise you not to be his friend, but you and Cain are different from you and me, Marduk."

"Ye and I never had the chance to bond while ye were alive, Father. I want something different with my son." Marduk took a long drag from his cigarette, and let out the smoke through his nostrils as he eyed Omega.

"If I had not been so foolish as to kill my brother, you and I might have had more time. My deepest regret in death, is leaving you unprepared for the duties of my Crown. You have struggled with the role of the Black Dragon every day of your life. Cain will not."

Marduk groaned and sat back in his chair. "I am aware." He ran his hands through his beard and sat forward. "Speaking of killing brothers. What am I to do with mine?"

"Set Krava free. He only acted out of fear for his mother. He never meant you harm, Marduk. He does not mean you harm now, and he will be the most loyal friend and brother you can imagine…if you treat him right."

"I suppose ye want me to give him a seat on my Council. Or should I just give him the fuckin throne?"

Omega sat forward and glared hard at Marduk. "Do not disrespect me, Marduk. And do not disrespect your only loyal brother because of your childish insecurities. You, Marduk, have always been my most beloved son. Always. I took you under my wing and have kept you there since the day you could walk. Aye. I love Krava. I love him because he is and always has been kind-hearted. He does not hate, nor does he love to the point of distraction. He is fair. He is honest. Like you, Marduk. I love Krava because he is like you."

Marduk sat back in his chair and closed his eyes as he sighed heavily, noisily. "I have always loved him for those same reasons, Father. Not because he is like me. Because he is like you."

"You and Krava are more like me that any of my sons, Marduk. Set him free. As to your other brothers… Herne is completely innocent. Seth is far from innocent, but he is less guilty than Lucian. Still, they are your brothers. Leave them where they are, and let the Elders serve them justice."

"Happily. But I will not let Samuel rot in that jail cell."

"Samuel was Lucian's pawn. The Elders will see this. He will be set free. But he must not follow in his father's footsteps."

Marduk's face fell. "I love that lad. I would put the Crown on Samuel's head before Cain's."

"Do you hear yourself, Marduk? You are openly admitting what you have just accused me of. Favoring one son over another, and wanting to place the Crown upon the head of the second son rather than the first."

"But I have the agreement with the Elders. My second son will inherit my Crown. Ye didn't have such an agreement, luckily for me." Marduk sucked his teeth and grinned sarcastically.

"He is Salem, Son of Cain. He is not your Heir. He is Cain's."

"I will not allow Samuel to fall under Cain's authority!"

"Cain is his legal father. But he is neither Cain's son, nor yours. You must not allow Samuel to wear the Omegan Crown. If you do, the Crown will eventually fall to Lucian's bloodline in Conall. The Crown must remain under your bloodline, Marduk. Even if that means the Heirship falls to Killian. Killian is far too innocent in the ways of the Incubi now, but he can be prepared for the duties of the Dark God. It cannot be Samuel. He does not have a drop of Omegan blood. Cain is the Heir, with Killian to follow."

"But the Elders have taken Cain's right to the Crown. Neither will wear the Crown, Father. It belongs to Declan now," Marduk answered solemnly

"Fuck the Elders," Omega said harshly and drained his wine. "They took my Crown." He leaned forward and filled his wine goblet again. "You will win it back."

Marduk grinned devilishly, then took a long drag from his cigarette. He remembered now where he learned his defiance to the Elders. "I'm gonna need a miracle."

Omega nodded slowly. "Secure my Crown, Marduk. I will never rest easy with the head of an Alphan beneath it."

Marduk heard a soft knocking on the door and looked away for a split second. When he turned back, Omega was gone, along with the bottle of pomegranate wine.

Draco poked his head in with a wide grin. "May I have a word with you, my liege?"

Marduk smiled warmly and waved him inside. "Ye just missed my father."

Draco's eyes widened as he plowed forward quickly. "It is not your time is it, Marduk?"

Marduk chuckled and shook his head. "No. He was here on a different matter. Have a seat Draco, I have questions. Is Cain behind my assault? Is Raven a mole?"

Draco groaned and sat across from Marduk. "I do not believe she is. She has not given us a day's trouble since she arrived here. Though is it a rather strange coincidence that she is connected to the red one, as well as Cain." Draco took the bottle of Scotch from Marduk and drank heavily from it. "I am more concerned with Cain's past with Lucian. Has he confessed everything?"

"Aye. Everything. He also offered to plot with me against Lucian. Dare I trust him?"

"It may be the only way to ensure Lucian's demise. And to prove Cain's innocence."

Marduk growled as he took the bottle from Draco. "Or his guilt. Set the stage, Draco."

"Aye, my liege." Draco took a deep breath and sat back in the chair. "I have another issue…" Draco blushed and squirmed. He couldn't look at Marduk.

"Ask and ye shall receive," Marduk chuckled, then took a long sip of Scotch while he read Draco's body language. He knew what he was going to ask for.

"I am getting no younger. I would like a household of my own. A home, and …a family." Draco glanced up at Marduk quickly. He wasn't surprised to see the wicked gleam in Marduk's eye. He groaned and squirmed again.

"Done. I have just the place for ye, Draco. A fine Palace in Marbh."

Draco smirked, then grinned like a schoolboy. "You know as well as I do that I will never leave Dorcha. Nor you." Draco grabbed the Scotch and eyed Marduk warily. "What I want is here in Dorcha. But she will be away again soon…if I do not act quickly."

Marduk chuckled and clapped Draco on the back. "Are ye asking for Mia?"

Draco closed his eyes and rubbed his hands over his face. "Aye. I think I am in love."

Marduk threw back his head and laughed loudly. "My condolences. Love is the blackest of all plagues, Draco." He took another sip of Scotch and handed it to

Draco. Draco took a long pull from the bottle and blushed a dark rosy glow.

"Your answer, my liege?" Draco asked softly, and placed the bottle on the table between them.

"Mia is not mine to give, Draco. But if ye're asking for my blessing…ye have it. Wholeheartedly. I can think of no one better suited for Mia than Draco, Son of Li Jing." Marduk lifted the bottle in the air, then drank heavily from it. "I would give ye the world served on silver, Draco. Choose the home ye want in Dorcha."

Draco's cheeks flushed again as he lifted himself from the chair and hugged Marduk tightly. "Thank you, Marduk. I have just the place in mind. It is only a stone's throw from the Lair. I will never be far from you, my liege."

Marduk cupped Draco's face and pulled him in for a kiss. "Aye. I know, Draco, and I love ye for it." He lit another cigarette and blew the smoke from his nostrils in heavy streams. "This was the easy part. Ye have yer home. Now ye have to win Mia's heart. Good fuckin luck."

Draco grinned widely. "I was hoping you would help me along."

Marduk groaned and drained the bottle of Scotch. "Ye set the stage to trap Lucian. I will set the stage to catch Mia." Marduk chuckled, then turned serious. "Draco, my father had some disturbing news. The Red Dragons. Mother and son are both mine."

Draco's face fell as he sat back in his chair. "This is not possible. The Cambion Project has never failed before. We always recognize our own."

"The Cambion Project did not fail, Draco. I failed. I should have recognized my own Cambion." Marduk turned inward again as he tried to remember the circumstances of that week of debauchery in New York with Declan, but the details were hazy at best. "Dig into this, Draco. Find out how this happened, figure out how to fix it, and set the stage. In the meantime, I will turn my son into the Black Dragon, and prepare him to kill my Cambions." Marduk sank deeper into his chair as the full weight of that truth settled on his shoulders.

"Aye, my liege." Draco's shoulders fell too as he realized the weight he would be asking Mia to carry with him if she agreed to marry him.

Marduk smiled sadly and handed the bottle of Scotch to Draco. "Cheer up, lad. Let's go catch yer lass with color in her cheeks."

Draco grinned and blushed. "My beautiful amber lass. I am deep into this romance, Marduk. I cannot fail to win Mia's hand."

Marduk shook his head with a wide grin. "Lad, ye're in good hands. I am the King of the Incubi. If I can't win Mia for ye, it's hopeless."

"No tricks, Marduk. I want to convince her to marry me, not obey some wicked call to the elements," Draco chuckled.

"No tricks?" Marduk asked with a furrowed brow. "Ye just cut yer chances in half, Draco," he laughed and led Draco out of the room.

Omega hovered in the dark corner watching them closely. He sighed heavily when they closed the door, laughing together like naughty schoolboys working on a deep, sinister plot.

"Do not get distracted by romance, Marduk. Ye have dragons to slay. Crowns to secure. Heirs to teach."

Chapter Twenty-Five

"Good morning, Amon, Makawee. I trust ye both slept well last night," Marduk said cheerfully as he and Lilith entered the Dining Hall, arm in arm. Marduk was happy to see the Hall back to its elegant décor, with all traces of the Dead Party removed, and the room spotlessly clean with a full buffet served in silver dishes, and onyx plates lining the table.

Amon stood and greeted Marduk with open arms and a sheepish grin. He couldn't look at Lilith. "You outdid yourself last night, Marduk. Party of the century." He clapped Marduk on the back and led him to the table.

"I cannot take credit. It was all Lilith's doing. Except for the Maze. I take credit for that."

"I imagine the Maze was quite a thrill."

Marduk's heart fell when he saw the blush creeping up Amon's cheeks. He groaned softly and held Lilith's chair out for her. "Aye. Thrilling, and full of surprises." He looked Amon dead in the eye and squinted slightly.

Declan entered quietly with Jade following behind him. "Marduk, ye twisted fucker, ye throw the best fuckin parties in the Colonies!"

Marduk greeted Declan with a hug and a tender kiss. "Where is your bride, lad?"

"Morning sickness," Declan winced. "Rory has rendered his mother useless today."

Marduk motioned to the Servant girl in the corner. "Have the chef prepare soft scrambled eggs, no butter, no cream, and a steaming bowl of bone broth for Queen Caraye. Take it to her suite straight away. Make sure she has plenty cold ginger ale, hot mint tea, dry toast, and salt crackers as well," Marduk commanded, then turned to kiss Jade's cheek softly. His grin faded as he scanned Jade with a slightly withered brow. It was obvious she'd been crying, but she had a brave face today that Marduk saw right through.

"I hope ye slept well in my Lair with no spirits haunting ye, Jade." He brushed the hair from her cheeks, then held her against his chest tenderly.

"Where are the coffins? The severed heads and body parts?" Jade asked solemnly.

"The room has been cleared until the next party," Marduk said with a chuckled as he led her to the table.

"I thought it was the permanent décor of the Lair. It seemed fitting." Jade blushed and looked back at the hallway. "Is Killian awake?"

"Not yet. Killian is sleeping in today."

"I really need to talk to him." Jade touched Marduk's arm and pulled him a little closer. "May I speak privately with you, Marduk?"

Marduk nodded and lightly touched her cheek. "Aye. After breakfast."

Lugh and Aaden entered the room noisily in matching, bouncy steps and wide grins.

"Little Lugh! Yer shining face in my Lair is a balm for my tortured soul," Marduk said earnestly and opened his arms. Lugh and Aaden both hugged Marduk fiercely. He winced in pain. "Careful, ye fuckin beasts. I'm still not fully recovered." He chuckled softly and pulled away slowly.

Aaden took the seat next to Jade. "Morning, Princess." He blushed and smiled slyly as he leaned forward to kiss her cheek.

"Morning, Aaden." Jade couldn't even look at Aaden this morning. She was more confused than ever, and desperately wanted to clarify her status with Killian before taking another step with Aaden. Her guilt over the kisses they shared last night weighed heavy on her today. She suddenly wanted to crawl under the table as all eyes were on her. She locked eyes with Lilith, who gave her a stern, disapproving stare as she huffed and pursed her lips.

"Where is my grandson, Jade?" Lilith asked with one raised eyebrow. "What have you done with Killian?"

Marduk touched her hand to put an end to Lilith's potential tirade. "Killian is exactly where he should be, my love. I sent a tray to his room, so he can recover in private."

"Aye. Exactly where he should be. In Dorcha, with those who love him." She cast a mean glare toward Jade and Aaden.

Marduk chuckled softly at her fierce attempt to protect Killian. He leaned in and kissed her sensuously. "My love, yer loyalty to Killian is very admirable, but Killian will return to Gael with Amon."

"Nope. I'm staying in Dorcha," Killian said adamantly as he entered the room with his hair neatly tucked into a tight bun. "Right, Dad?"

Cain grinned widely and draped his arm over Killian's shoulder. "If your mother and grandfather allows it." He winked at Marduk.

Marduk gave Killian a thorough appraisal and couldn't help the smile forming at the corners of his mouth. He was fully recovered and holding himself up like a true Omegan.

Marduk turned stern yet proud eyes toward Cain. "We will discuss this after breakfast."

"Nothing to discuss. I'm not going back to Gael." Killian marched toward the table, and took the seat farthest from Jade without looking at her.

"Are ye enlisting in Marduk's project, Killian? Maybe we can join together," Aaden said with a wide, friendly smile as he held his hand out to Killian.

Killian scoffed and almost turned away from Aaden, but his conscience got the best of him. "I don't know anything about Marduk's project. Seems I'm the last to know everything around here." He shook Aaden's hand firmly without meeting his eyes.

Cain sat next to Killian and draped his arm around his shoulder. "The Cambion Project is not for you, Killian."

"I'm old enough to make my own decisions. If Aaden joins, I'm joining too."

"Joining what?" Mia asked as she sauntered into the room in a pair of tight jeans that made all the Incubi at the table take appreciative note of her curves. Marduk stood and offered her his arm with a genuine smile.

"Nothing to worry about, Mia," Marduk said as he led her to a chair away from Cain and Lugh, who were both ogling her in lustful appraisals. "General Draco!" Marduk bellowed in a deep voice that rattled the nerves of everyone at the breakfast table.

Draco grinned when he appeared in the doorway with his arms crossed over his chest. "You yelled, my liege?"

"Join us for breakfast." Marduk waved his hand to the chair next to Mia.

"Thank ye, Marduk. I am a starving dog this morning." He grinned widely and bowed gracefully to Mia. "You are stunning in the morning light, Princess Mia."

"I know," she said playfully, but her cheeks flushed when she turned angry eyes toward Cain.

Draco chuckled as he motioned to the chair next to her. "May I?"

Mia raised one eyebrow and smiled beautifully. "Well, at least one man in Dorcha has manners. Of course, Draco."

"We are not men, Mia. We are Incubi," Cain said in a droll tone, then shot Draco a harsh glare.

"Not much difference from where I stand," Mia replied coldly. "So, what's this project, Marduk? I don't want my son caught up in his father's wicked ways."

"I'm not wicked, Mia. Just misguided." Cain shrugged and smirked.

"Where's Concubine Barbie this morning? Visiting with your wife?" Mia sneered at Cain through narrowed eyes. He groaned and closed his eyes as he hung his head.

"Wife?" Killian asked quizzically and shot Cain a harsher stare than Mia's. "What the hell, Dad?"

"It's a long story, Killian. Hurit is Salem's mother…and she isn't officially my wife."

Killian shook his head and sighed heavily. "I thought Salem was lying about that. Apparently not. Twisted secrets seem to be the norm in this fucking place."

Mia wrinkled her brow and pursed her lips. "Language, Killian. What the hell is your dad teaching you?"

Killian chuckled and finally looked up at Jade. He softened a bit at the tortured sadness in her eyes. "Morning, Jade."

"Can we talk in private?" Jade asked softly, then blushed when she realized how quiet the table was in that moment. It seemed that the entire room was holding their breath waiting for Killian's reply.

"Everyone knows we broke up, Jade," Killian replied in a sarcastic tone. "There's no such thing as privacy in this place. If you have something to say to me, say it in front of everyone," Killian replied as he sat back with a pout and crossed his arms over his chest.

"Killian… you're not being fair," Cain said adamantly.

"Fair? Is it fair that she flaunted her crush on Aaden in front of everyone last night? Is it fair that you paraded your whore in front of my mother? Fair that you have a wife as well as a whore?"

"Killian!" Mia shouted. "That's enough!" She lifted her chin and narrowed her eyes at Killian. "You're acting like a spoiled brat, and I know I raised you better!"

Killian withered under Mia's harsh stare, but squared his shoulders and reiterated his stance. "Whatever you have to say, Jade. Say it now. I'm not going back to Gael, so this is your last chance."

"What did I miss?" Amon looked around the table with a withered brow and hunched shoulders.

"Let me fill you in, Amon…Jade and Aaden have been lowkey vibing. You and I are the only ones who missed it, apparently," Killian said angrily.

"Vibing?" Amon asked quizzically.

"They're interested in each other. Romantically. She broke up with me because she wants to be with Aaden." Killian said sarcastically while rolling his eyes.

"But I thought you and Jade…" Amon's face turned beet red as he glanced at Jade and tried to smile. He wrinkled his brow and drank a huge gulp of wine. He was obviously disappointed in all three of the young humans at the moment. He opened his mouth to say something, but couldn't find the right words. Romance wasn't his area of expertise.

"I didn't break up with you, Killian! You broke up with me!" Jade said defensively.

"I let you go so you could follow your dreams." Killian replied sarcastically.

"I didn't ask you to let go of me, Killian. I didn't want to break up!"

"No? What did you want, Jade? To cheat on me with Aaden behind my back?"

"That's not fair, Killian," Aaden piped in. "Jade and I did nothing behind your back."

"And you think that makes it okay, Aaden? To flaunt your crush in my face? Fuck you both," Killian spat out.

The room suddenly become pin-drop silent as Killian's last words hung in the air. Nobody moved an inch, and it seemed that everyone held their breath while waiting for the silence to end, but nobody wanted to be the first to break it.

Marduk finally cleared his throat and put an end to the tension. "Killian, I love ye, lad. But I demand decorum at my table. Ye and Jade will speak in private. In fact, I would like to have a word with all three of ye after breakfast. Scotch as well. Everyone eat, for fuck's sake." He growled softly and cast a playful scowl at Killian.

"Is there room for one more at your table, Marduk?" Marduk looked up at Hecaté regally poised in the doorway in a stunning wine-colored gown delicately beaded across the bodice, with an intricately sequined triple belt that accentuated her long, slim waistline. The sleek skirt fanned out around her ankles like a bell.

Marduk grinned crookedly and stood to greet her, despite Lilith's sharp intake of breath and huffing sighs.

"Good morning, Hecaté. Ye slept well in my Lair, judging from the beautiful glow on yer cheeks." He bent to kiss her tenderly and growled softly. "There is always room at my table for my brother's wives. Where is Delphi?" He offered her his arm and led her to the chair beside Amon. He winked at Lilith and puffed up his chest at her obvious jealousy.

"Delphi is sleeping off a massive hangover. She drank half the cauldron of wine last night. Lucina will be down sooner or later. She's combing every strand of her golden hair, and trying on every dress in her wardrobe. She's as vain as her twin brother." Hecaté laughed softly, then winced slightly when she saw Amon's bright red blush.

Amon cleared his throat and stood clumsily when Lucina glided into the room in an emerald gown that hugged her long, lean frame.

"Hecaté, no one is as vain as Lucian. I will thank you to not compare us," she said in a haughty tone, but shifted her attitude immediately when Amon made his way to her with bright eyes. She smiled and curtsied gracefully, then leaned closer and kissed him softly on the corner of his lips.

"Lucina…you are stunning. If there is vanity in you, it is not unfounded," Amon said in a breathless whisper as he led her to the table and seated her across from him.

Makawee looked back and forth between Amon and Lucina exchanging furtive glances. She cleared her throat and nudged Amon with her elbow.

"Are you going to introduce me to your friend, Amon?" Makawee asked with more than a hint of sarcasm.

Amon turned bright red when he turned to Makawee and realized that she saw through him.

"Yes, of course, my dear. This is Lucina. She is Marduk's sister. Lucina is married to my middle brother, Inuus. Lucina, allow me to introduce Makawee." He waved his hands between them awkwardly.

Makawee raised one eyebrow as she assessed Amon's blushing cheeks as he stared at Lucina.

Lilith cleared her throat and let out a nervous giggle. "Lucina, Makawee is Amon's wife." She cast a triumphant glance toward Lucina, and a sympathetic one toward Makawee.

"Aye…of course. Makawee is my wife. Did I ...not mention that?" Amon stammered, then drank heavily from the wine goblet.

"You did not, my love," Makawee answered. She nodded politely toward Lucina as she gave her a thorough scan. Makawee shrank a little in her chair when she recognized that Lucina was everything she was not. Blonde, tall, elegantly slim, and graceful. "It is a pleasure to meet you, Lucina. You are my sister-in-law, though I have not met your husband, Inuus. You must visit us at the Crystal Palace soon."

Amon nodded clumsily in agreement. "Aye. You should come to dinner, Lucina. Makawee is an excellent cook. She works beautiful magic in the kitchen," Amon said as he patted Makawee's hand gently.

"Cook?" Lucina quipped incredulously "Amon, you have Servants to work kitchen magic. Makawee, I will visit, if for no other reason than to teach you the protocols of being the wife of a King. I was trained for that role from birth…to be the wife of a King," Lucina said arrogantly and lifted her chin slightly.

Hecaté made a small clucking noise with her tongue and shook her head. "Such vanity, Lucina. Especially since you never made it past the position of middle-grade Duchess. Makawee's kitchen skills are legendary in Gael. No one has ever complained about Makawee's protocols in her Palace, nor in her position as Amon's Queen." She winked slyly at Makawee.

Everyone at the table made a small fuss in agreement with Hecaté over Makawee's cooking, especially Declan.

"Aye, no one in the Palace can come close to the magic of Makawee's pots and pans." Declan smiled and raised his glass of wine to Makawee, who blushed softly at the compliment.

Amon closed his eyes and hung his head, then leaned toward Makawee and kissed her cheek softly. "Aye. My Queen runs her Palace as she chooses, and as I like." He wrinkled his brow, then draped his long arm over her shoulder and pulled her toward him for a tender kiss. "Forgive me, Makawee," he whispered softly for her ears only.

"We will speak after breakfast, Amon," she whispered back, then cast a slightly triumphant glance toward Lucina's withered face.

"Speaking again of vanity…" Hecaté said in her most sarcastic tone. "I would like to visit Lucian, Amon. May I please see my husband?" Hecaté asked solemnly. "Lucina, do you want to visit Inuus?"

"Absolutely not. If I never lay eyes upon that fat bastard again, I will be a happy Duchess," she said coldly, then dove into her breakfast, despite the gasps floating around the table at her remark.

Amon and Marduk exchanged glances and both nodded.

"Of course, Hecaté. I will arrange your visit to Lucian as soon as we return to Gael," Amon said sternly.

"Lucina, if you would like to divorce Inuus, I can arrange that," Marduk said in a formal tone.

"Please do so immediately, Marduk. I never wanted to marry Inuus in the first place," Lucina answered just as formally, but cast another soft glance in Amon's direction. "This marriage was forced upon me," she said as she sipped her wine. "As was Nahemah's," she added with an icy glare cast at Makawee.

Makawee immediately picked up on the insinuation and sighed heavily. She suddenly wanted to crawl away from the table, back to Gael and the safe zone of her kitchen.

Marduk cast an angry scowl at Lucina with one raised eyebrow. "Manners, little sister. If ye want to remain at my table." He drained his glass of wine, then rolled his eyes toward Hecaté, who looked a little too smug for his taste. He suddenly had the urge to wrap his hands around her neck, but he filled her wine glass instead.

"Are you seeking a divorce as well, Hecaté?" Lilith piped in cheerfully. She was thoroughly enjoying not being the object of Marduk's anger and disappointment.

"Of course not. I am in love with my husband." She lifted her chin and narrowed her eyes.

"Despite his shortcomings." Marduk winked and arrogantly sucked his teeth. Lilith chuckled softly and leaned closer to Marduk. He ran one finger across her cheek and leaned forward to kiss her tenderly. "*Mo ghrá gheal*, ye're stunning this morning in your very red dress." He winked, and she simpered flirtatiously as they stared lovingly in each other's eyes.

"Would you fuckin look at this?" Cain added with a chuckle. "Marduk and Lilith are the happiest couple at the table. Have we crossed over into an alternate universe?" He nodded approvingly and lifted his glass to them.

Declan cleared his throat and kicked Cain under the table. "My wife and I are happy as well."

"Aye, but…it's expected of you, Declan. That…" Cain pointed toward his parents. "Is nothing short of a miracle. Especially after a night in the fucking Maze, with everybody fucking anybody except their spouses." He chuckled and winked at Lilith.

Amon's shoulders slumped suddenly as his head began to spin. He began to wheeze heavily and he pulled on the collar of his robe as though he couldn't breathe.

"Are ye alright, Amon? Do ye need a wee hair o' last night's dog?" Marduk asked with genuine concern.

Lilith nearly choked on her wine, then giggled softly as she dabbed her napkin against her lips.

Amon blushed profusely as his breathing slowly returned to normal. "It seems that Dorcha is a bit more than I can bear. Makawee, we will away to Gael as soon as breakfast is over," he added with a sheepish grin. "Hecaté, I will arrange your visit to Lucian, but I must warn you… Lucian is unhappy with you," Amon said sadly.

"There's a lot of that shit going around," Killian said under his breath as he picked up his plate and headed for the buffet table in stiff, marching steps.

Marduk groaned again and marched toward Killian. "I understand that ye're angry, lad, but I will have no more discord at my table. I have little control over anything else in my Lair, Killian. Not another angry word, please," Marduk whispered.

Killian's shoulders slumped as he turned to Marduk. "She broke my heart."

Marduk draped his arm around Killian's shoulder and poured out a half dram of Scotch. "Don't let yer mother see." He winked slyly. "This will do wonders for yer disposition."

Killian tossed back the Scotch, then held it out for another. "My disposition needs more than a sip."

Marduk shook his head slowly, and poured another small splash into the glass. "Moderation, Killian. And decorum at my table. I will settle for nothing less."

Killian blushed and drank the Scotch, then sighed heavily as the warmth of the whiskey eased his anger. "Sorry for my outburst. I don't handle rejection well."

"Neither do I." Marduk drank straight from the bottle and grimaced, then locked it in his liquor cabinet. "My whiskey," he said fiercely, then smirked at Killian playfully. "It isn't the cure for what ails ye, lad."

"Is there a cure?" Killian asked sadly.

"Do ye like blondes?"

Killian shook his head quickly. "Not really."

"Hmmm…that's too bad. I have a dozen blonde lasses in my concubine room." Marduk raised both eyebrows and grinned devilishly.

Killian's eyes lit up. "A dozen concubines?"

"Aye. I am officially handing them off to my heirs. Lilith and I came to an agreement last night." He smiled and sighed dreamily.

"Happy for you, Gramps. But I'll pass. I'm sure my dad will be happy to inherit all your blondes. He's always had a thing for them."

Marduk chuckled and cast his eyes toward Mia. "Not always, apparently." He clapped Killian on the back and turned him toward the table. "What are yer thoughts on yer mother and Draco?"

Killian groaned when he glanced at Mia in a flirtatious conversation with Draco. "Great. Everyone's in love."

"Draco is a good Incubus. He will never hurt yer mother."

Killian shrugged his shoulders. "I suppose it's cool. As long as Mama's happy."

"I want ye to be happy as well, Killian. What is yer ideal lass?"

"Jade," he replied quietly, then returned to the table with slumped shoulders.

Marduk sighed heavily and rolled his eyes as he followed Killian back to the table. He caught Lilith's eye and noted a flirtatious yet anxious smile. He knew she wanted something. He raised one eyebrow and didn't even have to ask the question before she answered.

"I want Killian to stay in Dorcha, Marduk. He needs his family." She sidled up to him and kissed his cheek softly. "Think of all the things you and I can teach him."

Marduk shook his head slowly and grinned. "Little minx…I understand ye want Killian here, but that's not a very convincing argument, *mo ghrá*. The lad is far better off not knowing half the things we know."

The room turned rowdy again when the concubines entered the Dining Hall with wide smiles and tight dresses that shimmered as they glided toward Marduk.

"Case in point," Marduk said before he sat back and allowed the concubines to smother him with devotion and affection. It took every ounce of will power he had not to glance at Hecaté to measure her response to his bevy of blondes. He already knew Lilith's response. He carefully leaned closer to her to reassure her and to alleviate her claws digging deep into his skin.

Lilith slipped her hand in his and squeezed hard when the concubines gathered around Marduk with simpering smiles and bold kisses. He grinned widely and proudly accepted each kiss, then watched them walk away toward the smaller table in the corner with a wide grin. He finally glanced at Hecaté, who was staring vacantly into her tea cup, as though she hadn't noticed the blondes were in the room. He turned to Lilith's scowl and shrugged innocently. "I didn't have time to dismiss them."

Lilith raised one eyebrow and pursed her lips. "Now would be a good time, Marduk."

"There has been enough discord at my table this morning. I will dismiss them in private." He kissed her tenderly and brushed a stray curl from her face.

"Would you like me to do it for you, my love?"

Marduk grinned and cupped her face gently. "I will handle my lasses, Lilith. Ye handle yers," Marduk gestured toward Raven standing sheepishly in the doorway on Scotch's arm. The redhead twins were huddled behind them with silly schoolgirl giggles, with their eyes on Aaden and Killian. Marduk stood again and walked toward them with a wide grin.

"Good morning, lad and ladies. Welcome…make yerselves at home. Raven, Sherry, Madeira…please join Killian." He smiled boyishly and waved his hands toward the table, then draped his arm around Scotch's shoulder. "I feel 3000 years younger seeing this face in the Onyx Lair. Ye're the spit of yer father, Scotch."

"I have been dying to see this place since I was a wee lad, Uncle Marduk. My father had fond stories of this place. I am not disappointed."

"Perhaps ye'd like to stay here for an extended time. Killian is set on staying in Dorcha, and he could use a friend. Ye can stay in yer father's old suite."

Scotch smiled brilliantly as his eyes lit up. "I confess I hoped you would allow me to stay. Thank you. Aye. Absolutely. I will be delighted to stay in Dorcha with Killian."

"All settled then. I'll have the Servants open the Prince's Wing again. Ye and Killian will have the entire wing to yerselves." Marduk winked and clapped Scotch on the back. "I have a few household rules, only a few. Stay out of my Dungeon, unless I invite ye inside. Do not go anywhere near my private wing, ever…under any circumstances. And most importantly…stay away from my wife. If ye break my rules, ye'll feel my wrath, lad. But if I catch ye with my wife…" Marduk squeezed Scotch's shoulder so hard he began to buckle under the weight of Marduk's next words. Marduk grinned wickedly as his eyes turned white. "Ye will die. Painfully. Slowly. And no one will know what happened to ye, because my hellhounds never leave a traceable morsel behind. They eat bones and teeth like candy." He winked, then relaxed his grip on Scotch and smiled affectionately. "Other than that…welcome to my Lair, Scotch, Son of Seth. Uncle Marduk has a thing or two to teach ye."

Scotch swallowed hard and nodded. "Aye. I can live with those rules."

Marduk grinned as he led the young crowd to the seats on either side of Killian. "Three non-blondes to cheer ye up, lad." Marduk winked and chuckled softly.

"Hey, Raven. S'up, Scottie?" He held out his hand to Scotch and smiled sadly. Sherry and Madeira waved simultaneously, but immediately dove into their own quiet conversation.

"Marduk just invited me to stay in Dorcha. In my father's old suite in the Prince's Wing."

"Really? Dude, that's awesome. I'm staying too. I'll ask if I can stay in Marduk's old suite. We're gonna tear this place down."

Scotch nodded, but wrinkled his brow as he looked around the table. "What the fuck is going in here? You can cut the tension with a knife," Scotch said under his breath.

"Long stories short…Jade and I broke up. My dad has a wife and a concubine nobody knew about. Mom's being courted by Marduk's General. Marduk and Lilith have reconciled and the blondes ain't happy about it. Did I miss anything? Oh yeah…Hecaté and Lilith are fighting for the title of best-dressed blonde, and I think Amon's got a crush on Marduk's sister."

"I love it here already," Scotch chuckled wickedly.

"You and Jade broke up? Why? When? What the fuck did I miss?" Raven piped in over Scotch's laughter.

"Aaden," Killian replied in a droll tone and cast a hateful look at his rival soaking up Jade's attention.

"Aaden and Jade? When did this happen?"

"Apparently the moment he arrived in Gael."

Raven groaned sadly. "I'm so sorry to hear that, Killian. You and Jade were my inspiration. Did you say Marduk and Lilith reconciled? I guess that means…" Raven drifted off into sadness when she looked at Lilith hanging on Marduk's arm and his every word.

"Where you involved with Marduk too?" Killian asked quizzically. "My Gramps is the man," he chuckled softly.

Raven smiled sadly and slipped her arm through Killian's. "Not Marduk. Lilith."

Scotch leaned forward with an interested grin. "You're either the bravest or the dumbest lass I've ever known. I like you, Raven."

"I had Marduk's blessing," she said with a shrug.

"I am beyond impressed. You're getting some company in this place, lass. Killian and I are moving into the Lair." Scotch raised his glass of wine. "To the three of us."

"Hellions in Hell," Raven growled.

Killian raised both eyebrows and made of face of approval that faded quickly when Aaden leaned closer to Jade, who was laughing at a private joke between them. "I guess we've both been unceremoniously dumped, Raven. And the timing couldn't be better," he said playfully and managed to nudge a smile out of Raven.

Raven leaned in and cupped her hand over Killian's ear. "I know where Marduk keeps his stash of weed."

Killian grinned and bobbed his head. "I can't imagine anything better than the Devil's weed. Let's all meet up in the garden after breakfast."

Cain leaned in toward Declan and motioned him forward. "After breakfast, I'd like to talk to you in private," he whispered.

Declan wrinkled his brow. "Aye. But if it's about Mia…"

Cain shook his head quickly. "No. This is something more important."

Declan raised one eyebrow and smirked. "What's more important than my daughter?"

"The Red Dragon. We uncovered a disturbing connection last night. You need to know the whole story."

Declan let out a rush of air as a small shiver ran through his body. "Aye. After breakfast."

The remainder of breakfast was filled with happier stories, and bawdy accounts of the Dead Party, with even a few hints of the Maze activity, but not another angry word was spoken.

When the Servants came in to clean up the plates, Marduk stood from the table and motioned toward Jade.

"May I have a word with ye, lass? I would also like to see Killian, Aaden, and Scotch. Come along, children," he said ominously as he led them into his private study.

Cain glanced at Declan and motioned for him to follow. Draco caught the signal and decided to join the two of them to share his own discoveries about the Red Dragon. He leaned in to Mia with a shy smile.

"Princess Mia, I have business to attend to, but may I escort you to Queen Caraye? And…perhaps a stroll through the rose garden later this morning?" Draco asked politely, holding his breath while waiting for Mia's answer.

Mia smiled and nodded a little absently as she watched Marduk leave the room. "I would like that very much, Draco. I'll be with Caraye when you're ready."

Lilith glanced sadly at Raven and leaned toward her. "May I have a word with you, Raven?"

Raven nodded and sighed sadly. She knew what was coming. "My room or yours?"

"Mine," Lilith replied softly, then reached for Raven's hand under the table. Breaking off a romance was a first for Lilith, and she didn't know it would hurt so deeply.

She wasn't even certain she wanted to end her love affair with Raven, but she was certain that she didn't want Marduk to keep his lovers.

Lilith pulled Raven along gently, silently until she reached her suite. The moment she closed the door, she rested her head on Raven's shoulder and let out a small sob.

"I am sorry, Raven…not sorry that I loved you…and I did. I truly did love you, lass." She cupped Raven's cheeks and kissed her softly, tenderly in a series of breathless kisses that made her head spin with love. "But I have made a definitive promise to remain loyal to my marriage. You are free to love whoever you wish, Raven. I will give you…anything your heart desires, because…you gave me so much more that I can ever repay. You taught me how to truly love from the heart. You gave me love when no one else did, and for that…I will love you forever. But I can no longer be your lover."

Raven nodded and wiped away the tears from her cheeks. "You did the same for me, Lilith. I never knew that I was bisexual…full-on gay, even. And I'm not unhappy about it. I…didn't know why I never felt completely happy with men. Now I know why. It's because I prefer women. Is it okay to be homosexual here? Marduk didn't seem to mind."

Lilith sniffed loudly and nodded as she wiped away her tears. "Aye, my little bird…we hold no condemnation against anyone for same-sex love. You may love anyone you desire here, Raven. Marduk has only rule about sex…mutual consent between partners. There are many other lasses here in Dorcha who love each other. I will have them brought the Lair for you, if you wish. Would that make you happy?" Lilith stared sadly into Raven's eyes, and placed one more tender kiss on her lips.

Raven nodded. "I think so. I wasn't sure I wanted to stay here, but…Killian and Scotch are staying, so…yeah. I think I would love to meet others like me." She rubbed her soggy cheeks again and looked deep into Lilith's tender eyes.

"If things were different…I would keep you, Raven. Because I do love you…but I am in love with Marduk, and will never risk losing him again."

Marduk lowered himself into his chair with a groan as his knees and back cracked loudly. He waved his hands toward the sofa and waited for the young ones to take their seats. He snapped his fingers and his pack of dogs moved forward. They formed a tight line beside him.

"Puppies!" Jade said innocently and made a move toward the dogs, but stopped when they hunched their massive backs and bared their teeth without making a sound.

"They are not pets, Jade. Back away slowly." Marduk said ominously.

"Are those the dogs you spoke of earlier?" Scotch asked in a high-pitched voice.

Marduk raised one eyebrow and squinted at Scotch. "Aye. Heed my warning, lad."

"I will, Uncle Marduk," he choked out breathlessly.

"It has come to my attention that all of ye entered my private work area last night. Without permission." He lit a cigarette and fumed through his nostrils. "I will only warn ye once. That part of the Lair is off limits to all of ye. Do not step foot in there again." He sucked his teeth and glared at all four of them.

"We just wanted to explore the Lair, and we stumbled upon the room. What the fuck do ye do in there, Marduk? It looks like a torture chamber," Aaden said with a playful grin.

Marduk took a long drag from his cigarette and raised his chin. "It can easily become one, Aaden…if I ever find an unauthorized person in there again," he said in a dark, ominous tone. "Are we clear on that?" He sat back in his chair, then turned his squinted eyes to Killian sitting quietly with a sheepish face.

"Clear as that crystal dildo I saw in your torture chamber," Aaden replied with a small, cocky grin.

Marduk wasn't amused. He raised one eyebrow and pursed his lips.

"We didn't mean any harm, Marduk," Jade answered softly.

"We were bored," Killian added with a shrug.

"If ye ever find yourself curious or bored in my Lair again, come see me. I will find things for ye to do. But never, ever in that room." Marduk snuffed out his cigarette then sat forward in his chair.

"I led them there, Marduk. I assumed it was alright, since Omega was my grandfather. I just wanted to know more about him," Scotch said sheepishly.

"Scotch, I appreciate yer honesty. I also appreciate that ye want to know more about Omega, and perhaps even yer father's childhood. This can be arranged, lad. Killian, ye asked earlier if ye could stay in Dorcha…Aye. I would be honored and thrilled to have ye in my household. If yer mother will allow it, I will have my old suite prepared for ye. While ye're here, I would like ye and Scotch to have lessons on the history of the Omegan Tribe, and the Tuatha Dé Danann. Danu is the mother of our Tribe, and has a fascinating history of her own. Ye should know her story as well as Omega's."

"Do you mean it, Marduk?" Scotch and Killian asked almost simultaneously. Their eyes were bright with anticipation. "We can stay?"

"What about our training, Killian? The Revolution?" Jade asked. She was terrified of being separated from Killian.

"I can train here," Killian replied coldly.

"But…the gym is in Gael…your sparring equipment…"

Killian shot Jade an icy glare. "Aaden is welcome to my use my leftovers."

"That's fucked up, Killian…cheap shot, dude," Aaden spat out.

Killian turned red in the face as he and Scotch leaned toward Aaden and Jade with scowling grins as the four of them began a verbal free-for-all of shouted insults and hurled accusations.

Marduk groaned loudly, then snapped his fingers once and his dogs moved forward slowly with slight growls and bristled fur on their hunched backs.

The fighting stopped immediately and the four of them huddled together in fear at the six massive black dogs baring their fangs and licking their lips.

Marduk grinned crookedly and snapped his fingers twice. The dogs relaxed and sat gingerly in perfect formation. "As I was saying earlier…ye lads must abide by the household rules. One slip up and off ye go to the dog house." He cast his eyes on Scotch.

"There will be no slip ups, Marduk. I swear it." Scotch grinned arrogantly and Marduk immediately liked him for it.

"If ye'll excuse us, Scotch. I have some business with yer three amigos. This does not concern ye."

Scotch nodded politely and quietly walked as far away from the dogs as possible. He saluted once before he left the room with a superior smirk. He believed Marduk played right into his hands.

Marduk, however, wasn't fooled by Scotch a single minute. He knew the lad had been angling for an invitation to the Lair since he arrived. Marduk didn't want to refuse him the opportunity to learn about his Omegan heritage. Marduk was angling for a couple things himself. First, he hoped to earn the lad's trust to discover the true extent of Seth's participation in the Rebellion. Secondly, he wanted to ease Delphi's burden of raising a headstrong Prince on her own.

"So…about this love triangle... things are out of hand, and ye need to get it under control. We are Incubi, even ye half-breeds. Love is what we do. Incubi do not apologize for passion, romance, nor love. We do not restrict each other's right to love whomever we choose. With the appropriate lines of communication, any problem can be resolved. I demand that the three of ye work out a viable solution to this problem, where no one holds grudges against each other for things we cannot control. We do not control our passions. Our passions control us. There is no blame for it."

"But they did this right in my face!" Killian said loudly and moved away from Jade.

"We didn't do anything, Killian. We talked…we…kissed, but it's not like we had sex behind your back. It's not cheating, Killian. You broke up with me."

"Because you're in love with Aaden!"

"I'm not in love with anybody! I just want to be a normal girl in this weird freakin place we're stuck in. I'm confused, Killian. I need time to sort it out. But I can't lose you. You're my best friend."

"Oh fuck, you just painted me in the friend corner. After all we've been through!"

Aaden sat forward and made an attempt to shield Jade from Killian's anger. "Ye're not being fair. I know ye've both been through a ton of shit that would break a lesser person. Killian…I have so much respect and admiration for you for surviving all that…with your sanity intact. Ye handled yer shit, Killian. Jade's handling hers the best way she knows how. She needs space. Ye do too."

"That's rich, Aaden. How dumb do you think I am? Space between us is exactly what you want. You benefit big time from the wide open space between Jade and me."

Marduk shifted uncomfortably, but sat back to let the lads work it out between them. He suddenly felt his age. He also felt his youth when he remembered similar arguments with his brothers.

"That's not what I meant, Killian… Jade and I like each other, and we want to explore it. I like ye too, man. I don't want to lose your friendship either. Can we share her?"

"Share her? She's not a candy bar, Aaden!"

"I know that, Killian. I'm not asking to devour my share of her, I'm asking to spend time with her without ye butting in."

"Me butting in? Dude, Jade and I were fine until you came along…butting into my relationship!"

"Our relationship, Killian! A relationship by definition is between more than one person. My feelings matter too, ya know! You weren't the only one who got hurt."

"How the fuck did you get hurt, Jade?"

"Enough!" Marduk finally jumped in. "I will not have discord in my family nor will I allow either of ye lads to speak so harshly to Jade. That's crossing my lines. The three of ye will not become enemies over this. Lads, neither of ye are married to Jade…neither can claim her as yer property. That's silly human stuff."

"We're human!" Killian shouted.

Marduk glared at him with his stern, colorless eyes and didn't say a word. Killian withered under that stare, shifted in his seat, then changed his tactic. "You and Lilith claim each other," Killian said a little less impatiently.

"She is my wife, Killian. And even as such, I do not restrict her."

"Bullshit!" Aaden yelled out and grinned at Marduk. His cocky grin faded at Marduk's harsh glare and the low-toned growling of the dogs.

Marduk snapped his fingers again and pointed toward the cages in the corner. The dogs whimpered as they filed into the cages one by one. Marduk marched toward the cage and gently rubbed the heads of each one. "Ye're good lads, aye, good lads. At ease, my loves. Papa's got this one." He scooped up a mound of dried meat and filled a trough with the morsels as the dogs licked their lips, but didn't move into the trough without permission. Marduk locked the cage, then snapped his fingers twice. "Eat, lads, but no fuckin greed," he bellowed. The dogs walked toward the food in perfect formation, and noisily devoured the treats without fighting each other.

"My hounds set a good example, don't they?" He smirked and waved his hands toward the cage. "They share.

They do not fight over a morsel because they know if they do, their balls will be cut off, and they will never get another morsel again." He lit a cigarette, then blew the smoke from his nostrils while pacing back and forth in front of the trio. "There is a way to make everyone happy if Jade is willing to let both of ye into her heart. Aye. Share her. But let her be free to make her own choices without guilt." Marduk took another sip of Scotch and another drag from his cigarette. "Though I will warn ye…Jade is my granddaughter and I will not allow either of ye in her bed."

"I'm a virgin!" Jade huffed.

"I am aware of that, Jade. And I intend to keep ye that way until ye're handed off to yer husband."

"You're not my keeper! Grandfather or not, you have no right to tell me what to do with my body. My body! My rules!"

Marduk took two steps forward and towered over them. "Ye forget where ye are, lass, and who ye're taking too. I have every right as Chieftain of yer Tribe." He lifted his chin and narrowed his eyes.

"I'm not in a tribe! I'm a human girl! The only people in my 'tribe' are me, my mom, and Declan," she yelled.

"And I am Chieftain of Declan's Tribe."

"Fuck this." Jade stood up and started to leave the room, but Marduk quickly blocked her path with his arms crossed over his chest. Jade didn't back down. She raised one eyebrow and smirked while crossing her arms over her chest too.

"I'm not done talking, Jade. Have a seat."

Jade opened her mouth to protest, but Marduk's harsh glare sent shivers down her spine, and she sat down again.

"Lads…I would like to see ye both in Jade's life. I would like to see ye both romancing Jade, until she decides which of ye she likes best. At that point, the other lad will bow out gracefully. However, if I find out either of ye crossed my edict here today about Jade's virginity…ye'll get another glimpse of my Dungeon, and not as an invited guest." He sucked his teeth arrogantly. "Did I make myself clear enough? And if ye mention the crystal dildo again, Aaden, ye'll find yerself intimately acquainted with it."

Jade and Aaden exchanged glances and began to giggle like kids. Killian shrank into the chair and pouted with a sullen scowl as the two of them laughed breathlessly and hugged each other. Marduk relaxed his stance and grinned too.

Aaden nodded solemnly. "We'll handle this like men."

Marduk smirked and took a swig of Scotch. "I would prefer that ye don't handle this like men. Men are violent. Handle this like the fuckin royal Incubians ye are. No scandals. No fuckin fighting over a wee lass when there are thousands of them out there. My own fucking father killed his brother over a lass. I will not allow that to happen in my State ever again. Got it?"

"We get it. You want us to share Jade," Aaden said with a chuckle. "What do ye say, Killian? Can we work through this?" Aaden held out his hand. Jade did too.

"Let's just see where things go, Killian." Jade said softly.

"Nah. I'm going to make a graceful exit on that note," Killian said sarcastically, then stomped away from Jade and Aaden.

"Killian…c'mon. We can make this work," Jade called out, but he didn't stop.

"Killian…I did not dismiss ye, lad," Marduk said ominously.

"Yeah, well…I'm dismissing myself," Killian said as he continued toward the door. He stopped finally and held his hand over the doorknob as he hung his head. "I'm sorry, Marduk. That was rude. I know you're trying to make the best of a bad situation, but I'm not a kid. I can handle it." He turned toward Jade and Aaden with a firm jaw. "I'm officially bowing out. I'm letting you go, Jade. She's all yours, Aaden," he spat out, then marched out the door with stiff shoulders, slamming the door so hard, a mirror fell from the wall and shattered in a million pieces on the floor.

Jade started to run after him, but Marduk stopped her. "Let me handle him, Jade. Ye'll only make things worse at this point." Marduk sighed heavily and slowly made his way around the desk. He turned to Aaden with a fierce scowl, then a wicked grin.

"Keep yer fuckin cock under lock and key around my Jade." He leaned in and kissed her cheek softly. "Or ye'll face the hounds." He winked and raised his hands in mock defense. "I only want to protect ye, lass," he added when he saw Jade's indignant glare. "Now get the fuck outta here, and send in my blondes." Marduk grinned and raised one dark eyebrow. He chuckled as they gingerly lifted themselves from the sofa.

Marduk's eyes lit up when the simpering blondes danced into the room with swaying hips that tinkled when they shook their gold belts. The dogs began to howl, pant, and wag their tails wildly as the blondes fearlessly paraded in front of the cages.

Marduk moved toward the blondes in an easy saunter, fondling and kissing each one tenderly. He snapped his fingers again at the rowdy dogs. They didn't respond until Marduk yelled twice, then they finally settled down with panting smiles and whiny whimpers. "I have a commission for ye, lasses," he said as he pointed toward the window where he saw Killian pacing frantically in the garden.

"My grandson just had his heart broken."

"What would you have us do for him, Marduk?" Erin asked playfully as she sidled up to him with a sexy smile.

Marduk sat back in his chair and took her in his arms. He drew in his breath, then let out it again in a growling exhale. "Do ye need me to spell out for ye, Erin?" He grinned crookedly, then bit his lip as she leaned in closer.

"Aye. Talk dirty to me, Marduk." She laughed in a sultry voice as she straddled him and gyrated her hips slowly over his bulging kilt.

Marduk grinned wickedly and began to nibble on her neck, then whisper in her ear softly. "I remember a recent night, Erin, when a bold lass took me into the garden and stripped me naked. She ran that golden tongue of hers under my kilt, lingering over my Omegan charm, then she spread her thick, firm thighs and…"

"Marduk!" Lilith yelled from the doorway. "What are you doing?"

Marduk jumped up from his chair, dumping Erin onto the floor with a loud plop. He grinned like a naughty boy and shrugged as he helped Erin up from the floor. "I was giving them instructions."

"Instructions on what? How to seduce you? If they haven't learned that by now, they are useless." Lilith sauntered into the room with her hips swaying precociously.

Marduk couldn't take his eyes off her as she made her way toward him with a sassy smirk.

"Aye, they already know how to seduce me…obviously." He smoothed his billowing kilt and grimaced slightly as Lilith huffed loudly, but she never stopped swaying toward him. "But they needed instructions on how to seduce Killian."

"Really, Marduk? Have the counterfeit Liliths turned you into a spineless swine… and robbed you of your creativity?" Lilith raised one eyebrow, then snapped her fingers at the concubines. "Out. All of you. Marduk is no longer available to a single one of you, nor groups of you. You are all dismissed from my household, as well as my husband's bed. The concubine room is closed. All of you can return to your fathers, husbands, lovers, or the fucking gardens, for all I care. But none of you will remain in the Onyx Lair. None of you will ever again cross Marduk's threshold, and I want all my fucking dresses back," Lilith commanded. "Leave here as ye came. Naked."

The concubines all huffed and turned to Marduk for further instructions. He grinned widely at Lilith and pulled her into his arms fiercely. "That's rather harsh, Lilith. Let them keep the gowns at least. They earned them." He grinned and ducked as she playfully punched his arm. "Let's keep them in the concubine room for Cain's sake. Killian and Scotch will be staying in Dorcha. They'll need the concubines…"

"Dismiss them, Marduk. You can commission other concubines for the lads. Preferably those who have not been in your bed." Lilith raised one perfectly arched eyebrow and pouted slightly.

"Aww…anything but that pout, my love. I want ye to be happy and content in our new agreement. But Killian is in need of a distraction from Jade." He cupped her chin and bent to kiss her tenderly.

"Dismiss them, Marduk," she reiterated more firmly this time. "And have them return my gowns. I will never be happy otherwise." She lifted her chin and crossed her arms over her chest.

Marduk grinned as he lifted her off her feet, set her on his desk, lifted her dress, then spread her legs wide.

"Ye lasses heard my wife. Return her dresses and leave the Lair. Ye're all dismissed from my service. Titus will handle the details of yer departure." He groaned and growled when Lilith wrapped her legs around his back and arched her body forward as her hands slipped under his kilt. "Close the door on your way out, lasses."

Erin huffed as she placed her hands on her hips. "Marduk! You said I was on your list!"

Marduk never took his eyes from Lilith as his hands roamed over her body. "There's only one name on my list from this day forward. Lilith," he whispered, then kissed her savagely. "My Queen."

"Marduk…" Erin continued.

"Out!" Lilith and Marduk shouted at the same time, then collapsed against each other in laughter, but their hands and mouths continued to explore each other as though they were first-time lovers, and indeed this was the first time they'd dedicated themselves to being exclusive lovers.

"I rather like this agreement, Marduk. Just you and me," Lilith whispered against his grinning lips.

"Aye, *mo ghrá gheal*. Just the two of us is all that's needed to set this fuckin Lair on fire."

"My body is on fire, Marduk."

"It would be my pleasure to douse those flames for ye, Lilith."

"Only you can, Marduk." She grinned.

"Ye say that to all the lads." He laughed softly, then laced his fingers in her hair.

"Never again, my love."

"What of your skinny lass?"

Lilith sighed heavily and smiled sadly. "Gone."

"And your mysterious horny Duke last night, *mo ghrá*?"

She smiled seductively and pressed her breasts firmly against his chest. "I liked my horny Duke as well, but he is no match for my husband."

Marduk took in a deep breath and smiled as he kissed her tenderly. "Just the two of us then?"

"Just you and me."

Draco escorted Mia to Caraye's door, then held her hands in his and grinned sheepishly. He blushed a dark crimson as he stared deep into her eyes. He couldn't find his voice, but he desperately wanted to ask her to join him for dinner.

Mia smiled seductively and leaned in closer to press against his cheek. She was enchanted by his caramel and cinnamon scent and suddenly wanted to curl up in his arms.

"Mia…I…" Draco began, then swallowed hard and leaned his forehead against hers.

"You don't have to say it, Draco. You're a gentleman and you don't want to lead me on. I get it. You just wanna be friends," Mia said quietly and attempted to pull away, but Draco wouldn't let her out of his arms. He found his voice, finally, but kissed her tenderly before speaking.

"You have it all wrong, Mia. I want so much more than friendship with you. I want…a lifetime with you. I want…you…in my life every single moment of every day. But…that is so much to ask of a woman like you, so I will settle for quiet dinners, just the two of us…walks in the rose gardens…mornings in the sunlight, evenings under the moon, cuddles under a warm blanket, and soft kisses…until I prove myself worthy of you. May I have the pleasure of your company for an intimate dinner tonight?"

Mia giggled like a lovesick schoolgirl, then composed herself gracefully and nodded. "Yes. To all those things…Dinner. Moonlight. Sunlight. Blankets. Kisses. Yes, Draco…but…if you want to prove yourself worthy to me, all I need is a promise that I'll be the only one under those blankets with you. That's all I need."

Draco's starred at her, awestruck by her words, and cupped her face gently. "Mia LeBlanc…there is only one woman, one Princess in the entire world. You. Who else could possibly be under my blanket? There are no other women as far as my eyes can see."

"Good answer," Mia said breathlessly, then pulled Draco in for a deep, steamy kiss that set them both on fire.

Draco grinned slowly as he pulled away and bowed gracefully. "Tonight, Mia. Have dinner with me tonight in my private residence. I will cook an authentic Yoruban meal, from my mother's homeland."

"I accept… if you let me cook some authentic New Orleans food next time."

Draco chuckled and nodded. "Next time. I like the sound of that, and I love the idea of sharing food from our respective homelands, Mia. I want to share everything with you, lass."

Declan and Cain were leaning together over the desk, staring at the photographs of the redheads and Braedon when Draco entered the room with a dreamy smile. Nobody seemed to notice, as they were completely engrossed in the photographs of the Red Dragons.

"We might have a plan, Draco. It involves Raven, though. Can we get that cleared with Marduk?"

"No. Marduk will not allow Raven to be involved. I will not allow it either. The lass stays in Dorcha until this is cleared up."

"But Raven is my key to Six. I need her…"

"No. We cannot involve her. In fact, after what I've learned, I'm reluctant to involve the two of you. There's more to the story. A lot more."

"More than this?" Declan asked as he held up a photograph. "This is unbelievable. We were right there…in the same fuckin room with her!" Declan said in a breathless groan and sat heavily in the chair.

"She could have killed you both. Lads… there's more…" He pointed toward the photo in Declan's hands. "The boy is Marduk's."

Cain's face withered into a wicked grimace as he stepped closer to Draco.

"Marduk and Six? When? How?" His face was bright red. "How the fuck did Six find Marduk?"

"The question you should be asking is how Marduk found Six. Apparently…she is also his Cambion. Our first failure in the project."

Declan let out a howl when he picked up the pile of photographs and more of the pieces fell neatly into place.

"No fuckin way!"

Chapter Twenty-Six

Lucian arrogantly sauntered into the private cell with pursed lips and a tight jaw when he spotted Hecaté regally pacing on the other side of the bars, wringing her hands, and wiping the tears from her cheeks.

"Spare me your tears, Hecaté. You are not the one suffering in a locked cell. I do not believe those tears for a single minute," Lucian said coldly with no hint of adoration in his eyes as he thoroughly scanned his wife. "You have your revenge for all my sins and indiscretions over the years, just as you promised. I hope your conscience serves you well in your remaining days."

Hecaté's shoulders dropped significantly as she stepped up to the bars. "Lucian, please do not be angry with me. I never meant to hurt you, my love, and I am terrible sorry…"

"Not as sorry as you will be if I ever get my hands around your succulent neck, my dear." Lucian paced far away from the bars, glaring hard at his wife. "Why did you come? To gloat? To see for yourself the damage you have caused me?"

"Lucian, I take no pleasure in your situation. I came to explain."

"Explain? What the fuck is there to explain, Hecaté? You sided with my brother over me! Again!" He moved closer to the bars and tried to slip his hands through them, but the openings were too narrow. He could barely get his fingers through. He huffed and rattled the bars like an animal. "How long have you been plotting against me with Marduk?"

Hecaté stepped up as close to the bars as possible and laced her fingers over his. "I did not side with Marduk, Lucian, and I never plotted with him. The Elders…" She began, but stopped when Lucian pulled away abruptly, then turned his back on her.

"Do not lie to me, Hecaté! You have been to Dorcha. I can smell Marduk on you. Are you fucking my brother?"

"No!" Hecaté shouted indignantly. "I have not been in Marduk's bed since I left Tosú 3000 years ago, Lucian. I have been faithful to the protocols of our marriage! Can you say the same?" She crossed her arms over her chest and huffed loudly.

"Not the same thing, Hecaté!"

"How are the situations different, Lucian? You neglected your wife for your whores! But your neglected wife only sought solace in the arms of the weak-willed lovers you chose for me, instead of doing the task yourself! You treated me like any other of your concubines to be doled out small portions of love as you saw fit for me. Piecemeal, meager portions, Lucian. I needed more from you," she answered coldly, with a slight hint of remorse, but Hecaté never accepted defeat nor regret gracefully. Her claws were slowly peeking out, and Lucian knew exactly how to play his part.

"I never treated you like a concubine, Hecaté. I loved you! My concubines never received the love and affection I gave you! I laid my body at your feet, Hecaté, and instead of enjoying the feast set before you, you chose to belittle me…unman me into an incompetent lad. You squeezed my fuckin balls until they shrunk so far up my arse, I couldn't find them for days… every fuckin time I stood naked in your presence, Hecaté…you drove me one notch deeper into my darkness!" he hissed loudly. "You drove me to the fuckin concubines. I am a King…and desperately needed to feel like a King after leaving your presence. So aye… I took full advantage of my kingly right to concubines, and enjoyed every minute of it."

Hecaté stiffened her shoulders, and laughed quietly, coldly. "King?" she began as her claws came all the way out, but she toyed with him first. One little swipe to whet his appetite for blood. You are not a King, Lucian. You have never been anything more than a Royal Duke. A disenfranchised Duke at that. You had no right to the whores, Lucian. You took liberties. There's your difference." Hecaté yelled, then softened when she finally, truly noticed Lucian's tortured face and knew he'd just spoken his most honest truth. He shriveled up before her eyes, but the sting of it was still fresh and hadn't begun to overwhelm her, so Hecaté held her stance.

"I never meant to hurt you, Hecaté. I sought my concubines only to spare you my curious sexual proclivities. I did not want to disrespect you," Lucian said quietly as he slumped against the back wall of the prison cell. "I have been in bed with many, many bodies but have loved only you, Hecaté."

"Liar," she said in a soft, icy tone.

"Not this again…" Lucian groaned and rolled his eyes. "She was a deep infatuation, but it was never love. Not like you and my brother." He gave her a thorough once over with a budding sneer and small, angry sparks in his eyes. "Have you been to the Onyx Lair?"

"I just returned from visiting Akaia and Conall."

"And you wore that dress? Who were you trying to impress, Hecaté? Do not lie to me."

"I owe you no explanations, Lucian. I come and go as I please."

Lucian's cobalt blue eyes suddenly turned white with anger as he slowly sauntered toward the cell bars. "Unlike your husband, who is locked in fucking prison. You do owe me an explanation of your whereabouts, because I know for a fact that Akaia and Conall are in the Citadel. You did not go to the Lair to visit our daughter." Lucian's eyes narrowed fiercely when Hecaté's cheeks began a slow blush from the neck up.

"I attended a gathering in Dorcha. Amon was there. Delphi, Lucina. It was perfectly innocent."

"I cannot believe you are gathering with my enemies while I rot in prison!" Lucian took a deep breath to calm himself then continued in a calmer tone, but he was seething beneath the surface. "Only weeks ago, you betrayed me. You condemned me to the Elders, and my worst enemy, and last night you gathered with him and your brother…also my enemy. Nothing about that is innocent. The knife you shoved in my back is slowly bleeding me to death, Hecaté. You condemn me and consort with my enemies. I can never forgive you for this." Lucian doubled over slightly as the truth of his words hit him square in the belly. He took small, shallow breaths to ease his pain, then fumed as he paced frantically. He kicked the chair so hard it splintered as it hit the wall. "Fuckin whore!"

"You dare to speak to me of whores and knives in the back, Lucian? How many knives have you shoved into me?"

"Apparently one less than I should have. I wish I had killed you when I had the chance, Hecaté…and I had so many chances."

The room went completely silent for a full minute, but Lucian's words hung in the air. Hecaté finally let out her breath in a loud huff.

"You do not mean that, Lucian. You love me. You cannot deny it," she began to pace slowly, never taking her eyes from Lucian. I swear to you, I will do everything in my power to set you free again, Lucian."

"No games, Hecaté. I am sick of your games. Count your blessings that I cannot fit through these bars, otherwise I'd have wrung your pretty neck by now!" Lucian yelled until he was red in the face, sweating profusely, and itching to slam his fist into something.

"The Elders demanded this of me, Lucian! I had no choice!"

"Do not give me that bullshit drivel, Hecaté! You had many choices! You could have sided with your husband! Our family needed you! I needed you! But you turned your back on all of us to 'gather' with Amon and Marduk under command of the Elders, who never gave you nor our family a minute's reprieve! You had a choice, but you made the wrong one. Go back to Marduk. You are no longer my wife. Apparently, you never were. Your spell is broken, Hecaté."

"Lucian…hear me out. I can concoct a spell…"

"A spell will not fix this, Hecaté. I am already in prison because of your machinations! You made the biggest mistake of your life wen ye betrayed me, Hecaté. I loved you. And not because of your silly spell. I broke your spell the moment you cast it. I did not need the fuckin spell to love you, Hecaté. I loved you all my life. All your life.

Everything I did, I did for you." Lucian paused to collect himself, but the tears flowed down his cheeks faster than he could wipe them away. "I loved you even as you pushed the knife in so deep, I could not feel it anymore. That is the way of it in a fatal wound. There is more shock than pain. You did this, Hecaté. You not only betrayed me…you killed me. You killed us." Lucian whispered, then leaned heavily against the wall behind him. "I never want to see your face again."

Hecaté began to sob softly as she rushed to the bars and pushed her fingers through. "Please Lucian…hear me out. Do not push me away, my love. Allow me to explain." She stopped when Lucian turned his back on her. "I love you, Lucian, Son of Omega. Only you. You have always believed I loved Marduk, but I never did. I never loved him…I have loved only you my entire life. But the Elders forced me into this situation, before we were married. I agreed because I wanted fairness in our Colonies. Peace between you and your brothers, and my brothers as well. It was a commission from our Elders… I could not refuse them."

"Fuck, Hecaté. In addition to everything else you have done to me, now you are admitting that you only married me to fulfill a commission from the Elders! I knew something was terribly wrong when you agreed so quickly. I thought it was to save face from Marduk's betrayal, but it was even worse than that."

"That was not the way of it, Lucian!"

"You cannot take it back now, Hecaté. Do not lie to me anymore. You never loved me. I was a mark. A commission." Lucian doubled over again clenching his gut. "You have broken me beyond repair. Go away, Hecaté. Let me mourn the death of my pride in peace."

"I may have lied about many things, Lucian. But not about my love for you. I love you more than you will ever know. I will admit that when I married you, I did not expect to fall so deeply in love with you. But I did. And I broke more than your heart, my love. I broke mine as well."

"Oh please, Hecaté. Save your drama for the courtroom. I haven't the stomach for it. I can only imagine how far you will degrade me in your testimony at my trial. Go away. I do not want to see you again."

"Please do not shut me out, Lucian. I am the only one on your side. The only one who will testify on your behalf at the trial. Even your own son turned against you."

"Malachi would never turn against me, Hecaté. No more of your lies!"

"Malachi declared himself the One Victor. He abducted Aramanth, and claimed the Crown of Críoch for himself! He did indeed turn against you, Lucian."

"If Malachi claimed the Crown, he did so for his father! For our legacy! Do not come between me and my son, Hecaté. You do not have that right! He is not your son."

Hecaté's tears dried up immediately at Lucian's harsh words spoken in bitter cold anger. She stepped back from the cell with fire in her eyes. "I am well aware of that fact, Lucian. I have lived with your whores for 3000 years. You claim to have loved me, but never enough to give up your concubines."

"It is the way of the Kings, Hecaté! My own father kept concubines and had bastard children with them! Your father did as well! At least I loved you more than them. Which is more than I can say for Alpha. Calista occupied his heart, while your mother never did. I should have taken a page from his book."

"You are cruel, Lucian! You know good and well that I was not alone in your heart. I tolerated the whores in your bed, but when you gave a piece of your heart to her, you broke me!"

"Is that why you betrayed me? To avenge yourself for Morrigan? Aye, I did love her! I love her still. She never betrayed me! She gave me a son! But you ended our love with your magic tricks, did you not? Now you have put an end to my love for you as well. With your trickery."

"Aye! I ended your love affair with Malachi's mother! But not out of revenge, Lucian! It was my love for you that made me do what I did, and I am not sorry!"

"It might amuse you to know that every one of my lovers after her was revenge for your actions against Morrigan." Lucian sneered as he watched Hecaté unravel. He knew the exact buttons to push and pushed them all at the same time. "I loved her and she loved me much better than you ever did me, Hecaté, which is exactly why you hated her. You were so afraid that she would replace you…and I wish so fucking badly that I had placed her on the throne beside ye. I would have had an ally in the battle ground inside my own home! Morrigan was loyal to me!"

"Loyal? Did you know that she also graced Marduk's bed? And Seth's bed as well. She was not loyal to you, Lucian. She was loyal to herself, and her own pleasure."

"That is a lie! She never lay with my brothers! Which is more than I can say for you! Morrigan loved me enough to refuse Marduk! You did not!"

"My affair with Marduk was before our marriage! Seth…has not crossed my bedroom threshold…"

"I do not believe a word that comes from your mouth, Hecaté! Did you fuck Herne as well? How many of my brothers have you taken into your bed?! Did you laugh behind my back while you fucked them? Answer me!"

"What would be the point since you do not believe a word from my mouth, Lucian?" Hecaté said coldly as she paced the room with her head held high. "Did you laugh behind my back while you fucked your perverted whores?"

"Are you amused, Hecaté? Is this what you had in mind when you promised revenge for Morrigan? Is your pride whole again now that you have humiliated me beyond repair?"

"Aye, Lucian. This is exactly what I had in mind. But I have not even begun to humiliate you."

"You are beyond cruel, Hecaté. And stupid too, it seems. You may have wounded me, and stripped me of all pride and dignity, but you will suffer a similar blow to your pride. Everyone will know the truth now. Everyone will know the truth of your broken marriage alliance with Marduk. They will also know that you were never enough to satisfy me in bed. Despite all your love spells and tricks…" Lucian strutted arrogantly toward the bars, glaring viciously at Hecaté. "You could not even give me a son. Now the world will know it."

Hecaté fumed as her cheeks turned bright red, and tears stung her eyes. She wrapped her fingers in his hair and pulled until a thick strand of hair came loose. She grinned as she stuffed the hair into her satchel. "The world will also know of your twisted proclivities, Lucian. Candy is in Dorcha…as Marduk's prized guest. She has been given to Cain, I hear."

Lucian began to laugh wickedly. "Good. I am thrilled to hear it. Candy knows what you did to Morrigan, and will spill all the truths of your twisted magic."

"You cannot win against me, Lucian. Marduk knows nothing about Morrigan. She has not been discovered…your precious Morrigan is still locked away in my prison. Under my command and control." Hecaté pulled the train of her gown behind her and gracefully turned on her heel, then stormed out the door.

"Hecaté! Come back here!" Lucian yelled out, but it was too late. Hecaté had already left the room. Lucian let out a fierce growl when he heard the second door to the prison room slam shut with a loud reverberating bang.

Chapter Twenty-Seven

Draco danced around the kitchen of his new house, light-footed and graceful as he slid from pan to pot, wearing a black apron over his brand new suit, then sashayed from bowl to plate with a blushing grin on his face as he anxiously waited for Mia to arrive.

The moment he heard the soft knock on the door, Draco's calm, cool confidence danced away from him and he began to panic. He covered the pots, wiped the counter, lit candles, poured two glasses of wine, then struggled to untie his apron. He couldn't untie the knot and it wouldn't slip off over his massive shoulders. Mia knocked again, louder this time. He panicked again, and nervously answered the door with the apron on.

Mia's face lit up at the sight of him in casual clothes, Earth clothes, very stylish and worn well over his fine frame. But it was the black apron, splattered with orange, red, green, and purple smudges that made her heart flip as a genuine smile spread across her face. She fell into the first trap Draco set to draw her into his life.

Draco fell into her trap as well as he gave her a full body scan, slowly, awesomely enchanted as he melted into a bashful boy at the sight of Mia in a dark pink cocktail dress, beaded, sparkly, sassy, swinging tasseled, and very short. Her black heels were 7 inches high, and she still barely reached his chest when she stepped inside and placed a soft kiss on his cheek.

"Sexy apron," she whispered, winked, and stepped away, leaving Draco stunned, dazed, confused, with a wide-eyed smile.

"Glad you like it, because I seem to be stuck in it," he said with a chuckle. "I took the liberty of pouring the wine. I hope white wine is alright with you."

"White is fine. Thank you." Mia smiled as she lifted a wine glass and sipped it slowly while glancing around the room. She was pleasantly surprised at Draco's house and the beautiful display of unique African art and artifacts, even the display of weapons on the wall mesmerized her.

"I only recently moved into this house…it needs a little more time and energy. Marduk has kept me quite busy lately," Draco said nervously as he glanced around the room and realized how masculine it was, maybe even threatening, with all the weapons of war and destruction. Draco suddenly felt inadequate. He knew so little about life beyond war and the dark deeds he carried out with Marduk. He wanted to be a better Incubus for Mia, but he didn't know how to connect his world with hers. He picked up his wine glass and slowly paced around the room.

Mia was a bit nervous as well, so she stepped into the kitchen and lifted the lid, then took in a deep breath. "Oh my God, this smells divine…what's in it?" she asked in a soft voice.

Draco finally perked up when he realized they found common ground. Food. "So far, yams, corn, okra, beetroot, kohlrabi leaves, and a wide variety of African spices. I will add chicken and pork if you have no objections." Draco stepped up to the stove and scooped in a carefully measured and highly seasoned portion of meat, then sprinkled a fingerful of small grains. "Teff. Ethiopian lovegrass." Draco winked and grinned widely.

"Hmmm...Creoles in New Orleans use similar ingredients. We eat a lotta okra and yams in my home city," Mia said in a sultry tone as she stepped behind Draco and untied his apron. "As cute as this apron is, I wanna see what else ya been hiding under that thick uniform you're always wearing. I like this outfit. Lemme see what Draco's made of," she teased.

Draco turned slowly and faced her directly. He took off the apron, tossed it across the chair, and took two steps back. He held his arms out as he slowly turned 360 degrees while holding his breath. He smiled when he realized they found another common thread. Sex.

Mia held her breath too as she took in every firm, muscular inch of Draco's sculpted body wearing a soft, cotton dress shirt, tightly fit around his broad shoulders and thick arms, and wool trousers, easily displaying his high, firm buttocks and massive thighs. She was in awe of Draco's body, and had no words to explain the emotions running through hers, but she gave it her best Creole girl shot. She marched toward him in a sexy strut and slowly unbuttoned the first buttons of his shirt. "Nice suit, but...I wanna see more. I mean...I'm showing all leg tonight. Dat's half my body. I wanna see what's under dis fine ass shirt."

Draco held a straight face as she unbuttoned the rest of the buttons and slowly stripped off his shirt and let it drop to the floor. She stepped back with her jaw hanging open.

"Damn. I knew it was gon' be good, but I had no idea it was gon be dis good. You been hiding all dis? All dis time? Oh lawd, I am not mad at ya, Draco. Mmm, mmm, not mad at all." Mia chuckled and Draco closed the gap between them in one step, then grinned when his confidence came rushing back and he kissed her like she was the only woman in the Colony.

"I'll be damned. He cooks. He kisses. He looks good in a suit and out. You ain't never getting rid of me. I got eyes on you, Draco," Mia said in a sassy tone as she stood on her tiptoes and kissed him softly. "Dat's all I wanted to see. Put your shirt back on and get to cooking, mister. Ya woman is hungry, and you gonna have to earn the right to show me the rest of all dat." She grinned naughtily.

Draco laughed softly and bowed with the grace of sculpted art before he picked up his shirt from the floor, and spread his wings wide. "Your wish is my command, Princess Mia. Dinner will be served in 30 minutes. Will you dance me until then?" Draco held out his hand to her and snapped his fingers. Sam Cooke's voice suddenly filled the entire house. Mia squealed with delight, then they swirled and sashayed together around the kitchen in perfect rhythm, and the magic smells of Oshun's food wafted throughout the house to weave its long awaited love spell for a woman of Draco's own Tribe.

Chapter Twenty-Eight

Declan stepped out of the limousine onto the curb of his 5th Avenue hotel and handed five hundred-dollar bills to the limo driver. "Keep the change, Jerry."

"Are ye sure? That's the third $300.00 tip ye gave me this week, Mr. Eamon. Let me help with the packages at least." The driver's eyes lit up with excitement as he stepped out to take half of Declan's armload of boxes and bags.

"Yer wife's birthday?" Jerry asked with a wide grin and a heavy brogue.

"My daughter's homecoming, and the impending arrival of my son," Declan said proudly as he sauntered toward the hotel. Three bellboys with eager smiles ran toward him to take the packages from Declan and Jerry. The hotel staff knew that Declan always tipped in hundred-dollar bills.

"We'll take these up to your suite, Mr. Eamon."

"Thank ye, lads. Much appreciated." Declan handed them each a hundred-dollar bill, then turned back to the driver. "Keep the meter running, Jerry. I'll be back in about 30 minutes. I need to freshen up, then dinner and drinks."

"No problem, Mr. Eamon. Ye and I again tonight." Jerry said with a wide grin. He tipped his hat, flipped over his occupied sign, and leaned back against his limo with a smug grin aimed at his fellow drivers. They'd been fighting for Declan's attention all week, but he retained Jerry every day and night since he arrived in Manhattan a week ago.

Declan stepped into the elevator and tapped his foot impatiently while waiting for a large crowd of noisy people in business suits to file in, one by one. He scanned the crowd of strangers with a slightly sour face that melted when he saw one familiar face.

"Bridget?" Declan asked with a wide smile. He gave her a head to toe appraisal and was surprised at her appearance.

"Declan? You gotta be kidding me! I haven't seen you since '95! Where've you been?"

"Out of the country. For fuck's sake, Bridget. Ye haven't aged a day." He leaned in to give her a lingering kiss on the cheek.

"Neither did you. Those good Irish genes, eh?" She gave him an appreciative once over with shiny eyes, then sidled closer to him.

Declan laughed shyly and took one step back. "Still working on 65th Street?"

"Oh hell no. I'm in real estate now. Here for a convention," she said proudly. "Christ, that was a long time ago! I almost forgot that I worked there. The bar's still there, ya know." She flashed a flirtatious smile.

"Ye don't say? I haven't been there since…that night." Declan blushed and squirmed a little. "Haven't been to New York in 30 years."

"Welcome back to Manhattan. We should have a drink together at the bar. For old time's sake," she said boldly and flipped her hair over her shoulder. "I like the beard." She reached up to run her fingers through his beard gently.

Declan cleared his throat and squirmed again. "Sure. Why not? One drink at the old bar. For old time's sake," he said stiffly. "I have to run up to my suite to freshen up." He looked down at his shoes, then back into Bridget's hopeful eyes. "Meet me in the lobby in 30 minutes. I have a car on standby."

Bridget's face lit up as she smiled flirtatiously again. "You got yourself a date, handsome."

Declan grinned sheepishly and waved as she stepped off the elevator on her floor.

"Thirty minutes," she called out as she waved her fingers.

Declan bit his lip and groaned softly as he watched her walk away. "Still got that fine arse I wanna dive my whole face into," he whispered to himself, then blushed when an elderly woman huffed indignantly and took three steps away from him. He was a bit sullen when he stepped off the elevator onto his floor, then shuffled down the hallway with slumped shoulders and a heavy heart as the weight of his actions hit him square in the gut.

"What am I doing? If Caraye ever finds out…" He groaned loudly as he stepped into his room and clicked the lock, then leaned his head against the cold door and banged his head twice.

"Fuck."

Declan dragged his feet and slowly made his way toward the bathroom while stripping down to his underwear, but his heart was pounding with anticipation. It'd been a long time since he seduced a woman, and the thrill of it was more exhilarating than he cared to admit. He showered quickly, then looked at himself in the mirror critically. His boyish grin faded when he noticed the goosebumps on his arms and the already growing erection.

"Ye're an ass for doing this, Declan. Your wife is pregnant, for fuck's sake." He ran cold water on his face, brushed his teeth, dabbed oil on his beard, then combed it neatly. He sighed in the mirror again, and pulled his damp hair back into a neat bun. "She'll never know," he said sadly. He checked his watch, then marched to the closet for a clean shirt and suit.

"I fuckin hate myself for this, but goddamn it…that ass," he chuckled, then slapped his forehead and sat heavily on the bed. "Think it through, Declan. Think this through, for fuck's sake." He took two deep breaths, then stood abruptly. "Fuck it. I'm an Incubus. This is what we do," he said to himself, then squared his shoulders and marched out the room with his head held high.

Bridget was sitting in the lobby, wearing a tight black dress and red heels, and slowly sipping a Martini when Declan stepped off the elevator with a powerful stride. Her smile widened when she saw Declan scanning her long, shapely legs crossed at the knee.

Declan held out his hand and pulled her to him gently. "I can't believe my luck in finding ye here, Bridget." He leaned in and kissed her softly. "Did I tell ye how beautiful ye look tonight?"

"You just did. I don't mind if you say it again."

"Irish lasses." Declan grinned and slipped his arm around her waist as he led her toward the limo.

Jerry went from a smug grin to confusion, then a sly smile when he saw Declan with a redhead he knew wasn't his wife. He winked at Declan and held the door open for Bridget. Both Declan and Jerry couldn't help watching her legs as she slid into the limo gracefully.

Declan slipped another hundred-dollar bill into Jerry's pocket and grinned sheepishly. "For your discretion.

My wife can never know about this, and Bridget cannot know about the wife."

"I never saw her. And I know nothing about yer lovely wife," Jerry said softly. "This one's got legs for days, Mr. Eamon." He winked and sucked in his breath.

"Aye. It's not in my nature to resist long-legged redheads." Declan winced and hung his head. "Take us to 65th and 1st. We're going to an Irish pub."

"Straight away, Mr. Eamon."

Declan slid in beside Bridget with a sexy grin and pulled her close to him. "Real Estate, eh? I've been thinking of making some property investments in New York. Can ye recommend something?"

She smiled, handed him a business card, then slipped under his arm. "I can, in fact. I'd be happy to show you the city from a different perspective than last time, but not tonight. Tonight, we're on an official date." She lifted her face in the hopes of a kiss.

Declan leaned in and tenderly brushed her lips, then opened his mouth over hers passionately when she draped her body against his. Declan's pulse raced when she ran her hands over his chest, and he ran his hands over her entire body.

"Dammit Bridget, you're still as fine and beautiful as the last day I saw ye," Declan whispered before sliding his hand up her dress and pulling her closer for a passionate kiss.

Cain sat at the far end of a bar in Hell's Kitchen with his back against the wall, sipping his Scotch slowly. He was aware of every person in the room, especially Titus in the corner booth, but more so the rusty-haired man engrossed in a cell phone game that made obnoxious noises grating on Cain's nerves. When the door opened to a crowd of people, Cain noted a familiar face and groaned when she came toward him with wide eyes.

"Finn! I'm so glad you called me. What the fuck are you doing in New York? Is there a gathering I don't know about?"

Cain smiled his usual disenchanted smirk. "I'm the gathering you don't know about," he replied coldly, sipped his Scotch, then leaned forward to place a lingering kiss on her cheek. "How are you, Six?"

"Not so good." She took the stool next to him and ordered a spicy Bloody Mary. "Money problems. I'm about to lose my Brownstone. My son…ugh. That idiot is such a burden. My boss is a bitch, and I can't find another job in my field. I got problems, Finn. Need another trip to New Orleans. When are you going back? I'm thinking about leaving New York for good. And where the hell is Raven? She fell off the radar. Do you know where she is? That little bitch owes me a lotta fucking money."

Finn rolled his eyes and gave her a bored look. "I could've lived forever without knowing all that shit, Six." He drained his glass of Scotch and tossed a hundred-dollar bill on the bar. "Another Scotch. And whatever the lady's having." He leaned back and gave her a thorough once over. "You look good, darlin. Even with all your problems. Maybe you'd like to take your mind off those troubles for a minute." He winked and slipped a small bag of white powder into her hand.

"Hell fuckin yeah. I knew you'd be holding, Finn. Wanna go to my place to do this? I'm only a few blocks away. Nobody's home," she said flirtatiously.

"I've got a hotel room across the street. We can hang out there, but I don't mind if you get a head start in the ladies room. I've got plenty more where that came from." Cain smiled seductively and ran his fingers through her hair.

"In that case…I'll be right back." She slid off the bar stool and gracefully made her way to the ladies room. Cain watched her walk away and grinned devilishly when he thought about taking her back to his hotel room to have sex with her first. He shook his head as he thought better of it.

"She'll never shut up."

He drained his Scotch, nodded to Titus, and made his way out the front door as Titus made his way toward the back.

Declan and Bridget were highly aroused from their steamy foreplay in the back of the limo when they arrived at the pub. Neither wanted to break apart when the limo stopped.

"Is this the place, Mr. Eamon?" Jerry asked without turning around.

Declan looked up and grinned when he saw the bar, and the memories of this place came flooding back. "Aye. This is it. Can ye stick around, Jerry? We're only having one or two drinks," Declan said as he handed Jerry a wad of cash.

"I'll be right here. Ain't going nowhere without ye, Mr. Eamon," Jerry answered with a wide grin.

Declan stepped out of the limo first, then held his hand out to Bridget. He growled appreciatively when she swung her long legs out of the limo, then smoothed her dress. He slipped his arm around her waist and led her into the bar with a firm grip on her hips.

The bar was exactly as he remembered it, but the crowd had changed. Declan didn't recognize anyone. He wasn't sure if that was good or bad. He began to feel the weight of his actions settle on his shoulders, but pushed images of Caraye out of his head when he took a seat at the bar inches from Bridget.

"Irish whiskey, neat. Martini for the lady." Declan tossed a bill on the bar, then turned back to Bridget with a shy smile. "So, what's new in the life of Bridget? Besides your new career. Are ye married?"

"Nope. I'm a career girl. I like this much better than looking after a lazy man and bratty kids," Bridget said a little harshly, then looked at Declan's hand for a wedding ring. She breathed a sigh of relief when she didn't see one, but she knew how slick Declan was, and decided to test him a little.

"What about you? You probably have a dozen kids and a fat wife," she said with a wide smile as the bartender placed the drinks in front of them.

Declan hesitated for a second, then shook his head. "I have neither. Here's to the single life." Declan grinned as he lifted his drink, but winced slightly when her face lit up.

"Still a playboy, huh? It suits you, Declan. You're not cutout to be a husband and father."

Declan felt the sting of her words cut him deeply. "Apparently not."

"I have a confession." Bridget smiled playfully, and Declan's heart skipped a beat.

"Oh? Don't make me guess, sweetheart. I'm terrible at that sort of thing." He laughed softly and pulled her closer, running his hands firmly over her bottom.

“I saw you in the hotel earlier today. I kind of planned our accidental meeting in the elevator,” she giggled softly.

“Did ye really? Well, if ye’re waiting for me to be mad about that, ye’ll be waiting a long time, lass,” he answered in a deep voice. “I’ve thought about ye more than I wanted to over the years, Bridget. I’ve never been able to get this flaming red hair of yours out of my mind.”

Bridget laughed seductively and leaned in closer to his cheek. “Your scent. Fresh apples and ocean water. That’s what haunted me all these years.”

“Dammit, girl. I did miss ye,” he whispered. “I’m glad ye maneuvered your way into that elevator.” He kissed her softly and sucked in his breath. “I never thought I’d see ye again, but here ye are. As beautiful and tricky as ever.”

“I remember you being the tricky one. I was kind of surprised that you recognized me. There must have been thousands of girls after me.”

“I never forgot ye, Bridget. Ye were one of the special ones I kept in here.” Declan placed her hand over his heart, then lightly brushed his lips over hers.

“Don’t play with me, Declan. I know your type. Love ‘em and leave ‘em.” She smiled. “If I had truly been in your heart, you would have come back for me.”

“Life kept me a bit busy over the years, Bridget. But ye were always in the front of my mind. I swear it, lass.”

“We did have a lot of fun that night, didn’t we? Despite your troubles at home. What happened with your little sister? The one that was marrying the viper,” she laughed softly.

“Issa married her viper.” He wrinkled his brow and drank his entire dram, then waved at the bartender. “Another round, please. And keep ‘em coming.”

Cain strolled around the West side of Manhattan, with an arrogant bounce in his steps. He ducked into a dark alley, seemingly unaware of the man following closely in awkward steps. He grinned as he sent a signal to Titus waiting ahead. He slowed his steps, and when the man made his move, Cain turned quickly and wrapped his hand around the man's throat. His eyes lit up when he saw the fear in the young man's eyes.

"Why the fuck are you following me?" Cain asked in an ominous tone and squeezed harder. "Are you really that stupid?"

The man shook his head and tried to pry Cain's fingers from his neck, but Cain tightened his grip. He grinned wickedly at the bulging eyes and blood-red face inches from his. He laughed slowly as he pulled out a sharp ice pick from his pocket, then held it up to the man's eyeline.

"I'm Cain, and I'm gonna fuck you up," Cain whispered eerily, right before he plunged the pick into the man's carotid artery in three quick jabs. He laughed again as the blood spurted out in a fat stream, then ran down his hand. Cain laughed maniacally for a few seconds, then abruptly stopped, rolled his eyes, and pulled the ice pick out quickly.

"The high never lasts long enough," Cain said dryly then shoved the bloody body away just as Titus caught up to him.

"What the fuck did ye do? Ye weren't supposed to kill him here!" Titus shouted.

“One less body to drag to Hell. His cell will be in the Dungeon before we get back to Dorcha.”

“He’s Marduk’s Cambion! Marduk specifically said to take Braedon alive!”

Cain leaned over Braedon’s bloody body and scanned his face. “Exactly. Marduk’s Cambion. No fucking brothers.” He wiped his bloody hands on Braedon’s shirt, then squared his shoulders and stormed off toward the street. “Clean it up, Titus.”

Titus stared at Cain with wide eyes brimming with both awe and fear. This was more than vengeance; this was murder. Titus understood that Cain’s purpose was to avenge Marduk and protect the Omegan Crown, but this brutality was overkill and weighed heavy on his shoulders. Titus shivered when he looked down at Braedon’s limp, bloody body.

“Poor lad. He was just a simple fella.” Titus checked his pulse, smiled slightly, then waved his hand to open Marduk’s Gates. He first dragged Braedon’s body to the shaft, then carefully carried Six’s limp body into it. He looked around carefully and sighed heavily as he waved his hand again to close the Gates with Braedon and his mother in it. He looked back over his shoulder and groaned ferociously as he sprinted to catch up to Cain.

“This is not gonna end well.”

Declan and Bridget were deep into a flirtatious conversation while waiting on their 7th round of drinks.

“Then he takes my fuckin kilt and runs off after the lass I was eyeing all night before I had a chance to get out the door. Twisted fucker." Declan chuckled while Bridget giggled like a schoolgirl. "But he set her free in the end."

"You have to take me to one of those parties. Right up my alley. Your friend is quite the character. I'd like to meet him." Bridget snuggled closer to Declan and ran her hands through his beard. "Did you find her in the Maze?"

"Aye. I always get my lass." Declan grinned widely and wrapped his arms around her waist.

"Yeah. You're lucky like that."

"More skill than luck." Declan winked, then leaned forward to place a sensual kiss over her slightly parted lips.

"I remember your skills. Well …I don't remember, to be honest. The whole night is a blur. All I remember is that we were high. Very high." She giggled again.

Declan grinned like a young boy and ran his hands through her thick red hair. "I was hellbent on trouble that night."

"And tonight? Are you looking for another taste of trouble?" Bridget asked in a seductive tone.

Declan drew in his breath and pressed his forehead against hers. "Looks like trouble found me."

"Again," she whispered and moved an inch closer to his lips.

"Let's try to remember it this time." Declan kissed her softly, then held out his hand. He pushed away images of Caraye again, and smiled with just enough hint of sadness to push Bridget over the edge. Instead of taking his hand, she grabbed his tie and pulled him toward the door with a sassy, sultry swing of her hips that Declan couldn't stop grinning at.

They giggled like children as they approached Jerry leaning against the limo. With a wide smile and a sweeping bow, Jerry opened the door for Bridget, and once again admired her legs.

"Ye know the way, Jerry."

"Aye, Mr. Eamon."

Jerry drove away slowly, with a grinning eye in the mirror to watch Declan and Bridget kissing in the back seat. He turned off the main street and drove slowly toward the river, taking several turns, giving Bridget more excuses to lean against Declan. Their arms and legs were entwined, both in various degrees of undress with messy hair, sweaty bodies, and smeared makeup when Jerry suddenly pulled into a dark alley and flashed his lights three times, then turned off the engine.

Declan came out of the kiss slowly, with smoldering passion in his eyes, then pulled his hands from beneath Bridget's dress.

"Why are we stopping here? What's going on?" Declan asked as he looked around with wide, innocent eyes.

Bridget sighed heavily and kissed Declan passionately, then pulled away and rested her forehead against his. "Declan…I'm sorry to do this to you…" she whispered.

Bridget pulled away as the dark glass window slid open and Jerry pointed a gun at Declan's head.

"I'm a crack shot, Mr. Eamon, so if ye move more than an inch yer brain will be splattered all over this limo. It's a rental, so don't fucking move."

Declan lifted his hands and froze, staring into Bridget's sky-blue eyes sadly. "Why, Bridget?"

"Don't play games with me. You know why." She smirked.

The door of the limo suddenly opened, and a dozen armed men stepped inside and sneered angrily at Declan with their guns pointed at him.

"Be gentle guys. I don't want him hurt." She grinned wickedly and threw her head back in twisted laughter. "I do want him hurt, actually. But I wanna be the one to do it. Slowly. Not with the fucking guns. Too easy. Too fast. Bring him in alive and alert, boys, so he can feel everything." Bridget smiled smugly, then slid out of the limo gracefully. "You know where to go, Jerry. Shannon and I will meet you there." She turned to give Declan one last glance with a triumphant grin. "You got away the first time, but not this time, Declan. This time, you're gonna suffer," she said coldly.

"Ye knew all along?"

"Of course." She shrugged. "You've been the focus of my entire fucking life," she spat out coldly, then grinned wickedly as she slammed the door to the limo.

Declan looked around at the heavily armed men staring at him with a mixture of hatred and awe in their eyes.

"Fellas, we don't have to do it like this. I've got connections. Whatever it is you guys want, I can arrange it." Declan said softly as he held his hands up and scanned each hardened face.

Jerry laughed wickedly and cocked the handle of his gun, then steadied his position. "Shut the fuck up. The only meeting ye're gonna arrange is yer own meeting with the devil." Jerry winked. "Ye boys got this? I'm not moving until ye steady yer weapons."

"Got it, Jerry. Get us the fuck outta here. There's somebody walking around outside. Go! He ain't going nowhere!" A large man said right before he slammed the butt of his gun into Declan's head, knocking him out cold.

Jerry wasted no time in speeding through the alleyway toward the river, leaving Cain and Titus in the dust and smoke from the limo.

"What the fuck is he doing? This is the meeting place. Why the fuck is he leaving us?" Cain asked quizzically as he sprinted off behind the limo.

"Fuck!" Titus screamed as he pushed Cain out of the way and ran after the limo. He sent out an emergency signal to the Army, then climbed on the back of his motorcycle, leaving Cain in the alley with Bridget watching from the shadows.

"Oh, this is perfect," she whispered to herself. "This shit ends right here, right now. Tonight," she said with a wicked smile as she slowly made her way toward Cain.

Chapter Twenty-Nine

Declan woke to the sound of loud voices chanted slightly off-key. His splitting headache made him shiver as he tried to raise his hand to his throbbing head. He was dizzy, disoriented, and had a strange sensation of falling, as though he were about to topple over any second, but he couldn't move his arms to break his fall. It slowly dawned on him that both arms were spread wide and tied against something solid. He blinked several times to clear his vision, and realized he was upright with his legs tied together at the ankles, and his arms bound at the wrists by thick rope. He let out a loud groan when it dawned on him that he was nearly naked, several feet in the air, hanging on a cross.

As soon as Declan opened his eyes and lifted his head, the chanting stopped, but there was a rustle across the room as the crowds sat on the squeaky pews, whispering softly in hushed waves.

"Welcome back to Earth, Declan," an oddly familiar voice floated up to him, but Declan was still too disoriented to distinguish the individual faces of the crowd gathered below him. He blinked hard several times, then tilted his head toward the voice. He had a shocking flash of recognition when he finally saw the tall, dark-skinned man standing below him, and a dozen men holding crossbows aimed at his torso. "I don't suppose you remember me. But I have never been able to forget you."

Declan finally focused his eyes and fully recognized the man in full Native-American regalia. It was Cheveyo, Sekhmet's husband.

"This is not possible," Declan said softly. "How are ye still alive?"

"My woman shared her gift with me. And with her daughters that you did not take with you that day. You left them with no mother to guide them through this disease. You never came back to cure them either."

"I had no idea Sekhmet had children. Why didn't ye tell me? I would have helped ye through this if I had known."

"Shannon is also Sekhmet's daughter. You met her once. You did not recognize her. He did not recognize Shannon either." Cheveyo pointed to his right at Cain's bloody, lifeless body draped across a thick slab of black marble, tied with thick ropes across his chest.

Declan's heart sank immediately. Their rescue plan was ruined now. Cain was supposed to be his backup, but they were both in the hands of the Red Dragon Cult.

"Is he still alive?" Declan asked quietly.

"For now," Cheveyo answered solemnly. "He will not last long, however. Neither will you. He was not our target tonight. You were. But he crossed Bridget's path, and we could not pass up this opportunity. Soon you will both be dead. Marduk is already dead. Amon will be next. Then my revenge will be complete."

"Cheveyo, we never meant to harm ye, nor your daughters. Amon and Marduk made a terrible mistake with Sekhmet. They had to correct that mistake, but it took years to find her. As soon as they did, they sent me to take her back… before she destroyed all of humanity."

Cheveyo held up his hand to silence Declan as he walked closer to the cross. "They are Gods. They should not have made mistakes. They did not care for their creations when they sent the woman to Earth and left her there. My people suffered. My family…" he sighed heavily. "Gods should be infallible. If they are not, they should not be Gods." He paused and waved his hands across the room of people sitting stiffly in the pews of the church, ruminating over Cheveyo's every word. "We believe it is time to overthrow the Gods. Your father, and your wicked uncle are no longer fit to be our Gods. We, the people of Earth, will chose our own God. One God. One infallible God who cares for his children. Your family failed us, Declan. All of you must be eliminated."

"Amon and Marduk didn't send Sekhmet to Earth. She escaped…she…was sent here by mistake. My mother sent her to Earth by mistake. They didn't know where she was… they sent me…" Declan stumbled through his words in his clumsy attempt to explain the colossal mistake, but he knew the act of creating Sekhmet in and of itself was the biggest mistake Amon and Marduk ever made, and there was no way to easily explain or dismiss it. "I'm truly sorry for the suffering my family caused yours, Cheveyo."

"Not as sorry as you're going to be, Declan." Bridget stepped up with an angry scowl on her face. She was dressed in full Native regalia with a crossbow in her hands, and a quiver filled with steel arrows draped over her shoulder. She lifted and aimed the bow at Declan with a vicious grimace. "I'm in the mood for a game," she said wickedly.

"Bridget…talk to me before you do anything rash. Ask me any question. I will answer honestly, I swear it. We cared about each other once. Let me explain everything."

She shook her head slowly. “I never cared about you. I only wanted to kill you, Declan,” she spat out harshly. “Everything has already been explained to me thousands of times. You took my mother away, and left me and Shannon to suffer as outcasts for nearly 9000 years.”

“If had known, Bridget…I had no idea she had children. I knew nothing of Sekhmet until the day I was given orders to bring her back to Gael.”

“So, you admit your guilt in taking my mother away…to her death. Did you kill her yourself?”

“I was only following orders when I took her…and no. I didn’t kill her. Bridget, if I had known she had children…”

“Don’t fucking lie to me, Declan. Especially being up there on that cross and all. Sacrilege. You knew. You and this slimy piece of shit came here tonight to kill me and Shannon. But I got you first. He just happened to cross my path at the right time. You fuckers are so sloppy.” She lifted her crossbow, aimed it at Declan’s chest, then grinned as she lowered her aim and released the arrow with a soft whooshing sound.

Declan flinched, groaned, and braced himself for the arrow flying toward his genitals. He sighed in panting relief when the arrow curved at the last minute and landing with a small thud, just below his feet.

“Oops…let me try that again.” She laughed and pulled another arrow from her quiver. “Are those tears I see in your eyes, Declan? Awww… you scared of my little bow and arrow? And here I thought Declan, Son of Amon was so fucking brave. All those stories my dad told me about you. I expected more.”

"If ye want to see what I'm made of, Bridget, then take me down from this contraption and face me head-to-head. Let's make it fair."

"Fair?" She turned to the crowd and laughed wickedly. "What do you guys think? Have the Gods been fair with us? Margery…was God and his son fair to you when they took your little girl? She was just a baby when she was killed by that fucking monster, my mother. She suffered so much. Is that your idea of fair, Declan?" She aimed the crossbow at him again when the crowd bolstered her with claps, whistles, chants, and dancing.

"I didn't personally kill the child, Bridget! I have no control over life and death. It's mathematical…universal arbitration of probable laws that no one can predict."

"Here's something that wasn't arbitrary, Declan. You tricked my mother with your blood wine. Is that your idea of fair? You took my mother's blood, burned her flesh…so now we demand your blood and flesh in return."

"Bridget…take me down from this cross. Give me a fighting chance."

"My mother didn't get a fighting chance. Besides, you're the Son of God. It's fitting that you should die on the fucking cross. Again." Bridget doubled over in laughter. "This is too fucking easy. Where the hell is Shannon? She's missing all the fun, that dimwit."

Bridget's laughter rang out in echoes, but she stopped abruptly when the doors of the church flew open with loud creaks and clangs, and a flaming ball of fire shot through. Her eyes widened as the back wall of the church immediately caught fire, then she stepped away from Declan to take in the full specter of the fiery figure marching towards her.

"A church? Really? How fuckin cliché," Marduk said in a droll tone as he rolled his eyes and stepped forward confidently. A burst of flame shot up from the floor with each heavy step he took. The fire trailed behind him toward the door of the church where Draco and Titus were leading the Army of Dorcha into the church two-by-two. They seemed immune to the flames as they walked right through the fire, dipping their swords into the flames to light them one-by-one as the Soldiers spread out across the church among the screaming people attempting to run out the doors. The Army of Dorcha sliced their flaming swords through the panicked crowd that quickly went up in massive balls of fire and smoke that consumed them instantly.

Marduk paused to light a cigarette with a flame from his fingertip, then dramatically lifted his arms as flames shot out left and right, setting all the pews on fire instantly. The remaining members of the Red Dragon Cult went up in flames with them.

Marduk grinned and nodded with confidence. "Fuckin cool as shit. Thanks for the tip, Pops," he said as he glanced upward with a proud smirk.

His smirk faded slightly when he looked ahead and squinted sharply at Declan hanging on the cross with his head bowed in shame.

"Jesus fuckin Christ!" Marduk began to laugh wickedly. "I'm never gonna let ye live this down, lad. Ye're Heir to the fuckin Crown, get off that fuckin cross."

"Ye're late, Marduk," Declan said with an awkward chuckle as he pulled hard on his ropes, but they didn't budge.

"Allow me, Jesus," Marduk chuckled and lifted two fingers toward Declan and made a reverse sign of the cross. The ropes across Declan's wrists burst into flashing flames.

Declan yelled as his arms suddenly broke free and he fell forward.

"The fuckin feet first, Marduk!" Declan screamed as he grabbed hold of the cross and dangled precariously from it.

Marduk turned to Draco and Titus on either side of him with a wicked grin. "Is he wearing a fuckin loin cloth? For Christ's sake, where's my fuckin camera?" Marduk laughed fitfully as he watched Declan struggling to maintain his balance, barely holding on as he squirmed to free his ankles.

"Oh, this shit is going in my memory bank," Titus replied with a giggle. "Next fuckin party…Declan gets roasted to a crisp."

Draco cleared his throat and nudged Marduk in the ribs. "My liege…save the poor lad before he falls to his death."

"Or gets a splinter in his arse," Titus added as he and Marduk doubled over in laughter.

"Reverence, Titus. He is the Heir, after all," Draco replied seriously, but couldn't stop the small chuckle from rising up when he glanced back at Declan twisting in the air.

Marduk finally wiped the smile from his face and slowly shook his head, then pointed a fiery finger toward the ropes at Declan's feet. He was still laughing as he marched forward toward Bridget with a raging aura of fire around him.

"I am Marduk, Son of Omega. I've come to burn away your twisted knots." He bowed formally and grinned as he perused her from head-to-toe. "Ye're fuckin beautiful. Fancy a hot fuck before I kill ye?" He winked, blew her a kiss, then took a long drag from his cigarette.

"This is not possible. She killed you! Shannon killed you! Father…what is happening?" Bridget cried out as she moved toward Cheveyo's open arms.

Declan carefully shimmied down from the cross, then ran to free Cain from the sacrificial altar.

"Another fine mess ye got us into, Cain." Declan whispered angrily as he shook Cain awake.

Cain woke with a start and looked around with a wrinkled brow. He groaned loudly as he pulled himself up. "You lost control of her. My marks are both in Dorcha! You fucked this up!" Cain replied in a harsh whisper, then winced at the blinding pain in his head.

Cheveyo's men moved quickly to take hold of Declan and Cain, positioning them as shields as they faced Marduk in bold stances. Cheveyo and Bridget lined up beside their men with crossbows pointed at Marduk's entire Army, but they were terrified at Marduk's fiery presence and the preternatural Army standing behind him with flaming swords that had just taken out half the members of the cult. The roiling flames along the back walls made it obvious that no one was going to get out of here alive. The remaining men of the cult eyed the side doors of the church, carefully assessing their chances of getting out alive. Their stances were anything but fierce and steady.

"Holy fucking hell, Cheveyo. Ye didn't tell us we'd be facing the fucking Devil himself!" Jerry shouted as he dropped his crossbow and ran toward the side door. Several other men dropped their bows and followed Jerry. They fell to their knees in tears when the door went up in flames. Jerry's dramatic screams echoed eerily throughout the church as two of Marduk's Soldiers approached him and simultaneously brought their flaming swords down upon his shoulders. His body immediately burned up in a flash of fire.

The other members of the cult dropped their weapons and fell to their knees, holding up their trembling hands as the Army encircled them with their flaming swords, trapping them around the flaming altar.

Bridget pushed Declan to the ground and held a knife to his throat while glaring viciously at Marduk. "You killed my mother! Declan took her from us! My sister and I were going to kill you both that night at the Limelight…but you seduced my idiot sister, and she lost her nerve! Declan got away before I woke up. Do you know how long I searched for him after that night? Thirty fucking years! He fell off the face of the Earth. So did you. But your son was right under our noses all this time. He gave us the whole story of our mother's death when he bragged about his virus, and the source of it. Finn told the story to anyone who would listen…Shannon was listening. I will have victory tonight, Marduk. Rest assured, all of you will die before I do!"

"Bridget, look around ye, lass. Ye're defeated," Marduk said calmly as he waved his hands around the room, sending the flames higher. He hung his head and groaned softly. "I am truly sorry about your mother. I made a terrible mistake, but that mistake ends here. Tonight."

"You're damn right it ends. It ends when I kill Declan and your son, right before your eyes!" Bridget grabbed a handful of Declan's hair and pulled back his head, then pressed the knife closer to his carotid artery, but Cheveyo stayed her hand.

"Let him go, Bridget. Do not make things worse than they already are," Cheveyo said quietly. He took the knife from her hand and pulled Bridget backward and pushed Declan forward, then tightened his grip on Cain.

"Father, this is what we've worked for all these years! This moment! We have them all in one place!" Bridget screamed and reached for a gun a few feet away from her, but before she could reach it, Marduk sent a ball of fire toward it. The bullets in the chamber cooked off, spraying shrapnel within the circle of fire.

Marduk angrily blew a heavy steam of smoke from his nostrils as he stepped forward to pull Declan out of the circle of fire, then stepped into it himself.

Two of Cheveyo's men were hit by the flying bullets, and screamed as they ran wildly into the fire. Each one went up in flames immediately, then burned to ash.

"Are all of ye infected?"

"We are survivors of Sekhmet, and victims of God," Cheveyo said solemnly.

Draco pulled Declan behind him as Marduk faced off against Cheveyo in a firm stance. Marduk took in a deep breath and nodded reverently. "Red Dragon. Ye're everything I imagined ye would be."

"Black Dragon." Cheveyo returned the reverent nod. "You are also everything I imagined. I am Cheveyo, husband of Sekhmet."

"Marduk, Son of Omega, and I believe I am nothing like ye imagined, Cheveyo. It is my duty to rid the world of evil. I take no pleasure in it."

"You are all there is of evil, Marduk!" Bridget yelled from behind her father's shoulder. She didn't dare approach Marduk with his fiery aura that seemed to contradict his cool, nonchalant demeanor. He actually was nothing like she expected. She expected anger, brutality, wicked, violent, and bloody retaliation. His casually confident attitude was confusing, and his smooth, calm voice was more disconcerting than she expected.

Marduk shook his head and took a long drag from his cigarette. "I am not evil, Bridget. I don't take pleasure in killing. It's something I must do to maintain balance. I slay dragons to maintain the balance of humanity's evil against the innocent."

"My children were innocent. The children and wives of these men were innocent when your monster killed them. How will you balance that evil, Marduk, Son of Omega?" Cheveyo asked sternly.

"By mercy. Killing all of ye will be the ultimate act of mercy." Marduk took another drag of his cigarette and blew the smoke from his nostrils again.

"Not all of us are here, Marduk," Cheveyo said in an eerie tone.

"Shannon and Braedon are in my Lair. Your war is over."

"This war is far from over. I have your son, Marduk." Cheveyo stepped back and held his machete against Cain's neck. "If you kill my daughters, I will kill your son."

Marduk let out one short chuckle and shrugged. "Go ahead. Kill him. I have another son to take his place. Not all of us are here either, Cheveyo."

"Father!" Cain screamed out. "What the fuck? You're gonna let them kill me so you can place Salem on the fucking throne?"

Marduk shrugged again. "I'm just saying…they can't kill us all. I have a spare son. It's the fuckin truth."

"Then maybe you should've sent your precious Salem on this fuckin commission. Oh wait…you can't send him! He's in fuckin prison! I'm all you got! Un-fuckin-believable that you would bring up Salem while I have a knife to my throat!"

Marduk rolled his eyes again. "Fuckin brat," he said in a droll tone, addressing Cheveyo directly. "He thinks he's getting my Crown. I'm not giving up my fuckin Crown to anyone." He shook his head and advanced another few steps toward Cheveyo, who was staring at him in confusion as he loosened his grip on the machete and backed away from Cain.

Marduk took a long drag on his cigarette, then flicked it toward Cheveyo. A huge ball of flame shot up and the Army advanced quickly through the fire. Marduk finally pulled Cain out of the fire ring and handed him off to Draco.

Cheveyo's men scampered back toward their weapons, but Marduk waved his flaming hand toward the crossbows and knives; each one immediately went up in flames.

Cheveyo lifted his machete toward Marduk, but Marduk grinned sarcastically and flicked a fiery finger toward the machete, which Cheveyo dropped instantly when it became red hot. The men screamed and tried to run toward the doors, but the Army of Dorcha closed in on them with their flaming swords and began to swing wildly again.

"Your first mistake, Cheveyo. Ye took them to a church. I have more power than ye can possible imagine in these churches." He sucked his teeth arrogantly, with a slight hissing sound. "Fire and brimstone. Humanity assigned those weapons to me ages ago, and here I am bringing them down upon your heads, just as ye expected of me." He lifted his hands again and the walls of the church began to crumble. The flames shot higher and higher around Cheveyo and Bridget, who screamed in terror as Marduk advanced slowly amidst the burning chunks of the ceiling falling down around them.

Cheveyo wrapped his arms around Bridget as she screamed violent curses at Titus wrapping ropes around the two of them, binding them together.

Draco gave the order to fight, and the Army went into full military mode, slicing mercilessly through the terrified, screaming men and women huddled together near the flaming altar.

"You cannot stop us, Marduk. You cannot kill us. We are immortal! We have Sekhmet's gift!" Cheveyo yelled out as the fire inched toward them.

Marduk shook his head slowly. "I assure ye, I can indeed kill ye." He took two steps closer and stood at the edge of the fire ring encircling Cheveyo and Bridget. His pale green eyes reflected the fire and appeared to be shooting white flames toward them as he squinted fiercely. "I would have given ye the antidote had ye only asked. But instead…ye tried to kill me, and ye did kill my family. Revenge never fuckin pays, Cheveyo. For your sins against the Gods…ye'll die by fire, the same way Sekhmet died," he said as he pulled Titus from the circle of fire around Cheveyo and Bridget. "Make sure none of them survives this fire, Titus."

Marduk bowed gracefully once more, then sighed sadly. He closed his eyes to Bridget's terrified look, but nodded solemnly toward Cheveyo's brave face. "Ye're a true Warrior, Cheveyo. And a worthy foe. Thirteen fuckin years I looked for ye. Ye gave me quite a run. I thought Shannon was the Red Dragon the night she stabbed me, then later assumed it was Bridget. I never imagined Cheveyo, Son of Chogan and husband of Sekhmet would be the Red Dragon. Ye were an honorable man once. But my mistake made ye wicked. I take responsibility for that. For all of ye, because all of ye are products of the biggest mistake I ever made in my life. That mistake and the repercussions from it end here."

Cheveyo shook his head and let out one small chuckle with a groan. "I spent 9000 years looking for you, Marduk."

"Ye wasted a lot of time."

"Yes. I wasted my entire lifetime, because you are not the evil entity I believed you to be."

Marduk saluted Cheveyo with his fingertips to show his respect, then walked through the last ring of fire to stand directly in front of him. "My most sincere apologies to ye, Cheveyo, for my mistake that caused ye so much harm. I truly am sorry ye suffered. Ye'll suffer no more." Marduk took two syringes from his sporran and held them up to Cheveyo. "This will ease yer pain," Marduk said softly, then clapped Cheveyo on the shoulder. He gently touched Bridget's cheeks and smiled sadly. "Ye look like yer mother."

Cheveyo nodded in reverence, then took a knee to Marduk, dragging a reluctant and angry Bridget to the floor with him. "I did not think you were honorable, Marduk. I have been taught that you were evil, and worked from that premise. I see now that nothing is further from the truth. Bridget and I will die as Warriors, as we lived. We do not want your medicine." He gestured toward the syringes. "But Shannon and Braedon…they are not as brave. They will be afraid. If I may have one last wish, use the medicine on them. Please do not let them suffer."

Marduk nodded and slipped the syringes back into his sporran. "Ye have my word that they will not suffer needlessly, Cheveyo."

Marduk backed away slowly and gave one final order to Draco. "Burn this fuckin church to the ground, General Draco."

"Aye, my liege." Draco replied, then began barking orders to his Army. "Spare no one, and cover yourselves, Soldiers! This church is going up in flames, coming down in ashes."

Marduk shook off the flames from his body, then casually draped his smoky arms around Cain and Declan and led them away from the fray. "One day ye'll have to explain to me how ye managed to fuck up your first hunt together so badly. And then I'll tell ye about my first hunt. Fuckin disaster," he said in a droll tone and rolled his eyes. "Let's go home, lads. We've had enough fire and brimstone for one night, eh?" Marduk chuckled as he led them toward the shaft of light in the center of the church. He saluted his Army, then made one last sign of the cross toward Cheveyo and Bridget. The altar shot up in another massive flame, and the bodies of the Red Dragon and his daughter were instantly consumed in that flame.

"How the fuck did ye end up on a cross, Declan?"

"I don't have a fuckin clue. If ye tell anyone, I'll fuck your wife again," Declan said in playful anger.

"Ye got that wrong, lad. If ye ever fuck my wife again, everyone will know about this fuckin Jesus diaper." Marduk laughed heartily, then turned to Cain with a wicked grin. "Are ye alright, Son?"

"No! You mentioned Salem while he held a knife at my throat! For fuck's sake, Marduk. A spare son?"

"It was in the fuckin script ye wrote yourself, Cain! To throw them off! It fuckin worked!" He shrugged with a withered grimace.

"It was my line! And it was about Lugh! Declan's spare brother!" Cain shot back.

"Do ye see Lugh here, lad? They didn't have a knife to Declan's fuckin throat. I improvised, for fuck's sake. I saved yer sorry arse, didn't I?" Marduk sighed and rolled his eyes as they disappeared in a thick cloud of smoke.

They were still arguing when they returned to Dorcha and stepped out of the light shaft. "And on top of all that…you saved Declan first! I can't believe you actually said, 'Go ahead. Kill him.' That part wasn't in the script, Marduk!" Cain yelled as he stepped away from Marduk in heavy stomps. "I'm telling Lilith what you did," he said as he wagged his finger and huffed loudly.

"Come back here, ye fuckin brat! It added emphasis! Like the fire! I wasn't going to let them kill ye, Cain. Can't a father have a little fun with his son?" Marduk called out as he marched after Cain toward the Dungeon. "I'm sorry. Come here, lad. Don't tell yer mother. She'll lock me out of the bedroom! I'll let ye have the blondes…all of them."

Declan collapsed heavily into a chair and sighed loudly as he rubbed his face. He jumped when he heard a voice behind him.

"Ye did good, Declan. I'll never doubt yer position as Romeo of the Incubi again. Ye caught the worst of the dragons in yer romantic web in one fuckin smooth move."

Declan hung his head and groaned loudly as he turned around to meet Jerry's sympathetic eyes. "Not as smooth as it should have been."

Jerry shrugged. "Ye'll eventually get the hang of it." He handed Declan a garment bag with his suit neatly hanging inside. "Ye might want to get dressed before anyone else sees ye in that loin cloth. Marduk's never gonna forget this, ye know," Jerry chuckled softly.

"Aye, I know. Fuck." Declan took the bag from Jerry and shook his head. "Nice move with that dramatic run for the door, by the way." Declan smiled sadly.

"Power of suggestion. It works every time. I scared the shite of those lads," Jerry replied with a chuckle.

"How the fuck did I end up on that cross, Jerry?"

"Things got out of hand. I put ye up there to keep Bridget from slitting yer throat. I told her it would be a more fitting end to the Son of God."

"For fuck's sake! Ye might have warned me ye were gonna do that!" Declan huffed. "Was the fuckin loin cloth your idea too?"

Jerry shrugged and chuckled. "I had to improvise, Declan. But in the end, yer first dragon hunt was a success," he said softly.

"I don't like it. It sits badly in my gut."

"It's what we do, Declan. It's a necessary evil to rid the world of worse." Jerry sighed heavily. "It's not always this bad. It's easier when we catch them in the crime. Also easier when it isn't a woman."

"A woman I considered a friend," Declan said with a sigh.

"She was no friend of ours, Declan. She killed hundreds of our trackers, and thousands of innocent humans. She nearly killed Marduk, for fuck's sake. Ye can't feel sorry for the dragons. They're evil."

"My head knows this, Jerry. But my heart is fuckin breakin."

"I expect no less from ye, Declan. It's why we all love ye so much, lad. Yer all heart." Jerry smiled sadly, then let out a rush of air. "Do ye want to stay in Dorcha tonight? Settle yer nerves before facing the wife?"

Declan shook his head vehemently. “Take me back to Gael, Jerry. I can’t take part in the dismantling.”

“Ye don’t need to. Cain and Marduk will handle it from here.”

“That’s what I’m afraid of.” Declan hung his head and rubbed his eyes hard, then reached for a bottle of Scotch. “My wife can never know, Jerry.”

“I didn’t see a thing.” Jerry winked and clapped Declan on the back. “C’mon, lad. I collected the gifts from yer hotel room. All yer beautiful wife will know is that ye’ve been on a shopping spree.”

Declan groaned softly and took a long, hard swig from the bottle of Scotch. “I don’t deserve her.”

Chapter Thirty

Cain paced the floor of the Dungeon with an angry scowl while staring at Braedon lying on the slab. The knife wound on his neck had been cleaned, carefully stitched, and bandaged.

"You should be fucking dead," Cain spat out, then paced furiously as he waited for Braedon to wake up. He wanted him alert and awake to feel the pain he was going to inflict on him. "Oh wait…you are fuckin dead!" Cain grinned as he scanned Braedon's naked body lustfully, then shook his head and groaned.

"Marduk will never allow it."

He paced in a full circle, then grabbed a glass of ice-cold water and slowly poured the water over Braedon's nose and mouth. He laughed when Braedon woke up choking and coughing.

"Welcome to Hell, Braedon. I hope you enjoy your stay with us," Cain chuckled. "Just joking. You're not going to enjoy this at all."

"What in the world? Where am I?" Braedon asked as he tried to pull himself free from the straps. "Where's Mama? You have no idea who you're dealing with, mister! My Aunt Bridget is gonna hurt you! Where's my Mama? What did you do with my Mama?" Braedon asked in a sobbing whimper.

"Shut the fuck up." Cain stared at Braedon with a fierce scowl, then leaned close to his face. "Allow me to properly introduce myself. I am Cain, Son of Marduk."

"Son of Marduk? We killed Marduk. He's as dead as you're gonna be when my Mama shows up," Braedon said as he fought against the straps again and growled in frustration when he couldn't break free. "Mama!" Braedon cried helplessly.

Cain laughed evilly and loudly. "You're in my territory now. You have no power and your Mama isn't going to save you. You're wrong about my father. Marduk is very much alive, and he's a little angry with you, Braedon. You've been a naughty, naughty lad. You kinda pissed him off when you shot him. A little tip for you, brother. Something I learned the hard way. If you're gonna fuck Marduk, have the balls to finish the job." Cain laughed and pulled Braedon's straps tighter.

Braedon's face froze in terror when the room went eerily silent except for the slow, thumping footsteps in the hallway, getting closer and closer. He braced himself and gasped when he looked up to see Marduk filling the entire doorway.

Marduk leaned against the doorframe and sucked his teeth arrogantly. He had a bottle of Scotch in one hand, a cigarette in the other. The Omegan Crown was regally poised on his head. Braedon was blinded by the flash of gold and jewels when Marduk nodded and took one step forward. Braedon froze with his mouth hanging wide open.

"Surprise," Marduk said softly without smiling. His face was stoic as usual. But inside, Marduk was a bloody mess. His mind was on all the blood spilled by Braedon's hand. His included. His mind was also on the blood that flowed through Braedon's veins. His included.

"That's not possible. You're dead. We killed you," Braedon said innocently, and shook his head. "Where's Mama? Where's Aunt Bridget? Did she kill Declan?"

Cain's sinister laugh echoed against the walls as he walked toward Braedon in slow, steady steps. He grabbed him by the hair with one hand and pulled him forward.

"Seriously…how stupid are you? Did you really think Declan was unguarded?" Cain pulled Braedon closer with a wild look in his eyes.

"Cain. Step away." Marduk said in a deep, even tone that resonated eerily against the cold Onyx walls.

Cain turned to Marduk with an open protest on the edge of his sharp tongue, but when he saw Marduk's scowling squint, he pulled his hands away from Braedon and backed away slowly. Cain knew that look well, and knew better than to cross Marduk in this mood.

Marduk advance in a slow, panther-like swagger. He opened the bottle of Scotch and took a long drink, never taking his eyes off Braedon.

Braedon was terrified, but in complete awe of this dignified, noble figure in a black leather kilt and black boots, wearing an ancient crown of the purest gold he'd ever seen. He shivered when Marduk finally reached him. Marduk unstrapped Braedon's hands, then held out the bottle of Scotch to him.

"Mama says whiskey is the devil's brew," Braedon said in a staccato jerking voice.

"Your Mama's right about that, but a wee sip will calm your nerves, lad." Marduk held the bottle up to Braedon's lips.

Braedon's hands were shaking when he took the bottle. He could barely bring it to his mouth. Marduk reached out to steady his hand and helped Braedon take a sip. Braedon immediately began to cough, gasping for air.

"Cain, get the lad some wine. This Scotch is too strong for him."

"Really, Marduk? We're gonna kill him anyway. Let him suffer. He deserves to feel the pain he caused you," Cain replied in a droll tone. He crossed his arms over his chest and glared at Braedon. "Not to mention our trackers…and Maddie."

"They were evil! All of you are evil! God will avenge the righteous!" Braedon shouted, but immediately regretted his words when Cain moved forward with an angry scowl. Marduk blocked Cain with one arm.

"Wine for the lad. Take yer time."

Cain huffed and marched out the door with a murderous glint in his eyes.

Marduk sighed heavily and sat on the stool near the slab. "I'm very sorry for my son's actions, Braedon. He's new to this kind of thing." Marduk chuckled softly.

"How did you survive?" Braedon asked as she shivered. "You lost so much blood. I mopped it up myself."

Marduk shrugged. "I actually didn't survive for a minute or two. But luckily, I have a connection with God." He winked and grinned. "Are ye cold, Braedon? Do ye want a blanket?"

Braedon nodded slowly. "Yeah. It's chilly in here, and I don't like being naked." He sighed softly when Marduk placed a thick, warm blanket over him, and gently tucked him in with a sad smile.

"Better?"

"Yeah. Thanks." Braedon opened his mouth to say something, but hesitated while closely studying Marduk's face. "Mama says I'm your son, Marduk. I don't look like you, except maybe my big hands." Braedon flashed a goofy grin and held his hands up. "Marduk, I really don't wanna be the son of the Devil, but… ye don't seem so bad. Not as bad as the preacher says you are. But you might be tricking me. Mama says you're a wicked trickster. I don't trust you, Marduk," Braedon said innocently.

Marduk sighed heavily. "I'm sorry ye feel that way, Braedon. The Cambions I created are supposed to reveal the truth to the world about who I really am. I'm not evil, Braedon, but…I am a bit of a trickster." He chuckled, then wrinkled his brow sadly. "The truth is…I fight against the evil of the world to protect the innocent."

"Like me, Marduk?" Braedon asked in wide-eyed awe.

"Aye. Exactly like ye, Braedon."

"Mama says I'm innocent because I'm stupid. Aunt Bridget says I'm stupid because I'm innocent. Which one do you think I am, Marduk?"

"Innocent," Marduk replied softly, then gently held Braedon's hand and let out a ragged breath. "Braedon, I have it on good authority that ye are my son. I truly am sorry about that. I failed ye. I failed yer mother as well. Yer mother's grudge against me wasn't unfounded. I made a huge mistake a long time ago when I created yer grandmother, Sekhmet, from my own flesh and blood. I hurt yer family without even knowing it. For all of that, I am sorry, and I understand why ye hate me." He lifted Braedon's hand to his lips and kissed it tenderly.

"I don't hate you. I don't hate nobody. But Mama says I have to bring you down if it's the last thing I do. I have to kill you, Marduk," Braedon said sadly. "Sorry," he added in a soft whisper.

"Ah, Braedon. A good soldier knows when to admit defeat. This…is the last thing ye'll do. More's the pity. Ye and I might have been good allies, if ye hadn't tried to kill me." Marduk winced and ran his hand over Braedon's ruddy cheeks. "I'm going to let ye in on a little secret. Something everyone should know." He cleared his throat and took a drink, then a long drag of his cigarette. "We are a race of Incubi. A superior race of living beings, though sometimes when I look at my son and a few of my brothers, I doubt the part about being superior beings." He rolled his eyes as he took another long sip of Scotch, then flicked his ashes on the floor. "There are two Gods, Braedon. Two of us who work the system designed billions of years ago. My partner is Amon. He's the one ye believe is God. The White One. Amon and I are cousins…sons of twin brothers. Amon is my best friend." Marduk smiled and let out a quick chuckle.

"God is your best friend? But…the Bible says you and him are enemies."

"Amon and I have never been enemies, Braedon. We've been confederates all our lives. We were groomed to rule together from the day we were born. It took a few years for us to become friends, but we did. Our friendship began when we were about 20 years old." He chuckled and took a long drag of his cigarette, then snuffed in out in a red glass bowl. "We've never left each other's side for more than a few years at a time since that day."

"I wish I had a friend like that. I ain't never had a good friend. Siobhan was my friend for a little while, but Mama ran her off. She never came back. She was the only girl who was nice to me. I love her. Do you love anybody, Marduk?"

"Aye. I love my wife and my children. I love my entire family. But more than anyone, I love Amon. I understand why the world loves him, too. But he's not the God ye know, lad. Amon is kinder than that God. He's my light. And believe it or not. I am his guiding force. His shield. I take on all the dark and wicked things in our world to keep Amon innocent of it, pure. And he is. He is a pure, innocent soul…Amon is all I know of good." Marduk paused and smiled genuinely. "I would like for ye to meet him, Braedon," Marduk said quietly as he gestured toward the door.

Braedon gasped again, then broke into tears at the sight of the White One, Amon, Son of Alpha regally poised in the doorway in an ornate sapphire robe and the Alphan Crown on his head. It was the same crown Marduk wore. Amon stepped forward with a withered brow and blushing cheeks.

"Hello, my name is Amon. I am so sorry we had to meet under these conditions, Braedon."

Amon tried hard to keep a stoic face, but this was the first time he ever met a condemned person, an incorrigible soul, and his anxiety was raging. Amon clasped his hands behind his back and tapped his fingers against each other as he stepped forward gingerly.

"You're really God?" Braedon asked in a breathless whisper as tears soaked his cheeks. He tried to sit up, but he was strapped down tight. Marduk unbuckled another strap, and helped Braedon into a sitting position.

"I am one of two Gods, Braedon. Marduk is the other God." Amon touched Marduk's shoulder and smiled sadly at him. "We are equals. We rule side-by-side, but he bears the heaviest burden of our duties. I love him more than the world will ever know. He is more my brother than my actual brothers."

"We are not enemies, Braedon. We never have been. Except for that time he gave me pepper salve for my rash, without telling me what it was. He's a fuckin beast." Marduk's eyes twinkled as he leaned in and kissed Amon on the lips. Amon smiled brilliantly and cupped Marduk's bearded cheeks.

"And the time you stole that lovely blonde from me, Marduk."

"I did ye a favor. She's fuckin crazy." Marduk and Amon both chuckled like little boys. Amon took the Scotch from Marduk's hand and took a small sip.

Braedon was confused by this display of affection between God and the Devil, and had no idea what to think.

"Am I dead?" He scratched his head and looked around at the pristine Dungeon that looked like a surgery room, except for the dark, Onyx walls. "This is a joke, right? Mama sent you, didn't she?"

Marduk and Amon exchanged glances, and both sighed heavily.

"No, Braedon. This is no joke," Amon replied sadly.

"Is Mama here?"

Marduk nodded solemnly. "Aye. She's in the next room."

"Can I see her? Where am I, God?" Braedon's face was tortured as he looked back and forth between Marduk and Amon. "What's gonna happen to me?" Braedon asked softly as tears began to roll down his ruddy cheeks.

"Braedon, dear boy…I am so sorry that you fell for the lies of the Lesser Gods. You believed that Marduk and I were enemies, and you believed you had to choose sides. We understand that you followed the only path that was given to you. If you had not taken it to extremes…you might have been spared. But you killed many people, lad.

Some of our own. You, your mother, Bridget, and your grandfather brought false messages to the world. The truth is what you see before you. Marduk and I have no value without each other. Half coins don't have half value. They are void of all value. When you tried to kill Marduk, you tried to kill me. Braedon, you are in the Dungeon of Dorcha, the place you believe is Hell. As punishment for the crimes you committed against humanity, as well as the Incubi, you are condemned to eternal death. Your suffering will only be temporary, but it will be harsh. After you are dismantled, your life force will be extinguished forever."

"No! I don't want to die! God, please…don't let the devil kill me! I'll change! I swear. I'll never hurt another person as long as I live," Braedon cried like a wounded child.

Amon leaned in and kissed Braedon's cheek softly. "Marduk is not the devil you believe him to be. You would be lucky to have Marduk dismantle you. But because you tried to kill him, you must suffer the consequences of what would have been if you had succeeded. Be at peace, Braedon. You will not suffer for eternity." Amon sighed heavily as he walked out the door slowly with his head hung low.

Marduk turned to Braedon with sad eyes. "I'm truly sorry it has come to this, Braedon. I'm a Romantic. I cannot bring myself to hurt ye. Ye're blood of my blood." He smiled sadly with a withered brow. "Because of yer actions against me, I cannot emotionally nor physically dismantle yer body. This is what ye set in motion yerself. My son, Cain, will dismantle ye, and he is no Romantic Devil."

Marduk strapped Braedon again as he cried softly in shock and fear. Marduk tried to ignore the tears, but Braedon's wailing broke through his stoic façade. He pulled out a small vial and a syringe from his sporran, then tied a black tourniquet over Braedon's arm.

"This will ease yer pain, Son." Marduk slowly plunged the syringe with a lethal dose of morphine into Braedon's arm as Braedon stared up at him wide-eyed with an innocent smile. His face softened and his tears stopped as the drug began to take effect.

"Marduk, I'm sorry I tried to kill you. I was just following Mama's orders. Thank you for letting me meet God, Marduk." He smiled genuinely and curled up under the blanket, blinking slowly as his eyelids grew heavier and heavier.

"Sleep well, Braedon," Marduk said softly.

"Good night, Daddy," Braedon smiled widely. "You know what, Marduk? I ain't never said those words before," Braedon whispered, then fell into a deep, peaceful sleep he'd never wake from.

Marduk's face withered in misery and emotional turmoil as he leaned over Braedon's serene face. "I'm sorry, Braedon. Ye'll rest in peace now, and so will I."

Chapter Thirty-One

Shannon tried her best to sit up, pulling hard at the straps holding her on the cold, metal slab. “I can change! I can change everyone in the program. Even Bridget. She’ll give the order to the Elite members, and they’ll bring the message to the followers. The Orthodox Fascists are worldwide, and they believe in us…in our prophecy, and our vision. Don’t you see? We control them! The Red Dragon controls all the forces of evil on Earth. They won’t stop until they control the entire world, unless the Red Dragon tells them to stop. Send me back, I’ll put an end to the war against you. I swear it! We have power! Bridget and I have all the power!” She stared back and forth between Marduk and Amon, but she knew she was getting nowhere. She began to panic as she felt the adrenaline rush and heard the buzzing in her ear. She knew what was coming.

Marduk shook his head and furrowed his brow. “Shannon…yer war is over. Bridget is dead. All the heads of yer organization are dead as well.”

“You’re lying! There’s no way you killed Bridget. She’s well protected!” Shannon yelled. “We’re way too big for you to kill us all. The Orthos are world-wide! You can’t possibly kill us all.”

“I don’t need to kill everyone in yer cult, Shannon. I only need to kill the leaders, then the cult will fail. Tonight,

I personally ended the lives of Bridget along with all the elite members of the Red Dragon Cult. They are all dead."

Bridget snarled and laughed wickedly as she pulled on her straps and glared angrily at Marduk. "Bridget isn't the head of the cartel. You have no fucking clue who the head is, do you? You're weak. Ignorant. Ineffective. You cowered like a wounded animal when I stabbed you in the thigh. Didn't even have the stamina to fight your own son…we got the best of you, Marduk. The Red Dragon Cult isn't over.

"Except that it is over, Shannon. I know neither you nor Bridget were the Red Dragon. It was your father, Shannon. He is dead as well."

"There's no way your killed my father. You might have killed some of the elite, but not my father. You don't even know who he is. Nobody does," she replied with a knowing smile.

Marduk lit a cigarette and blew the smoke from his nostrils. "Cheveyo, Son of Chogan of the Akokisa tribe. He was the husband of Sekhmet, your father, and the Red Dragon." Marduk sucked his teeth and adopted an air of arrogance with a small grin. "Ye picked on the wrong devil, Shannon. I'm an expert dragon hunter, lass. I will admit it took some time to bring your father down, but I always win in the end. I've just been a little off my game lately." He shrugged and smirked.

Shannon's eyes widened in fear as she shook her head slowly. "No…please tell me you didn't kill my father. Please, Marduk…he's all I have!" Shannon cried. "Where's Braedon? What did you do with Braedon? He's your son, Marduk!"

Marduk groaned softly and hung his head. "Braedon did not suffer," he answered quietly. He couldn't look at her.

Amon stepped forward and held her hand. "Braedon was brave, Shannon. He and I had a lovely conversation, and he understood that his deeds could not go unpunished. Braedon is at peace, and he did not suffer," Amon said softly.

Shannon's face turned bitter and angry as she fought against the straps. "You owe me! You took my mother from me! You killed her! Now you killed my son! My father and my sister, too! You killed everyone I ever loved!" Shannon began to foam at the mouth as her face turned vicious with anger and something else Amon was afraid to identify as he backed away slowly.

Marduk grabbed her arm and held her down as best he could, but she fought viscously, trying hard to dig her teeth into his flesh, but Marduk had covered himself in a silver coating that kept her from puncturing his skin. He held a thick syringe in his hand, but couldn't keep her still long enough to inject her.

"Don't fight this, Shannon! I'm trying to ease yer pain, lass…as I promised yer father… though at this point, I'm tempted to let ye suffer. Ye stabbed me like an animal…of course I reacted like one. I am merely a mirror bearing yer own reflection, Shannon. Ye're fuckin wicked, and I simply made ye see yerself."

"I am not wicked! I do what my body tells me to do, Marduk! Isn't that what you had in mind when you created my mother? Bridget and I are made of the same material. We only did what the cells you implanted into my mother told us to do! Kill. But my father turned us around. Cheveyo said the only way to truly avenge ourselves and rid ourselves of this bloodthirst was to kill you…and the White One. I had to save myself! That doesn't make me evil!

Marduk grabbed her by the throat and held her back long enough to tighten her straps. "I nearly died because of ye, and Braedon did die because of the things ye made him do. Ye don't deserve this medication to ease yer pain, but I promised yer father, so fuckin hold still!" Marduk bellowed, but he had to back away quickly when Shannon became monstrously enraged and broke through the strap across her chest.

Amon slowly backed up to the wall with wide eyes when he saw Shannon's animalistic grimace. He and Marduk exchanged glances and read each other's minds clearly. She was heavily infected with the virus and would have to be put down quickly, like an animal.

"I am not an evil, wicked creature who takes pleasure in killing, Marduk! I fight the urge to kill every fucking day of my life! But some days, I have to feed this monster inside me! This what you created in your virus, Marduk! And you, Amon…how many fucking mistakes did you make in the design of Sekhmet? How many fucking mistakes did you both make when you sent Sekhmet into the Akokisa village? I know exactly how many mistakes you made in taking her back. One. Actually, two. My sister and me. Declan took our mother from us when we were just babies, not even two years old. We were left behind in the wake of her destruction, forced to live as outcasts in chains! We were just children, but we couldn't control our lust for blood and raw flesh. We had no mother to guide us through this wicked virus you cursed us with!"

Marduk rubbed his hands over his face and sighed heavily. "Shannon…releasing Sekhmet was not in the plan. She escaped…by an unfortunate mistake. I am deeply sorry for what ye and Bridget suffered. Had we known Sekhmet had children, we would've taken ye both back to Gael."

"To kill us? Like you killed my mother? Am I supposed to be comforted by that?" Shannon spat out angrily, as she broke free from another set of straps. "My father told me you were gonna try to worm your way out of this. Nothing you can say will make up for what you did!" Shannon spat out as she pulled on the last set of straps that began to give way.

Amon panicked when he saw how close she was to escaping. He knew he had to do something. He stepped in front of Marduk, and held up his hands in surrender. "If you must take a life to avenge your mother, take mine. It was my fault, Shannon. Marduk and I were not the ones who released her, but it was my fault she was released. Your mother was never bound for Earth…that mistake costs us both more than you will ever know. But it was my fault. Take my life if you must…"

"Save your breath, Amon! The two of you couldn't possibly have suffered more than my sister and I, living 9000 fucking years with this disease!" Shannon screamed, then pulled on her straps again. She let out a wicked howling yell and finally broke her last strap.

Marduk pulled Amon away quickly and stood ready to take the brunt of her attack, but Cain rushed into the room at that exact moment and stepped in front of both Marduk and Amon. Cain grinned evilly and waved a silver sword above his head, then pointed it directly at her.

"I was hoping you would break those straps! You fucking bitch! You killed Maddie! And you treated Raven like an animal her entire life! And then you tried to kill my father! Did you really think you could get away with that? You're either the most evil or the most stupid person alive.

Which is it, Six? Stupid? Or evil?" he teased as he jabbed at her with his sword. Cain's eyes were shooting fire as he glared at her distorted grimace. He laughed wickedly, then sliced through her arm, leaving a bloody gash that set his heart racing as the blood flowed onto the floor. He was fascinated by the deep, red hues, and the smell of it sparked his appetite, but he knew he could resist. His bloodlust wasn't overwhelming, but it was still there.

"I say stupid…you know why? Because I am the most evil person alive," Cain said in a droll tone.

Shannon laughed as she circled him and lashed out with her claws. "Are you sure about that, Finn? I was right under your nose the whole time and you didn't recognize me. You sat in the same room as me and told the entire story of my mother, You left no details spared…it was everything I needed to fuel my hatred of you and your family. So, who's stupid?"

Cain grinned devilishly. "Let's play a little game, you and me…which one of us is badass? Which one is stupid?" He held the sword directly aimed at her heart, but she sidestepped and lunged at Cain, biting into his shoulder.

Cain laughed wickedly as he pushed her off him and stepped forward two paces. "I'm immune to your disease, Six. You cannot hurt me."

Cain sneered wickedly when he lifted the silver sword, then swung it like a baseball bat, slicing it across her neck, which severed her head from her body instantly.

Cain's eyes were bright with a touch of madness as he watched Shannon's head roll toward the wall and stop with a heavy thud. He raised his bloody sword high in the air and grinned proudly.

"Did you fuckin see that? It came clean off with one fuckin strike!" Cain stomped over to Shannon's severed head and stabbed the sword into her ear, pushing deeper until her head was firmly planted on his sword. "Being that I have your fucking brain on my sword and splattered all over my floor, Six…I'm gonna go ahead and call it. I'm the badass," he chuckled and drove the sword the rest of the way through.

Marduk vomited when Cain picked up Shannon's head with his sword and waved it around the room proudly. He vomited again when the blood and brain matter oozed and dripped onto his sterile floor. He stepped away quickly when a long stream of blood flowed toward him.

"Fuckin bloody hell!" Marduk screamed as he doubled over. "Ye're a fuckin animal! Control yer devil, Son!" Marduk's knees buckled, and he broke out into a cold sweat. Cain's devil was the cruelest he'd ever seen. Far worse than Omega, who was renowned for his savage butchery. Marduk knew Omega was right. Cain needed a conscience. He desperately needed balance.

Amon held up Marduk and shielded him from the blood dripping from Cain's sword. "How did this happen, Marduk? What just happened?" Amon asked in a breathless whisper as he absently waved his hands in the air with a blank, withered stare at the bloody walls and floor. "This nightmare has no end!" Amon cried softly as he looked over the bloody mess in front of him. He'd never seen this kind of carnage before.

Marduk leaned heavily against the wall, gagging violently as the smell of blood drifted into the air. He stormed out of the room as quickly as possible and ran right into Draco, carrying two silver food trays. He set them down immediately, then ran toward Marduk with a furrowed brow.

"Are you alright, my liege?" Draco got a cold chill when Amon stepped out of the Dungeon a moment later with a confused, withered face, and Cain's wicked laughter echoed against the Onyx walls. Draco helped Marduk stand upright, then propped him up against the wall.

"No, I'm not fuckin alright!" Marduk yelled as he tried to steady himself.

"I understand, Marduk… but…we have another problem," Draco said with a heavy sigh.

"Aye, we have a fuckin problem! My wicked son is a fuckin problem! Handle it, Draco. I cannot."

"Cain is not the problem I'm referring to Marduk. The problem is bigger…" Draco began, but Cain's fiendish laughter drowned out his voice.

"Her head bounces!" Cain said incredulously, then his laughter faded into dry, humorless groans. "Do I have your permission to begin the dismantling, Marduk?" Cain called out dryly.

"The virus, Cain…I cannot let ye near the virus again." Marduk made a move toward the door, but he couldn't bring himself to walk through it.

"My liege…" Draco interjected nervously.

"I'm immune, Marduk. I survived the virus. I took the antidote. I'm probably the only one not at risk."

"Marduk…" Draco said as he pulled on Marduk's arm, but once again he was interrupted.

Cain poked his head out the door and grinned playfully at his father's pale, clammy face and limp body wavering on the edge of collapse.

"I forgot about your blood phobia, Marduk. Sorry. But it had to be done. Shall I proceed?" He chuckled and clapped his bloody hand on Marduk's shoulder. Marduk shirked away with a scowl as Cain laughed again. "Now we're even for that 'spare son' remark." He winked and shrugged. "Can't a son have a little fun with his father?"

Marduk glared at him with a withered face. "Evil. Pure fuckin evil." He shook his head slowly, then gagged again, but managed to pull himself together. "Aye. Dismantle her, but leave Braedon alone. Draco will handle his dismantling." Marduk groaned as he doubled over in distress.

Draco sighed heavily and pulled on Marduk's arm, but Marduk shirked away from him to face Cain directly.

"Ye don't have to literally dismantle the head and limbs from the body, for fuck's sake." He paced slowly and wiped his sweaty brow while holding back another wave of nausea. "Drain her blood. Keep what's left of her intact and burn her body. Burn the blood as well, but separately from the body. Don't send her to the Vortex. The body must be burned to ash." Marduk glanced up at Cain and was disturbed by the wicked gleam in Cain's eyes.

"You'll be avenged before nightfall, Marduk," Cain called out in a solemn tone as he headed back into the Dungeon to finish his task.

"Draco, see that every detail is carried out exactly as I said. And for fuck's sake, make sure he keeps his devil under control," Marduk said quietly as he moved away from the Dungeon

"My liege…a word with you?"

"Give me a minute to recover, Draco," Marduk said a little harshly.

"Marduk…this won't keep."

Marduk dismissed Draco with a wave of his hand, then led Amon away from the Dungeon in slow steps.

"What have we done, Marduk? What have we done?" Amon cried softly as he leaned heavily on Marduk's arm.

"I can't believe the repercussions from Sekhmet are still beating us over our collective fuckin heads! Fuck! How did we miss this, Amon?"

"We have to end it, Marduk. Once and for all. We have to calculate every detail of what we've done, and finish it. There may be others," Amon said dramatically

"Should we take this to the Elders?"

"Aye. This time we will not go against the law. No skirting the Elders this time, Marduk. We have lost too much already. I will not lose another child, nor will I give up my Crown."

"Prepare for a long stay in the Citadel, Amon. We may be held there while they assess this from every angle."

Amon was suddenly alert at Marduk's warning, and began to pace in circles anxiously.

"If we are to be held indefinitely…there are so many things I must attend to. Declan and Caraye. Aramanth's child. Lugh. The young lads and Jade." Amon groaned loudly when he realized he might have to answer to the Elders for another transgression. "I must also make amends to my wife. I must confess…" Amon said under his breath, then marched away from Marduk.

"Amon!" Marduk yelled out. His face fell when he saw Amon's withered brow and slumped shoulders. "What must ye confess?" Marduk asked hesitantly.

Amon's cheeks turned bright red, and he couldn't look Marduk in the eye. His tiger-eyes filled with warm tears. "Marduk, I am so sorry…" He held up his hands sadly. "I was in the Maze. I couldn't help myself…"

Marduk sauntered toward Amon slowly with clenched fists and an ice-cold demeanor. Marduk grabbed Amon by the collar and slammed him against the wall. He stared into Amon's teary eyes in disbelief. He didn't want to ask the next question. He was certain he already knew the answer.

"Who were ye with in the Maze?"

Before Amon could answer, Draco stepped in and pulled Marduk away from Amon with a quick jerk of his arm. "Marduk, there are more pressing issues to worry about! Two of the members of the Red Dragon cult have just arrived in the cell room. Intact."

"What? That's not possible, Draco. We burned them all. They were all destroyed in the fire." Marduk replied while glaring back and forth between Draco and a red-faced Amon who was sweating profusely and visibly shaken.

"Not these two, my liege. The cells are asking for you by name. Come with me, my liege."

"Not now, Draco! Handle it, for fuck's sake!" Marduk barked as he dragged Amon down the hallway by the collar of his robe.

Draco's shoulders slumped significantly as he watched them scurrying away from him. "I cannot handle this on my own, my liege." Draco whispered to himself as he picked up the silver trays, then slowly made his way to the Dungeon, looking over his shoulder to make sure no one was around. He unlocked the secret door and slipped inside with the trays stacked on top of each other. He held up his lantern and nodded reverently to his prisoners.

"I know I am late with your dinner. Please accept my apologies. The Lair is ablaze with activity, and I cannot trust anyone else to care for you." He slipped the trays through the slot and winced visibly when the two men grabbed the trays and began to devour the food like starving dogs. They both stared curiously at him, speaking to each other in a foreign language as they huddled together in the dark corner. But the language wasn't as foreign to Draco as he wanted it to be. He drew in his breath and braced himself as the bold one with a tangled mass of black curls finally stood and cautiously slinked toward him while sizing him up, but not in a predatory or offensive way. He held his hands up and walked so slowly, Draco was certain he was walking on air.

The hair on Draco's neck bristled as he watched him. He knew he was facing a fellow warrior, and immediately admired him for the power he held in check as he stepped further into the light. Draco stood perfectly still with his arms at his side, limber, with just enough tension in his body to spring into action if need be. He stared directly into the dark stranger's eyes without blinking for a full minute. The stranger broke the silence in a deep voice and familiar accent that startled Draco, but only the sudden widening of his eyes gave him away. He remained as still as the dead.

"I mean you no harm. I only wish to speak to Marduk. We are not part of Cheveyo's cult. We were invited to that church for one night. Cheveyo said he would tell us where to find our lost family. We are victims of the Wendigo. Sekhmet…took my family… but… Cheveyo said our family is alive. Here, in this place I knew nothing of until today. Whether by chance, accident, bad luck, or good… we are here, and I see it in your eyes, man of Death… you know who we are." He waved his hand toward the other man hovering in the corner. "We are here for our family. Ahanu and I have come for Makawee and her child. I am Kuruk. I am here for Hurit, and Samoset…my son."

17641432R00289

Printed in Great Britain
by Amazon